IRON ANGEL

GABY

BOOK III

A Novel

P.F. BUSCH

Trenton, Georgia

Print ISBN 978-09854419-2-0
E-Book ISBN 978-0-9854419-3-7

Library of Congress Cataloguing in Publication Data
Busch, P.F.
Iron Angel Gaby Book III by P.F. Busch
Library of Congress Control Number: 2023909554

This book is a work of historical fiction. Names, characters, places and incidents relating to nonhistorical figures are products of the author's imagination or are used fictitiously. Any resemblance of such nonhistorical incidents, places or figures to actual events or locales or persons living or dead is entirely coincidental.

P.F. Busch
First edition 2023

Cover design by Todd Engel, Engel Creative
Front Cover photo by iStock photo
Author's picture by Sherigeoffreys

NOVELS BY P.F. BUSCH:

THE LYRICIST
IRON ANGEL THE FRENCH YEARS BOOK I
IRON ANGEL SORDID AFFAIRS BOOK II
IRON ANGEL GABY BOOK III

COMING SOON
IRON ANGEL THE TRIAL BOOK IV

GABY

A NOVEL IN THE IRON ANGEL SERIES
BOOK III
By
P. F. BUSCH

1876

A novel depicting the life of a remarkable Louisianan Diva, a woman of profound artistic gifts and untamable passion whose life intermingles with the likes of Sarah Bernard, Berthe Morisot, Gide, Baudelaire, Manet, Flaubert, Bizet, Debussy, Gounod, in a recovering City of Light, Paris, still shattered by a not too distant history of societal divisiveness, despair and hopelessness.

To Carl, my love, thank you for your unending support.

Thank you to Laura Taylor, editor extraordinaire.

Great appreciation to Todd Engel, the cover is beautiful.

In memory of my parents, grandparents, aunts and uncles who imparted in me, as a young child, the rich history and culture of France, its beautiful land, its profound literature and its proud people.

CHAPTER ONE

DECEMBER 1876 Paris

Upon his return from the United States, Jean-Louis-Pierre de Pleyssis, Duke de Bourbonne, stopped in Rome to personally deliver documents to Cardinal Philippe Thornsen, his former wife's cherished cousin. Gabriella de Conte-Thornsen, the former Madame de Pleyssis and Duchesse de Bourbonne, was presently in Venice, singing in La Fenice Opera House to an adoring international audience.

The prelate refused to acknowledge the provenance of the courier. Instead, an aide had rudely grasped the papers at the door. An invitation for a private audience with the Cardinal in his lavish apartment had not been extended.

Inconsequential, reasoned Jean-Louis-Pierre de Pleyssis. He knew Gaby was on her way to Paris. Hence, all of the lies propagated by cousin Philippe had no effect on the end result. He'd paid a fortune to purchase Gaby's singing contracts; six to be exact—two in Italy, one in Milan, one in Rome and another in Austria at the Viennese Opera House.

Living without Gaby in Paris, or anywhere else, proved unfeasible. The ancestral grand *hôtel particulier* in Paris, their residence after the wedding, elicited passionate emotions he longed for. He'd purchased a new apartment close to the new opéra house on the Grands Boulevards. Strolling past the house that she'd purchased after their separation was Calvary.

Gaby had sought comfort in the arms of another man, while he'd been detained under house arrest all these months in late January 1871. *Eh bien.* That was the past, and it could not be allowed to oversee and control the future. Perhaps he should have believed her when she'd revealed that she would have slept with a thousand men if the final price had been his freedom.

Regardless, only Gaby could fill the void he endured daily. Gaby in his life forever was his plan. Life without their love seemed an absurdity. Despair had haunted his days for the past five years. He could not be the sole person in this relationship to feel so terribly distraught? She still adored him, he felt certain. Great loves never ceased to be; passion could never be forgotten!

The old English Chesterfield chair accommodated his large stature. He sank back in it and reached for his favorite cigars, the latter enclosed in a golden box engraved with their wedding profiles. The arrogant brat would hide his cigars as he absently reached for the box while reading. He'd look up, annoyed as she'd stood before him, brazen with a cigar hanging down the side of her sensual pout! The box had followed him these past five years-a Christmas gift from Gaby.

After their separation, he attended many of her concerts in Austria, Milan, and Naples. Crushing guilt plagued him at the thought of his refusal to allow her to perform her art. Supernatural was the term that came to mind when she sang. An angel—her audience trembled at the end of an aria. Jealousy might have played a role in his repudiation. Perhaps the adulation she received from her fans, as well?

Eh bien, she now had a taste for fame and adoration. He would never refuse her anything—not ever. To hold her in his arms remained his sole aspiration. In less than a month, his queen would arrive in Paris!

The stacks of papers on his smoking table required his immediate attention. His investments abroad and at home in France had skyrocketed beyond all expectations. Alas, his pretty former wife was all he could think about.

He glanced at the newspaper to his right. A photo of Gaby graced the front page of a Roman Gazette, 'Signora de Conte-Thornsen, in all her glory as she arrived in Rome. '*Brava*' proclaimed the headlines. Socrates as well, her new dog, a pretty white Terrier she held in her arms made the gossip column, as well.

He scoffed at the portrait facing him—Aristotle and Plato, the two lonesome cats Gaby had rescued from God knows where still counted as his dependents. These two had been lucky; they had not landed on someone's table during the Prussian siege and the latter tragic days of the *Commune*. Lofty Greek philosophers' names would have to be downgraded if her obsession with stray animals persisted.

Satisfied with his decision to have her back in Paris at any cost, he stood and strode to the fireplace to rekindle the logs. Golden flames burst forth in the hearth, the crackling of the scorching wood turned to ashes carpeting the dark stones of its inner wall.

He stared down. "Patience. Let us await the grand arrival of my Duchesse!" he proclaimed hopefully.

No illusions. He expected an uphill battle, but the decision had been taken. He wanted her back in his life, in his home, in his bed. A smirk on his handsome face and a furtive glance toward his bed displayed his obstinate nature. He turned on his heels, ambling to the nearest window.

The weighty gold and cream brocade draperies were parted, revealing the Parisian sky in a deep shade of blue, while the Seine down below picked up its color as several loaded flat-bottomed *chalands* returned slowly to their moorings. The captains stood on deck, guiding their charges with care, always on the alert for large chunks of submerged ice that often damaged the hulls of their barges.

Unlikely fair weather for November, Jean-Louis-Pierre mused. He thought of The Tempête moored in Brest, the refitting experts giving her a complete overhaul. He loved the sea and the freedom it afforded him. Here in Paris, he felt compelled by society's rules, and there were far too many.

The Second Empire had fallen, the Emperor dead in England, an early death over essentially a simple operation; his son, the Prince Imperial dead as well, fighting under a foreign flag, England, cut down by Zulus in Africa, and now the former Spanish bred Empress Eugenie had no qualms about vacationing in the South of France, often accompanied in Nice by her close friend, Queen Victoria.

The aristocratic world that he'd been born into essentially continued their charmed lives not much different from the early and later years of the Empire, less festive for certain, but Paris more resplendent than ever, courtesy of the magnificent work devised by Haussmann, was still a divine lady, who honored the culture of the French aristocracy. Presidents came and left, the populace complained and often changed their representatives. Yes, the atrocities of the Commune had enveloped the city with a veil of apprehension and prudence, but the lives of his kind saw little change.

With both hands he rotated the gilded golden handles on the casement, pulled the double panes of the floor to ceiling windows in opposite directions, and walked across the spacious balcony overlooking the Seine. Bitter cold bit his face. He inhaled deeply, leaning his elbows on the thick marble balustrade that rimmed the terrace. In the street below skirting the river, carriages bowled down the streets. Security guards re-directed servants to other passages, these poor souls had most certainly taken a shortcut toward their masters' houses. Life was brutal for many. A better existence for the next generation was assured if France resisted its infatuation with the Monarchy or vengeance wars.

Trees were mostly bare of greenery; a few remaining burnt copper leaves unfurled from crooked limbs and caressed the soft grass until the soles of *flâneurs* foiled their last stems in the mud. Others landed in choppy waters where most often a brutal current submerged the stragglers. Unlike Gaby, Jean-Louis-Pierre rarely allowed himself moments of reflection. He thought of his friend Baudelaire, who had died much too soon nine years ago. The famous flâneur and poet had coined the word *modernité* in his renowned work of lyric poetry, *Les Fleurs du mal*, one hundred and twenty-six poems reflecting the shifting, decadent, and erotic landscape of beauty. The Emperor had been offended by it—of all people! The tall aristocrat smirked. Meanwhile Manet, Bazile, Renoir, and Degas, through their palettes, captured these fleeting moments.

Gaby belonged to that world; *les artistes* were her friends. He would change his ways for her. She certainly had; she'd given up her passion for him. He now wished he could have understood her complex nature. He sighed. Mistakes on his part produced repugnance when his thoughts probed past errors. Promptly he pushed away from the balustrade. An invigorating walk was the answer. He strode back inside, ran down the staircase, grabbed his coat from the waiting butler and marched out the door.

CHAPTER TWO

December 1876

Under a cloudy gray sky, miles and miles of frozen land furrowed by tortuous lanes of train tracks bestowed an air of solemn dignity to the surrounding landscape. Gabriella de Conte Thornsen, the former Madame de Pleyssis, Duchesse de Bourbonne sat by the window in the train as it returned to Rome from St. Petersburg, where she had been invited to sing at the Mariinsky opera house. A new contract had been drawn, and she carefully reviewed it in her private compartment. The director of the Palais Garnier, Auguste Emmanuel Vaucorbeil and Maître Goriot, had forwarded the offer to her private secretary. The Palais Garnier, the new opéra house in Paris, was located on the Grand Boulevards. She'd read it once, but now read it again.

Dearest Gabriella,
The opéra will have its grande fête for Christmas and the New Year. It would be our most fervent wish if you'd agree to be the shining star of our first season. A new opéra has been written just for you, Gabriella. All has been prearranged with your other contracts, only your signature on this parchment will give our new Paris' house of tragedy, comedy and everything brilliant its stellar diva. All of us, your most cherished and loyal friends, beg you to accept our invitation. Only you will make this historic opening a grand commemoration. You will love it, Gabriella! And for us, it will be the pinnacle of a splendid season.
Amitiés, chère Gabriella,

Alphonse Goriot. Je vous attends avec impatience.

She leaned back and reclined her head against the well-cushioned red velvet bolster, smiling at her friend's excessively flamboyant theatrical demeanor. Her thoughts returned to the heady days in the splendor of the sumptuous *hôtel particulier* she had shared with Jean-Louis in Paris.

The Maître would argue for hours with Jean-Louis—she'd shortened his first name a bit. "Way too long, Jean-Louis-Pierre," she'd proclaimed with grand theatrical demeanor—to grant his permission for her to appear on stage as the 'exquisite soprano' in the many operas performed in the old theater. Futile!

Goriot had always been there for her. The same day that the separation had made the papers and the Gazette, he had appeared in her new home.

"Gabriella, here is a contract for you to sign."

She'd decided not to accept. At that time, she'd contemplated a reunion. Their great love affair could not end on such a simple note. But it had.

Looking back, her escape to Rome from Paris had been the right decision as her sanity verged on despair. A few days later she'd written to Philippe. He'd begged her to immediately return to the Eternal City. She'd left three and a half months later, Élyse, her forever friend, had accompanied her, while all of her well-wishers and colleagues worried about her will to live.

The train struck the rails as the snow spattered on the side of the many wagons. Was she sufficiently composed to return to the City of Lights? she wondered. Only time would tell. Her former husband remained somewhere in India, she'd been told. A six months stint in Paris would be heavenly *sans* narcissist beast Jean-Louis! She'd come to adore Paris and its people. France was now her home where her friends had supported her artistic ventures. Paris would become her home in later years.

At this late date, she still had not received the musical score. She wondered about the story and libretto. Perhaps it awaited her in Rome. Her engagement with the Teatro La Scala in Milan had been purchased for the holiday season, as well as a four-weeks solo appearance in Naples.

Five years had passed since her estrangement from Jean-Louis. Could a new opera have been written about their passionate love affair? Her work was now her sole passion. And it was a grand passion! She loved to sing. It transported her to diverse worlds, different cultures, worlds where she was truly amazing. Crowds loved her wherever her musical talent led her. Freedom, independence and exuberance ruled her life now, and she was the better for it—essentially, the stage and singing were the reason she had traveled to Paris, even if there had not been an interlude with Jean-Louis.

At times, heartfelt pangs of her former self as the Duchesse de Bourbonne flashed through her mind. Her life then compared to an inexplicable, brilliant gem that would shine forever! Loving Jean-Louis had been first and foremost; nothing else counted. Contemplating their years together still touched a tender spot in her heart.

"If you have forgiven a man for everything he's done then it means he is done for, Madame!" a young student in psychiatry called Sigmund Freud had told her during an engagement in Monrovia. She recalled fondly the man who'd been a guest that evening, highly entertaining as he rattled on with amusing but veracious quotes that she had memorized in order to heal her broken heart.

A tragic love their passion had been. Oh, so pure at first! Yet, as the years passed, it had blown away like a glacial Parisian rain shower. The ones that pelted the capital as droplets disappeared into the mighty

Seine, flooding valleys on its northwesterly path and causing famine to its farmers.

Jean-Louis's pride possessed no boundaries. He'd shattered her young life. Their marriage had been a charade. She nodded and shook her long mahogany curls to clear away the painful memories. The past held no meaning. Had she ever known anyone who had learned from it?

Wars still shattered lives. Old men spoke and young men were sent to war and died! Malice, ignorance and poverty still reigned king in many countries. Women treated as chattel was a common sight. The old adage, join the nunnery, marry well, procreate, a boy naturally for the aristocratic lineage. For the peasant woman, breed, work the fields or the *boulangerie*, or run away from it all and join a *maison close*, become a well-kept courtesan perhaps or a *demi-mondaine*.

For the pretty soprano, simply, luck of birth—being gifted with an amazing voice and a well-stocked bank account—provided some cherished moments after the Civil War in the United States, where she had been born and raised. Driven by the insouciance of youth, she'd offered it all to Jean-Louis thanks to her innate passion. Her youthful innocence had played in that ghoulish scenario.

"Live the moment," she whispered to Socrates, her adored white terrier, resting on a hassock. At the sound of her voice, his ears perked up and quickly he jumped on her lap to receive her caresses.

The train continued to roll across the plains, her head lulled from side to side on the sturdily padded bolsters. A butler entered the compartment.

"Madame, your repast is ready. Monsieur Montellier is awaiting your invitation. Should I respond that he should join you or that you will be available promptly or perhaps... later at your convenience?" the young man questioned with a staunch Russian accent.

"Yes, I'm on my way to meet with him."

The servant departed to announce her arrival to the historian recently assigned to her staff. In the richly decorated corridor, she strolled as the train headed through the frozen fields crisscrossing the hunting forests of myriad summer castles of the Tsarevich Alexander the II and his family.

The Romanov's dynasty had started in 1613. It was now 1876, almost two hundred and sixty-three years of the Romanov's absolute power. It was one of the most luxurious courts in Europe.

"Bonjour, Monsieur," she greeted him as she entered the lavish dining room whose walls, covered in white and gold satin coverings, displayed tapestries of hunting scenes woven with golden thread on a deep burgundy background.

She recognized the profile of the current Tsar, his youngest daughter, the Grand Duchess of Russia, Anastasia, mounted on a miniature pony which resembled a unicorn. She recalled the magnificent pieces she had seen at the Winter Palace, where in 1764 Empress Catherine the Great had begun housing her priceless art collections.

"It smells delicious. Has the chef shared our *menu du jour*?" she questioned the historian, a rotund man sitting in the far corner, bent over a pile of books piled high on a small rectangular table pushed against the far wall, close to the window. He raised his eyes to her.

"Non, Gabriella, I appreciate the sumptuous feasts they surprise us with daily."

And that he did, indeed! She smiled, the historian's corpulent stomach spoke volume. He pointed at a castle emerging from the dusk.

"This expanse is the summer home of the Tsarevich Alexander II and his ailing wife the Tsarina Maria Alexandrovna of Hesse and by Rhine.

"Yes? I understood that the Russian royal lovers had an affection rarely seen in these circles? It did not last long!"

"No. Amid gossip of infidelity, which were proven correct, Alexander had entered into a very heated relationship with Princess Catherine Dolgorukov. He'd moved her into the Winter Palace as he sired four children with her."

Memories of her memorable passion with Jean-Louis-Pierre de Pleyssis re-surfaced. Catherine had given the Emperor children. She lingered on that last thought as she glanced down at Socrates, who had followed her down the corridor. Perhaps it had been divine intervention. Being childless had somewhat sweetened the bitter pill. She shook her curls as if to erase painful memories. "Let bygones be bygones, Gabriella," she whispered to herself.

Socrates barked at the closed door as her artistic entourage awaited a formal invitation to enter the dining room. Vocal coaches, musicians, lyricists, historians, all accompanied her. At the Winter Palace, the stage's creation had been awe-inspiring. She'd worked closely with the artists and architects who created the space in which she sang.

Russian ballets from the acclaimed Marlynsky Ballet appeared during many interludes, giving new unrivaled dimensions to the spectacle. Saint Petersburg, although bitterly cold, was a sensational center of the arts. Its unique museum, the Hermitage, assembled an array of painters, sculptors, their protégées and the accolades of phenomenally gifted artists.

Catherine the Great had acquired Jean-Jacques Rousseau book and Denis Diderot's library and his edited work of the Encyclopédie ou Dictionnaire Raisonné des Sciences, des Arts, et des métiers, as well, it was said, as the long letters of Voltaire, who had corresponded with the Empress for over two decades. It sealed the great shame to the proud French nation. The affront lingered as the Empress disembarked in Paris.

The train rolled out of the station where they'd stopped. She gazed at the splendor of the palace; the small châteaux where the Tsar and his family spent a good part of their summer vacation in the Alexander's palace.

"When did Tsar Alexander II grant emancipation to the muzhiks?" she inquired as the train began to regain some speed.

"In 1861," her historian replied.

The new historian was an interesting fellow, although much of what he said she had read on the international news.

A private train with a lovely salon had been placed at her disposal; her meals were delivered in a spacious and magnificent dining room where she usually invited her vocal coaches and the many artists that had traveled with her to dine. Flutes filled with Cristal, her favorite French Champagne, cluttered the tables already adorned with silver plates.

She reached for a glass and listened to the comments of her traveling troupe—talented men and women dedicated to the world of opera but most importantly impassioned by her singing. All were enchanted with the change of venue. Paris titillated their artistic souls.

To open for the new Palais Garnier was no small accomplishment. She recalled the many hours she'd spent working her voice with the sopranos, mezzos, tenors, in the old opéra house in Paris. How she had yearned to have been permitted on the stage. Of course, Jean-Louis would not hear of it. Maître Lauriot, along with Goriot, had pleaded and pleaded to no avail. Eh bien, she had taken the good with the bad! Essentially the good had abounded. No regrets.

An hour later she decided that she would dine alone after all. A bit of solitude. Walking back to her private dining area, her thoughts flashed back to her first train ride in France from Villefranche-Sur-Mer to the Principality of Monaco. Jean-Louis had been with her. Then, too, she'd questioned the great social divide existing between the classes. The aristocrats always boarded and disembarked first. Eh bien, she was one of them now! Her train passed hundreds of stations where she noticed peasants who undoubtedly had been waiting for hours to bring their crops to towns.

Life was hard for so many in this age. Taxes were paid to the aristocrats and the Empire, tithes required to be given to the Catholic Church, and the Orthodox Church, rations from the peasants' fields were offered to the Seigneurs for the privilege to live on their lands, furthermore, on a whim, conflicts amongst the Seigneurie devastated entire villages and towns. The populace subsisted.

***

Philippe, the Adored, as commonly intoned by Jean-Louis, waited for her in Rome. Perhaps he would travel with her to Paris. Her usual immovable performance itinerary had been rescheduled. In Rome her repertoire for the prime minister of Italy, Mr. Minghetti, had been rescheduled, as well as the operatic season in Vienna at the Austrian-Hungarian court of Franz Joseph and his Empress Elizabeth.

Out of the blue, the director of the Palais Garnier opéra in Paris wanted her to open the opéra season in the City of Lights. The French had offered an enormous sum to both the Romans and Austrians to buy out her singing engagements.

Since the repudiation, she had not returned to France. She missed it immensely. Paris was her home. A city she had learned to adore after much tribulation in the early years after her arrival. True, changes had occurred. The young and naive ingénue who had given up her singing dreams for a fleeting passion had matured. She smiled at the very word. Her *exuberance and joie de vivre* had survived.

Jean-Louis-Pierre de Pleyssis had been, and would remain, her life's great love. Every woman deserved to love as passionately as she had. Although the unexpected and abrupt estrangement after his trial had seemed at times insurmountable, had it not been for her deep faith in God, she surely would have ended her life. But yet... after five years, Jean-Louis no longer held a special place in her life. He was just a memory. The final separation from a man for whom she would have given her life for had been the second time in her young existence during which she had been wounded beyond comprehension. She vowed that it would be the very last.

The butler and a young maid entered the compartment after a faint knock.

"Will Madame dine in the salon, or should the servants accommodate a tray?"

"I will eat alone this afternoon. I would like to rest prior to our arrival."

She called out to Socrates, a white puffy ball she had rescued while visiting one of the Ernestine duchies of Saxe-Coburg-Gotha. She adored the small white dog of uncertain pedigree. It ate what she ate, followed her into the most glamorous restaurants and State Courts, in her loges even as she took pleasure in the latest plays or symphonies.

During a concert, he'd escaped from his keeper and appeared on stage at the end of one of her performances, making his way to her while paying close attention to the parterre of strewn roses whose thorns had nicked the pinkish pads under his paws. She'd even ended relationships with several lovers on the only account that Socrates had an aversion to their one or many personality traits. He was her child, and she spoiled him to her heart's content.

Two days later, the train rolled in *Stazione di Roma Termini.*

"Did you know, Gabriella," Monsieur Montellier questioned, "that in 1868, Pope Pius IX started the construction of the station prior to the loss of his Temporal Power to Emmanuel II? The station has been in operation since early this year."

The historian wanted to instruct the young soprano, but the train had finally stopped. He annoyed her.

"Fascinating!" she replied curtly. "I have not seen my cousin in three months, we will talk later. As you know, our plans have changed. Paris is our next destination. I appreciate your erudite comments, Monsieur Montellier, but please, remain intent on the history of the opéra's époque. Have a lovely time in Rome, Monsieur. I am staying with the Cardinal."

CHAPTER THREE

The train had come to a complete halt. The cool Roman breeze caressed her long curls and made her skin tingle. Hundreds of people on the platform were arriving from or departing to unknown destinations. The excitement was palpable. Lovers embraced passionately, others with grief embedded faces walked sternly away from loved ones, perhaps never to be seen again.

Quickly she turned and ran to the window. With both hands she rammed the glass pane down and glanced outdoors. She spotted Philippe as he searched for her private train. She waved a white foulard to draw his attention as the train initiated the convergence to its proper rails.

The Royal Carabinieri cleared the platforms of the common men, a bronze cable chain parted all ranks. Slowly her train was allowed to advance into the station. The *opérateurs* of the many stations throughout the continent were competent and responsive to their duties, accustomed to royalties from Russia, Bulgaria, and Austria, who often stopped in these very locations on their way to Monaco or Nice, both coveted warm winter destinations for the royals of many nations.

Finally, Philippe spotted the train.

"Philippe!" she shouted.

Their eyes met. He hastened his pace and then began a swift run, waving his arms as stunned onlookers followed the tall cleric's glance. Caught in a euphoric moment, he promptly switched back to a dignified slow pace.

Gaby scampered down the corridor, lifting her midnight blue bouffant skirt and running the final few steps from her compartment onto the platform. Philippe's arms extended to her as he reached and encircled his dearest cousin tightly to his chest. His long black cassock swayed gently along his tall and lean physique. Had it not been for the biretta and the bright red sash that rested around his waistband, a Cardinal vestment, he would have appeared to be a lowly priest, which would have suited Philippe just fine. But in these precarious times as the Church's influence waned, all prelates wore their rightful habits.

"Gaby, welcome home, my dearest!" He pressed her to him ever more tightly, then gently pushed her away, stared at the beautiful woman facing him and kissed her on both cheeks. "You are more radiant and beautiful as the years pass. I missed you so, my dear cousin."

While her servants and musical entourage disembarked, Gaby slipped her hand under Philippe's arm and walked through the building and out the door where a carriage awaited her arrival. She waved to all who tried to catch a glimpse of the famous soprano as she returned to Rome. Drafters and photographers drew and flashed away.

"Madame, I hear you will begin the season in Paris, at the new opéra house, the Palais Garnier?" one of the French journalists threw out as she made her way to the carriage. She smiled, questions left unanswered. She had made that mistake upon her arrival in Rome five years hence. Within days her entire life had been revealed in the many gazettes of the city. It had been terribly painful. Her security quickly urged her into the carriage.

Philippe followed close behind, and Socrates jumped onto her lap. She tossed her white mink toque on the opposite bench as a mane of long mahogany curls unfurled on a vanilla silk, intricately woven, Alençon lace blouse.

"Implausible, Philippe, I only found out about the change last week. Do you know anything? I'm delighted and extremely proud. France is really my first home, Philippe, I love and miss the country like no other. Maître Lauriot gave me my first chance at the stage. And now with the first production in the new opéra house... what a wonderful surprise! Bernard, you remember Bernard, my favorite vocal coach, he shared that the tenor's role has been given to Tomaso Perini." She burst out laughing. "We make magnificent music together!"

Philippe, who followed her every performance when she sang in Rome, and often followed her to nearby countries, was not as thrilled as she was about the change in venue. He knew a lot more than she did.

"All are awaiting your arrival in France. It will be a homecoming like no other, Gabriella. I was one of the lucky ones to visit the Opéra just last fall. Resplendent - that is the perfect word for the magnificent venue. Gaby, you will be its reigning queen. And rightly so," he added. "Have you given some thought about your former husband? I understand he has returned to France and is now living in Paris. For how long, I do not know."

She looked up to him for an instant, rendered speechless by the news. Then a great big smile promptly dismissed the dark cloud that had startled her.

"You know quite well that I have moved on, Philippe. Look at my wonderful life now. My joys and the wonder of this beautiful world would have never materialized if I were still Madame de Pleyssis. Seriously, Philippe, all will be perfect, and I hope that you will attend the third or fourth performance. I have to be in Paris before the 17th of December. A gala for dignitaries, regular patrons and members of the *Presse Nationale* will attend. I will sing the first performance on New Year's Day. I know your presence is needed here in Rome, but please come and celebrate my triumph." She stepped closer and hugged him close to her heart.

Both cousins stayed in each other's embrace, Gaby delighted and Philippe conflicted. He had never in his life wished for another human to have gone on to the other world but with de Pleyssis... Gaby would be safer and much happier with the beast completely out of her life. Within seconds great pangs of guilt shook his entire being. He berated himself. He did not deserve the holy habit he wore.

CHAPTER FOUR

ON A TRAIN TO PARIS

Less than two weeks later, Gaby was back on a northbound train to Paris. Letters from her many friends had arrived in Rome while she was away. All celebrated and delighted in the knowledge of her prompt return to the City of Lights.

"Jean-Louis-Pierre has returned from his travels and apparently he is in Paris?" Philippe had shared.

While in Rome these past three weeks, she had denied his presence in the French capital. Recently, her memories of the idyllic times they'd shared rattled her spirit. Why couldn't she recall the suffering after the rupture? Soon, their confrontation in Paris would become a reality.

Total ignorance of him, wherever he happened to be, would be the line of defense. She refused to be deterred. But... would he ignore her, as well? A shiver shook her. She stiffened her spine, her hands lifting to her heart. A passion, oh so pure, had blown away like a glacial Parisian shower. The very same that often pelted the capital savagely as it quickly diluted in the mighty Seine, flooding the river banks, the valleys, destroying the crops and causing famine to the farmers.

Jean-Louis's pride had no boundaries. He'd shattered their lives, listening to his grandmother's salacious rumors rather than assent to her loyalty and her dedication to their union. Their marriage had been a charade! Tragic! It was the past, she reminded herself.

She felt blessed and thankful that her dreams had come to pass. An entrance in Paris's new opéra house. A score dedicated to her and an adoring audience awaiting her arrival. The future was happy and bright. She tapped her hands on the bouffant velvet skirt, she loved that fashion, promptly Socrates jumped on her lap.

"You will love Paris, my little darling," she whispered in his ears, her hair tumbling across his thick, white, curly fur.

The train swept through Tuscany stopping for a few hours in Lucca, a picturesque medieval town surrounded by stone ramparts. They stopped to partake in gastronomic delights of risotto, fresh lettuce hearts swimming in balsamic vinegar from Modena and a local wine that filled her mouth with a savor so delicate that she allowed herself another glass.

They also spent a few hours in Cinque Terre, the five villages built in the mountainside on cliffs that dropped down into the sea. The scenery was spectacular, natural beauty indescribable. Tomorrow to Verdi's hometown right outside Milan, a night at Lago Maggiore, and then off toward the mountainous Alps where they would switch over to the Glacier express to experience the grandiose Swiss Alps. Then, on to Beaunne and Paris.

***

Munching on little round loaves of German strudel she had purchased earlier in a Swiss *patisserie*, she sat entranced by the magnificence of the scenery, Montellier's entrance to the salon of the bakery was unnoticed.

"Hello, Gabriella, may I join you?" the historian intoned.

"Naturally," she responded. She did not particularly like the Academic. His arrogance truly annoyed her.

"We should arrive in Beaunne early tomorrow morning. Some of the best meals ever, I do not believe I ever ate a bad meal in Beaunne. Have you ever been there?" he asked. Before she could reply, he continued, “The history of Franche-Comté is rich, it must be very attractive to you. Have you ever visited the Abbeye of Cluny?”

She wanted to respond, “take a breath”, but the stout historian continued his diatribe with very little concern of his audience. “The Romanesque architecture is phenomenal, its role within the church,” he sighed, “the division of Church and l’État, n'est-ce-pas, quite telling, I’ll advance.” He suddenly turned his attention back to the banquette to find Gaby engrossed in one of her music books.

“Are you done, Mr. Montellier?” She glanced upward, sideways and then back to him in great distaste. “Yes, my cousin, Cardinal Thornsen educated me in the special role the abbeye played. I also know that it was William the first, Duke of Aquitaine, who founded it in 910.” She grinned back at him and held his gaze.

The academic’s face turned bright red. “I am sorry, Gabriella.”

Her hand dismissed him as she nodded and let the anger pass.

Had she ever visited Cluny? What an erudite idiot! Academically advanced but socially inept, she wanted to retort. Her enthusiasm for Montellier had never been too great. He’d lost the last bit of approval. She wondered why they had not replaced Bernard, her former historian, with another Frenchman.

“Have you heard about the new opera? I am curious about its historical setting. Have you received any correspondence from Maître Lauriot or Maître Goriot?” she prodded.

“No, they’re keeping it a secret until our arrival. Do not fret. I am well versed in most historical periods.”

She shot a dubious look upward and held his gaze again for a short moment. “Very well, always good for the cast to have an expert on hand. Tidbits of important historical movements eases the production along. We appreciate your quick arrival after the horrific incident Monsieur de Levelant experienced on the slopes. You must have been close by.”

She smiled sweetly but stared fiercely into his eyes. "Where were you born, Mr. Montellier? I understand your studies took you to Boston and then to Venice early in your profession."

"Virginia," he replied.

The focus had changed drastically for the impertinent historian, her interrogative statements throwing him a curve.

"Richmond, outside of Richmond actually, Gabriella. I cherish Europe with its rich history and sophisticated society, but I also miss home at times." His voice had gone down a few octaves in a matter of seconds.

She detected a certain amount of insecurity. Good, she thought. I am more than a pretty face with a fabulous voice. Promptly he regained his insolent demeanor as he expertly skipped over his personal history and that of Monsieur de Levelant's accident and his personal proximity to the location of the freakish accident.

"Yes, I look forward to our arrival in Beaunne, as well. A lovely town, indeed. Marc shared that you were in Paris during the Siege. Is that right?"

She nodded.

"I was in London for most of the war," he retorted, "and I traveled to Naples to the San Carlo opéra house soon thereafter. A large community of castrati relentlessly work their voices in the Monastery of Santa Chiara. I remained there during the war and the Siege of 1870."

"Yes, I heard," she responded coolly.

Mr. Montellier had been a new addition to her staff just before their arrival in Rome. He was an American, from the South like her, but had moved to Boston to study Art history at Harvard.

"You know," he continued "the castrati were researched all over Europe. For a couple of centuries, every court in Europe had several to illuminate their soirées. The Choir in the Sistine Chapel still has quite a few. Have you ever heard one sing, Gabriella?"

"No," she lied, displeased.

The horror of Philippe's ordeal flashed through her mind. The 19th century had put a damper in the sub-human practice of gelding young men to keep their voices high and pure. Most never reached the fame of a Facinelli, a famous and adored castrato of the time. Kings, Queens, and aristocrats willingly showered these renown artists with great wealth, gold, precious stones, castles, lands, sculptures in their own likenesses for the sole reason of keeping them in their courts. On the flip side of the coin, many, like her cherished cousin, were sent home, back to their family in a mutilated state. The practice had destroyed so many lives.

Take a breather, Gabriella, she instructed herself. Montellier was solely trying to forge a lien. Suspicion of the world that surrounded her was always at the forefront. Why? Italy, most likely. Jean-Louis had secured her immediate circle of comfort and security but the kidnapping in Venice had left marks—traumatic marks.

Although arrogant, and there were many men in that category in this day and age, the historian just wanted to develop a relationship, she prompted herself. Her former life had titillated the press. All that happened in one's existence left a remnant of conscious and unconscious memories, not unlike a soft cashmere blanket that envelops one's being, the fears, the loves, the ambitions until one decided to fling it open for all to see... or not. She stood and returned to the seat near the window.

"Like a writer, Monsieur Montellier, I cherish solitude. Let's meet later during the day." She dismissed him curtly.

Later that afternoon he reappeared, his arrogance no longer as obvious. He actually asked questions and her opinions of the many European stages. She'd have to suffer him a while longer. Surprisingly enough, his questioning returned back to the Prussian siege of Paris in 1870 and early 1871.

"Marc recently shared with me that you suffered the Siege in Paris, Gabriella. You know I have studied this time in history in great detail. The horrific events that occurred during the Commune, after the Siege of Paris and the defeat of the French in January 71' by the Prussians were ghastly." Montellier pursued.

She nodded.

Jacques and Juliette, her costume adjustors, had entered the compartment as well. "I was caught at the border and forced back to Paris," retorted Jacques. "The hunger that I experienced is inexpressible. I recall fighting. Yes, fighting my way amongst lines of men and women to be first in front of the gutters? I waited with my butcher's knife for the starving rat to inch its way out onto the street. I'd cut his head right then and there, blood spurting from the fallen head across the broken cobblestones. It was a ritual. To my utter surprise, even then, one day a boy reached down in between my legs to grab the bloody head of the rat with its beady eyes and placed it whole in its mouth. Fires were lit and stoked all over Paris, but that child had not waited for the head to be roasted, his intransigent hunger had thrown all rules of civility, humanity into the great basin of survival. That thought lingers to this day in my head. Wars, conflicts come and go, but humans are never the same after living through hell! Let me ask you, Montellier. You were in England, what were the English saying? Why not come to our aid? What about the Americans who maintained the Prussians in their Embassy in Paris and served the Prussian cause? They, too, had forgotten their first friends!"

An awkward tirade coming from an otherwise quiet and gracious man, left Gaby feeling ill at ease.

Montellier swallowed hard as he fell silent.

Juliette lowered her eyes.

The war with the Prussians had lasted from July 1870 to September 1871—just six dreadful weeks. Napoleon III was captured during the Battle of Sedan, abdicated and was taken prisoner by the Germans. The Prussians had released him to England in March of 1871. The Empire had fallen but nevertheless the war against Prussia had continued until January 1871 when the French surrendered and signed the Treaty of Versailles. Jean-Louis had been there. She had stayed behind in Loire. A Gazette's vignette showing the tall aristocrat smiling at a female guest nearby had started a drama that had almost gotten her killed. She'd taken a Montgolfier balloon into the city and had been swept toward the sharp promontories of the Normandy's coast—almost crushed on its jagged coastline. Oh, the past! she considered and sighed. Never rehash its tragedies.

Lost in her thoughts, horrific moments raced in her mind. She repeatedly shook her head, trying in vain to permanently erase the unending judgments firing like fire crackers on the Fourth of July. The aristocracy with their solid financial backing was still a considerable and influential factor of the Parisian establishment—thank God! She looked off into the distance, tucking a stray hair behind her ear, unable to harness the emotion that came firing with intensity at the very thought of the Siege and then the Commune.

The Civil War after the Siege had lasted approximately six weeks—twenty-four thousand Parisians had died. The retributions from Thiers, the leader of the provisional government in Versailles, against The Fédérés, an unorganized band of revolutionaries, many young and uniformed young men who did not deserve to die, had been appalling! The askance had been a return to the Constitution drafted in 1793 during the years of the French Revolution. Many of the dead had been members of the National Guards.

Tragically, these young men had been called from the provinces and were not trained as true soldiers in the great military schools.

Instead, they'd been replacements for the valiant soldiers who perished and gifted their nations with the ultimate sacrifice during the Franco-Prussian War. The battles and hostilities with Prussia—gruesome. Hundreds of Parisians had eaten their horses, dogs, cats, and even rats. The large elephants from the Paris's zoological gardens had been butchered along with many other wild animals.

"Rats?" the historian exclaimed.

"Yes, rats. The citizens would wait in long lines with their hammer and knives ready, kneeling down in the gutters, vigilant, waiting for the rats to make their nightly appearances," she stated sadly, recalling with abhorrence these ignoble days, "some lucky habitants of Paris would call their roast—sami d*e rat,* some even mortgage their mattresses for four ounces of milk on the black market! *Le marché noir* was fierce, for a few extra *sous* many would walk outside the wall and buy at outrageous prices food for their families, sellers would wager their lives for goods that their families needed, to be sold like an indentured servant for the very rich who could afford it. In many *quartiers* in Paris, *épiciers* would buy much of the stolen goods and hide their loot in basements. It sold at outrageous prices but the secret would be divulged in the streets very promptly and many of these *canailles* lost their lives. The price of war! The restitutions to the now Germanic kingdom with Prussian leadership had been fierce. In addition, the loss of the Alsace and The Lorraine were sour points in the French soul. So much dignity lost." She gazed into the distance, yearning to release the great anxieties that trounced her entire being.

"Manet, Degas and Renoir stayed in Paris while many artists fled to England," Montellier said with awe in his voice—a rare departure from his otherwise pretentious demeanor.

"Manet as well as Degas served in the Parisian National Guards," she replied.

"Manet? A son of the high bourgeoisie possesses Republican tendencies?" Montellier questioned, clearly incredulous.

"He felt a duty to shield his wife, Suzanne Leenoff, a Dutch born pianist who tutored him as a young man. His mother and Suzanne traveled with him to the Southwestern part of France."

The stories they told were heart wrenching. Jean-Louis had fought on the warships that tried in vain to obliterate the Prussian army advancing upon Paris. She had been fortunate to have crossed into Paris twice, the first time she had flown back in a balloon from the Place Saint Pierre in Montmartre. The second time, she'd taken a balloon a month later after Gambetta's first voyage to Tours, where he planned to round up the national forces outside of Paris. He was Minister of the Interior, consequently the right man to ask the provinces to '*levée en masse*' to save the patrimony, namely Paris from the Prussians.

One of the servants who took care of her needs, sat across from her, staring. She must have appeared distant as she recalled some of the sordid stories of the siege. The Provisional government, or Government of the National Defense as they called themselves, liberated Jean-Louis in late December 1870.

The proletariat, which made up a large force of the National Guard, was weary of seeing an aristocrat as part of the National Defense government. She lifted the heavy damask curtain from the side window of the cabin and gazed at the snowflakes falling on the rugged road she traveled. So cold, she thought, as a knock at the door brought her out of her rêverie. The maid had departed but Montellier was still there staring at her.

"It must have been some trying times," he murmured. "I understand that the government was not prepared for such an onslaught."

"Unfortunately, these men had joined the National Guard without much soldier training. Essentially yes, the guard was large but out of the 300,000 soldiers that made up the force only 100,000 had been soldiers who were accustomed to severe discipline."

"Trochu, the general in charge of the forces made strategic errors." She sighed and paused as dark memories filled her spirit. "One blunder after another," she retorted. "He'd entirely lost his tactician intuition." Now seated across from her with his usual plum *Eau de Vie* by his side, Montellier looked confused.

"The Duke de Bourbonne had assistance as he mollified the Reds," she pursued, "the proletarian force had descended on the Hotel de Ville in early October and burned it to the ground. An erratic act, indeed, which essentially erased a great deal of French citizen's history." She recalled these darkest of hours. A dark cloud hovered the pretty American soprano. "I will never understand war, and... gossip that destroys human beings and their place in history."

"The war against Prussia had essentially been fought with the fear of the Reds taking over the government," Montellier stated in his grand arrogant style. "In my humble opinion, Gabriella, after the extravagances of the Second Empire, many highly placed aristocrats reaped what they sowed."

Rage bottled up inside her, she stared him down, nodding at the two doors. Shame spiraled through him, she assumed at first, as he hung his head forward in a contrite mien, but he promptly retrieved his aplomb. The historian stood, confident in his beliefs, it appeared, as a smirk hung down his full lips. The butler outside the compartment opened the French doors. Montellier exited.

An overcast gray sky settled over the rolling plains. The rattling carriages lulled her into a melancholic mood. She gazed outside as the sound of a whistle announced to the shepherds on the flatlands that they should gather their grazing animals as the train crisscrossed their pastures at a high speed. Picturesque Alpine valleys dotted with small villages, churches and breathtaking castles at the foot of majestic snow-capped mountains rolled by.

The daily afternoon dessert, usually *petit fours,* was normally served at four in the afternoon. She sighed and spooned the last of the fresh cream covering an apple compote.

Vivid memories of the passionate nights they had shared as the war thundered in the city, destroying all in its path. Nothing much to eat, although she had bought some food on the black market. Where the *boulangers, patissiers, and épiciers got* the food? No one knew—no one cared. She'd formed a close relationship with Elihu Washburn, the American Ambassador who'd refused a transfer back to the United States. All was lost by then—the Krupp had bombed Paris and civilians had died.

Later in February of 1871, in Versailles, a newly elected National Assembly had a royalist majority mostly from the provinces, which had opposed Charles Louis Napoleon's war from the very beginning. Were they to blame? Certainly, not a time to question their allegiance.

All representatives were there to terminate the war against Prussia. Otto von Bismarck, the old King Wilhelm I, and his nephew Wilhelm II made it a point to sign the treaty of the unification of all the German States in the *Gallery des Glaces* in Versailles. Jean-Louis had been in attendance while she was still in Loire. Another huge injury for the proud French. The reparations had been immense for a nation thirsty for freedom from an invading nation.

The last insult the defeated French endured was the painful of viewing the Germans soldiers as they marched one last time down the

Champs-Élysées. The city was draped in black. The reparations cost France five billion francs, which was disbursed in a little less than two years, the final payment in September, 1873. She recollected the festive spirit amongst the troupe that accompanied her. She'd been in Rome with her entourage. The imbibing of French Champagne had not prohibited the extravagant celebration—the final exit of the Prussian army from French land!

CHAPTER FIVE

Weeks later, upon their return to his ancestral home, Jean-Louis had tried to prepare her for the devastation awaiting. He'd clasped her waist. "It's only possessions, Gaby, we'll be just fine. Thousands have lost their lives."

The massive wooden doors opened into the courtyard. Flabbergasted, she'd assessed the unimaginable destruction and ruin left behind. The grand ball room had been used for butchering farm animals. The same sort as Adolphe Thiers's mansion, the first president of the Third Republic. Priceless artwork stolen, canvas stained with animal blood torn from their gilded frames had been used as tablecloths, shattered sculptures cracked in innumerable pieces, scattered across the marble staircases that led to the guests' rooms and the *apartments particuliers* of the family.

Irreplaceable books reduced to ashes in the library's fireplace hearth. The stables emptied. All bottles in the wine cellars were confiscated and carried to Germany. The soldiers had not had the comfort of a bottle of Crystal. A scholarly handwritten note with the seal of the Hohenzollern had been left on a table close to the staircase leading to the main cellar. It read, 'Will enjoy immensely. Merci!' For no good reason, the apartment in the Faubourg had been left intact.

The city appeared frightened. An eerie calm pervaded at every street corner and avenue, generating gloom and despair. The Parisians were as stunned as if an asteroid had landed on the Arc de Triomphe, whose construction had been finished in 1836.

Her jealousy had almost landed her on the guillotine—American or not. The streets were lawless! Jean-Louis had forced her back to Loire while he stayed in the capital.

She had been certain that he was having an affair and was about to start a double life. She'd escaped down to the south of France to embark on a ship bound to the United States. Naturally, the servants and her security had alerted the Grand Monsieur, which prevented her return to America.

Upon arriving in Paris once more, the Communards had taken him prisoner and accused him of treason based on his hasty departure from a most important meeting at the Élysée Palace. Why had Jean-Louis not been killed? The man had escaped death a thousand times.

CHAPTER SIX

Three days later the train reached Paris. Her arrival was just as flamboyant as the one she had received in Rome, maybe more so. Her friends, *les artistes,* all were awaiting. Her home as well, the servants aligned in the courtyard as her carriage entered the large house on the Quai Voltaire.

She had been apprehensive about setting up house in her former home where so many tears had been shed. But the servants, Elise and her new husband Jean-Luc, Camille and Claude Monet, Madame Manet, the great tragedienne Sarah Bernhard, the painter, Whistler, with whom she'd share a short dalliance in Venice, before the love of his life had appeared in his debauched life—all had traveled to Paris to greet and welcome her.

The servants had adorned a beautiful table.

"For your first night back in Paris, Madame," her cook Madame Bonnard said.

Their joy touched her heart. Yes, Paris was her home, a welcome like no other. She wished Cunnan had been here as well, but he was most likely with Jean-Louis. No one spoke about him, certainly not in her presence. Musicians, writers, sopranos, the great financiers who financed the Rubens Gallery, Renaud, who had just returned from England—all in attendance. The music and the dancing lasted well into the night. Around four o' clock, un petit déjeuner was prepared with great care and served to the stragglers. A novelty, for sure. She was amused, all wanted to stay with the taste of champagne and petits canapés.

As carriages began to line up outside the main entrance, Gaby bade goodbye to all and slowly climbed the formal marble staircase to her apartment. Essentially nothing had changed, white roses, her favorite Marie-Josée, were scattered all over the sitting room and bedroom. They had not forgotten. Her maid entered and without much ado removed her scented gloves, untied her dress, removed the petticoats, released her beautiful hair and stripped off with rose water the last of her maquillage.

A lacey nightgown in a pale vanilla color and designed by one of her favorite designers, Worth, was draped across her bed. It caught her attention, reminding her of the design she had chosen for her wedding night. Not that she had worn it! But... in her inebriated state.

She approached the bed where the négligé lay, caressed the raised white roses embroidered by the Bayeux factory, and wondered if the servants wrote every one of her likes in a special notebook. She had been right to preserve their rights and paid for their lodgings during the Commune. Not one of them had left her service.

One of the scullery maids had been impregnated, the father dying on the wall after being shot by the Fédérés. Gaby had given strict orders against all advice not to dismiss her. Juliette was now an apprentice to Madame Bonnard, she'd seen her tonight serving and she'd been wonderful.

Tomorrow would be another day. She'd call a staff reunion since her main butler had returned to Jean-Louis's estate. Five years was a long time and yet the servants were just as wonderful as when she had left. She shook her hair back as she removed her earrings, and then let herself collapse across the bed.

"Oh, Madame, I am sorry. Please let me." The young maid extended her hand, and Gaby released the earrings into the crook of her palm. "It will not happen again," she apologized in an overly contrite demeanor.

"All is well and thank you. Your help was appreciated"

"Good night, Madame."

"Good night, Juliette."

Startled to hear her name, the young girl continued to snuff out the wicks in the remaining candles and quietly left the room.

CHAPTER SEVEN

In a magnificent venue in the new Opéra on the Grand Boulevards, Gaby stood mesmerized at the talent of her favorite tenor. Entranced by his passion for music, his presence, the power and flexibility of his booming voice, she sighed with lust. They made beautiful music together, both on stage and in other more intimate venues.

Last month, after years of being denied by yours truly, he'd decided to propose to his old paramour, the patient and adoring young woman had accepted his marriage offer on the spot. Perhaps she should have given it more thought, Gaby thought as she pondered the instinctively eclectic artist. She loved everything about him.

Alessandro was witty, an avowed libertine who loved women, erudite and extremely handsome but... love was not in the cards with this incredible man. She sincerely hoped they would remain friends. Thirsty, she glanced from the corner of her eye at the flute of champagne that hovered to her left on a silver plateau. She reached for it, ready to clasp the glass as a shadow umbrage the light. She'd recognized that distinctive manly scent anywhere. One that she would identified the world over. It lingered and emanated all around her private space. Shaken, she shifted sideways, confronting her former husband's icy blues as he stared down at her.

Five years of emotional turmoil flashed before her eyes. A frisson of shock shook her body. She stared back. His all too familiar sensual smirk warped her stomach. Unwilling to let her raw sentiments unravel, she flashed a grand smile back at him, and as self-assured as her acting skills allowed, remarked, "Ah, Jean-Louis, a pleasure to see you. I heard you were back in Paris!"

He stared down to the bottom of her soul. Her performance acting was unsustainable. On a *Louis d'or*, a heavenly interruption from Alessandro drew the revelers' attention to the temporary stage that had been set up in the center of the ballroom.

"Mesdames, Messieurs, hiding from us is the dreamiest soprano the world has ever heard. Gabriella is back in our beautiful city!" he shouted as he strode across the room to her.

"Hiding, n'est ce pas, Madame?" Alessandro declared. He'd presaged the unfortunate encounter as he surveyed the room and realized that de Pleyssis had cornered his favorite partner.

All eyes now turned promptly to the singers who cavorted back to center stage, hand in hand. Others stared at Jean-Louis. After all, Gabriella and her former husband had been at the center of Parisian gossip five years prior.

Secured in the tenor's presence, she nodded, smiled to all in the room and quickly stepped toward him. In a grand romantic theatrical demeanor, he clasped her hand, gathered her tightly to his heart, and amorously placed a sensuous kiss on the crook of her neck as they swept away from the back of the room and reached the stage.

Jean-Louis swallowed hard, his jaws clenched as he took a step forward in the couple's direction. Presto, Alessandro disengaged. After all, even now, many remembered in the enchanting salon, de Pleyssis less than kindly nature when the stake was Gabriella de Conte Thornsen, the former Madame de Pleyssis—his Duchesse.

Alessandro loved his partner dearly, but he adored his own face even more! Poor Cardinal Thornsen had almost been killed for the sole error of embracing his dear cousin. God had been on his side. He'd watched the tall aristocrat's fiancée politely set her hand on his clenched fingers, his chin jutted forward, he scanned the room, smiled and eventually calmed down. All wondered why in the world he'd proposed marriage to Marie-Hélène de Grisaille. Rumors had it that

Gabriella was affianced to Alessandro and that their impending marriage would take place at the end of the season. Jealousy, the word was out! The gossips found it all quite delicious, and the Grand Monde reveled in it!

"My dear, let us delight this magnificent *parterre* of opéra aficionados and give them the diversion of their lives, n'est-ce pas, ma chère?" Alessandro repeated, keeping Gaby at a safe distance as he strode to the pianist and handed him a new score. The musician with his long fingers on the clavier sat motionless, mesmerized by the continuing spectacle developing a few steps away from his brilliant black grand piano.

Gabriella's voice filled the room. A coloratura soprano with the highest tessitura, her voice entranced the sternest critic. As the last long Italian syllables filled and bounced off the magnificent painted wooden panels in the room, the shatter of a glass falling to the floor resounded, then another registered and all at once myriad shattered Saint Louis flutes clattered down on the parquet floors.

Mesmerized, the audience lifted their eyes and stared at the orchestra. The sound of the crashing glasses felt to many that another instrument had been introduced to the orchestra. Jean-Louis stood, awestruck with bits of crystal shards remaining in his hands.

Gabriella burst out laughing as the servants rushed to clean up the fallen glasses. Obviously, it had not been the first time that the phenomenon had occurred.

"Ah, I see, Gabriella, another one of your tricks to mesmerize the crowd!" Alessandro quickly intoned a new aria.

Unaware of it but the former lovers had glanced at one another. The duet and arias, Un Di Felice, and Sempre Libera, were the same operatic melodies that Jean-Louis-Pierre and Gaby called their very own.

Ah, fate! Jean-Louis pondered. How often had they sang and danced in their vast ballroom to that very tune? Gaby sang with a new facility that now positioned her at the apex of her profession. He had had to pay a surprising sum of money to annul her contracts. Her voice was honed to near perfection if that was even remotely possible.

After that last glance, the one that had caught the 'thorn birds' by surprise, never once for the remainder of the evening did Gaby gaze toward her former husband.

En revanche, Jean-Louis could not look at anyone else until he realized that the drafters were sketching his every emotion. He smiled at his new fiancée and regained some *composure*—not for long as Alessandro began to serenade the love of his life with languorous words of love and passion, which sent the crowd in a state of longing to hear, feel and want a great deal more.

Gaby, as charming and beautiful as ever, shook her thick mane and swayed gracefully to the tune of the music. Alessandro moved into her personal space, held her close and kissed her on her lips.

The shocked and irate aristocrat stepped forward once more. Conscious of the uproar it might cause, he froze and, with barely restrained fury, turned on his heels and began to cross the vast ballroom. He scaled the stairway two steps at a time, soon reaching the very top of the foyer where guests had been announced prior to the beginning of a soirée.

He marched outside to his carriage when... it dawned on him that Marie-Hélène still stood alone, certainly aghast at the situation at hand. He returned promptly, smiled the same dazzling smile that so few women resisted, sweetly took her elbow and led her to the staircase and into the waiting carriage.

The Gazette and the Figaro had not lost a single instant of their first encounter. Tomorrow all papers would be filled with photos and commentaries on the de Pleyssis's new adventure. Jean-Louis-Pierre de Pleyssis slipping conspicuously a flute of champagne to his former wife. The kiss from the tenor, the departure *sans fiancée*. The applause had not stopped by the time Jean-Louis and Marie-Hélène reached the entrance of the mansion. The butler waited. The footman awakened from a short nap, opened the doors of the coach as the coachmen prompted the horses forward, and then advanced the carriage to the grand entrance.

Marie Hélène stepped in the elegantly decorated interior. She sat and waited for Jean-Louis to follow, glowering at the tall Frenchman when he appeared.

"I find your demeanor this evening horrific and terribly upsetting. I will ask you to never again place me in such a humiliating situation!" she murmured both pained at the very thought of the mortifying role she'd been obliged to tolerate in front of a famed parterre of Parisian luminaries.

Jean-Louis-Pierre sat across from her, his long legs reaching the opposite side of the burgundy upholstered bench, his mind lost in distant thoughts.

The ride to Marie-Hélène's house was silent. She touched his knee as the carriage stopped. His polite demeanor springing out of habit, he helped her out and followed her to the portico.

"Good night," he said as he turned on his heels ready to return to the carriage.

Marie-Hélène caught his arm. "Are you coming in?"

"No," he murmured gently and smiled, "I have an early meeting with a colleague tomorrow." Feeling remorseful he returned back to her and posed a tender kiss on her lips.

"Good night, Jean-Louis-Pierre," she whispered as her eyes filled with tears.

"Good night chérie." He turned on his heel and walked away.

As he stepped back in his carriage, his imagination returned to Gaby. The expression on her face had not told a lie. Gaby still loved him. She had never been able to hide her emotions from him. But would she ever return to their former lives... unknown.

Gaby did not forget nor did she forgive. Eh bien, he would wait. He had all the time in the world now to woo back the only woman he had ever loved and surely would ever love. His thoughts returned to Marie-Hélène. It would cost him a 'pretty penny' as they said in America. Why had he gotten engaged? To entice Gaby's jealousy? Seriously? The thought alone was disconcerting.

Once again, the pretty little American had made him behave like a child? At this stage, however, he was troubled. Gaby might marry Alessandro to show him and the world her utter indifference—her pride had no limits. She just might. Before returning to his estate, he redirected the driver and decided to ride by her house.

The party had continued. Lights glowed in every corner of the property, and music had been piped outside. Eh bien, Gaby had many friends.

Philippe had arrived yesterday. Again, the press had picked it up. Cardinal Thornsen, one of the few survivors of the Massas's prison massacres during the Commune, had not perished during the Civil War. He must have been part of the festivities at the pretty soprano's home!

Anxieties assailed him. Perhaps he had dreamed of the look of love on Gaby's face. Perhaps Gaby had forgotten him. Perhaps she was truly in love with her libertine tenor. He swallowed hard and rapped his knuckles on the upper part of the window. Immediately the coachmen bowled the horses down the arteries across from the river.

CHAPTER EIGHT

For the following few weeks, Gaby's singing captivated Paris. Her encounter with Jean-Louis had been upstaged by all the stories coming out of the opéra and the myriad parties given in honor of the young soprano enjoying her climb to stardom in Paris.

She'd returned to the city of lights for the grand opening of the opéra Garnier. Rumor had it that she would marry her tenor at Notre Dame at the conclusion of the season. Her cousin, Cardinal Thornsen, would perform the ceremony. Then Renaud, just back from the Orient, was the next in line.

As well, she would return to the New York Metropolitan Opera in September. Tickets to all of her performances had been booked for months. Many in Paris would attend, traveling aboard the British ocean liner, The RMS Britannia, to the *cotée, very much in vogue* American city.

Rare was a non-aristocratic woman's social comeback, particularly after having been scorned by a former husband as influential as the Duke de Bourbonne. *Confusion* was the word of the moment. The Duke appeared to be distressed over the separation and acted unlike his usual unperturbed self.

Gaby had seen him once with some friends; a mature couple along with young girls had applauded forever after her performance. The sighting had been more difficult than she had expected. Jean-Louis looked older. She wondered if she appeared older to him as well. Cease at once, Gaby thought. One more week of commitment and she would meet up with Elise and Renaud, perhaps Luke as well. Élise had been in London, and Luke and Ribaud would stop in Paris prior to vacationing in Nice in the South of France and the Principauté of Monaco.

Tomorrow, the banns of Alessandro's marriage would be published. She shook her head. The gossip columns would go on a rampage. Odd feelings stirred. She presumed that Sandro would not be as accessible; his wife would make certain of that. It was good for him. She had been involved with all the arrangements. Tonight, a private room had been reserved to bury his bachelor's days.

Strong doubts surfaced. A man like Sandro would not be confined to the marriage bed for long. Beauty, money, wit, talent, kindness would go only so far! Juliette would understand, she would endure and, in the end, accept his hot-blooded lifestyle. She had promised Juliette to surprise him with the many arias they had sung together.

Life was good. She loved Paris although the carnage that the forces of Versailles had inflicted upon the revolutionaries of the Commune remained tender among the population. Twenty-five thousand people had been murdered during la Semaine Sanglante, the Bloody Week. That was in May of '71—over five years ago—Paris, the city of lights had burned. What would it portend for the future? A return to the monarchy or the continuation of the Third Republic? No one knew.

CHAPTER NINE

The group of artists filed into La Goulue, an end of the century restaurant in Saint Germain known for its Tarte Tatin. Gaby, who had arrived earlier to organize the party, was told by the Maître d'hôtel that Monsieur de Pleyssis also had reservation with Mademoiselle de Grisaille. Was it a game? Jean-Louis appeared at every venue she'd attended. Unfazed, she continued on her merry way, flirting openly with Andrea Perini, another adored tenor.

As the guests arrived, she greeted them and murmured a few secrets, or adventures to divulge during ensuing celebration at her behest. Her graceful fingers crossed over her mouth and her expressive eyes spoke volumes, indicating the amount of mystery. The future groom, her favorite tenor and partner in the present opéra, La Traviata, entered in a grand fashion. He embraced Gaby, who returned his amorous sweetness with gusto.

All was not lost on her former husband, who entered the establishment at just about the same time with his fiancée, Marie-Hélène de Grisaille. They were seated in a private adjoining room with a good view of the large banquet room where a musical event was obviously in process. Jean-Louis, envious and perturbed that an invitation had not been extended to him, eyed the large grand piano and observed Gaby, joyous and magnificent.

Great laughter and merriment animated the *en vogue* restaurant. Arriving politely late, a beautiful young woman appeared and gaily joined the group. Incensed at all the gaiety across the room from him, Jean-Louis could not help but stare at the new arrival. He fumed at the theatrics his former wife flaunted with one of the top earning and celebrated tenors in the operatic world. To his astonishment, the pretty young thing walked to the tenor, enveloped him in her arms and kissed him passionately on the mouth. She turned to Gaby, smiled and strode to the talented soprano, giving her a warm embrace as well, *sans la bise*.

Jean-Louis stared, not quite certain what to make of this new development. The young woman sat with Alessandro at the place of honor while Gaby settled with friends further down the table. *Croquembouche*s, petits canapés of Saumon fumé and Foix Gras, along with Cristal, of course, were presented to the artists seated at the long table covered with highly starched, white damask tablecloths. The *piece de resistance was served and the customary conical Piece Montée de choux à la crème,* the traditional engagement and wedding cake in France, was brought in and devoured immediately by all.

Jean-Louis watched as all settled back in their fauteuils with their Cognac and *fines, the tasty liquor brandy savored after a gastronomic feast*. Finally, the room was cleared of the long banquet tables and the piano was rolled back center stage.

Jean-Louis waited, impatient for the next elaboration. He smiled as he recalled the last pastry. It was definitely Gaby's choice. She simply adored *les petits choux* with *crème fraiche.* He smirked, recalling their own wedding in Loire. She had almost left him at the altar!

Oblivious to the tall, elegant blonde next to him, he was now ecstatic. Gaby's melodious voice began to echo throughout the private rooms. In essence, Gaby was the organizer of the celebration given in honor of the tenor's engagement. Consequently, the field was free, and far sooner than he'd expected. The rumors about Alessandro or Perini. All false. Without an iota of remorse, he promptly excused himself to Marie-Hélène, stood to his full height and strode to the vast banquet room where Gaby leaned against a brilliant black grand piano, her favorite pianist playing the joyful tune.

The tall Captain entered the room. Stunned, all turned to him, anxious for the dénouement. Jean-louis walked to the piano where his former wife now stood motionless, staring at him and awaiting his next move. He smiled at her and quickly motioned the pianist to move over.

Gaby gazed, amused at the obnoxious behavior, as her former husband took his place on the slick black bench. She'd imbibed a bit too much, but... what harm could come out of simply flirting with a man she knew almost everything about. The slight musician, forcibly shoved to the very end of the bench, nodded, visibly annoyed, took the hint and walked away, a grimace on his face courtesy of the aristocratic arrogance.

Jean-Louis played a few notes and solicited the accompaniment of Gaby. He slid a bit to his right, lifted his eyes to Gaby and winked. "*Eh bien*, Madame, *continuez*!" he exclaimed with a grin. "Am I good enough to join your artists' friends, Gaby? Great surprise, chérie, I have been practicing my musical skills."

"You've improved," she quipped back, tickled by his challenge. "But you still have a long way to go!"

Great bursts of laughter broke the awkward moment. He used it to reach for her hand and clasp her wrist, pulling her gently round the piano. As the talented diva slid next to him, he gathered her sweetly to him and stole a kiss while lifting the lace of her décolleté closer to her throat. "Then re-marry me, Gaby! I need to practice with the very best."

"Never!"

"That bad, *n'est ce pas*?" he teased. He swallowed, hiding his disappointment in a well-rehearsed, confident demeanor.

"No, I..." she began and ceased immediately as she spotted Marie-Hélène striding into the room. "No." She straightened her torso and looked up at the future Madame de Pleyssis. "It was a wonderful time in my life, Jean-Louis... but now it's history."

Gaby recalled the tender touch of Marie-Hélène de Grisaille's hand over his as they'd entered the private club. Their eyes had met. Jean-Louis's fiancée's resentful glare had spoken volumes. To redress the moment, she began to sway away from him on the bench to remove herself from a difficult situation until his clasp forced her back down on the seat next to him. He continued to play.

"Eh bien, Monsieur, it is impossible for me to follow your cacophony."

He smiled again, redress the ever-plunging neckline that teased his gaze and lifted his eyebrows. "Fair!" he said good-naturedly in English.

Marie-Hélène, who by now stood right behind the former enf*ants terribles*, placed her gloved hand on his shoulder. "Why, I thought it was euphonious and grand, Jean-Louis. You're so gifted."

Gaby turned her head and acknowledged with an ironic glance the future Duchesse de Bourbonne. "Since rumor has it that your engagement is imminent, Jean-Louis, I presume, Marie-Hélène, that you will have to send the Duke with his many talents to my former theater to practice his great gift!"

"There will be no need for him to serenade anyone," the blonde beauty replied. "Jean-Louis and I have decided to turn your theatre into a nursery wing, Gabriella!"

A pin could have been heard falling on the shiny parquet floor. Gaby's eyes began to fill with unshed tears. Taking hold of herself, she swallowed hard and smiled grandly. "In that case, Jean-Louis, make certain to call Maître Lauriot. You know how much he adored the Grand Piano. He would love to take it!"

She winked at him as a tear escaped from the emerald eyes he loved to kiss shut.

"Magnifique!" the pretty American soprano exclaimed. "Another one in a million de Pleyssis in the making." She smiled, her trembling chin and lips bearing the agony her heart could not reveal.

Jean-Louis stood and rounded the bench as he approached Gaby and posed a kiss on her cheek. "My regrets, Gaby," he apologized as he grasped Marie-Hélène's elbow none too gently and escorted her out of the restaurant.

Less than a week later, the dissolution of the engagement of the Duke de Bourbonne and the aristocratic Marie-Hélène de Grisaille was announced with great fanfare in all Parisian publications. Gossips abounded in salons. Marie-Hélène departed for London.

CHAPTER TEN

A fortnight hence, as fate would have it, Jean-Louis-Pierre was waiting for old friends to arrive in an *en vogue auberge, La Maison Fournaise*, close to the *Châteaux of Malmaison.* The magnificent estate had been sold during the Second Empire to Charles Louis Bonaparte, the former Napoleon III.

The gardens had been an absolute joy to Joséphine de Beauharnais, Napoléon I's Empress. Bonaparte, appalled at the large sum of money she'd spent on the Estate while his army died on the Egyptian shores, had nevertheless learned to adore the beauty and intimate corners of the Château. The government had been moved to the charming castle. Many evoked this period as one of the happiest times in the Conqueror of Europe's life.

Jéan-Louis-Pierre had not much to do with the little Corsican tyrant, but he often said, "The Corsican was part of French history." His words inflamed many of Gaby's friends, the artists, who adored Napoleon Bonaparte's humble roots and his astounding climb to the apogee of power throughout Europe. He did not care. She'd excoriated his 'pretentions, his *Ancient Régime* ideals,' of no value. His only response—amusement at her Republican principles.

"Vraiment?" she'd responded as he recalled the altercation. "The '89 Revolution, the Directoire, Napoléon's first Empire, then... another three Kings, a President for another two years, who essentially crowned himself Emperor! A war loving Emperor at that," she'd declared "who'd gotten played by the wily Prussians? What has that accomplished, *mon cher* husband?"

"The French Revolution, Gaby? Its manuscript, supported by many of us aristocrats, darling, will go down in history as one of the most astute and freedom giving documents ever written. One huge problem, the populace was not ready for it all. Your turn, what has that accomplished?" He'd responded calmly as the recollection of some of the wonderful moments of their lives together popped into his mind.

"Much, Jean-Louis."

"Yes? My imprisonment? Less than one hundred years later? Another revolution? Famine? The death of twenty-four thousand French men, remember *la Semaine Sanglante*? No, Gaby, the aristocrats would have protected the common man from these revolutionists. Had anger, hunger, the dismal discourse of another great revolution at hand, one that would liberate the have-nots from their pitiful state, had these men been given time to ingratiate into laws their views of accelerative goals for the nation, none of these horrors would have happened. A State needs to ease into modernity, led by men with integrity and the love of their nation at heart."

Rather than accept a learned viewpoint, she'd left the room. He smiled at the thought of her excoriating antics. She'd laughed out loud when she'd agreed with him, not willing to utter the words, "You're correct." How he wished his jealousy, his possessiveness had not led her away to distant lands. To have her back in his arms at any cost was the design.

He'd made plans to join a boar hunting party. He sat in the *guinguette*, overlooking the river ballooning out of its bed onto the sloping, slippery banks. The trees, their trunks partly hidden by the mounting water, appeared to have sprung out of the water. The winter rain or flash downfall had flooded villages, bringing misery and deprivation to many peasants and their families.

Paris, as well, experienced the intemperate weather. The chalands returning to the capital from the provinces struggled to deliver much-needed fresh food destined for *les Halles* market. Their berths, often inaccessible and no longer visible, extended the time it took to disembark the provisions.

On the cultural venue, many of the *Louvre*'s paintings and sculptures held in basements had been relocated on the first floor of the museum. Nevertheless, today, the air was fresh, the sight spectacular, and although the habitants of Paris were reserved and many still traumatized at the very thought of the 71' civil war, life and its many pleasures continued for the well to do.

The government kept tight control on many activities. While Jean-Louis-Pierre waited patiently under the dried, copper brown, ivy trellis awning, for the group to arrive, a young waitress with a long white apron advanced toward him.

"Monsieur, Lord Ribaud and Lord Luke and Mademoiselle Élise de la Grangeade were here less than an hour ago. We are preparing their lunch baskets. Monsieur le Chef asked if we should prepare one for you, as well, Monsieur?"

"Please do!" he retorted, pleasantly surprised. He stood, returned to the oak bar inside and asked for a whiskey. Under the *tonelle*, lively music and scores of men wearing straw *canotiers* and women donning their 'garden' hats, as his grandmother referred to the new millinery, danced to the sprightly beat of an accordion.

He scribbled a note to his friend, Jean-Marc, on the polished mahogany bar, stating that he might join the party later but his plans had changed. At the end of the path facing the auberge, a young *garçon* waited, he handed the parchment to the young boy and strode outside. His horse harnessed, he mounted it. Just an inkling, he thought, but perhaps the former Madame de Pleyssis might have joined them.

The reason for the silence. "Ah, Gaby, you cannot escape me. Fate has a way of bringing us back together," he scoffed aloud.

In fact, Ribaud and Luke had invited Gaby to go boating in Chatou with Élise. A week and a half of unlikely warm winter days had melted the ice on the river. The boats, usually locked in and iced in the frozen river, bobbed about in the snappish water undulations.

The sun was high in the sky and the cold winter air naturally blushed the women's cheeks. The four friends sat on a wooden bench facing a dark wooden table, awaiting their lunches before heading down to the river. Soon the water would freeze. Luke and Ribaud looked forward to their winter vacation in Nice.

"Like two good English aristocrats," Gaby mocked. "Nice is the destination *de rigueur. Why else* would the path bordering the crystal-clear water of the Méditerranée be called 'the Promenade des Anglais'! You own it all, Your Graces!"

Legend, or partly true stories, had it that unusually brutal weather had brought beggars to the temperate south, and the English had put the beggars to work building a promenade next to the sea in the South of France.

Socrates, Gaby's dog, scurried every which way in the clearing surrounded by willows stripped of their leaves. For no apparent reason, he began to bark in a frenzied manner. All turned around at the same time as a recognizable voice thundered behind them.

"What a great surprise,'" Ribaud exclaimed.

"It would not have been had you invited me in the first place!" Jean-Louis-Pierre derided as he tapped his friend on the shoulder while placing his large body between Ribaud and Gaby. "While waiting under the *arbor* for a group of friends... we had decided to go hunting, the boars are plentiful this season, I was told about your arrival."

Stunned, Gaby kept silent.

"Bonjour, Élise," he said, "guarded as well... I see. I remember that you almost drowned in that same river down the ravine until yours truly saved your life! Who are we pledging alliance to, my friend?" Jean-Louis-Pierre thundered, amused.

Élise burst out laughing. She stood quickly and came around the bench to greet him. She bent down and kissed him on both cheeks. "I am delighted to see you, Jean-Louis-Pierre. Sit with us, I'll share my lunch with you," she said as she reached for the white Sancerre they had been served. She poured a glass and inched her way next to him.

"Am I being displaced once more, for this grand Monsieur?" Luke burst out laughing as he took Élyse's seat across the bench. "Will we have to share our food, as well? Going a bit too far, Jean-Louis-Pierre?" he said as he chuckled.

"No need. The chef is preparing a basket." He took a sip of the wine and glanced down at Gaby.

Stunned, she could only stare back. Dismal. Perhaps it had not been the best idea to accept the engagement in Paris. She recalled Philippe's warning in Rome. Jean-Louis would not let her rest. She questioned her "I've gone on, Philippe" and sighed.

His next sentence was directed to her. He placed his arm around her waist and brushed a kiss on her forehead, lovingly he parted the short curls that hovered on her shoulders. She shrugged and moved further away on the bench.

"Eh bien, Gaby, we have made the front page once more," he murmured jovially.

"Yes, rightly so," she derided. "I would appreciate it if you stayed away from me from now on."

"Truly, Gaby," he murmured, "I am terribly sorry for the spectacle last week. Marie-Hélène and I have gone our separate ways."

"I presume that it is hard to keep your dear privacy, my friend," Élise remarked, "It was plastered in every newspaper in Paris. Down to the last payment you paid for her grand house in London! I presume priorities took the place of honor." She nodded down toward Gaby.

The tall aristocrat did not respond. Instead, he turned his back to her.

Smirking, Élise returned to her seat, next to Luke.

"But I can assure you, Gaby, that I still have hope that perhaps one day soon you'll grace your stage in our home once more!"

Gaby did not offer a retort to the egregious impertinence, but her eyes and demeanor spoke volumes. She lifted her skirts and whirled away from the bench where both sat and stood behind him, a brazen expression on her face.

"Jean-Louis, first, do not ever touch or kiss me again! And frankly, why don't you go and fight a war, beat, get beaten and die! This would be my most fervent dream! As far as my wedding present," she emphasized with a trembling voice. As soon as the words leapt out of her mouth, she knew she'd revealed her sadness, and the words stuck in her throat. "Maître Lauriot would absolutely love to transfer much of the theater to the Palais Garnier."

Shocked, the friends sat frozen. Perhaps Gaby may not be as removed from her painful experience as she'd like to convey. The two Englishmen remained silent.

Jean-Louis-Pierre roared with a great burst of laughter.

"Cher amis, now you know how I was abused!" he boomed. "I was told more than once that my death would be music to her ears, and... *N'est ce pas, Gaby*?"

"Jean-Louis," she exclaimed, "how can you?"

"Let truth fall where it must, Gaby. Luke, you asked some time ago why Gaby's plantation had not been razed during the Civil War? Eh bien, dear friends, the answer is that Gaby's reputation preempted her—too fierce." He turned and came to stand by her.

Her eyes swept up to him, not knowing what to make of it. Brazenly he gazed back. His lips breezing closed to hers, "I know all about it, Beauty, I heard it first hand from your friend, Martin, the barrister on your plantation."

Powerless to the emotions the proximity of his presence bore, his scent and his incredible aplomb, she pushed his chest away from hers and caught Élise's glance. She lifted her skirt and looped around the bench toward Ribaud, a half smile on his face. The Duke straddled the bench and reached for the dog still barking at the intruder.

Immediately Gaby stood and returned to the dog, grasping it away from his lap. He clasped her elbow and then her hand, "no need to..."

He lifted his head and noticed the young and pretty *serveuse* as she struggled to push forward a wide wheelbarrow lined with a red and white damask tablecloth. Packed inside were the picnic baskets. A thin young man followed the waitress with bottles of red wine cradled in his apron.

"Stay, Gaby, I was teasing. It is nice to have you here in Paris. You look magnificent. I will eat with you and our friends and be on my way," he promised.

Observing the happy expressions on her friends' faces, Gaby let go of his hand, snatched Socrates away from his lap, and sat back down closer to Élise.

The young waitress set the silver cutlery, porcelain plates and crystal glasses on an embroidered white damask tablecloth that she spread over the wooden table. All received matching white, heavily starched napkins as the waiter began to serve the already sliced roast pheasant, spooned the plump red new potatoes sautéed in a buttery sauce and the thin *haricots verts* covered with sliced almonds and chestnuts split in halves. These tasty bits were placed expertly in a large platter around the bird.

Crusty baguettes cracked in several large pieces by the server were positioned in silver baskets at each end of the table. In another dark brown basket lined with white napkins, large chunks of peasant bread and an assortment of apples, pears, walnuts and large brown figs were ornamentally arranged. The barman who had followed the young woman to the clearing began to pour red wine into their glasses. All appeared normal.

Quiet had returned, and the six friends began to eat and drink. Élise noticed furtive glances from Jean-Louis-Pierre, which at times were returned inconspicuously by Gaby. All asked about the Duke's trip to India and his banking interests in America.

"You were in the United States?" Gaby questioned. "What banking business? Where? In New York?"

"Both in Boston and New York," he responded simply.

"I thought you had gone to India?"

He nodded. "I did for a short period after you left for Rome. But I like your country much better, Gaby. The big Four are essentially my neighbors in Newport." He smiled as he referred to the railway tycoons. J.P. Morgan and I met in late '72. I had a lot of money at my disposal and voilà the deal is working well. I own quite a few banks in the States. But let's talk about you, instead. All are expecting you with great excitement in New York. I understand that you will open the season at the Met in late September?" She nodded, certain now that he knew far more than she wanted him to know.

The wine mellowed her restive spirit.

"I will," she answered distantly. "I will return to America in June on the RMS Oceanic."

He smiled. Both knew exactly what the other was thinking. He stared at her.

"I could make the Tempête available, at your service," he replied, gazing at her sensuous lips.

She glanced away, sipped the wine and uncomfortably glanced at Ribaud and Luke. "Thank you, dear friends. The food is scrumptious, the conversation always fun and challenging... well, until a certain

Duke infringed impolitely on our serene surroundings." She glowered at Jean-Louis, who began to roar with laughter.

Her eyelashes fluttered, and she shook her head. "As I said, the setting is spectacular, you are my truest friends and truly I am at my happiest when you are near!"

She beheld her friends lovingly for a long moment. But then, as if she had forgotten the presence of her former husband, she turned to Jean-Louis and stared into his imposing blue eyes. "Time for you to go. My previous statement did not include you!"

"But Gaby, dessert has not been served yet!" he replied amused. "You know how much I love it!"

She shot a hatred-filled glare in his direction.

"You hate it, hypocrite!"

"Ah, Gaby... I'd gulp down a *Piece Montée* spiraled with a thousand cream puffs just to keep you near me, Chérie."

"I hate you, Jean-Louis." She spoke with such vehemence that he did not retort.

A few hours passed as the afternoon sun began to lose its luster and a cold briskly air settled in.

"Friends, let us go," she said as she stood and strode to her horse. "Let us enjoy the freezing cold but glorious rest of the day. Even this brutal Parisian cold cannot compare to the ruthless Russian winter."

"Eh bien," Jean-Louis mimicked, "I drank too much. I will join you instead, lest Gaby's sordid dream materialize. Impaled by a boar, not a pretty picture!" he stated implacably.

Swift on his feet, he strode behind Gaby and clasped the reins. "My horse is back at the auberge, let me ride behind you."

"Absolutely not!" She mounted her horse promptly.

Just as agile, her former husband held on tightly to the reins.

"Let go. We do not want you," she remarked sternly as she raised her whip ready to smack him.

Effortlessly, he clasped it, forced the lash down and climbed up behind her.

"I understand that I was just invited to join the boating party!" He struggled against his mirth as he dug his spurs down and then firmly in the horse's flanks as he led the charger at breakneck speed downhill. All began to laugh, and even Gaby was forced to break a half smile at his force of character.

Instinctually, the divine soprano lowered her face closer to the horse's mane. He observed her every move. God, how he loved her. He noted her long torso, miniscule waist, although covered by a moss green velvet cape as she lay against the spine of the horse, and he recognized the thrill of danger in his ex-wife's demeanor. He refrained from placing his hand on her back. He had pushed her to her limits—of that he was certain.

A touch now might set him back another month, if not forever. Still amused, he continued to stare down at the shapely body before him. He recalled having been surprised while riding to Nice years ago upon their arrival in France. He tightened his grip around her waist. Ah, Gaby, he thought, we were made for one another.

***

Having reached the docks at the very bottom of the hill, the group spotted the two boats reserved for their outing on the lake and their return to the *auberge*. Both multicolored *barques* were moored by the river bank.

"Well, very well," Gaby said in English as her former husband lifted her down from the saddle. "Your journey ends here, Jean-Louis. As you can see, there are only two boats. I doubt that your attire would be appropriate for a swim in these murky waters."

A great roar of laughter answered the pretty soprano ironic comments.

"You've appropriated my best friends... now seriously, chérie?" He smiled tenderly at her. "I adore you, Gaby."

"I wish you dead," was the curt answer.

The three friends lifted their eyes to the heavens at the two *enfants terribles.* The amused twinkle in the Duke's eyes was not lost on any of them. Ribaud reached for Gaby's elbows as he strode toward the small boats to embark.

The rest of the group reached the riverbank as Luke burst out laughing. He'd presaged Jean-Louis-Pierre's next move by following the big guy's glance. They boarded their respective barges, Luke with Élise and Ribaud with Gaby, and the boats promptly began to sail down river.

Tightening her white fur *toque* around her face, Gaby heaved a long sigh. She clasped Socrates and covered him with her cape.

Shortly into the crossing... a familiar voice shouted, "Gaby," she heard her former husband shout.

All turned toward the bank they had left just minutes ago. Jean-Louis in a very small yellow barge with green and orange stripes on its sides, his long legs clad in dark suede breaches rolled up to his knees hung down from the sides of the boat while he rowed away trying to bridge the gap between him and his friends. As she took in the sight, she shook her mahogany curls and her smile spoke volumes.

"*Voilà,* my dear friends, allow me to present to you, the powerful Capitaine de Pleyssis!" the diva proclaimed in her grand theatrical demeanor.

"A sorry sight, my friend," Ribaud intoned.

All turned as they surveyed the sight, laughter echoing across the slippery slopes.

"I'm glad you're back!" Élize shouted. "I missed you so."

The rest of the day continued as planned, but with Gaby's former husband in tow. As they returned to the inn, the last rays of the winter sun shone on a few straggly leaves suspended on the stripped tree limbs lining the path to the inn. The dancers were gone, the large sunflowers embroidered in the damask adorned the sofa and its matching chairs facing the fireplace. Gaby marched to its hearth and stood pensive in front of it as she warmed her hands in front of the dancing yellow flames.

"After Saint Petersburg, one would think that my southern blood might thicken slightly!" Her crystal-clear laughter brought a smile to all present. "It was a wonderful day, dear friends, thank you," she said.

"Welcome home, Gaby," Élise remarked as she came close and hugged her friend.

Years ago, upon Gaby's arrival, they had started on uncertain ground in Cannes. Yet their friendship had flourished throughout the years. They had been inseparable during the trial of Jean-Louis, the difficult times of the Commune and even afterward.

Élise and Ribaud had followed her to Rome when she left for the Eternal City. She had been so fragile then. The three had fought to secure Jean-Louis's freedom, and yet the big man had chosen the lies fed to him by his grandmother—her nemesis! Oh well, that was the past. She'd survived.

"You know, Élise, Paris is my home. I miss it so when I'm away. My singing engagements have taken me to splendid cities, fascinating royal courts. I admired Saint Petersburg, the lavish castles of the Tsar summer residences, the incredible art collections amassed in the late 1700's in the Hermitage by Catherine the Great." She sighed and looked down at Socrates, who'd followed his mistress. She bent down, picked him up and gathered him to her heart. "Vienna and its many opera houses, Rome, Naples... but Paris has my heart."

"Well said!" Jean-Louis-Pierre remarked. A venomous glance followed his statement.

"Diderot and Grimm were the celebrated Empress's art dealers, chiefly in Paris, n'est ce pas, Gabriella," the pretty blonde said. "They chose phenomenal works of art for the museum."

"*Oui, en effet, Élise*, her gardens as well were awe-inspiring. She loved flowers, well-trimmed bushes, waterways that did not deter from their natural flow. She was a true aristocrat in every sense of the word and, like you and Jean-Louis, never denied it. She actually believed that an autocratic monarchy was the only way to govern and to protect the populace. I think she may have been quite liberal and enlightened at the start of her long reign. She suffered in that very court under Empress Elisabeth, her children taken away and a husband who wanted to entomb her in a convent.

"Things changed after the Pugachev's rebellion that was dealt with in 1775. It frightened her, and because of it she gave a lot more power to the nobles surrounding her. She needed them. Her dreams of giving the mujiks their freedom never came to fruition. Actually, building nations, taking territories, sacrificing large groups of soldiers for the good of one's land was the right way to govern in her eyes. Her wars with Turkey and Finland appeared to have been to shield her nation from the many western European conflicts," Gaby explained.

"It was reported that the French Revolution affected her previous enlightened ideals and her vision for her Empire. She wanted to assuage the sort of the populace but essentially never trusted them with matters of state and administration."

"Who can disagree with that?" Ribaud retorted. "These people were uneducated farmhands, most of them anyhow. It would have been foolish for the nation and the aristocratic realm to leave such a vast mass of land to peasants to govern themselves."

Gaby nodded. "Nevertheless, I would have loved to have been presented to her court. Quelle femme! What a woman!" she repeated in English. "You are aware that the Russian Court spoke only French?"

All acquiesced, and Gaby burst out laughing. "But of course, I forget the long aristocratic lineage that you, my great friends, represent!"

Ribaud winked at Jean-Louis.

Élise shot him an enigmatic glance.

Supper was served in the main dining room. Later that night they all returned to the sofas and comfortable chairs in front of the hearth with their glasses of brandy and Champagne bottles.

Jean-Louis ordered a magnum of Cristal, Gaby's favorite. The war with Prussia, the civil war—the Commune, the trauma still felt from losing *l'Alsace* et *Lorraine*, the spirit of revenge ingrained in the French laid raw below the joyous surface. Gaby felt it, all five years hence as they discussed these memories of uncommon misery.

"It happened so promptly," she said. "A gilded age, really. A time of balls, plays, operas, 'bonne table', great exhibits of young painters, *Les Impressionistes* assumed the role of observers of their society through their paintings and sculptures of modernity and amusements of all types."

Together the five friends stared at the remaining embers that crackled their dying sounds in the large stone-covered hearth.

All of them could have completed her implicit words—la bonne vie. All that *joie de vivre* was replaced suddenly in July '71 by a Declaration of War with Prussia asserted by the Emperor Louis Napoleon III. Over what? Yes, France had been frightened by the placing of a Hohenzollern on the Spanish throne, fundamentally a momentous event since the French nation would have faced the Prussian on the East and South West, but the Prussians agreed to remove the appointed leader. Was it one of Bismarck's sly hoaxes? Who knew?

Six weeks later, the war was lost, the Emperor had abdicated and was incarcerated in Germany, a provisional government governed France while the Prussian laid a siege on Paris, intent on waiting until the Troffu government, the new French head of State, agreed in January to accept defeat. Those who had stayed in Paris, had been plagued by starvation, one of the most rigorous and brutal winters in its history and the complete disarray of the rule of law. The Communards had tried in vain to re-establish a government by the people for the people. As a final point, 25,000 thousand French men and women had died.

"Paris feels like a silent city," Gaby murmured. Her voice sounded so grave that all but Élise, who sat next to her, questioned her last statement. "Parisians exhibit towers of strength in their daily lives, but the traumatic air that swept the city before my departure five years ago is still present. The distress experienced after the Commune extends to this day to all walks of life."

"Where were you, in Paris, Gabriella?" Ribaud questioned. Recalling the difficult times, he paused. "I am terribly sorry, my dearest Gabriella. I recall the selfless struggle you fought for Jean-Louis-Pierre as his prison sentence was in contest. What a time!"

"Oui... what a time!" She sighed, glowering at her former husband. "I stayed in Loire, as well," she responded curtly to Ribaud.

She stood and strode to a side mahogany buffet where a silver pot of freshly brewed café sat, positioned next to it an unusually large container of sugar. She lifted the silver spoon and dipped it twice into the sugar bowl.

The barman smiled, his expression seeming to say, you are showing your roots, Madame. Unconscious of the silence surrounding the group of friends, a wave of desperation scorched her entire being. Her extreme jealousy had begun the denouement of their idyllic union. A sigh escaped from her expanding breasts and a dark cloud passed over her pretty features.

Jean-Louis-Pierre remained silent.

"Let's be happy those desperate days are over. No need to recall a destructive era." Élise perked up, bent forward to the table and lifted the Champagne from its silver bucket. "A nous tous! To us all!" she cheered.

"Artists are filing back into Paris mostly from London, Gabriella, and also the South of France, Nice primarily," Ribaud declared, stunned at the rapid transformation. "I spent a lot of time there during the war. No one dared to broach the French nation's demise. A harrowing time, indeed."

The grandfather clock chimed twice.

"Dear friends, up I go. We will meet early tomorrow," Luke exclaimed as he stood and grasp the whiskey bottle sitting on the table. "Anyone," he called out. Both Élise and Ribaud declined as they slowly uncurled their inebriated bodies and commenced a slow saunter to their first-floor rooms.

Gaby stood up.

"Stay down here a while longer Gaby, please?" Jean-Louis asked. The collar on his shirt halfway open, she stared at the chain that hung down from his neck.

"I never took it off." he murmured.

She glanced at the gold chain and medal of the angel Gabriel. The locket had been her wedding present, their initials and pictures engraved by the Maison Cartier.

She hesitated for an instant and reached for the Champagne flute as she reclined, deep in the soft cushions on the canape. 'Watch yourself Gabriella,' Philippe's voice echoed.

"We have nothing to talk about." Promptly, she picked up the coupe and drained it as she bent forward, reached for her leather bag, and slowly curled out of the deep-seated sofa. She stared in his baby blues for a long time. He did not attempt to flicker a muscle until she turned her back to him. Quickly he stood, wrestled her bag from her grasp with one hand and clasped her elbow while directing her toward the steps leading to the rooms.

CHAPTER ELEVEN

Unwilling to attract attention to themselves, Gaby followed his lead under the stunned scrutiny of the front desk clerk's glances.

"I recall letting you share my room once, on a certain ship, ma chère. I hope you'll return the favor."

He stopped her on the winding staircase.

"I don't share, Jean-Louis. You can return downstairs and sleep outside on the frozen benches for all I care."

Silent, he swallowed hard and without much ado, he picked her up, bags and all, and brought her upstairs.

"Les clefs, the keys, please?" he requested, his hand extended, a smile on his gorgeous face.

She hesitated. "You always win the battle," she reflected aloud as she offered him the bronze set of keys.

He stared down at her and stole a kiss. Her breasts heaved. Resigned, she handed him her reticule. He opened the door and placed her on a settee parked on a dais in an alcove in between two windows facing the large bed. A full moon glowed high in the sky. He looked outside for a split second, spun on his heels and ambled toward the bed. He settled on it as he adjusted the pillows behind his back, intertwined his hands behind his head and stared at her.

She stared back. "Tell me, Jean-Louis, what is wrong with this picture? This is my room. I paid for it, and you're lying on my bed?" she remarked in a tight voice.

Her glare persisted.

"Why did you divorce me, Gaby? Never in a thousand years would I have started such proceedings and renounced my wedding vows." He lifted the gold locket.

"To save your life, Jean-Louis," she retorted. "You should know that, I repeated it enough times. You preferred the falsehoods spread by your grandmother," she countered with resentment. "After what I had gone through, I had no fighting spirit left in me. You chose to believe I had lovers! The will to fight deserted me. I did not have your trust... consequently, our marriage was a sham!"

Her breasts throbbed as she clasped her throat, her emerald green eyes scanning the painted ceiling. She returned his focused gaze. "I no longer dwell on the past," she remarked coldly. "Now, I want to know about your statement today, about my plantation and Martin."

He decided not to pursue the vein of the conversation. Soon enough, he would return to it. Giving up on Gaby, a tragic error and one that would never ever be repeated."

"Stop the happy talk, Jean-Louis, I want to know why you traveled to the Justine? Who did you talk to? Did you meet my father?"

He nodded.

"As you know Cunnan and I left for India after you left for Rome. We negotiated some good leads for international economic affairs but neither one of us wanted to deal with the poverty and the conflicts on the Indian continent. At that time, England had a good hold on the culture and, like the French India company of yesteryear founded by Louis XIV's finance minister, Jean-Louis-Colbert, we could not compete with the English and the Dutch. They are still well entrenched in business there after the demise of the French East India Company and the English nationalization of the Company. We sailed back to the United States instead. I was in Boston for a while. I bought a summer home in Newport and in early fall I attended a financial conference in Washington. I like your *Capitale* and visited a friend in Virginia."

She glanced awkwardly at him.

"I met newlyweds who actually saw one of your solo repertoires in Florence as they toured Europe during their *lune de miel*," he explained.

"All these meaningless details have no importance, Jean-Louis," she interrupted, "go on." He smirked. "Eh bien, I met John Young Mason. Do you recall, we met him in Cannes years ago? He was the Ambassador to France at the start of the Empire. We talked about you and our time in Paris. I decided to revisit New Orleans, maybe meet my father-in-law or rather my former father in law," he retracted. "Perhaps even ride down to your place of birth, Gaby. I had time to explore."

"And?" she demanded, stunned.

"At the Cotton Exchange in New Orleans, I asked about your land. I received more information than I needed to learn, rose early the following morning and rode to *La Justine.* The reception was somewhat less than I expected, since your lawyer friend barred me from your land. 'Leave the premises and never come back!' were his exact words. Although, as I rounded my horse down the imposing oak trees alley, I was stopped by several of your sl... servants. All knew of your marriage and asked about your life and your possible return."

Gaby sat motionless, a million questions popped in her head, but her pride prevented her from uttering one word. Although Jean-Louis gave her time to inquire, she remained silent.

"An older woman came out of the marsh as I rode away and waved me to stop. She asked if you were happy."

"Who was it?" she questioned.

"I do not know, but a small child pulled on her skirt crying and a young man came quickly and chased me away. I checked out Philippe's plantation as well and tried to visualize both of you as children, riding your favorite horses on the banks of the Mississippi."

His sensuous smile and well-timed eye twinkle lightened the sober conversation. "The reception... eh bien, Gaby, was not much better. Consequently, I rode back to New Orleans."

Dazed at the revelation, Gaby attempted to make sense of this incredible turn of events. The valorous Captain de Pleyssis was in a narrating mood, however.

"I remembered you spoke well about the restaurant *Antoine's*. I decided to give it a try. You were correct, and I dined there often. New Orleans has a provincial atmosphere, every little detail of life on the Mississippi is reviewed and recounted with great folklore. I really enjoyed it. They remembered Philippe, but many more remembered 'the Voice' at the Cathédrale on Christmas Eve. Extraordinary. One of these times, one of the waiters who tended to my needs expressed that a Mr. Thornsen, a well-known *personage* and regular client in the Vieux Carré, was on his way with his family. Would I mind moving to the covered patio? Stunned, I agreed and asked for a table which would give me a clear view of the inside dining area. I was also informed that the family usually returned home after the meal and that your father stayed behind to conduct end of the week business with large groups of cotton brokers. Whether or not the Maître d'hôtel knew more than I perceived—perhaps? I asked a lot of questions, and I was not secretive about our relationship. Here and there I'd noticed that the regulars stared at me conspicuously. I do not know. Even without prior knowledge nor physiognomy of the man, I would have recognized your father. The resemblance is fierce. A bit short." He sneered, a twinkle in his eyes.

Gaby remained silent. Her breasts rising and falling, her fingers fiddling with her skirt, she glared at him.

"He must have been told who I was," Jean-Louis pursued "for he curiously glanced over at me increasingly through the glass French doors. So much so that the whole family began to stare in my direction," Jean-Louis continued, his tone controlled. "A short while after your stepmother and brothers left, I saw him gesturing to the waiter. An elegant note changed hands, whereas your father requested my presence at his table. I welcomed the occasion!"

Jean-Louis continued, "I accepted the invitation as I ambled inside. We introduced ourselves, he offered a cigar and two whiskies and two desserts. Beignets and Bananas Foster were brought over. Your father expressed great pleasure in our 'per chance' meeting. We spoke about his businesses, my businesses; he even apologized for not attending our wedding. All was going well until he stated that he knew that a person like myself must have been attracted by your beauty and charm, but that all in New Orleans knew the marriage would not last! Too headstrong... like her foolish mother," he stated.

"One of the few times he showed good judgment," Gaby mocked. She bit her lips. Burning tears ready to stream down her face filled the expressive green eyes that faced him. "I wish that very strength of character had resurfaced after you asked for my departure from our home. I was broken, Jean-Louis, your jealousy and pride never gave me a chance to explain. I asked God to take me, had it not been for Philippe, Élise and our friends, I'd be no more. Your stories and countless perfidious apologies will never assuage the hatred that I feel for you! I have heard enough. Get out of my room!"

Incensed, she rose from the cream satin settee, lifted her skirt and began to cross the room, her long hair unraveling down her back. She snatched from the floor and brandished one of the many satin umbrellas that matched every one of her costumes, as she approached the bed where Jean-Louis half reclined on one of the pillows as he calmly recounted his turbulent days in New Orleans.

"Three furies wrapped in one! Are you Alecto, Megaera or Tisiphone?" he exclaimed, knowing his former wife's fiery temperament. He rolled over and stepped down from the elevated platform where the bed rested.

"Why have you escaped death so many times, Jean-Louis? I wish I had never met you," she shouted as he gently clasped the umbrella, tossed it across the room and gathered her body close. "I wish you were dead!" she gasped with venom.

He swallowed hard, his well sculpted jaws tense under her tirade.

"I deserve it, Gaby, but... I am quite pleased to be alive and well and to hold in my arms the woman I adore." His lips descended gently down her uncovered décolleté.

She turned her head and looked up, stunned by his désinlvoture.

"And furthermore, Gaby," he continued, "I will never, ever allow you to leave my sight again."

"You are mad, Jean-Louis!" She untangled herself from his embrace. "There are laws in France that will put you behind bars and throw away the keys!"

He roared with laughter.

She continued, "Or better yet, lock you up in an asylum to indulge your follies! Do you think I care that you met my father and his family? That it will establish a link for us to rekindle? I abhor the man, Jean-Louis."

"Just a difference of opinion, Gaby," he stated calmly, changing the subject. "Do you truly believe that my compatriots, after I devoted my life to France and to my renown ancestral lineage, that my countrymen would revoke my right to Liberty, Equality, Fraternity? I think not, Gaby."

"You have a very short memory, Jean-Louis! I recall distinctly visiting you in prison, taking great physical risks to insure your release. You had fought for your country then, as well, but the Communards were not too impressed with your service. What happened to the likes of you during the '89 Revolution? Many were shortened a bit, lost their heads or were torn to pieces!"

"Correct, I owe you a great deal, Gaby. These were horrific times. but we fought a second Revolution, Gaby, to guarantee that these distasteful incidents will never come to pass again. The Empire has fallen. France is a Republic and... but please let me finish the story." He tried to gather her to him and draw her small body onto the bed, but she refused. She returned to the settee, while he stretched out on the bed once again.

"Now, where was I? Oh yes, Mr. Thornsen would be lying six feet under with his foolish wife had it not been for his friends who came to his rescue!"

"You didn't, Jean-Louis?" she whispered.

"Yes! Given the chance, I would have killed him! I paid dearly for it but it was well worth it!"

"They dragged you to prison?" she questioned.

"They did. New scars on my battered body!" He laughed heartily. "The corrupt bastards enchained my feet and hands, threw me into a solitary cell and made my life a living hell for a month! Had it not been for my contacts in Washington and the integrity and legal know-how of your friend Martin, I would have rotted in the reeking prison!"

His grasp of the language was impressive. She looked at him embarrassed at the thought. Jean-Louis appeared more American than she. She did not know how she even felt about this tragic turn of events. She had not thought about her father in so many years, which was good.

"The advocate took pity upon me and I recuperated at your plantation," he continued, "I rode Tempest every day, became quite friendly with your servants and slept in your bed. Quite nice Gaby. I must say, the home is well-appointed, your land is beautiful and from what I could see well established and lucrative. I would have stayed much longer had I not been ordered out of the state and driven to the border in shackles and chains. My friend, the Senator from Virginia, was quite embarrassed. Needless to say, I'm persona non-grata in Louisiana."

"Quite an ordeal, Jean-Louis," she remarked, her voice emotionless. "But you of all people should not have been surprised. I am happy Martin took care of you. It was the right thing to do." She nervously patted her skirt. "Not everyone in my state is corrupt and lacking moral fortitude."

He stretched out fully on the bed. The great de Pleyssis was in a talkative mood.

"More exploits?" she mocked, torn between wanting to throw her former husband out of her room or continue the intimate conversation which essentially was all about her.

"Before I returned to Paris, I stopped in Rome to deliver to Philippe documents sent by Martin." He continued, anxious to reach the end of the story. "Your cousin would not even see me. I gave the package to an aide and was thanked in passing by the presence of a priest who essentially kept me company as we dined in a restaurant across the way. The fellow asked a lot of questions about my itinerary. I told him I was on my way to Milan, to catch one of your performances at the Theatre Regio Ducale. Two nights later, I was ambushed and beaten by a group of thugs who left me lying in a pool of blood in a gutter across from the Teatro Regio Ducale. Neither money nor valuables were stolen! Unusual, don't you think? Seriously, I wonder about dear cousin Philippe?"

"Jean-Louis, cease! It's scandalous! Poor Philippe. How dare you? He dislikes you immensely for good reasons, but Philippe is a rare angel!" she replied lovingly as her cousin's handsome face flashed in front of her.

"Although by some still unknown reason, I was found—in the gutter, that is—and taken to a very nice local hospital. I must say the sisters treated me quite satisfactorily. Gaby, one of the nuns told me I had Cardinal Thornsen to thank. Bizarre, *n'est- ce- pas*? I never saw your exceptional performance, instead I read all about it a few days later in the paper. You were already on your way to Saint Petersburg to fulfill your chanting contract at court!"

"Jean-Louis, did you have anything to do with the sudden modification of my singing engagement redirected to Paris?" she questioned, suddenly very aware of his influence in the capital. The many interactions amongst the myriad groups stirring in the same direction perturbed her immensely.

Silence prevailed.

She stared at him, all too aware of the intense moments spent agonizing over their rupture. Philippe, her most fervent confidant, had not been able to lift her tortured spirit from suicidal thoughts. Her soul vanquished, her heart bleeding, only the hours spent on stage singing the words of love and betrayal that spilled out of her throat offered respite. Too weak to foment her own death, she had taken outrageous chances with her life. Leaving the opéra in the early hours of the morning, walking the streets in her mink coat and jewelry in sordid areas of the city—all hours of the night.

She had even prayed for someone to kill her to end the agony! Her death wish would most certainly have become a reality had not Philippe heard about it from one of his aides. Her cousin was a saint. He had taken leave and set himself up in the house that she had rented. He was in the *coulisses*, offstage, during and after the end of her performances, he ate with her, spent his days with her, accompanied her to the theater, to her recitals, and prayed with and for her.

He had not stopped in just Rome but had accompanied her to Milan and Naples. His constant appearances with her had even provided fodder for a few gossip magazines. The Paris incident had been mentioned more than once. Poor Philippe, his only desire was to protect and save her from herself. She loved him so! A year and a half after her departure from Paris, the energies of her indomitable spirit seeped back into the fibers of her being.

She became amenable to tours outside of Italy and away from Philippe. An invitation from an Austrian Prince had been extended. She'd accepted it. Philippe had returned to Rome. Even Ribaud and Élise had found her in much improved spirits. No allusion to Jean-Louis-Pierre had been attempted. She had lived an idyllic life, giving up her dreams, her passion for him, but he had deserted her in a moment of insane jealousy bolstered by an old dowager intent on erasing a relationship that would have stained the illustrious family's name.

Socrates barked. She looked away. The darkness enveloped the hillside outside. Jean-Louis's gaze, intent and determined, pinned her. She swallowed, cast a skeptical regard in his direction and heaved a long sigh.

There were streaks of gray on his temples and a new scar right above his eyebrows. He had been silent while she recalled these troubled times.

"Why didn't you fight for our love, Gaby? I asked myself that question incessantly. Why your departure to a foreign country...? To retrieve Phillippe? I just needed a little extra time to make sense of these new accusations against your person while I was in solitary confinement. You knew that nothing would have kept me away from you."

Stunned, she remained voiceless for a moment but fury re-surfaced à *grand chevaux,* at great length.

"Are you humoring me? Why did I not fight for our love? I fought with every fiber of my being for six long months. Not knowing if the firing squads would spare you or sentence you to the ultimate punishment!" she shouted.

"The divorce, why, Gaby?" he murmured.

"You want a reconciliation and, after all these years, you still doubt my words!"

"I just want the truth, Gaby, I know I was wrong but I do not understand the lack of money, the *cours* de Pleyssis, I am a wealthy man and so were you by extension of our marriage. I would never have broken our solemn vow."

She sliced his last word.

"You want the truth? Eh bien, let me repeat it once more with details." She sighed and for a long moment appeared to be drowning in a chasm of despair. Why did she even need to give him an explanation? He did not deserve it! The flow of emotions mired with indignation boiled in her veins.

Jean-Louis-Pierre remained silent and serene. He lifted his torso to rest it onto the blue silk and gray satin-canopied bed.

"I was disconsolate after fighting for your freedom incessantly for almost six months through most of the Commune." She stopped, not quite certain whether her heavy heart would let her unravel the torturous moments she had endured.

"I would like to know, Gaby," he murmured so low his words were almost imperceptible.

She nodded. "No trust. You'd accused me of an affair first with Philippe, then Jacopo and then with this ghost of a lover invented by your grandmother. You believed her over me. My life had been placed on hold for you. Our accounts were frozen or the ones that I knew about in Paris. I asked your grandmother for loans. She denied me, insisting instead that I was lying. 'All banks will extend credit to our illustrious family!' she exclaimed, essentially calling me a falsifier, a swindler! My lawyers advised for the divorce to save my plantation and my own financial assets."

Jean-Louis stirred uncomfortably on the bed with a questioning glance.

"My money paid for your litigation," she responded, then heaved a great sigh. "Furthermore, let me add another dimension to 'my not fighting for our love' libretto."

She pursed her lips, and paused for an instant. She was not certain she wanted to share, but she'd gone too far. He wanted to know. Well, she would lay it out clearly in his court! "I expected our child—again—Jean-Louis. This time, the pregnancy lasted a bit longer than usual. I thought that perhaps God would save that child, in the event that you would be condemned to the firing squad."

The bones and muscles on his jaws tensed. His chest slumped and rose again rhythmically, his sculpted arms resting behind his head tightened, and his piercing blue eyes glared at hers. Melancholy and fear all wrapped up in one expression. He looked somber.

"As I crossed the street in front of the apartment Luke's grandmother had lent to me, I jumped in front of a carriage bowling around the corner. Many thought I would not survive. The Duchesse de Pleyssis included. In my semi-somnolent state, I believe that she visited me. Dr. Durand was close to my bed as she gave him explicit orders to send the child to an orphanage should he survive!" She paused, her memories beyond painful.

"Durand refused. She threatened him. He had her taken away. I was strong enough to beg Durand not to do her bidding, under any circumstances. I was prepared to sign over my plantation and everything I owned to him. Durand, bless his heart, brushed my forehead with a kiss. 'You and the *bébé* will be just fine, dearest Gabriella,'" he cajoled. That very same night I lost the baby—again," she mocked. Her facial expression and the continuous, nervous twirling of the layers of her multicolored skirt betrayed her.

She shook her hair back, an old habit from when her luxurious mane reached her waist, instead the shock of mahogany curls returned to frame perfectly her celebrated and refined Grecian features. “A little boy, I was told. No great surprise in the loss. If death should take me, so be it. But... I survived and within two weeks, I returned to reaching out to all levels of the administration and military services to secure a meeting with you.”

She stood, descended the dais and strolled to the window closest to the bed where he sat. She parted the drapes, the bay windows had been left half open, the water of the creek down below rumbled across the rocks. “You wanted the truth, Jean-Louis, voilà.”

The silence of the night appeased her torn spirit. She cracked open the French windows a bit more and inhaled the cool breeze. Perhaps a new gust of wind could sweep the painful pangs the remembrance of those agonizing moments unfurled. At that moment, almost imperceptibly, the two doves balanced on one of the branches reachable from the balcony flew away to their nest.

Two strong arms encircled her waist and gathered her small body tightly to him. She could hardly breathe. A powerful spasm shook his body, warm tears wet the crook of her neck.

“I am repentant, Gaby,” he murmured, “wretched... offer me another chance, I will follow you the world over. I will make it up to you... all the time that we have lost... the memories that we did not make, I will be there for you, Gaby, forever.”

At the very same moment she felt strong hands pressing her back and gathering her abdomen against his impassioned manhood. Lust surged. In each other's arms and both emotionally drained, they fell together across the bed. Guilty pangs of *faiblesse* tortured her, *while* he caressed her cheeks with tender kisses, searching for her lips.

She wondered, why deny herself a few moments of happiness? She was strong and could handle another separation now. His kisses made her happy.

Jean-Louis was a magnificent, sensual lover, but she was no longer in love with him. Philippe's voice haunted her. No, she was no longer a young girl who could be manipulated with visions of the perfect love, she had had many lovers over the years for lust and amusement, so why not? This is how she'd handled her life after the denouement.

Jean-Louis would not be any different. He was just a man now, not the hero of her youth! Sexually, they were great partners. Why deny herself a few moments of pleasure? Jean-Louis pleased her, and she did not want to be anywhere else. It was insane to live with anger and reproaches. Her life was glorious. Jean-Louis had essentially done her a favor!

As he penetrated the depths of her body, he clasped her hands and lifted them above her head. He pinned her to the bed, her back arched, her breasts exposed and ready to be loved. His lips gravitated from her eyelids, to that very tender place behind her lower lobe that only he secreted, to her alabaster throat and alighted to the large mounds of soft and sensuous skin as he pressed and pulled on her hard nipples. She fully surrendered herself to his lust.

Old guilt pangs, however, lurked around the outer edges of her mind. She hated herself for being in his arms, and even more so for being in his bed while her traitorous body was incapable of resisting her craving to caress his muscular back and to press his chest to her breasts.

She assured herself of her independence. Then, she rolled him over onto his back, climbed astride his large torso, rubbed her breasts across the most erogenous parts of his physique, and made love to him as he'd so expertly taught her. He smiled and stole a kiss at the height of pleasure.

No, she did not wish to let him go—at least not quite yet.

CHAPTER TWELVE

The following morning, followed by Socrates he walked out of the bedroom. Down in the dayroom, tables were magnificently dressed for the *petit déjeuner*. Élise and Ribaud sat drinking a cup of *café au lait* and English black tea respectively.

"It is breakfast, American style!" Jean-Louis told Élise and Ribaud as all three stared in amusement at Socrates eating eggs and filet mignon. "Gaby is fast asleep."

"Have you reunited? I presume our plan worked? I thought she'd have more resistance in her," Élise remarked, a hint of disappointment in her girlish voice.

"I am never quite sure with Gaby," he murmured. "Let us see how she reacts without the Cristal in her heavenly body this morning."

"You have no right to utter another word," Élise exclaimed. "You are fortunate that Gabriella even talks to you!" She stared at him until he looked away.

Élise stood, came closer to her old-time friend and gathered him to her. She kissed him tenderly on both cheeks.

"*Eh bien*, it is time to go. Do not spoil our plans!" she ordered as she turned away, grabbed her flowery satin umbrella from the servant and ran svelte and light toward her waiting carriage. Another thought appeared to pop up as her eyes glanced back at the handsome Frenchman. She rejoined him on the steps.

"Promise!"

"I will change," he repeated, thoughtful as he massaged the back of his head.

Élise was correct. He grasped the unimaginable pain he had inflicted on the person he loved the most in the world. "I will change, Élise, I adore her and always will," he whispered.

"For your sake, I hope that you can, but I'm uncertain that Gabriella will go along with the scenario. Be prepared, my dear friend." Once more she came up to him and unabashedly gathered him close and kissed him again on his lips as she whispered softly, "I will do everything in my power to help you recover the love that you so flippantly tossed away. I love you, always have and always will. Do the right thing, Jean-Louis-Pierre." She hugged him to her voluptuous breasts for a very long time. Socrates, perturbed at the show of affection not directed towards him, began to scratch at his leg and bark fiercely. "I'll write as soon as I get to Nice."

Jean-Louis scrutinized the ground below him, nodded to his cherished childhood friend, tensed his perfect jaw and resolutely bent down and picked up the dog.

"Élise, Mon Dieu!" shouted Ribaud, "Come, we've ridden twice around the *Place* for Madame to reappear!"

She clasped her skirt, lifted it above her shoes, ran back and climbed into the carriage with Ribaud. As carriages waited their turn to return back toward Paris, Luke announced he would stay behind just in case Gaby changed her mind. His bag was removed from the carriage by the footman. He grabbed it and placed it on a nearby bench. The coach attempted to pass five or six carriages traveling in the same direction. Élise waved one last time from the open window at her two friends.

Slowly, Luke and Jean-Louis, Socrates in his arms, strolled inside the *auberge and* sat at the table.

"*Un carré d'agneau,* and *un œuf brouillé,* American style—pour Monsieur." He smiled and pointed at the dog. As the waiter bent down to serve the dog his second morning dish, Socrates scurried along and ate to his heart's content while Jean-Louis and Luke perused through the main headlines of the paper that had been left on the table.

A quarter of an hour later both dog and lover climbed back up the twisting staircase to Gaby's room. Near the fireplace, a large silver tray displayed warm flakey croissants nestled in white napkins in a silver filigree basket. Six small crystal pots containing wild raspberry, blueberry and peach marmalade were set on a table, along with a silver coffee pot, milk and cream carafe, all appointed on a heavily starched white damask tablecloth and matching napkins.

Bright-eyed in bed, his former wife watched him stroll in the room along with Socrates.

"He appears to like me immensely, Gaby," Jean-Louis said, dipping his head, smiling at her favorite pooch. "He will have to learn how to forgo his daily morning croissants upon your return to the United States. Quite difficult to find a decent *patisserie* in New York."

She smiled, turned her back to him and fluffed up her pillows. "Thank you, will you pass the tray? I'm ravenous." Obediently, he brought a cup of coffee over in a white cup designed by the Sèvres factory nearby.

"Wasn't the design on these cups designed by Alexandre Brongniart, in honor of our marriage?" he questioned, routing his forefinger on the cup, Renaissance in its motifs but definitely Second Empire in its images, "Here you are, Chérie. Look, they captured your face perfectly right down to your emerald eyes and your unforgettable smile as you shared your elation with our guests!"

She glanced upward and scoffed at his imperturbable pretension. Cup still in hand, he rotated it around and then inspected the matching saucer.

"But Chérie, where am I?" He chuckled. "*Eh bien*, even then, Gaby, it was all about you. A good omen?" He came closer to the bed and kissed her. "Our love inspired a new generation, Gaby. We can't run away from it, Chérie."

She wrested the cup away from him to examine it. "Yes." She smiled, remembering the special moment. You were about to feed me a *choux à la crème* from our wedding cake!" She looked up to him, full of the love she still felt. A moment passed... She wished she could surrender and let their love blossom once more. Forever.

A vision of Philippe appeared, her *sang froid* and logic resurfaced. No... no... no... she thought, this is just great fun, passion has passed, I have been in many compromising positions these past five years. This is just one of these situations. This, too, will pass. Enjoy yourself, Gaby! That is what life is all about. She stared at him.

"*Mon peignoir*, please," she requested, nodding at the satin and lace vanilla robe thrown on the Louis XV white and gold trimmed *canapé*.

He did not budge. She swung her shapely naked legs down from the bed and onto the thick carpeted flooring. Instinctively, Jean-Louis followed her every move and deliberately caressed the curves closest to him as she passed by. He stood and retrieved the silver pot filled with the bubbling hot aromatic black brew—strong black coffee—Gaby's favorite. He poured another steaming cup and handed it to her. "A good start, *n'est-ce pas*? I have not forgotten, two in a row."

She returned back to the bed, her curves enveloped in a white satin negligée not quite tied up at the waist as the belt hung down her legs. A few more instances as she was not quite yet willing to dismiss the escapade.

She reached for the cup and lifted it to her lips as she looked up to him in good spirits.

"Our sexual chemistry will never wane, the connection..." she began, then stopped. An interior conflict stirred wildly within. He probably had heard her statement last night, at the height of pleasure.

She'd disclosed emotions that she now wished could have remained unspoken. It had been truthful at the time.

Trusting Jean-Louis once more still evoked passions that left her breathless and wanting in a moment of weakness she now regretted immensely. The scent of the crusty croissants in the basket was too scrumptious to forego. She reached for one and pulled off a large piece, which she offered to Socrates. Then she reached for the scrumptious treat and proceeded to spread confiture on its flat glazed surface.

Whether he grasped her internal conflict, he quickly approached the bed, and kneeled down next to her. "I love you Gaby, I always will."

"Until the great love ceases," she responded with bitterness.

The comment remained between them. "Our reunion is my deepest desire, Gaby." He came closer, lifted the fluffy eiderdown and kissed her breast. His lips ascended slowly to her throat, delicate jaws, and he forcefully licked the comfiture from her lips.

"Why, now? You've had five years to mend your demented conduct." She pushed him away.

"Yum, raspberry marmalade, *n'est ce pas*? To die for!" he murmured, letting the comment fall on death ears. He could sense her body wavering, retreating and finally surrendering.

Desire leaked out from every pore of her shapely figure. She pulled on his white unbuttoned linen shirt and slid her hand below it and around to his back. "Kiss me," she demanded. The response was immediate—the tray was quickly picked up and placed on the nightstand as he rolled in next to her, his body searched her warmth, his lips hungrily pressed hers, her breasts arched and pressed against his chest. Chemistry—oh yes, but a whole lot more. She still adored him.

A few hours later, Jean-Louis held his former wife's back close to his chest, his face buried in her dark wavy mane, his hand on her soft sensuous breast. Both stared at the lonely bird chirping on an ancient oak tree stripped of its greenery right outside their balcony. "Most probably his friends have left him behind," Gaby remarked sorrowfully.

"I was that bird, Gaby," he whispered. "After you left, no one could fill the void, like this little fellow I was looking for my life partner." Some unshed green leaves wavered across the window pane as the lonely bird stared back, then decisively opened his wings and flew away.

Jean-Louis gathered Gaby even closer to him. She wanted to push him away, ask him to leave. "Just a few more hours, Gaby, Enjoy, the good times should linger' her treacherous inner voice whispered.

And she listened.

"I will make it up to you, Gaby, all the time that we have lost, all the memories that we did not make. I will change. I will live for you and will follow you everywhere, I will be devoted to you and you alone," he murmured as his lips brushed her eyelids shut.

Once again, she hated herself for being in his arms and even more so for wanting him so fiercely. Helpless against her adulterous body, she caressed his hand and forced it close to her breasts, reluctant to let him go—not just yet.

A spray of dog bark right outside her window sliced the passionate moment. She lifted her head pushing him back.

"Where is Socrates?"

"Resting his full to the rim stomach on the chair next to the hearth in the salon." He chuckled. "He was served breakfast American style. I had the chef reheat and serve him a *faux filet,* they had not baked the croissants yet." He called out Socrates as if they had become the best of pals.

"I have a great idea, Gaby. You mentioned yesterday that you did not have to return to Paris before Wednesday, how about going to Beaunne—together?"

"No, I need to return, Jean-Louis. Besides, I do not have any clothes." She tried to roll out of bed but he curled her back close to him.

"What do you have to lose... for old time sake? I sent out for a more comfortable carriage and asked the driver to stop by your hôtel particulier to assemble a more appropriate wardrobe. The new carriage, as well as your clothing, should arrive here in early afternoon. Meanwhile, the last foxhunt of the season is being sorted out on the outer edges of the woods. Let us partake in the fun this morning. Madame Bonnard promised that she would have the raspberry tarts ready upon our return. Come, Gaby, we will have much fun."

About to refuse categorically, she looked up at him and... relented. Why pass on a few extra moments of happiness? Jean-Louis made her happy. She did not want to be anywhere else. It was foolish to live with anger and ill feelings that essentially had been forgotten. Why not enjoy a few days with Jean-Louis?

She would return back to the opéra in just a few days and the following week she would be in Monte Carlo with Pirelli. She loved spending time with the amusing, adventurous tenor. Although a miserable rider, he possessed great know-how in bed. It would be easy to forget her tryst with Jean-Louis. All good, she told herself. Just a few more hours with Jean-Louis, she surely would continue to pursue her happy life after her return to the capital. She nodded to him in the affirmative.

"I love you, Gaby. I will follow you to the end of the world." He repeated as he rolled her in his arms and stared at her wide-open eyes, expecting a response.

"Our chemistry is..." She gasped under his tender touch, "... it will never wane. Our love was uncommon, Jean-Louis. But now, the pleasure I derive from my independent spirit surpasses our previous happiness. I will never in a million years give up my wonderful life for anyone... not even you, Jean-Louis."

"You speak as if I kept you in a dungeon stashed away from all but me, Gaby. You were one of the most independent wives in Paris and, now that I know a lot more about your country, I would even advance that you were certainly one of the one percent if you resided and married in the United States! I refused the public stage to you solely out of security concerns."

She lifted her eyes to the heavens, shaking her head.

"It is absolutely true, and I do not need to rehash the unfortunate incident that occurred while in Venice. You almost died for the very reason that I relented on your security. You had your own theater in Paris, you directed many sopranos at the opéra, you had free rein in Paris with your friends and colleagues. I do not think that you were a prisoner because of my insurmountable jealousy!"

Realizing that his defense was too harsh, he softened his tone and drew her even closer. "How strange, Gaby, that I always thought I was born without an ounce of jealousy until I met you. Odd, I fell in love and married the most independent spirit in France and now I'd give it all up to spend the rest of my life nestled on your breasts!" he announced sweetly.

"What drama, my dear! You'd be a pauper had you decided to go into the dramatic arts! I, yes, I gave up everything for you, my life, my friends, my profession... what more could you ask for? You asked earlier why I did not fight for our love? Emotional and physical exhaustion sapped my energy and my will to persist. I just couldn't. It dawned on me that your love for family and country was greater than all we had shared. You chose your grandmother's lies over my love and utter dedication to you!" He did not answer. She pressed. "You gave me two weeks to move out of our home. You left to hike in the Pyrénées. The very thought of those insufferable days is ravaging."

"I was wrong, Gaby. I told you so after my return. I would have been amenable after the trip to listen, but you had given up on me. Rightly so, perhaps," he murmured almost to himself. "I begged you to stay, to cancel Milan..." He recalled seeing her dash off in the interminable train in the *Gare du Nord* on a dreary late summer day. He swallowed hard, his chin jutting forward as he recalled the pain she'd meted out. "I have been paying for my grave error ever since. You mentioned a while ago that you had forgotten how handsome I was," he mocked.

"*Eh bien, ma chère.* You're always with me, your photos, your paintings, your letters, the newspaper clippings of your opéras, I engaged in a moment of pure insanity as I heard of your impending wedding to Adolfo Pirelli upon arrival in Paris." He swallowed hard and reached for her chin, lifting her face to face him as he placed her fingers on the chain. "My wedding chain has never left my chest. I will always adore you, Gaby." He kissed her mouth sweetly. She was clearly emotional.

"Let's spend a few days together, Gaby, before your return to the stage on Wednesday."

Her questioning eyes gave him some concern. "For old time's sake," he quickly added, feeling a twinge of uncertainty. "Let's go to Beaunne, the food is scrumptious, the Champagne, *eh bien* you know it is better than most, and the riding trails in the nearby forests are challenging but so beautiful."

Her ghastly weakness was repulsive, but the denial of a few extra days of happiness seemed irrational. She nodded. In the train that had taken her to Rome, she had sworn that she'd accept whatever pleasure that came her way. No need to sulk! Whatever made her happy, she would pursue. That very philosophy had lifted her out of a deep depression and most certainly had saved her life. Today was no different!

Silent, he rolled her onto her side, clasped her breasts and kissed her hair. "*Eh bien*, Gaby, let's get ready!" he exclaimed in English.

He rolled out of bed and pulled the cordon to request a servant. Quickly, a pretty young *soubrette* knocked at the door and entered the room.

"Pour a hot bath for Madame." Jean-Louis summoned.

"Oui Monsieur, de suite!" the pliant young maid turned back on her heels and retreated through the open front door. Minutes later she returned with baskets of fancy soaps, aromatic bath oils and lavender scented lengths of white toweling material. She placed it all and turned on the water in the stand-alone mosaic tub nailed down to the floor tiles by large bronze lion claws.

Both were left alone once more. He ambled to the side bar, refilled his coffee cup and poured in a splash of pear brandy before he downed it. Prior to his return to the tub with the baskets, he tossed some sweet-smelling scents into the steaming water.

"What do you think, Gaby? Could I make a decent living wage as a butler? Your butler? How much do you pay?"

"You still have a lot to learn, Monsieur. Furthermore, I much prefer you in my bed!" She returned his smile coyly.

"I could make myself available for both, Madame!" he retorted, retaining in one hand the lavender *vaporisateur* with its golden cord dangling on his well sculpted thighs. Without missing, he uncoiled the opening of his cognac suede breeches, stepped out of them and undressed fully. She smiled, her gaze filled with erotic expectations.

"Voila, Madame, at your service." He came close to Gaby still stretched out in bed, brushed her lips with a kiss and picked her up. Gently, he dipped her toes in the scented tepid water. A questioning glance materialized on his handsome face. "Eh bien, *parfaitement*, Madame?"

Amused she nodded.

He slid her body into the colorful porcelain tub, then stepped in by first moving in behind her and then lifting her onto his enlarged manhood as he slid his long legs along the tiles. Before she could ask, her hair was unexpectedly pinned up in a chignon and tied with the rose ribbon that had encircled the soap. He cupped her visage sideways to him and stared, "very cute indeed." he declared, apparently quite pleased with himself.

The soap and oil massaged along her body facilitated the many indecent improprieties he seized upon and elicited moans of ecstasy from the pretty brunette as he delighted her in the most private of places.

"Touch me, Gaby," he demanded.

Filled with yet unfulfilled promises, she turned on him cat like and brazenly clasped and thrust his swollen sex deep into her most private spot. The warm water filtered gently in her womb before his distended manhood blissfully filled her.

"You're adorable, Gaby," he gasped before pleasure engulfed them both. "I love you!"

Less than one hour later, she removed herself from the hot water in the tub and stood nude, watching his every move. She regarded him, unconvinced. His regard left hers and wandered down the curvaceous body facing him. He swallowed hard, sighed, rubbed the back of his head and winked at her, lifting his eyes back to her.

"I will follow you to the end of the world, the only certainty in my life is that I want to be with you wherever you are. I adore you, Gaby, always have and always will."

She lifted her chin as she met his gaze. "Only until you don't!"

He fell silent.

She sat on the edge of the tub and slipped her feet into her satin slippers. Seductively, she glanced back and promptly turned on her heels. The round firmness of her derriere spoke to him.

"What are you doing, Gaby?" he questioned as his passion spiraled and his manhood throbbed with excruciating unfulfilled desire.

Undaunted, she ambled into the bathroom, turned on the faucets, poured a lavender sachet into the sink and cupped her hands to splash scented warm rose water on her face. Tears rolled down her cheeks.

"No, it will not happen! I will return to Paris," she whispered to the reflection in the mirror.

CHAPTER THIRTEEN

The carriage was waiting for the return journey to Paris. Serious and sad, and staring at Socrates, Jean-Louis approached Gaby and clasped her elbows. "Wait, let us go to Beaunne. You loved the town, its beautiful hills covered with vineyards as far as the eye can see."

Visibly shaken, Gaby brusquely shook off his hold, returning a cruel glare as she walked away. He pursued her, reached for her waist and turned her to him. The cordons that fastened her straw hat below her chin came undone, lifted by a swift gust of cold winter wind. Stunned, she watched it fly away high toward the heavens and then drop down just as promptly into a muddy puddle.

"Gaby, we have wasted five long years on account of my jealous nature," he whispered in her ear. "You still love me, and I'll always adore you. Last night meant something to both of us. Why persist in this play of sorrowful events? Come with me to Beaunne, I will get you back in time for your performance. Please let us retrieve our lives. A love like ours is seldom found, Gaby."

She tensed. His warm breath on her naked throat still had an effect that she wished she could deny. She looked up to him.

"Gaby," he whispered, "what do you have to lose? Moments of happiness..."

As this last sentence was uttered, visions of her time in Paris after the rupture, the agony of the many weeks while she tried to avert a situation she did not think she could ever reemerge from, her desperate days after arriving in Rome, her wish that God would take her, her endless hours on the banks of the Tiber wishing that she could be strong enough to end her life. Never, never again!

God had given her a second chance to repudiate the dark tentacles that seem to adhere without any end in sight to women's emotions. No, last night had been just like another night of wonderful lovemaking, the very same that she'd enjoyed without culpability these past few years. It had meant to be her life as she'd left New Orleans. She had never wanted to be tethered with a husband and children. She swallowed hard at the thought of little ones clasping her hands, hiding in her skirts... she had Socrates. Her cherished little terrier loved her unconditionally. Her singing, her artistic friends, Élise, Philippe, Ribaud, these were the people she loved, who loved her. Jean-Louis could never be trusted—not ever again.

"What could I lose?" she questioned, cold, staring emotionless in his deep blue hopeful eyes, "My life, Jean-Louis, my very life." She gazed up once more, tears swelling in her emerald gems he loved to cover with kisses. "We will never be again, —of that I am certain. I no longer love you," she enunciated in an imperceptible murmur that only a pained expression confirmed.

A gentle smile accompanied the purr, one she knew caused emotional agony in her former husband's heart. She nodded, secure in her demeanor as she turned on her heel and flipped her light blue velvet skirt forward. She did not turn back as the footman lowered the steps to the carriage. Luke, who had presaged the dénouement, extended his hand to her. She sat down across from him, and he grinned and winked at Jean-Louis. Knowing the stubborn Frenchman well, he promptly reached for his cane and rasped at the door. The carriage moved on.

Jean-Louis-Pierre stood alone in the cold air, pensive as the horses trotted down the path across from the small lake ebbing the inn. "We will have to see about that." He spoke the words aloud to himself. Reassured, he spun around and entered the inn.

He was starved. As he passed, the workers of the inn pretended a keen interest in the mighty cold of the western Parisian suburb, he grinned and remarked in his loud, commanding voice, "*Rentrez Messieurs, Mesdames, l'opéra est terminé.*"

The Maître d'hôtel and the young horse trainer caught by surprise had stopped to watch the amorous development of the famous couple whose love affair less than five years ago had shaken the aristocratic roots of the Tout Paris. All had seen her descend into despair before her return to Italy and her art. She had been in this same establishment with the Countess de Gambryeres, her close friend Élise, slim as a rod, imbibing too much Cristal and Absinthe. All had thought at the time that the beautiful colonial with the golden voice had just been a short-lived passion in the Duke's life. Perhaps a bit more—she had gotten her wish of becoming Madame de Pleyssis.

"But here they are again," Madame Saccarde in the kitchen lamented.

"They shared a room. Sophie said the sheets were crumpled and stained to such an extent she had never seen before," the cook recounted.

"The Duke even brought down Madame's white cotton ball puppy, Socrates, for an early breakfast, "*entrecote avec des oeufs aux plats à l'Americaine, il l'a demandé!*" And now, another argument. These aristocrats have no better things to do. They should work as hard as we do for a meal!"

The old lady reached for a transparent jar filled with flour on a nearby shelf, then returned to her kneading table where a circular piece of dough lay on a large wooden plank. She sprinkled a bit more flour on the dough and rotated her rolling pin up and down a few times to flatten and soften it, a few expertly placed pinches on the outer crust molded the corners of the pie where the sliced apples, sprinkled spices and sugar filled the cavity. Happily, she slipped her flat spatula below the pie and slid it in the warm and heated to perfection oven. She checked the time on the carillon. "Should be ready in forty-five minutes. It's your favorite, Jacques, I'll save you a few pieces, I made extra for your little sister."

The young stable boy did not lift his eyes. Instead, he peered at the journalist from the Gazette that he recognized instantly standing behind the wood casing of the large windows in the morning room. Good, he thought. This episode would bring in a few sous, maybe even a gold coin to round off his meager salary. His mom, who worked as an ironing maid in one of the castles nearby most of her adult life, was on her dying bed, and petite Claudine needed to be fed and clothed.

He caressed the mare to quiet her down and continued to watch unaware that his keen interest had also been caught by the Maître d'hôtel. He heard the master clear his throat—loudly, the young boy turned around and saw the Chef with his white, heavily starched apron who now stood next to the owner.

The Maître d'hôtel's glare spoke volumes. He followed the big man's eyes pointing at his boot. He knew quite well that silent language, the young boy caught the reins of both horses and continued his slow stroll to the stables, peering whenever possible at the drama unleashing in front of his eyes. He gyrated slightly with the pull of his keeps and noted the continuous glare of the owner and Maître d'.

His wages were too significant to the family, pay consistency was imperative versus jumping at the chance of earning a few extra sous for gossip. He lowered his casquette over his eyes, positioned himself between the two horses, offered to his favorite mare the last remnant of the carrots given to him by the cook and he gave a sharp pull on the reins. The head of the stables would gossip about this new development, at least he'd add a few bits of interest himself. Anything to endear himself to those in service he belonged to and would most certainly served for the remaining of his life.

***

Meanwhile, as a heartwarming déjeuner was placed in a private dining area reserved for the grand of this world, Jean-Louis formulated a plan. Gaby's wardrobe, which he'd ordered surreptitiously the night of his arrival, had arrived in Chatou. She had no reason to return to Paris for six more days, so he felt certain a small change of plans could be accomplished.

He called for his carriage to be harnessed. He knew the coachman well. An hour later at breakneck speed, the Duke of Bourbonne was giving chase to his former wife's carriage. It did not take long for the carriage to be overtaken. At the sight of the celebrated captain, Gaby's coachman stopped immediately. His carriage, which had passed them less than a quarter of an hour ago, now barred the path with Jean-Louis on one of his untethered horses.

Stunned, the coachman stopped his horses. "Monsieur?" he exclaimed loudly.

"I'll handle it from here!" the Duke replied as he slipped down from his horse and crossed over to his friend Luke's rented carriage. He opened the door with his winning smile.

"Désolé, Luke," he said as he grinned, "Gaby will have a much better time with me in Beaune!"

Without much of an apology, he did not even unfurl the steps. Instead, he reached into the carriage, gathered up Gaby's petite body and transferred her to his waiting carriage. Her bags had already been conveyed to his coach.

Georges, the young coachman who had just recently come under her service, turned to the footman who'd come around to sit next to him.

"Do not worry, nothing will come of it. Put that gun away. She'll go willingly, they spent the night together. Here in Paris, you will learn quickly that the aristocracy still carry a heavy clout. Pay attention. The

Duke de Bourbonne is a great man, a great Frenchman who has fought for us, the little people. One of the few I admire."

The shocked coachman did not budge. Instead, he held his horses and prepared to return to Paris.

Inside the carriage, Luke shook his head. "Some protector I am, Gaby! Proceed," he shouted to the young groom as he tapped his cane to the window.

A stunned Gaby did not utter a word.

Pleased with her silence, Jean-Louis sat across from the love of his life. He extended his long legs across the banquettes and cushioned his gorgeous head against the well-padded bolsters.

"We will have fun, Gaby!" he said in English. A phrase she was not accustomed to.

She stared in disbelief and burst out laughing. "You are deranged, Jean-Louis!" she shouted in English. "You could have been killed at the speed the horses were traveling."

"I escaped a thousand deaths, Gaby, and you're my reason d'être, ma chérie." He smiled and comfortably reached for the brandy bottle set on a red leather covered bottle warmer. He poured a glass that he offered to Gaby, then another for himself. "I love you, Madame!"

The crystal-clear laughter he adored resounded in and about the carriage. She lifted her glass. "To fun. Just fun, Jean-Louis!" Her new interpretation of the word sounded hollow.

"Trés bien, with great pleasure! I will ensure that your most fervent desires be consummated." Quickly he hopped onto her side of the banquette and kissed her. "Nothing but remarkable 'fun' for the former Duchesse de Bourbonne. Your wishes are my command, Madame."

The elegant coach carried on slowly on down the road to Beaune while the lovers inside let their passion stir.

CHAPTER FOURTEEN

It was a beautiful day, a winter day. Gold and multiple shades of copper and rust-colored leaves carpeted the hilly path the carriage had taken. A few song birds flew from one tree to the next—late birds for certain who had missed their migratory rush.

Jean-Louis stared down at Gaby, who had decided to be as charming and 'fun' as ever, regaling him with stories about her life spent in many of Europe's capitals. His decision not to return to Paris had been right. Gaby might have changed her mind. A couple of 'splendid days together' might soften her disposition.

There was hope, but it all rested upon his shoulders. At the inn, the party he was to meet the day before to go boar hunting, had lingered. He'd arranged a ride in the nearby woods while waiting for his carriage to arrive with her clothing.

He just needed to keep her challenged. By early afternoon, the clothing had arrived. Gaby loved Champagne and he'd written a fast note to the Abbot of the Bénédictine Cluny Abbeye Monastery. The refectory there was still one of the best gastronomic tables on the Côte d'Or. The viniculture of the region lent itself to superb gastronomical feasts.

"A meal reserved only for the Dukes of Bourgogne," the Abbot's servant had quipped flippantly years ago, which in turn had provoked a well-deserved admonition from the Abbott. "Monsieur de Pleyssis is one of our Grand Monsieur, Serge, do not ever forget!"

His prompt and well-prepared plan had worked nonetheless. By two o'clock both were on their way to Beaunne.

Ensconced in the elegant carriage, Gaby spotted the steeple of the church bordered on all sides by large fields of well-trimmed vines arranged in rows of eight, so as to absorb the sun's golden rays. These vineyards spread as far as the eye could see.

"France is so beautiful, Jean-Louis; its diverse landscapes, historical villages and vineyards often within a day's ride of the capital imbues me with awe."

The carriage rocked on the yellowish packed dirt of the road taking them to Beaunne. As usual, conversation was not difficult. It flowed on the life of their common friends, their preferred readings, why they loved a certain play, a certain artist in a particular role. Jean-Louis was always talkative and imaginative in social settings, and Gaby never lacked subjects to explore, repeating gossip in amusing anecdotes. Both laughed easily and essentially had an identical 'funny bone'.

They stopped at an auberge in the village of Veselay, and enjoyed the traditional cuisine de Bourgogne, the home of the boeuf Bourguignon and its many dishes *en meurette*, cooked in red wine adorned with small strips of pork fat, that Gaby truly adored. They had dined and had stayed there often during their years together.

Earlier in the day, Jean-Louis dispatched a servant to accommodate a déjeuner reservation that included cold bottles of Cristal—her favorite champagne. Nothing left to chance, a grin lit his manly face after the last drop of the simply flawless Cristal passed down the sensuous throat of the pretty soprano.

The Duke chose not to tackle the sensitive and misinterpreted dispute that had severed their personal life. The carriage continued on its way as the tall aristocrat stretched his long legs across the tufted banquette, resting his head on the velvet squabs. His deep blue eyes focused on the pretty artist across from him as she untied and removed her hat, gloves and scarf while settling in for the remainder of the ride to Cluny.

The de Pleyssis's hunting lodge, which overlooked the vineyards surrounding the estate, suddenly appeared on the horizon as if suspended in the clouds. She looked out, sighing as she recalled myriad happy days spent in this lovely setting following their marriage.

"Jean-Louis, did you know that Cristal is the favorite Champagne of Tsar Alexander II? Supposedly he chose the clear bottle and flat bottom so that no bombs could be inserted into the grooves of the bottle!" She lifted her shoulders, not quite certain if the rumors dispensed of the fine Champagne were real or legendary. "It flows profusely at all the great events celebrated by the court in Saint Petersburg."

"Like yourself, Gaby, the Tsar has a refined palate."

She winked and smiled. "Yes, that refined palate has landed me in a few difficult situations."

"Don't share more than that, Chérie," he retorted curtly, "wallowing in your escapades is distasteful to me."

She was about to snap back that he was not her confident and would never again be privy to her adventures. But instead, she remained silent, reached for Socrates and began to caress his fluffy flanks. Jean-Louis's volatile personality when it involved her friends and now her numerous, highly publicized affairs had not diminished.

She'd acquiesce to a few days with him. Let's keep a light tempo, she thought, Jean-Louis never stayed angry for long. She shook her hair away from her face and shot a half smile his way before parting the heavy tapestry curtains. She peeked out at the vast flat plains with hundreds of vines spiraling on their wooden stakes in perfect little rows—all were stripped of both grapes and leaves.

The gray sky, the bare stalks, the lack of domestic animals roaming the land, all contributed to a sad and lonely paysage. She had ridden close to the borders of desperation, not unlike these sights, which now appeared to experience an insurmountable amount of despair. Yet, less than four months from now, a new birth would emerge, large scrumptious fruits, white, red, pink would hang amongst the bunches, children of farmers would stop, peek in opposite directions for security guards and feast on the still tart but firm and juicy grapes.

Fragrant blossoms from surrounding orchards would fill the air with hundreds of aromatic scents! This was how she had retrieved her *joie de vivre*, accepting the passage of time and the healing that it brings.

She glanced at him every so often, always catching his piercing blue eyes ogling her every move. Jean-Louis loved her. She knew that, but his pride surpassed all. There was no use lying to herself. At the moment she did not want to be anywhere else but here, in his arms. She let her body control her resolute mind for just this once, for lessons learned the hard way were inculcated in her mind--never to be dislodged. Trusting the man she loved, and most likely always would, was no longer in the cards. He would hurt her again. She was no longer willing to take that chance—not ever.

"A gold coin for your thoughts, Madame. You appear, oh so far away, Gaby, I hope the happy glance I just spied on your pretty visage was of the memorable moments we spent in this beautiful region together." He moved over to her side of the banquette, encircled her in his arms and kissed her tenderly on her temple. "I would not exchange this instant for any other in a billion years. I am in love, at peace and next to the woman who makes me whole and gives me infinite happiness." He tightened his embrace. "Do you still feel the uniqueness that we had, Gaby?"

She stayed silent. He did not press her for a response.

As usual, time passed. The horses bowled down the serene *campagne*. Like in the past, there were no awkward moments. The silence felt right. The rhythm of their bodies in unison, his heart beating alongside her breast, his mouth nestled in the crook of her neck. "I love you, Gaby."

She did not respond. She knew the rejoinder, but was not ready for the commitment. Not yet. Jean-Louis sensed her uneasiness. He did not pursue the thought. In four months, she would sail back to New York. He had plenty of time.

The gossip she'd missed while away from Paris was being recounted in all its decadent colors by none other than yours truly.

"You've missed a lot, Madame!"

"And you, Monsieur, with all your travels and time in my country, how is it that you're so clairvoyant?"

"I have free transportation at my disposal." His smile made her smile. That very facial expression, 'childish, boy-like, vulnerable,' all words she had heard too often employed to describe Jean-Louis-Pierre. The hearts of so many had been pierced forever. She recalled the gossip recounted during their courting days, so and so knew she had what was lacking in his life... then so and so knew his affluent but strict childhood had had an '*effet sur son charactère*,' oh yes, she considered, all had been discarded—on a moment's notice!

She had suffered the same after two years of marriage and a trial that had pushed her to the limit of madness. Little did she know then that sinking into a chasm of despair was just around the corner. In effect, why would she even be in such close quarters with him? She looked up at him. He smiled down at her. She parted the curtains and gazed away.

"Actually, I returned often, Gaby, with the most ardent hope that you'd be in Paris."

"I removed Paris from my thoughts, my senses, and my life, Jean-Louis. I obliterated it all. And finally, I became very good at letting go. Essentially, I knew I was not ready. Even now I doubt my decision to return," she replied candidly. "As you know, my contract was bought out by the Palais Garnier. I could have refused, but the offer was too tantalizing. Such an honor!"

He nodded and promptly changed the subject. That's all that was needed at this moment of indecision. Gaby was not an easy woman to comprehend.

"Oh, Jean-Louis, here it is." She pointed to an old wooden pole with the arrow directing visitors to the old town. "Beaunne, less than fifty kilometers from the Medieval City," she continued to read, "the vineyards and its *coteaux*, the Canal de Bourgogne, the Abbey Cluny... the hold of the Benedictine order... didn't it repudiate the submissive attitude of the Clergy to the King in 910?" She smiled and winked. "You taught me that."

"You know your history fairly well, Madame, your memory never fails you," he replied, "good or bad, I will let history reveal its apothéose, grand finale, as you call it. You know my sentiments when it comes to The Church, the movement insured the independence of the Catholic Church and its prelates."

Not willing to begin a conversation that would create a stormy cloud, she asked, "Do you recall our horse racing on the banks of the Canal of Bourgogne in late September?" One can never forget the fiery colors of the trees bordering that lovely waterway. What wonderful days we spent here!"

She glanced at him. Yes, he remembered.

"You remember it well, Gaby?" he quipped in English "Eh bien, a perfect time for a stretch." He tapped a long wooden cane on the inside panel of the carriage. The horses came to an immediate halt. "Would you like some refreshments, Gaby?"

"No, I'll save myself for later. I can taste the subtle delicacies we will be offered in the monastery." She smiled sweetly and then winked devilishly, keeping him on his toes. Why did she even need to flirt with him? Oh, well. She shrugged her shoulders. Just a few days, she reminded herself.

God, how he loved her. For the first time in many years, he invoked the God he had been raised to adore above all else. Mon Dieu, let us return to our former life, and retrieve the joys that we once had, he prayed silently.

Back in his carriage, he assumed the same position, holding her tiny body close to his. She did not resist. Instead, she clasped his forearm close to her breast, her cheek resting against his chest. He kissed her lightly on her forehead and gathered her ever more tightly to his chest.

"Gaby," he whispered, "you asked earlier why I waited this long to try to mend our relationship? Eh bien... the truth is that I owed it to you. It was your time to shine and share your voice with the world."

She glanced at him as he removed himself from the comfort of her arms and slid onto the bench across from her. The intense stare in his deep blue eyes stilled her. He sensed her disbelief, but he pursued his thoughts and laid out his considerations.

"You certainly have the right to doubt my intentions, Gaby, but it is the truth."

He spoke with such emphasis that she gave him the benefit of the doubt. She reluctantly reminded herself that Jean-Louis never lied. She relaxed her head on the burgundy velvet squabs.

"You recall that last day as you embarked for Rome? Your train veered to a distant land, I sunk on the narrow cement platform divide, mindless of time and space, longings within my soul called for me to run, to take another train and follow you to the end of the world, but imaginary iron chains strapped me down to the rails amongst screeching sounds of stricken steel, reeking scents of burnt wheels, eardrums blasting, whistles and trains trailing one another preventing me to follow you. I acknowledge the wrongs that I inflicted upon you, Gaby, the dreams unfulfilled, the denial of your life's visions."

He paused and looked away into the distant bouncing hills the coach traversed. "In great part for your safety, but mostly for my possessiveness of your entire being. I needed to let you go, to step aside and allow you to fulfill your *rêveries*."

Gaby sat motionless and silent.

Jean-Louis continued. "You are not a simple woman with ordinary gifts, Gaby. I recognized that early on... and yes, I wanted to make amends. But... never five years' worth of amends!"

"What kept you away? I was in Milan for a year, so you could have come. I nearly died of a broken heart. Philippe, Élize, Ribaud, all came to see and console me as best they could. Instead, you left for India and then America."

"I saw you on stage five times, Gaby. Berlin, Vienna, Naples and again at the Scala in Milan. Had I stayed and tried to convince you to return, your dreams would never have materialized."

"I was that whipped?" She shot him an ironic sideways glance, unconvinced. "And now?"

"I no longer have a choice. My life has lost all meaning, it's futile, no more need to carry on, I am a lost soul without you, Gaby." He stared at her so intently that any movement was a release. She adjusted herself on her banquette, then promptly stood to pour a cup of fresh orange juice into a tall Saint Louis crystal glass. Lifting it to her lips, she downed it in one long gulp. A few minutes were required to regain a semblance of reality and her position in it.

"Give me more time, my heart pulls in one direction... to you, but my sense of logic urges to charge like lightning far, far away."

He swallowed hard, nodded and playfully pulled and untied the large bow tied behind her back.

"Come and sit next to me." He clasped his hands around her waist, gently tugging her body closer to him.

"Jean-Louis, my glass!" He quickly grabbed it and placed it on the table next to him without releasing her. Drawing her into his arms, he pressed her to him and posed a sensuous kiss on her neck that gravitated to her lips. At this very moment, he envisioned a reunion. The purchase of the contract had been the right decision. He would tell her one day. He knew that Gaby felt the same way. It was time to admit that their lives had been written somewhere in the Book of Love. He would do the right thing.

CHAPTER FIFTEEN

Gaby descended the steps rolled out by the coachman.

Along the wide paved courtyard, on a black wrought iron bench by the entrance to the Abbey, an elder churchman sat, rosary in hand. Upon the arrival of the couple, he slowly stood, rearranged the crucifix hanging on his cloak, patted it and began to stroll toward the Duke and his former wife, who had just stepped down from the carriage.

Both stopped, basked and marveled at the magnificence facing them. The Benedictine Abbaye de Cluny, founded by the Duke of Aquitaine in 910, had the largest monastic empire whose authority, at the peak of its power during the 11th and 12th centuries, governed over eleven hundred priories and ten thousand monks.

The Abbaye had financed the Reconquest of Spain, countless pilgrimages, the Crusades, while essentially influencing every aspect of politics and history. Many Abbots from the Abbaye had been advisors to kings and Popes. Although its role and architectural design had been greatly curtailed during the French Revolution, the beauty of the land and the sanctity and reverence emanating from its very walls and garden were awe inspiring.

"Monsieur, Madame, great pleasure to see you once more. We were delighted when we heard of your arrival. How long has it been, Monsieur?"

"Six years at the very least, too long, mon Père," Jean-Louis replied.

"*Et bien oui, Monsieur, le temps passe vite*, time soars," the old monk smiled good- naturedly.

A second, taller, and leaner brother, who'd just turned up from behind one of the Abbeye's curved stone pillars, strode promptly to them. He faced Gaby with a great big smile on his handsome and youthful face. "*Un grand plaisir, Madame*, I understand that Cardinal Thornsen is in Paris," the younger cleric questioned.

"He will arrive in late January." Gaby hinted, "the Holy Days are upon us. His responsibilities are to his flock foremost." She smiled in greeting.

Father Agueras had a deep but pleasant voice, heavily accented. Spanish perhaps, she thought.

"We were delighted to hear that the Cardinal's life had been spared from the firing squad during the horrifying Civil War, Madame. Your cousin gave his heart fully to our Father Superior, who had been imprisoned in the same cell. Father Orsini just passed, Madame. He would have been proud to meet you."

Gaby nodded. In effect Philippe as well had been taken and defrocked with many clerics by the National Guards in Belleville during the Commune. Often, he had been prepared to die 'the following day... or the next hour,' just to have his life pardoned at the very last moment. All Republicans in the Constitutional government were not atheists; although many had crossed the line to join the Commune, particularly many of the men in the National Guards.

"*Eh bien,* it is getting late and we have a wonderful dinner awaiting you and Monsieur de Pleyssis. You will be delighted."

They all walked inside the large hall. An immense fireplace with a significant cauldron within its hearth took up most of the far wall. Large religious tapestries hung on the wall. Gaby's eyes rested on one of the panels—the Apocalypse from the Book of Revelation, the last battle between good and evil.

"Your glance says it all, Madame. It is on loan, as well as many of the priceless Bayeux tapestries over there, so many of these works of art were burned or destroyed during the first revolution in 1789, a good many of them to extract the golden or silver threads the crafters used in the design. The Castellans in Angers loaned these panels to us, they foresaw the conflicts that set Paris aflame during the dreadful six weeks of the Commune."

Gaby nodded. "Horrific times... on a happier note, I have been in Paris these last few weeks and the resilience of the Parisians is formidable." About to divulge a bit more about her travels throughout Europe, she stopped.

The old monk continued. "I can see that you are appreciative of our great cultural history, Madame. Let me summon the Abbé. He will give you a most informative tour of our latest acquisitions. A fabulous collection of illuminated manuscripts has been brought upstairs for your pleasure. Pure magnificence!" the monk declared with genuine pride and joy in his voice.

"With great pleasure. Merci, Mon Père," Gaby replied.

"Stay here I will call Abbé Sébastien." He showed them to a small salon where a low round table was covered by a semi-circular velvet tablecloth. Gaby danced her fingers over the knitted pile. "The weave, how intricate and subtle," she said to the faithful holy men. "I had not noticed the figures of the Holy Family."

"You will see much beauty on our walls, Madame, delighted that you appreciate it!" The Abbé, a young, tall slender man with blond hair and vibrant blue eyes, showed up. Gaby and Jean-Louis were taken to ancient rooms where the glory of the Church and of France were exalted.

Two hours later, a monk with a white apron covering his stout abdomen appeared. "Eh bien, after so much information, I hear your stomachs growling. Be prepared for a wonderful feast that I, along with the great gift that our Father bestowed upon me, prepared especially for you. The short and doughy monk held three small liqueur glasses and escorted them to a rounded sofa facing a fireplace.

"Here let us begin our wonderful adventure, starting with the ancient culinary arts of Cluny. Sit down, please. I have brought you a taster of the liquors. Enjoy our fine dark plum liquor infused on site by our monks."

He smiled and in one swig swallowed the sweet liquor. He poured another. "For good measure!" he exclaimed, smiling widely as he placed the tip of the glass to his lips and downed the alcohol in one straight gulp. "Ah, pure delight!" He signed himself and laughed, a big hearty burst of laughter. "It is not perfection... ah, but so close!" His eyes lifted to the heavens.

The dampness and darkness of the cavernous refectory initiated a peculiar fretful sensation in Gaby, but she managed to remain quiet and serene. "It will pass," she murmured to herself.

Leaving the corner of the sofa, she slid nearer to Jean-Louis, reached for his hand and clasped it tightly. Pleasantly surprised at the gesture of affection, he gathered her to him and stroked her hair.

The monk offered another small glass of the plum liquor, which she downed rapidly. A sudden warmth and comfort enveloped her body. Absolutely, she reflected, all was well.

After all the introduction and amiable lectures on the food, its origin in their on-site gardens and their secretive preparations in even more secretive chambers, Jean-Louis was ravenous. As a young man, he had studied in great detail the artistic and political impact the Abbeye had had on the medieval world. He stood, nodded to Gaby and came around to help her away from the large fauteuil where she sat. Taking the initiative, the Abbott also stood.

"Eh bien, it is now time to descend into the caves. A wonderful meal awaits us," he declared, leading the way across the vast carpeted sitting room.

Jean-Louis clasped Gaby's hand as he followed the cleric and guided her toward an obscure narrow stone stairway that led to the fermentation caves.

As she began to negotiate the first stone staircase that gave way to packed dirt steps, the darkness of the grotto terrified her. Stomach cramps began to contort her abdomen, heat burned her cheeks and chest, her breathing labored with each descending earth filled steps. Her chest heaved, her head shifting from side to side as she reached for the dark wooden railing to retrieve a sense of security.

Jean-Louis had already reached the long corridors filled with the scent of the fermenting wine barrels of the Nuits-Saint-Georges. She felt him reach back and clasp her hand as a monk dressed in the brown monastic tunic of the Benedictine order directed their glances to the dozens of wooden *tonneaux* where approximately nine hundred liters of fine wine matured. A wide wooden cross with a silver Christ sculpted in it hung from a cordon tied around the waist of the brother.

"This very Abbey was founded in 910 by the Pious Duke of Aquitaine, Madame. As you can see the style is Romanesque, but our Cluniac reforms quickly spread to encouraging the arts and caring for the poor," he said, speaking in a kind and tender voice. "Our Abbey here in Cluny at one point covered over 25 acres, before the radical pagans destroyed most of it during the Revolution. A great sadness, indeed."

Gaby straightened and nodded.

At the very center of one of the long, low ceilinged corridors appeared a narrow, winding staircase leading to a rounded cave. From top to bottom, rows of short, tapered tunnels were dug in the packed mud where bottles of wine lay. A small intimate table flamboyantly adorned in thick white damask embroidered with the Monastery's name stood in the cave's center. Large silver plates and silver goblets adorned with enormous forks, knives and spoons were positioned upon a magnificently woven tapestry that told of past hunting scenes by the Dukes of Bourgogne. Myriad scents spread across the large halls.

Unsteady, Gaby followed Jean-Louis and the Brother. She heaved a great sigh once more. Leading the way, the monk stepped down into the abyss. Heat began to gravitate from her head down to her chest, spine and stomach. She heaved deeply to regain control and lifted her arm to grasp the iron banister along the walls where large wooden drums were stacked side by side, rows after rows.

One of the steps was wider than most. To regain some inner strength, she stopped and looked down. She touched the cold stone above the iron bannister. The swirling staircase had begun to widen, down below the area was illuminated. Nothing to fear, she straightened and steadied her torso as she continued her descent. Her cheeks were burning.

Jean-Louis turned to her and smiled. "Oh, Gaby," he touched the large gray, irregular stones, "if these walls could talk, the stories they could recount."

Weak and dizzy, the elegant, long rectangular table with a vanilla lace tablecloth just off the end of the stairwell came into proper focus for Gaby. Quickly, she followed her former husband. She tried to steady her trembling limbs on the side bannister close to the awaiting monks already seated at the dining table. The long climb down appeared to have no end.

A few more steps, she told herself. She grasped the marble covered by a long red velvet runner; her gloved fingers glided on the cloth that she attempted to grip to foil a disaster. Everything atop the marble was swept to the ground with a thunderous and echoing resonance of broken glasses, plates, wine bottles and silverware.

Gaby fell on the white gravel that covered the floor of the caves along with the candelabras, bottles of wines, plates, glasses and liquors. Jean-Louis sprang to her. The monks sent servants for smelling salts. The pretty soprano was carried and seated on a large king chair with wide wooden armrests decorated in multi-colors velour patches. The servants returned and swayed the voile sacs filled with salts back and forth like a pendulum in front of her face. She slapped the bag away as she regained consciousness. Haggard, she pushed aside the monk, and jumped down from the dais where the throne rested.

Long corridors bordered on both sides by immense tunnels filled with additional large wooden barrels of fermenting wines gave her room to maneuver. Her arms flailed in all directions, her body shifted too fast for the stunned men to react. She bolted down one of the alleys, contorted, running sideways, hitting the barrels, looking down and behind her. Oblivious of the men following her, she swatted her lower legs as if she wanted to shoo away some imaginary beasts gnawing at her feet.

Jean-Louis followed her, although Gaby's red kid shoes remained on the dais that she'd escaped minutes ago. Her small bare feet struck the cobblestones like lightning—blind to everyone and everything in her current state. Fortunately, a large barrel stopped her flight.

Jean-Louis grabbed her and enveloped her small body tightly. With his former wife lifted in his arms, her head nestled in his chest, he strode back toward the dining area, quickly turned and began to scale two by two the steep stone steps to the sitting room and foyer.

Gaby's cheeks were on fire. She held on to him as if her life depended on it as she hid her face deep inside his chest to obliterate the horrific pictures that danced a macabre waltz in her mind. Minutes later, Jean-Louis emerged outside in the garden. Although brutally cold, the sun still shone bright. Almost immediately, the unnerved vibrations of distress he felt as he held her near began to ease as her body retrieved a tranquility he knew all too well.

"You're fine, Gaby, I'm here," he whispered.

He had forgotten her terror of the dark but this episode had been graver than any other he had witnessed before. Gaby held a dark secret. He wanted to make sure that this episode would not be disclosed. Of all places for her to experience such an incident! He smiled and quickly felt awful about such an outrageous contemplation. His former wife still in his arms, he called out to the two remaining monks who had just re-emerged from the caves—stunned.

"You will keep this dire incident to yourselves. Be certain that all reparations and the cost incurred will be fully recovered. My secretary will contact your Abbot."

Quickly he nodded to the gatekeeper to have the carriage brought in front of the Monastery. The hunting lodge was less than an hour away. He also had a wonderful friend who owned a castle nearby. They'd ride the short distance to the larger estate.

CHAPTER SIXTEEN

Gaby reacted quickly to the brisk cold air and stared into Jean-Louis's eyes.

"It was horrific," she murmured, her cheeks flushed with shame. "I relived a momentous event in my life. I am not sure if it occurred, but it was too real to put aside." She fell silent as she parted the curtains to stare at the road disappearing under the horses' pounding hooves. "My mother's body was hanging from a rope in a dark courtyard. Her eyes were following me, Jean-Louis."

"All will be well, Chérie," he murmured. A strange moment in his life in which silence seemed of the utmost importance.

"I dispense with my guards when I am with you. I allow you to be my protector, and I always end up losing control of my emotions," she admitted.

Jean-Louis remained silent.

"I do not recall ever having been in this fearful situation... Villefranche, perhaps—in the rue Obscure, was the closest... while riding... but there was some light at the end of the rounded dark gray stone-covered grotto. Crouched on old rattan hassocks mending their men's nets, fishermen's wives sat and used the wall to rest their backs. *The pas de l'âne helped* me recover."

Jean-Louis nodded. "Do you have any other memories of your childhood that may have precipitated the incident, Gaby?" He studied her as she remained glued to the window, lost in her contemplation.

"I saw my mother hang... they..."

"They? Who are 'they', Gaby?" Jean-Louis questioned, stunned.

"Men in suits. They handed me her clothes in a neat pile... in a small dark room. My father was there, his hand on my shoulder. The clamor in my head was deafening as we rode back in the carriage..."

"We?" Jean-Louis interrupted again as he removed his long legs from the banquette next to hers and slid his body on the opposite leathered covered seat, his knees coming into contact with hers as he faced her and reached for both of her hands.

"My father. I was numb." She nodded. "I remember now... all of it, Jean-Louis."

She turned her head away from the window where she'd been staring at the rolling *coteaux,* the hillsides filled with desolate vineyards. Her glance veered his way as she took in his expression of concern.

"I remember," she whispered, returning her gaze outside of the carriage. Her voice now, more assured and distinct. She wanted to talk.

He would listen.

"I was just thirteen years old when my father came to pick me up one autumn afternoon. I had known that my mother had been taken prisoner on account of her abolitionist views. Aydan, her lover, had fled a few months earlier to his native Boston. Not wanting to scare me, Tita, my servant, the woman you obviously met when you resided on my plantation for a short time," she focused on his hands clasped around hers and exhaled deeply. "Tita and her husband, Auguste, were my caretakers. I adored them." She stopped once more, trying to retrieve some order for the thoughts that rolled in her memory like a wild torrent.

"Anyhow, Tita, a person that I adored, mentioned Aydan would return with the power of the full extent of the law. 'All will be resolved upon his return,' she'd say calmly. I believed her."

Gaby paused, but after a few moments of silence, she continued. "After all the agony this demon has caused you, now your pain will never again reoccur. Your mother will be hung at five this morning, Gaby. We will be in attendance." My father announced sternly.

"I always believed that Aydan's lawyers would win the case—always. I had prayed fervently for it. I was stunned with the verdict."

"I do not want to attend, Father," I recall saying. "I cannot Father."

"You will, Gabriella." He then turned to my former slave. "Tita, have her ready by four."

He kissed me on both cheeks. "Be strong, my child. This nightmare will soon come to an end." He sounded almost gleeful, Jean-Louis. He departed in the direction of his waiting carriage stationed in the middle of the alley facing our grand entrance. Tita, Auguste and I stood on the portico as we watched him, step into his carriage."

Shock kept Jean-Louis silent.

"The following morning," Gaby said as if she needed to tell it all, fearful that the nightmare might once more recede into some dark corner of her mind. "Tita and her daughter helped me into my clothes. I wanted to take my horse and flee. Philippe was in Rome, but I had stayed."

Gaby was not talking to anyone now, the blank expression on her face revealed that she was reliving the horrid story of the past. Jean-Louis clasped her hand. She gripped his.

"Tita brought me down to the dining area the following morning at dawn," Gaby murmured almost inaudibly. "She came closer and handed me a large mug. I drank the mysterious tincture she poured into my café au lait.

"'To make you strong, Gaby,'" Tita said, "and when the moment is at hand, lower your bonnet or close your eyes.' I drank it to the last drop. My father was already waiting for me, dressed in black from head to toe."

"Come Gaby, this is not easy for either of us." He led me by the elbow. The coachman lowered the steps, I stepped in and remained silent for the hour ride. It was still dark outside when we arrived at the prison. We took our respective seats outside in the frigid courtyard and waited.

"My mom was taken out first. Her hands were bound behind her back. I heard her gasp as she saw the gallows and became reticent, standing still, not willing to take another step. The priest took her hand and whispered in her ear. She lifted her eyes to the outdoor gallery where we stood."

Gaby's hands began to tremble. Her legs were glued tightly to the banquette.

"My father placed his hands on my waist, lifted me to a standing position and placed my two hands on the cement balustrade. He said: 'Gaby, be reverential of this moment. She is your mother, after all.' I stared at my mother as she mounted the nine steps to the platform. She took one last step and stood erect, glaring at my father. She turned her head to me, a sad half smile on her still beautiful and serene face. Her fear was gone.

"Remove my cords!" she ordered the executioner. The man was about to push her toward the final knot, but the priest held him back. "Do as she said, she has not asked anything of you other than this small last request. You will be rewarded in heaven for your consideration. Give this good deed up to God."

The burly man nodded, crossed himself and grudgingly, while glaring at the condemned, cut off the ropes. She stood still for a long moment, massaged her bruised limbs, opened and closed her fists, and then glanced one last time upward to me. Her will and lack of trepidations gave all of us a moment of respite. Within seconds and without being prodded, she strode to the gallows. The executioner followed her. She lifted her long and elegant neck to the noose, and he coiled it around her neck, tightened it.

"She had refused the eye patches. 'I want to see the world I am leaving,' were her last words, according to her priest, her confessor, who had followed her footsteps from her Baptism in the City State of Piedmont-Sardinia, where King Victor Emmanuell II was Monarch and then just recently as you are aware, Jean-Louis, he was installed as the new King of a united Italy. The cleric was present at her execution in the sordid square where the plank would fall out below her and her life would be no more."

Jean-Louis moved across the seats and gathered her small body into his embrace. She stayed, her head close to his chest for a while, seeking solace, he thought. "No need to go further, Gaby. These atrocious moments should not be relived. Look at your world now, all that you have accomplished."

Ignoring his plea, she pushed him away and resumed her story. "I wanted to wave, to send a kiss, to run down to the courtyard and beg the magistrates for a reprieve, for the executioner to halt this execution, but I couldn't. I was immobilized... but I called out to her... I watched the priest finish the prayer. He blessed her. The *bourreau* pushed her forward onto the platform that would fall beneath her and seal her death. My mother nodded and crossed herself, then looked up one more time. I took one step forward and held on to the balustrade, minutes later a rolling of a trap with a loud boom sounded off in the large courtyard. Within seconds my mother's lifeless body was dangling in space.

"Down below, I heard heartfelt sobs. Aydan Hartley wept openly, his face in his hands—a broken man. 'You coward!' he shouted at my father. 'You will pay dearly for this ignoble act." As they closed the trap, the executioner walked to my mother's side, holding her broken neck upward. Another man lifted her frail body out of the noose. Without a word, we were led toward the entrance door This was the last I saw of her. She had a closed casket. Aydan showed up as we waited in our carriage.

"You son of the devil!' Aydan shouted again to my father and the magistrates. 'You will pay dearly for this act of cowardice. I will see to it.' He turned his back on us and walked briskly across the street where his carriage waited, sobbing every step of the way. My father, clearly disturbed by the embarrassment of being challenged by the cutting words of a wealthy northerner, in front of some of the city's most honorable members, lifted his head and marched toward the last carriage left on the empty road. A young clerk called out to us, a document in his hand. My father clasped it, read it and signed it."

"Miss de Conte-Thornsen needs to sign as well, Sir!" Without returning a single glance to the clerk, my father took my hand and pulled me in the direction of the carriage. The coachman lowered the steps, we climbed in and returned to my plantation. I knew then, Jean-Louis, although I was only thirteen, that he had made a grave mistake—in my favor.

"As we drove down the Alley to the great house, parked in front of the flight of stairs, carriages were stopped and waiting. I recognized one of the carriages, it was Aydan's. Many men were already sitting in the women's sitting room. Two walked by my father's side, three others walked around the table and came to sit across the way from my mother's former attorney. One was obviously waiting for me, holding documents. I marched in and sat alone near the fireplace.

"Miss de Conte-Thornsen, the last testament will now be read. I understand that in recent months you have been given the power of majority in the Louisianan-French legal interpretation. Emancipation, as it is called in the Louisianan legal system, that is closely related to the Napoleonic Code, gives a white thirteen-year-old, the legal and financial rights that a twenty-one-year-old possesses for financial and legal purposes."

"I nodded. 'In effect, Maître,' I responded, 'my mother bequeathed me full possession of this plantation—the Justine.' My father stood. Both lawyers, standing on either side of him gripped his shoulders and nodded to his chair. He sat back down. Angels must have been watching over me, Jean-Louis, because Aydan had returned with lawyers of his own. I won, and I kept the Justine."

But she had not, Jean-Louis thought, her dark and hidden secret had now been revealed. What next? He stared at his former wife. She was in the room. Gaby was recounting the ordeal. She had lost all awareness of time, he thought. He sat quietly on his large leather chair. Gaby appeared subdued, serene. He wondered if she'd recover fully from the ordeal—a trauma like no other.

After a long pause, she returned to her previous statements. Long contained memories reappeared in a haphazard order.

"When we arrived back at the plantation, lawyers were waiting," she repeated, her eyes and demeanor now centered on a particular event.

He stayed calm.

"All wanted me to sign my plantation away to my father. I refused over and over." Her voice took on the tone as if she was there, speaking to strangers who were trying to break her spirit. "Tita intervened, attempting to shield me from these overbearing thugs... a massive man, appearing from the side door of the dining room, slapped her down to the polished parquetry, then kicked her and dragged her away outside in the kitchen. This ordeal lasted for quite some time, Jean-Louis, when finally, as dusk fell, my father lost patience. He clasped my arm and led me outside the house to the underground shed... pushed me down the stairs as he shouted, 'let us see how long you'll last with the nightlife underground.' Then he slammed the double doors of the hurricane shed. I heard the click of the padlock securing the two flaps. It was dark, very dark.

"Almost immediately, fur brushed my leg. I tried to swat it away, but was bitten. I shouted to the top of my lungs. Was it a mouse or a rat? I will never know. There were many, all around me. I stood up, mice, rats, twirled around my feet, toes, legs, sticky spider webs around my arms, fingers and head. My shrieks went unanswered. In the dark, I screamed and supplicated God, the Virgin, my mother up above, my father, all the names I could remember. I was kept in this inferno until the following night, when again, I refused to recant.

"Once more the large double doors of the shed closed upon me. There were large rats, Jean-Louis. Tita would come at night and place food as far away as possible from the winter stalks of wheat I slept on and yet I was bitten... I had to keep moving all night to fend them off. When the double doors re-opened, the following day, I slowly hobbled outside. Angels must have been watching over me, because Ayden had returned with his Boston lawyers. He quickly came to me and embraced me."

"Aydan? Your mother's lover?"

"Yes, the documents he provided, or rather copies of the originals, confirmed that my mother had signed over the plantation, La Justine, to me. I was legally recognized as an adult, emancipated just before her imprisonment. She probably realized by then that her abolitionist's ideals would land her on the gallows. Tita was told by my father and his friends to take me out after their departure. Auguste went to the authorities, they would not believe him, of course. He was darker than the inner earth. Instead, they denounced my mother as an ardent abolitionist who worked against the laws of the State.

"The freedom of her slaves had not been approved by the Assembly. Consequently, they had been emancipated solely on the Justine plantation. Their freedom was ephemeral, most planters feared a revolt by their slaves. It is hard to believe that what happened has been a total blank all of these years."

All the recollection of that day had been laid bare. She did not take her eyes off the passing road. "I am content that she died imagining her slaves had become waged servants."

Silence was of the essence.

CHAPTER SEVENTEEN

The Count of Monteyrre, a very good friend of Jean-Louis, owned a nearby castle. He gave the coachman new instructions. Meanwhile, the ashen faced Gaby was now silent. He cradled her on his lap, her cheek pressed close to his heart.

"All will be well, Gaby. All will be well, the past cannot be undone," he murmured, "you have kept these horrid memories for much too long. You learned early in life to conquer your fears, which is good. Look at your life now, ma chérie."

She squinted and stared down at the tips of her laced up brown boots.

The horses thundered down the narrow streets of the town, the sound of the coachman shouting at the pedestrians to clear the way echoed in the air.

Nestled in his arms, Gaby said not a word as the carriage traveled to the castle. Her shame at her demented behavior was too immense to even broach the subject with Jean-Louis. Perhaps it was time to explore this corner of her life that had indisposed her so terribly. Indisposed. She smiled. What a soft word to describe the powerful emotions that permeated every cell of her being.

Jean-Louis as usual, magnificently adept at compartmentalizing all deceptions after the occurrence, seemed to have forgotten the incident in its entirety.

"Look at the magnificence of the undulating hills ascending. They're dotted with rows of frozen and barren vines that will reach their multitude of red and white shades later in the upcoming spring. The tiny green minute balls are still enveloped in their green leaf blankets and attached to their respective stems. They demand sun and water to achieve their maturity in the upcoming spring in the cisterns of the many wineries."

Jean-Louis wished she could have enjoyed the beauty of the countryside. Gaby, who celebrated the smallest hint of nature's grandiosity, now lay wounded in his arms. What other horrific drama was concealed in her subconscious? Now was not a good time to ask. He continued to stroke the long curly mane that hung down her back.

"I do not know, Jean-Louis. I just do not know. The war..." She let the words hang, as if reading his mind. Often simplistic moments revealed the great traumatic events in one's life.

"You are fine, Gaby. It was my fault, I should have remembered your fear of the darkness."

"You should have!" she suddenly shouted. "Why in God's name did you bring me to that catacomb? Did I need to be subdued? You wanted control over me? If you can't have me willingly, then all bets are off! You'll make me heal? Was that the reason for this senseless trip?"

"Gaby, I am not evil," he declared, clearly aggrieved, "this deduction is devilish. Why would I want you to agonize over anything? I love you more than my life. Be reasonable."

She pushed him away, stood, fluffed out her dress, and slid across from him, directly opposite to the window he peered out. She lifted the curtain and focused her offended spirit on the sloping hills. Jean-Louis was not at fault. He had remediated a possibly injurious story with his usual *sang froid*. And she did not believe that his intent had been to subdue her usually indomitable spirit.

A moment later, she turned and stared at him. He was looking away, his well sculpted jawline revealing disappointment. In a change of heart, she returned to his side of the bench, placed her hands over his and rested her head on his chest. He did not utter a word but he gathered her tightly to him.

This too will pass, he thought.

The carriage arrived at the spectacular château. Recognized by both of the gatekeepers, they let the carriage pass through while they sent two couriers to the big house to announce the surprise arrival of Monsieur de Pleyssis.

A middle aged man, straight as a rod, appeared with a large smile at the very top of the marble arch. As the carriage approached, two footmen materialized and the butler descended the steps to attend to Jean-Louis.

"What a great pleasure, Monsieur will be delighted upon his return. You know Monsieur entered into marriage last year. Monsieur's father in law is from Bordeaux."

"From *Bordeaux*?" Jean-Louis questioned. "When will the Count return?"

"Anytime, we have a lavish *soirée* planned for tomorrow night. Madame's sister was in Paris for a week."

Not willing to give the head butler more standing, Jean-Louis began to start toward the great entrance. Both were greeted by the house servants.

"Can we prepare a déjeuner for you, Monsieur, Madame?"

"No, we will wait for the Count to return. Please let the Count know that we have arrived."

"Very well, Monsieur, your apartment will be ready within the hour, meanwhile Leonie here will attend to your wishes," the butler nodded and quickly disappeared, ignoring the young girl.

Jean-Louis started toward the salon. "You will bring a flute of Cristal pour Madame, and a brandy for me."

« *Très bien Monsieur, de suite.* »

Jean-Louis clasped Gaby's elbow, crossed the room and led her to the balcony, the *paysage* was stunning, spectacular manicured gardens faced her, out in the horizon, large vineyards stretched under the sunshine as dusk settled on the property. Small guérites, sentry boxes, transformed into workman's brick or cement slab huts could be seen at the very top of the hill. "Let's walk over there, Gaby," Jean-Louis said softly, "the view is splendid."

She bent over and picked a few sprigs of lavender that still had some light *parme* blossoms. Even in the brutal cold winter of eastern France, these hardy plants offered their distinctive scents to all who strode in their magnificent fields.

"Beautiful," Gaby whispered.

They began to walk silently toward the lowlands. Gardeners were hard at work in the flower beds, carriages and horses ridden hard under the sharp eyes of mechanics and horse trainers.

Jean-Louis liked these fields, he had spent many a wonderful summer here with his friend. The Count's father came from a long aristocratic lineage, married to a distant cousin, who loved his family, his land, his people and his country. The merging of lands had been ordered by both parties. Now the count spent an enormous amount of time teaching his only son the way of the world.

"Gaby, let's sit and..."

"Monsieur, Madame, the Count has arrived," a breathless servant shared with the couple. He has sent a coach to take you back to the castle."

"Thank you," Gaby answered as she promptly strode to the carriage, happy to have been saved from a difficult conversation.

Jean-Louis sighed. Both got in and rode the short ride back to the big house. Count de Monteyrre waited for them, clearly unable to contain his immense joy. He ran down the steps as the coach closed in.

"*Cher ami*, dear Gabriella, it has been way too long, dear friends. We saw you in Milan, Gabriella. You are divine, divine! Your celestial voice mesmerizes all of us who have had the great chance and immense pleasure to have seen you on stage."

Jean-Louis did not react to the comment nor the bear hug that followed thereafter. De Monteyrre smiled and lifted his head to his friend. "Shame, shame on you, Jean-Louis-Pierre, to hide this angel's talent from all of us! I understand you had your own theater in your home in Paris, Saint Louis and yet, not once this selfish man granted us the great pleasure to listen to one of your favorite arias?"

Gaby smiled coyly.

"I expect a *grande soirée* on our next visit to Paris."

Another smile replaced the need for less than a candid answer. So many in Paris had already made up their minds that the separation had been mandated by their station in life. A man like Jean-Louis-Pierre de Pleyssis, scion of an illustrious family, needed an heir, and the pretty American was either unable or unwilling to forgo her very attractive life. Different backgrounds, different expectations, but the relationship endured.

"Abnormal," the gossips concluded.

"Love conquers all," youthful aristocrats would sum up.

"What an awful legacy!" the old ones advanced, "land and money wasted on those who need so little."

The assessment from above had not changed much in the last five hundred years!

"Eh bien, bref, perfect timing we are having a soirée tomorrow night," de Monteyrre announced, looking directly at Gaby. "Could we request an aria or two, Gabriella?"

Before she could answer, Jean-Louis made his wishes known. "I know that Gaby would never say no, but her musical coach has forbidden her to sing until next week's performance. The reason why we are here in your beautiful province—to rest." De Monteyrre smiled, knowing his friend's possessiveness of the pretty American soprano.

"Jean-Louis-Pierre, I understand you were in America very recently and doing quite well?" the Count changed the subject promptly.

"Yes, a great country, interesting people, very proud of their lands and accomplishments. If I am not mistaken, your grandfather had some vivid encounters with Franklin while he was in Paris, looking for large gifts to continue the revolution? A very convincing fellow, I understand. A new kind of society for certain."

"Oui, *absolument*, come and meet my Juliette."

"And you are from the South, Gabriella? La Nouvelle-Orléans? You own a cotton plantation, I heard?"

"No, sugar, although New Orleans is renowned for its cotton plantations. My father owns two large ones up river. La Justine deals solely in sugar."

"Small one, I presume?"

Gaby knew where he was going, and she was ready. "Not so small, we do not rival the fertile grounds of the Caribbean islands but it is solvent and well managed. Our location overlooking the entire Mississippi Valley is splendid for trade and all of our workers have homes and small farms on my land."

"Slav... former slaves?"

"Yes, former slaves who were given their freedom papers by my mother long before Mr. Lincoln issued the Emancipation Proclamation of 1863 during the American Civil War."

The Count de Monteyrre followed the couple inside the foyer. His lovely wife patiently waited at the top of the marble staircase. Juliette was not as young as one would have surmised, considering the Count's vivaciousness and youthful allure, but her elegance and sense of good manners preceded her.

"Quelle grande surprise Madame, Monsieur, entrez, je vous en prie."

The friends walked back inside the foyer.

CHAPTER EIGHTEEN

The *au revoir* had been done, the party the night before had been a great success and great fun as well. In effect, Jean-Louis had recognized how much his relationship with Gaby had changed. The singers hired to provide entertainment were enchanted to meet 'HER'.

Amusing, he considered, Gaby had been the luminary of the night and as the many guests approached to meet the couple, the leading light, his former wife, had been the one who was '*recherchée*,' sought after. All eyes on the prodigious soprano. The Grand Monde, his world appeared tickle silly and much honored to have been introduced to her. Not a singular omen that Gaby had Piedmont-Sardinian aristocratic roots on her mother's side of her family.

"Eh bien, Gaby, I have to take second stage," he'd announced in English, "a new order, Chérie."

She'd shrugged.

"Very French, Chérie, the divine Mademoiselle Gaby!" he'd scoffed.

"Possibly so, Jean-Louis!" she'd leered, Cristal flowing through her veins.

"The arrogance as well. What happened to the young ingenue I saved from a sordid fate years ago?"

"She grew up and has been adored ever since!" she'd responded arrogantly while the diamond necklace with the heart pendant that embraced her poitrine was removed. Who had given it to her was a *mystère*? A charity will be happy to receive it. He frowned. Immediately, he'd purchased a much nicer one while he'd advise her favorite Cartier diamantaire to be on the lookout for the jewelry she'd most surely held in high regards.

Jean-Louis-Pierre smiled as he recalled their first stop in Nice, after his ship moored in Villefranche sur mer. They had gone to Nice for a grand party given in his honor. As he slept, she had gone on a shopping spree. He'd hardly recognized the pretty colonial's transformation in just a few hours. How adorable she was after he'd questioned why she had taken so long. He recalled being less than happy to have been forced to wait for her. Furthermore, at this pivotal time in the relationship, he'd distrusted the man whom she'd been with as he'd observed her getting out of Renaud de Beauvaur's coupé.

The seductive Beauvaur was a wealthy aristocratic landowner from Provence, financially routed in the construction of the new railroad projects. They'd only met the evening before, for Christ's sake! Had she arranged an afternoon reunion with Renaud, who'd gallantly offered to be her guide on the many diversions offered in the south of France.

He recalled looking away at the bright, blue Mediterranean Sea, annoyed at the time he'd spent questioning this young girl's every movement and motive. Stop immediately, Jean-Louis-Pierre, he'd murmured to himself as he'd spun on his heel and strode back inside the hotel room. Two or three more weeks of this lovely interlude, and they'd go their own ways. He would introduce her to the Parisian society so as to soften the rupture. He'd just wished he had not taken her virginity. Who would have known then, the immense transformation, this pretty, talented and charming woman would create in his life? He gazed at her for a long while.

"She was adored then as well and never forgotten. I loved you then, Gaby, I idolize you now and will worship you forever," he said solemnly, capturing her chin and gently turning it to face him.

"I love you, Gaby, and you love me, too. I know! We are the missing blocks in our charmed and affluent life. Remember?"

She did not respond.

The trip back to Paris was quiet. Unknown to Jean-Louis-Pierre, Gaby had taken a major decision. Her life needed to go on without this man, who created chaos in her well-orchestrated life. Accepting his invitation to Beaunne had not been wise. She would never admit to him that she still loved him far too much and that the suffering of years past remained tender. Her heart required shelter. Philippe had been correct. She would still offer Jean-Louis anything he asked of her. The emotions were raw, she loved being in his arms, she never wanted to be anywhere else when he held her, when he made love to her, the tryst that he had planned had turned into a major emotional trauma.

More important, the realization that the pain she'd experienced five years ago was right below her emotional surface. She would comply with her contract and leave Paris shortly thereafter. Perhaps even preempt her trip to New York, spend time in New Orleans and return in late August to open for gala performances at La Fenice in Venice.

Meanwhile, she was the present Belle of Paris. She'd fill her life with joyous company, she had many solid friends in Paris. Enthralled by the magnificence of the Côte d'Or, she remained seated and lost in reverie of passionate time gone past. The randonneuring on horseback they had enjoyed years ago in late Autumn as they galloped on the bank of the canal de Bourgogne still vivid, under the brilliance of the fall colors, crossing les grands crus *de la Côte d'Or,* Pommard, Beaune, Vougeot, Gevrey-Chambertin, Vosne-Romanee, Nuit-Saint-Georges - she recalled those years of total abandonment to leisure, to passionate moments with a man she adored.

Motionless and staring out of the window as the carriage stumbled on the mostly paved road on a beautiful early winter afternoon, peasants were busy with their shovels and scythes. They cut down the remaining stalks, attaching small limbs of vines to the main trunks, re-digging rivulets flattened by the December rains for irrigation and thinning unnecessary budding leaves, the remnants of last year's harvest.

The few apple orchards had already shed all their leaves, their limbs had been shortened to increase the upcoming year's blossoms.

Jean-Louis reached out and clasped hers as he brushed a kiss on her cheek. "I adore you, Gaby. I always have, and I always will!" he murmured.

She stared down at her skirt, and she did not respond.

CHAPTER NINETEEN

They arrived late at her home. The footman unfurled the carriage steps and opened the door. Jean-Louis stepped out promptly and assisted Gaby out of the carriage as the servants grabbed the few pieces of luggage he had sent for in Chatou.

Both stepped forward to the grand foyer. Looking forward to their first night together in her home, he approached her, reached for her waist and brought his lips to her mouth. She disentangled herself from his embrace.

The servants dispersed promptly to continue their usual chores. Gaby strolled into the petit salon where a well-stocked mahogany bookcase rounded a corner, nearby a large brown chesterfield fauteuil facing a grand fireplace.

Jean-Louis stared at the chair. "Who sits in that gargantuan chair? Certainly not you, Gaby. Could it be you purchased it with *moi* in mind?" he probed.

"You're incorrigible, Jean-Louis. A half smile brightened her pretty features. "Eh bien, non, I happen to like it immensely."

She pursued her search for the novel she'd started three nights earlier and sat down on the large chair that engulfed her small stature.

With a smile on his manly face, Jean-Louis passed by her and caressed the hair that tumbled down across her shoulders. He stopped by the side board where two crystal carafes, a bottle of Cognac, champagne flutes and rounded bottom glasses were set up on a silver tray. Jean-Louis poured a brandy and brought it around with him as he positioned a chair across from her. He sat, his long legs stretched out over a low table that separated them.

She continued to peruse the pages as she waited to acquire enough nerve to send him away forever. He gulped down a few sips, grinned and nodded at the book.

"I don't believe you will need a novel to lull you to sleep tonight, Chérie."

The butler entered the room. She watched him move to the long glass double doors, which opened onto the garden, in order to part the drapes and let the winter sun shine through. As the man returned back to the foyer and closed the door behind him, she found her voice.

"Jean-Louis, we need to talk!" She exclaimed a bit too loudly as she stood and directed her petite stature to the windows. From this second-floor vintage, she caught a glimpse of the many chalands that traversed the Seine.

His questioning blues eyes watched her stride for a moment and simultaneously trailed behind obediently. As he reached her, she promptly turned around to face him.

"Jean-Louis, I should not have agreed to our trip to Beaune. These past few years I've handled my life quite freely... "

He placed his two fingers across her mouth. "I dislike the turn of this conversation. Your past life after our wedding and separation and... ensuing divorce is disagreeable. Pray no more divulgations."

"Very well," she said, finding an inner strength unfamiliar to her a few moments ago. "Jean-Louis, I never promised a reenactment of our previous relationship, I just agreed to a cheerful few days. And it was great fun..."

Her voice began to quiver. She swallowed hard. She was accustomed to taking control of her emotions. Being on stage had taught her well. "The truth, Jean-Louis, is that I no longer love you, of that I am certain. Consequently, a reunion is pointless."

She turned away from him and pulled herself up straight as a rod, focusing instead on a little bird in the tree across from her as it sat on a denuded branch. Incapable of facing his guarded emotions, she tapped her long nails on the circular rosewood table on her right looking for a flute of Champagne.

Slowly, he obliged. He returned to the side board, uncorked a cooled to perfection bottle of Cristal left behind by her butler, and brought it back to her.

"Thank you, "were the sole words she could utter without a quiver in her voice.

"Look at me, Gaby." He bent down, gently turned her around and raised her chin so that he could see her face. "Why, Gaby? I do not believe you. You're frightened. Is it the incident in the monastery that disturbed you? I heard you last night, you thought I was asleep 'I love you so... I wish that I could trust you again.' You whispered these words to my heart, or... do you still believe that I devised this whole scenario to have you heel to my wishes? It is insane, and you know it."

"Jean-Louis, I NO LONGER LOVE YOU," she enunciated slowly, gaining strength in her conviction that she no longer needed to abide by his wishes. To deny him the reunification plan he'd set in stone was absolutely appropriate—a huge error in retrospect, although the days spent together had been unforgettable—good at first but irreparable at the Abbey. Although, if the revelation of her past trauma had to be exposed, she was content that Jean-Louis had been her confidant.

He would not divulge her secret—of that she was certain. All worked out perfectly, she reminded herself. Her other indiscretions always ended amicably, consequently there would not be any divergence in her comportment toward her former husband. This time she stood and faced him. "Please leave, Jean-Louis. You agreed to just 'amusement,' my sole request for our little escapade." She removed his hand from her chin, stood and prepared to take her leave.

His hand dropped to his side, and he stared at her once more.

Facing him, she prepared to amble away.

He strode closer and clasped her wrist as he turned her to him. "Very well, Gaby, I'll leave now. But I will return tomorrow and the next day and the next day." He dropped a kiss on her lips, turned on his heel and marched out of the foyer, down the marble steps onto the wide driveway where his carriage waited.

"Follow me, I will walk home," he shouted to the coachman as he reached the waiting carriage. He tossed his coat to the footman.

CHAPTER TWENTY

True to his words, he returned to Gaby's *hôtel particulier* the following day.

"Madame is gone," her young maid told him.

"Where?"

"I am not at liberty to disclose, Monsieur."

"Place this letter on Madame's secretary. I will return later."

Two hours later he was back and like earlier, Gaby was nowhere to be seen. By five he decided to stop by the florist. Her favorite white roses, the Marie-Josée, were sent to her loge and hôtel particulier. He planned to meet her at the opéra shortly after the delivery. She was singing tonight, and he knew her work ethic. Gaby would have practiced in the early afternoon and rested prior to her performance.

Half an hour prior to the performance, he rushed down the spiral staircase of the Opéra to the diva's suite. A couple knocks at the door brought her assistant to the door.

"Please, Monsieur..." Quickly Jean-Louis pulled her young servant out of the loge. He walked in and closed and locked the door behind him.

"Jean-Louis? How dare you? Leave immediately, these types of disgraceful scenes are abhorrent. I will call secu..." His lips pressed upon hers as he gathered her into his arms while marching to the small sitting room that served as a quiet room.

"Please, Jean-Louis, we can't," she whispered, "it's scandalous! *J'entre* en scene in forty-five minutes. My fans have never waited."

"I have waited and waited and waited again for many great performances. It's my personal revenge on the likes of you."

He placed his wide body on hers and, unwilling to speak another word, he tore her satin robe from her body while kissing her passionately. Her shameful body did not respond to logic. Their passion deepened as they interlaced, kissed and ceased to think—logic replaced by flaring desire.

Angry knocks whacked the closed door as she let herself be loved. Time passed, their sexual passions ignited. The world stopped. Finally taking deep breaths, she turned her head to him, her body spent, her mind blank, dewy, translucent, pearly beads of perspiration covered her breasts, neck and cheeks. For the twinkling of an eye, her world stood still and splendid, until she heard the angry shouts behind the door. They reminded her that a full house awaited her grand entrance.

"Oh, Mon Dieu, Jean-Louis. Move, it is late. I need to dress; the costume dressers are outside the door."

He rolled on the narrow fainting sofa and watched her collect her robe from the floor. She opened the door. The stage hand stared at him angrily. Gaby stood on a dais and, as if through no fault of her own, she pressed her dressers and make-up artists to hurry. Finally, in costume and made up, she slipped on her satin heels and hurried through the large door opening that accommodated extravagant costumes for the stage.

Amidst all of the commotion, Jean-Louis shouted to her. She looked back and watched him wave the black filigreed bonnet she had forgotten. He rolled off the sofa, approached her, lifted her mane inside the cap, pulled her even closer and dropped a kiss on her nose. "I love you." He turned her toward the door, gently tapped her bottom as she hurled murderous glances his way.

"I will see you after the performance. I adore you!"

"Go burn in hell!" she mouthed in English as her handler, who carried her wardrobe changes, hurried behind her.

CHAPTER TWENTY-ONE

He returned to his loge almost certain that they would mend their ways. Many friends joined him as he basked in the joy of the moment. Gaby had sung with a passion that mesmerized the audience. The woman was born to sing and to love him! Regrets scratched his soul for a short second. In essence, no one could outperform the heavenly sounds that came out of her lovely throat. She shone like the brightest of stars amongst the greatest of divas. She had been 'the voice' in New Orleans. She was 'the light' in Paris! That was his new life. He liked it very much.

Years ago, his fear for her safety had been monumental, perhaps there could have been another way. Singing was such an integral part of her being. He wanted to make up for the wrongs that he'd committed. Gaby had been young and pliable. He excused himself and looked at his watch. Gaby should be ready now.

Once more at the diva's door, the same maid opened with a smile on her face. He entered and gazed to and fro, searching for Gaby, behind her paravant, in the sitting room. The young girl was clearly enjoying this moment. She watched him in silence, a sneer on her face.

Let him explore, the glance appeared to say, you will find her gone, Monsieur.

"Madame left an hour ago with Monsieur Renaud de Beauvaur, who is just back from India. She will return next Sunday," the maid said, basking in her knowledge.

He was about to question their whereabouts. Instead, he spun on his heel and stormed out of the loge, shocked at how untrustworthy Gaby had been. This time, he felt certain Renaud was most probably a lover. Less than three hours earlier, she had basked in his arms, the recipient of his caresses and kisses.

Eh bien, it was over. That would be the last time he would submit to her treacheries. Fury emanated from his entire being and distress filled his broken heart.

CHAPTER TWENTY-TWO

Gaby's five days in Nice with Renaud had been a joyous occasion to spend with great and loyal friends. Élise, Ribaud, Luke luxuriated in the cities that bordered the temperate and magnificent Méditerranée. Nice, Cannes, Monte-Carlo, all attracted the well to do who spent a great deal of their lives in the frozen tundra of Northern and Eastern Europe.

Jean-Louis was missing, and she was thrilled. Her heart deserved a reprieve from the emotional chaos he inflicted. No one had asked about or referred to him, not in her presence anyway. Too short of a voyage, she murmured to herself as the train veered toward the capital. Her feelings toward a reunion with Jean-Louis mounted. She loved him with all her heart still. No question. Perhaps, just perhaps she should let her guard down and follow her heart.

An inner voice, that of Philippe, echoed, 'do not allow this monster to hurt you again. He will, Gaby, if he gets a second chance. Be strong, my dear cousin.'

She swallowed a few sips of Cristal and rested her head on the fluffy down pillow the butler had just brought in, along with the bedding. A decision would need to be taken the following day. Meanwhile, sleep worked its magic. She let herself be lolled into a dreamless slumber.

Upon her return to Paris, a full ten days passed without a sighting of Jean-Louis. As she rode along in her carriage while returning to her *hôtel particulier*, she would furtively glance at the large wooden doors of her former home, unfortunately save the guards in the *guérites*, the gates were closed.

Jean-Louis was in town, she'd heard of soirées where he would make his grand entrance, but he would remain absent from the myriad of late-night gatherings she attended.

Several weeks later, an invitation to a ball given in honor of Madama Juniel, an interesting writer Gaby had met in Milan, arrived in the early afternoon. She looked forward to her lecture. Tonight, she'd explore the theme of her new book—Altruism. The host and hostess begged Gaby and her favorite tenor to make a short appearance.

"My friends," she proclaimed, melodramatic, "it has been said that the well-being of your neighbors is as important as your own well-being. Enlightened humans who practice selfless actions should be copied by all, by us, yes by us, towards the laundresses, the dancing girls, the demi-mondaines, yes, *mes amies*, God knows some of us in our aristocratic salons use their services regularly!" She sniggered at her own witticism. "Eh bien," she continued, "I am no longer certain of the philosophy. After much research, it seems that a selfless act always has an unconscious ulterior motive—guilt, reward, love, attention..." Gaby listened intently until she heard the butler announce Jean-Louis' arrival.

He looked magnificent in a stylish black suit with dark velour's lapels, alone as usual, but with the confident glance that told of the certainty that someone might be the fortunate lady of the night. After short conversations with friends, mostly of the political world, he followed the former President and members of the Senate, who were ushered into the great dining room to partake of the gastronomical feast. Seated halfway down the opposite side of the table, he gave the impression of being happy, humorous, the life of the party.

The author had been placed to his right, and they engaged in a lively conversation. Her eyes veered to him several times, always the same, great laughter as Madama Juniel gathered all of his attention.

Just as well, Gaby reflected, my heart would have been broken once more had I accepted his lies of unconditional love.

She turned to her partner, Victor Marie Hugo, the learned and much acclaimed writer of Les Misérables and Notre Dame de Paris. Gifted, musically inclined as he shared with her his love for operatic music and his *dada* of the time, the abolition of capital punishment. She liked him immensely.

Like so many Romantic writers, dramatists, and poets of his time, Victor's interest in politics and his fearless position to engage in the fiery denunciation of Charles Louis Napoléon, the former Emperor of France, had forced him into a nineteen years' exile. He'd escaped first to Bruxelles and then to the Guernsey Island in the English Channel for calling Napoleon III a traitor, in response to laws passed that set in motion the Emperor's absolute control of the government.

"Madame," Victor Hugo said dramatically, "you will enthrall us with one of your favorite arias, n'est ce pas?"

"With great pleasure," she agreed, "under one condition, that you read with tone your favorite poem. We have missed you so terribly, Monsieur Hugo."

He smiled, turning to the small venue and then back to her and with his grave well-appointed voice, he regaled the *parterre*.

"How can I refuse anything to this diamond star?" Applause and laughter filled the room. Jean-Louis' stern face showed a crack, but quickly he recovered and beamed his winning smile.

Later that night, she received repeated requests to perform more than one aria. She pleased so many with her art, she thought, and it gave her such gratification.

Her contract with the opera had elapsed. Recitals were held mostly for friends' soirées and tonight had been such a night.

All moved to the ballroom, Gaby picked a flute of Champagne from a circulating servant, as she started a conversation with some of her closest friends.

Jean Louis walked over to his circle of male friends, toward the cigar room, to avoid the high pitch voices of the many inebriated invitees, meanwhile not a glance at his former wife.

Henry de Sanges, a senator, turned to the tall aristocrat.

"What a splendid creature," Henry de Sanges, Jean-Louis's grandmother's companion continued admiringly. "Who would have known? You and the beauty before us. The love of the century, they'd declared. She worked tirelessly for your release... and that smile, oh that teary smile when the judge granted you your freedom! *Eh bien, you see, the eternal recommencement,* you got tired of it all. All were stunned in Paris when your marriage broke up. Gabriella did well for herself. Look at her now. Never been so beautiful!"

Jean-Louis-Pierre remained silent and stared at his former wife, who chatted with all who surrounded her after her glorious solo. He looked around the room; all were making their way toward the returned sensation, save a few old men in the salons who still spoke of a return to a Monarchy. If it had not happened after the Commune, Jean-Louis thought, France would never again crown a monarch.

He continued to stare at Gabriella. The newspapers had placed her in Monaco last week, gambling away with the ever so attentive Jean-Marie-Gabriel de Lancennes. Less than a week ago, she'd been moaning in his arms. Was she in love with Jean-Marie-Gabriel?

"You see," the old de Sanges pursued, "I am correct, there is no such thing as lasting love for a man. Affection makes for a good marriage. I am happy I married Celeste to Lord Byron in London. She hates my controlling demeanor now, but will be grateful in the years to come. Better let the old ways prevail." Henry turned to Jean-Louis, surprised to find him intently staring at the pretty soprano.

Slowly the crowd moved away from Gaby to allow her to walk closer to the grand piano. Her return to Paris had been magical and tonight in this small but élite venue, the Grand Monde, yes it still existed after the civil war—the horrific Commune—had given her a welcome like no other. Her escapades to Italy and the myriad of world stages she'd adorned had not thwarted the adoration of her Parisian fans. For the loyal French, Gaby had chosen to break her contract and open the Palais Garnier, the new opéra house on the Grand Boulevards. That's all that was needed to warm her devotees' hearts.

"Paris is the city I miss the most. I am home, my dear friends, thank you," she'd exclaimed to an adoring public in her first interview after her return.

Tonight, the host had mentioned a surprise when he'd extended the invitation, Jean-Louis-Pierre had thought of a political announcement. He had not divined that Gaby would be the acclaimed guest of honor. She was gorgeous in a canary yellow flamenco dress with bountiful layers which required her admirers to stay several meters away. The ever-present plunging décolleté was also part of the very charming attire. He would have liked to have lifted it round her neck!

Her voice lifted to the heavens.

Jean-Louis-Pierre stood emotionless. No one would have guessed the jealousy within that torc at his heart and soul. Gaby had achieved her dreams. She would never allow him to direct her career and select the venues. Never, ever again. He had been so sure of his plans in Chatou. The pangs of insufferable emotional pain had been laid to rest. He'd imagine them returning to their idyllic love affair, which should never have been interrupted.

Two days later she'd renounced her love after a well-staged escapade that he had turned into a heavenly romantic three days in Beaune. Upon her arrival in Paris, he had thought all was mended and that finally their love for one another would triumph, the lovemaking in her loge had guaranteed a precious place.

Eh bien, the little devil had escaped to the South of France with one of her tenor's or worse, Renaud de Beauvaur, the man she had met just a few days upon their arrival in the South of France. He knew his kind well. They ran in the same circles. 'I no longer love you, Jean-Louis,' she'd said coldly. How could he have been so wrong? Across the vast ballroom, here she was in all her splendor and talent, perhaps in love with Jean-Marie-Gabriel de Lancerre, another of his philanderer social relations.

Collected, Jean-Louis-Pierre remained charming, with the ease of standing for a man of his aristocratic lineage. Many women flocked to his entourage and all were greeted with witty conversation, polite banter, and gracious flirtation. All a well-rehearsed theater, while his mind reflected on the pretty brunette he simply adored. Gaby was in Paris because he had purchased her contract. Now, he realized she was no longer the innocent young girl he had fallen madly in love with. Without guile, she'd left him to spend time in Monaco with a lowly Count!

Lost in his thoughts while her melodious voice charmed the audience, a sensual smile from the pretty soprano chanced his way. He remained cold to the advance and followed a friend into the smoking salon. Consternation flashed in her appealing emerald eyes... elegantly, she left her favorite tenor to direct herself toward the cigar room where she gracefully moved in the circle of friends he had joined. The euphonious music piped in from the nearby ballroom had her swaying to the rhythm of the violins.

"Gentlemen," she called out arrogant with a resplendent smile, and a flirtatious grin directed at her former husband. "You departed from the ballroom? You dislike my choice of arias, Messieurs? Please give the pianist your list. I want you to stay," she admonished the four men leaving the ballroom. "Classical music affects creativity. Please remain with us," she demanded with sugar in her voice, accentuating her charming American accent while she gazed into Jean-Louis's eyes. He shook his head, and smirked.

"But of course, well said, our boring conversation certainly can wait, dearest Gabriella. We were miffed by your lack of attention to our grand lineage, ah! ah!" de Sanges professed; Jean-Louis-Pierre's grandmother's great friend laughed. "We old men love these cultural caresses!" he said loudly.

"Eh bien, just for your grand lineage!" She approached them. Her swan neck lifted to the heavens, and she reached a note that chilled all who stood nearby.

"Bravo, Madama!" the guests shouted, their flutes lifting to the firmament, chorusing with her in the early morning hours.

Gaby's attention remained on Jean-Louis. "Will you dance with me, Jean-Louis?" she murmured.

He stared at her for a long time. The brouhaha silenced. All eyes descended on the former lovers. Long, embarrassing moments elapsed, motionless at first, gesticulating uneasily as seconds and minutes chimed. She stroked the multitude of yellow voile layers that adorned her dress, her meaningful glare fixed stubbornly on Jean-Louis. He was not amused, she pondered as his icy blue eyes didn't bat an eyelash.

"Eh bien, I presume that dancing is not in the cards!" she ventured, a shy smirk directed his way. She lowered her eyes, smiled at him, ready to pivot and return to the stage. In an unexpected quick recovery, Jean-Louis removed himself from his respected circle, strode round his friends to his former wife. Silently and measured, he clasped her elbow and engaged her willing body to the dance floor.

She drew in a deep breath, continuing the aria with gusto as she strode with Jean-Louis to the dance floor.

She raised her eyes to him.

"That was bold, Gaby," he muttered, a half smile appearing.

She looked up, taking in the immensity of the act. She might have to pay for it later.

"Ouch, you stepped on my toes, Jean-Louis!" The spontaneous interlude shattered.

"Your pace was off, Gaby!" he countered. "Your dancing skills need a practiced coach, ma chère. Your return to Paris was well clocked."

Her diva glance, alien to questions regarding her artistic aptitudes, surfaced.

He stood his ground. "You missed your step," he repeated.

"Dance!" she replied.

A loud deep throated laughter erupted. "With pleasure, Chérie. Follow my lead!" He winked at her and gathered her closer to him.

"I love dancing with you, Gaby," he whispered sweetly in her ears.

She scanned the ballroom and swallowed hard. "You're a wonderful dancer, Jean-Louis... but... watch your step. You were at fault this time!"

"*Toujours le dernier mot, Gaby*? Always the last word, n'est ce pas?" He lifted her up, stole a kiss and looped her body in the air until bursts of crystal-clear mirth altered her mood. Slowly he returned his former wife to the dance floor.

Vanquished, she declined to answer, but followed his exacting lead. A demanding Strauss Waltz intoned, the music flowed through the pages of her past life in the ancestral home in Loire, melancholic thoughts of the two of them dancing in their ballroom flashed before her eyes. They had been too happy to even question their future.

He glimpsed at her contented allure as he guided her across the room to the foyer. He smiled down at her, his warm breath must have caressed her as she lifted her head simultaneously and beamed back.

He continued to hold her through three more waltzes and then directed her away from the dance floor.

"Jean-Louis, will you come and sit with me for a short while?" she murmured sweetly.

No answer came from the grand Monsieur. Jean-Louis glanced away.

"As to avert an embarrassing moment?" she pleaded, "I will be greatly humiliated otherwise. Please?"

He remained silent and continued to lead her away as a former General of the regime stopped him. Aware that she was no longer his confidante, she began to move away alone. Instead, he reached for her waist and curled her back to him. He caressed her upper arm.

"I cannot spend more time on the issue as Gaby and I have plans. I will call on Tuesday," Jean-Louis stated flatly as he gently led Gaby toward a large settee. He sat in the far corner of the bergère, scrutinizing every inch of her body.

"Where are we going?" she questioned.

"Nowhere," was the curt answer. Gaby glanced at the other guests with a pleasing smile.

"Stop staring at me this way. It's perverse." she admonished.

Not deterred, he kept on staring. "I know every millimeter of your body and yet my desire for you is unrelenting—flagrant."

"You adore me," she replied flatly.

Shocked at her forthright response, he sat upright and turned his glance to the grand salon.

"Eh bien, Gaby, who are we making jealous this evening?" he glowered at Matthieu du Marchais, the man she had vacationed with in the Hautes Alpes. Few people knew that they were the best of friends but, and it was a well-kept secret for the handsome aristocrat, Matthieu loved men.

She lifted her shoulders and bent forward to lift her dress and move away. Two steely hands clasped her wrist and forced her down the settee. He noticed the crowd unremitting interest in their demeanor, an enigmatic sneer broke on his manly face. Annoyed, she smoothed the layers on her dress.

"Jean-Louis, look at me," she said, her gloved fingers reaching for his chin and gently turned it to face her. "If there is any chance for us, your absurd, jealous fantasies will need to terminate. First it was Phillippe, my cousin, the Cardinal, then Jacopo in Italy, then the ghost lover who destroyed our idyllic love affair. Cease, for God's sake!" she declared in English.

"I adore you, Gaby, but you are pushing the limits of civility. May I remind you who you are talking to?"

He stood amidst a row of drafters and photographers who had been attracted by the interaction of one of the most celebrated couples in recent history. Jean-Louis strode to the large spiral pink veined Italian marble staircase. All eyes upon him.

To avert the commotion, the music director asked Gaby to sing a second duo with her favorite tenor.

Arriving at the very top of the stairs. Jean-Louis stopped and listened to her melodious voice wafting through the enormous town house. His departure would assure the loss of his former wife forever. He asked for his carriage to be brought forward. The yellow diamond two string bracelet he'd bought for her a few days after their Chatou's and Beaune's encounter was still on the back seat. The jeweler had engraved her initials in an intricate heart design. She would love it. Saved by Cartier!

Swallow your pride, Jean-Louis-Pierre, he scoffed as he slammed the carriage door and turned back toward the hôtel particulier, the black velvet elongated box in his coat pocket. He climbed the stairs of the elegant home two at the time under the amused glances of the servants.

A former member of the Government of the Defense and his new paramour were walking up the staircase onto the introduction foyer. The man had passed the inebriated state.

"Tell us de Pleyssis," he shouted, swaying on the stairs. His pretty, raven hair companion rescued him from a precarious fumble down the marble staircase.

Jean-Louis-Pierre clasped the minister's hand and rotund body, and he dragged him to the main platform, calling a servant to help return him safely to his coach.

The former general would not follow. Instead, he gripped the gilt bannister. "le tout Paris is asking if you and Gabriella have mended your parting ways?" he shouted.

"Our affairs are not of the tout Paris's social commerce, Gaston," he responded coolly as he continued his descent down to the filled ballroom waiting for Gaby to finish the melodic aria.

The applause resounded across the halls. He walked behind her, gently placed his hand on her wrist and wrapped the diamond bracelet around it. The crowd gasped. He kissed her flowing mane and smiled.

"Like it?" he asked.

Clearly stunned, she replied, "Very much." She caressed the stones with her gloved fingertips. Without much to do he handed her his champagne flute and guided her away from her adoring audience.

Not so quiet murmurs and gossips measured *les enfants terribles* as they passed the revelers. Paris adored titillating moments in intriguing love affairs. The attendees of the salons would warm their throats for weeks to come!

"They fooled us, the conniving pair, the broken marriage was a charade! They wanted privacy. All a dramatic play to fool journalists and gossips," many in the crowd professed.

"I knew it all along, but my great admiration for passion and privacy prevented revealing the secret of this most modern couple. You know how we French love history, but yet contemplate with great yearning the future of relationships," a young woman proclaimed with great drama.

Gaby passed by and winked.

Within the hour all believed that the relationship had continued to flourish under the unknowing eyes of the Beau Monde. But it had not. Jean-Louis was much too proud to forget it all. He politely accompanied her to the carriage, stood by as the footman unfurled the steps to let her pass. He stood proud, not moving a centimeter. She stared at him, not knowing what to make of this new development.

"Good night, Gaby." He strode to his own waiting carriage a few feet behind hers.

Stunned, Gaby rapped the window with the golden baton engraved with her initials. Jean-Louis had gifted it to her on her twenty-third birthday. The carriage still held the de Pleyssis's coat of arms on its side. Perhaps it was the end of their love affair. She had pushed him too far. Teary eyed, she lifted her slender fingers to her throat. It was for the best, she told herself. Why did it have to hurt so much?

While in Nice, Élise had impressed upon her that perhaps love was too seldom recognized between two individuals, who essentially could not care less about aggrandizing their families' fortunes. Not to give their relationship a second chance might have been a grave error.

CHAPTER TWENTY-THREE

Two weeks later, all the resolutions made by Jean-Louis were swept away by the winds of passion. He could not wait to see her. Yes, Gaby had gone to Nice. Yes, she'd probably spent time with Renaud de Beauvaur, but Renaud was seen all over Paris with many women, and he knew for certain he savored *l'amour libre*.

He would attend the de LaGrange's dinner party. Gaby was the honored guest. He sighed, swallowing his pride as he took the stairs two by two to dress for the event.

His English friends, Ribaud and Luke, along with Élise, had just returned from the South of France. They had spent many happy moments with Gaby. He would ask questions, although Élise did not mince her words. He loved her and would forget it all, which she also knew. The three friends had met in their favorite restaurant, *La Grenouille*. Jean-Louis had been drinking heavily, and Élise suggested that they should return to his house.

"I will put you to bed, Jean-Louis-Pierre." She laughed as she cajoled and tenderly kissed him.

"No, I will go to the de LaGrange's ball and watch my former beloved sing her melodious arias," he whined.

Filled with disdain and jealousy and yes, unbearable passion, he stumbled into Luke's carriage. Ribaud, Luke and Élise stood on the balcony together to help him stand straight as their presence was acknowledged by the guests. Their names and titles were called out. Élise held tightly to Jean-Louis-Pierre. He skipped a few stairs, almost falling flat on his face had it not been for Ribaud, who stepped in front of him. Gossip and laughter made the rounds. Unable to stay and watch this once great military genius reduced to this sorry drunken state, Gaby gathered her dress, her shawl, and bid good night to her hosts.

Renaud surprised her in the foyer, clasped her arm and escorted her to her carriage. "Let me take you home, Gabriella."

She smiled. "I love you, Renaud, merci. Philippe is arriving tomorrow. I can't wait." She came close and kissed him on both cheeks.

"Gabriella." he said as he hugged her and lowered his lips to hers. "I love you too, way too much."

Renaud was an amazing kisser, but he would have to wait after Philippe returned to Rome. "Bonne nuit." She blew a kiss prior to entering the carriage.

At home and feeling distraught, she questioned Jean-Louis's demeanor. He now showed up at so many parties inebriated. Was she the reason for his despondent state? Philippe had been right. She should never have accepted this new contract. Where was Philippe now? Hopefully on his way to Paris. Christmas had passed... and the New Year. She'd celebrated with friends in Paris. On Christmas Eve she'd entertained the parishioners and many attendees from various part of the nation by singing the Ave Maria in Notre Dame. *Naturellement*, every paper had sung her praises.

"Mademoiselle," the Monseigneur secreted, "you should be French!"

She'd placed her long fingertips on the very top of his chasuble. "But I am, Mon Père. In spirit." They'd both laughed.

She attended many balls and grande *soirées.* At times Jean-Louis showed up late, surrounded by friends but never a particular paramour or lady friend. Renaud had invited her to Nice after her last performance in early February. She intended to go, finish the season and embark for America. The great adventure had ended. She wished Jean-Louis had no business ventures in her home country.

After New York, she had a contract in Chicago, back to the Palais Garnier in late September, then to Venice, Milan and at the end of the year, Notre Dame. A few repertoires in Paris, she'd accept and then... who knew where her singing might take her. However, her home base would remain in Paris. She had wonderful friends who truly loved her, and she loved the brilliant cultural aspects of the city. She truly loved Paris. She loved France. Of course, Jean-Louis... but his many businesses would keep him traveling a good part of the year.

She would adapt when he remarried. Others had loved passionately, suffered and accepted their new existence. She would, too. Life was good. Gazing at the flames rising high and streaking the smoke darkened back stones of the fireplace, a frisson shook her. She reached for the woolen scarf and enveloped herself in it. Her maid, who studied her demeanor intently, strode to the fauteuil where the diva sat and offered a cup of tilleul. The Tilden tisane was her go to after too many flutes of the silky texture and fruity aromas of the several *coupes* of the Cristal Champagne.

She reached for the tisane from Juliette's silver platter, savored it for a long time as melancholy emotions encircled her being. She shook her mahogany mane and stood, paused as she stared at the Sèvres tea cups that commemorated their marriage. She climbed the stairs to her private suites. Socrates followed closely. He jumped on the sofa while she undressed.

"Just you and me, my dear Socco," she said as she stopped to caress her very best friend. "Another adventure awaits us." She slipped into a satin night shirt embroidered by the Bayeux workshops, her fingers smoothing over the bas relief embroidery. She finished the tisane and climbed into bed.

"Jean-Louis has not been parading his paramours at the soirées that we attend," she whispered to Socrates as he crawled on her pillow and nestled his furry muzzle in the crook of her neck.

***

As the deep rose colors of dawn bared the quiet streets of Saint Louis, a loud, grave-sounding voice woke her up. Jean-Louis, his voice thunderous voice as he shouted at the butler, maids and guards to move out of his way as he stomped up the staircase. She froze in her bed, wakened out of a deep slumber, her reaction to the unpredictable Captain delayed. Jean-Louis burst into the sitting area and then into her room, servants and security following in his wake.

"Order them out!" he shouted in English. "Or I will and it will not be a pretty sight, I assure you."

He staggered through the room, collided with a circular rosewood table and knocked off a crystal vase filled with her favorite Marie-Josée. The water, vase and long-stemmed roses spattered on the parquet and carpet as her former husband took a forward plunge.

Luck of the intoxicated, the rose satin sofa softened the blow as his head struck first the embroidered pillow and then quickly rolled onto the floor, adding another scar to his perfect visage. Placing his hands on the floor, he tried to straighten his large body, but crystal shards pierced his skin. The alcohol must have subdued the pain as he halfway uncurled his torso. This time, his body landed fully on her bed. She reclined quickly on her pillows.

"Leave us!" she ordered the confused servants.

Maids talked in the boulangeries, épiceries, so no need to aggravate this very uncomfortable situation. All left the room quickly, happy to return to their quiet quarters.

In his drunken state, Jean-Louis smirked. A win at last.

"What do you want, Jean-Louis?" she murmured softly.

He did not answer. Instead he shifted to her side of the bed, lifted the matching satin covers and flung his weary body next to hers. He curled her small body into his and positioned his heavy leg on her thigh, his long fingers posed around her breasts. "Just you, Gaby, just you, I want to hold you."

He gathered her even closer and on those last famous words, within minutes the great de Pleyssis sighed, his lips buried in her hair, and he happily surrendered to his drunken stupor.

Gaby's turn to sigh. She closed her eyes, felt his labored breathing on her shoulders. Torn but not willing to be anywhere else in that instant, she reached for his fingertips, then arranged her hand over his. One more night of happiness. She would think of something later that day. Sleep routed all thoughts.

CHAPTER TWENTY-FOUR

When she awoke, the household was alive and working like a well-honed steam engine. Even her carafe of coffee had been kept hot with two cups on a silver platter adorned with the lover's profiles on each corner of the tray. Steam rose in twirling vapors out of the delicately curled silver spout. The servants must have noticed Jean-Louis, the two interlaced love birds in bed—with her. She rolled onto her back and stared at her former husband, who was still sound asleep. He was good for a few more hours if his sleep pattern had not changed. They would talk then.

Confused was the word of the moment. A subtle inner voice whispered to give reconciliation just one more chance. Both were miserable without the other. Why, not? Life was filled with disappointments and painful attractions. Jean-Louis loved her, of that she felt certain, but her fear of a second rejection paralyzed her. She could not, would not... and her attraction to her feelings was replaced by a traumatic, gut-wrenching pain that recalled the torment exacted after their break up.

She had fought judicial and administrative forces to obtain his release from prison. Their parting had been de Pleyssis' recognition for her travails. She still hated him. There would be no reconciliation; she'd leave with Renaud. He was bound for Nice in February. Fun was the name of the game whenever they spent time together. She pushed aside Jean-Louis's hand and rolled off her bed. She reached for her peignoir, tied the belt around her waist and walked to the rosewood table where two breakfast settings had been placed.

Two settings? The shattered vase, roses and shards—nowhere to be seen. Instead, a silver carafe of piping hot coffee set sat next to an oval Saint Louis crystal bowl filled with luscious blueberries to its center and a heavily threaded silver basket loaded with warm flaky croissants replaced the damage. She poured herself a cup, and walked downstairs. The day room was scenic, it overlooked the Seine and the quays, lots of movements.

She never became bored or lonely when she sat in the alcove overlooking the river, its commercial chalands, Notre Dame and its elegant flying buttresses invented in the 11th century, the many lovers kissing on the benches of the river bank. At the moment four lovebirds embraced, two sitting side by side in the fork of the limbs, two more down below on a bench, the bitter cold and the drifting snow from the bare oak limbs aged their feathers and hair color to snowy white in minutes. She recalled how often she and Jean-Louis had sat on that very spot, unaware of the world around them. She lifted her fingertips to her throat, her soul chock full of romantic episodes, her heart recalling the passion of days gone by.

"Jean-Louis," she murmured, "why, oh why, did you become the slayer of my heart?"

"Monsieur, Monsieur, Madame is in the morning room," Juliette shouted after Jean-Louis.

Gaby pivoted just in time to watch him stomp down the steps, snatch his coat from the butler and stride out the front doors and into the midday brilliant sun. He detached one of the horses from his carriage, mounted him bareback and nodded to the security to open up the large wooden doors—in minutes he was gone. So much for an explanation! She should have listened to Philippe and declined Palais Garnier's invitation.

Always the same refrain, fatigued from incessantly placing blame on herself, she spoke aloud, "No, Gaby, it is your every right to enjoy

Paris. Reproaches should be tossed out the window. Jean-Louis was the one who asked you to leave the ancestral home, not the other way around. Let him suffer. I have every right to be in Paris. Mea Culpa should be his daily awakening phrase!"

Book Two

CHAPTER TWENTY-FIVE

LEVENS

Close to death and residing in a small yellow house in Levens, a small village in the backcountry of the Basses Alpes, Jeannette Eveline knew that the end was near. She gasped for breaths of fresh air sifting through the open window.

The suspended jasmine trellis clinging to the buttress of the many terraces of the picturesque village imparted sweet scents in late January. How she loved the South of France. Fields of fat bright purple lavender flowers faced the farm house. As a young child and the only daughter of a country doctor, she recalled filling her lonely Sundays and summer vacations picking the lavender blooms and placing the pretty flowers in cheesecloth to dry out, often giving the sachets to her mother and grandmother on Mother's Day.

Daffodils as well grew wild alongside long weeds by the side of the road. The scent was ingrained in her brain. It embalmed whatever gardens or room one would find themselves in while reading, contemplating, playing with her young cousins.

Spring is in the air, she thought, my favorite season. Funny that she had lived an upright life most of her existence. Dr. Durand and his family, whom she had met while they spent their summers in their Normandy country house, had taken a real interest in her life. The good physician had taken her to Paris as his assistant when her father had died. She loved them all and had rewarded the doctor with total devotion and dedication to his research center and practice.

Even her marriage had been approved by the family. Jean-Claude had been a hardworking man then. He'd worked as a carpenter, an amazing one at that. He had been one of the advisors to the architect of Empress Eugenie's boudoir.

They'd met one Sunday afternoon at an outdoor dance on the Place at the Louvres, where dances and music concerts were held every Sunday. He was a wonderful dancer who noticed everything beautiful. He would spend his Sunday afternoons, if he did not have a commission, painting in Chatou or in Chartres. He'd admire the grandeur of the most venerated Gothic French architectural Cathédrale, its altar, its sculpted wooden pews that lined the grande allée.

In those heady days, she'd often observed him in fervent prayers to the sculpture of Notre Dame as he lighted a candle to the divine Mother. In his uncle's house in Chartres, his artistry would blossom. An artist he was! This creative sense had first attracted her to him. His most ardent dream was to paint with the grandeur of his world.

They had gotten a small apartment and lived a charmed life until his addictive usage of absinthe began to turn a romantic interlude into Dante's Nine Circles of hell. He'd commenced by gambling his art, his profession, his carpentry, his tools, anything to pursue his dependence on the green ferry and yes, he had used her to provide, as well. She'd decided to walk to the village to pick up a baguette, because there was no delivery on Sunday. She liked to have a few pieces of bread to dunk into the soup Madame Sarton, her housekeeper, prepared.

The fragrant scents of the trellises of jasmine wafting upward and about the terrace was a nice reprieve from the foul odors that drifted up from the farm animals that lived below. Away on the hills in front of her were the colorful lavender fields that stretched as far as the eye could see. How she had loved picking the fat purple flowers in her time off from the hospital where she had worked ever since her arrival in Provence, seven years ago.

She had followed the love of her life. What a grave mistake it had been. A sharp pain in her lower right side reminded her that the consumption was lurking around the corner, giving her no rest until she finally expired. The thought of that horrific night never left her now. It was a cancer that tormented her. She had spent countless hours in the église Saint Jean in the center of the village. Candles burned to the Virgin night and day. She never let it go unlit. Today, upon her return from the *boulangerie*, she'd warmed up her soup in the dark coal oven and brought it back with her in front of the window. She sat on the green wooden garden chair.

The image of the tiny miraculous child, premature, delivered at seven months, ALIVE, a miracle, snatched from her arms and replaced with a large purple velvet bag filled with gold coins tormented her. She had needed two arms to hold on to the heavy loaded bag that swapped the tiny life she'd clasped in her arms. A woman's hand, a nun or one dressed as a nun, firmly curled her fingers alongside the velvet cover.

Two clerics had appeared on the scene, one rotund, another so short and skinny the shoulder of his tunic slid down to his forearms. Their faces were hidden entirely in the voluminous pleats of their cloaks. The large one held the child. He escaped through the anteroom and waited for the nuns to join him.

Words resounded in her weary spirit to this day. "Tell her to leave France immediately. If only one-word trickles down about this ordeal, I will make sure that their lives, hers and her husbands, are destroyed—in a very unpleasant way."

"Seigneur, we should make her disappear now. How can you trust a woman of the people to keep such a secret?" asked a man from the populace. He spoke in broken sentences with an accent from the Massif Central, which resembled her mother's.

She remembered the anxious retort of the large man. "I am a man of the cloth, I cannot do more than what I am doing tonight. I will burn in hell because of it. Dispose of her and her husband in a reasonable manner, but do not kill them!"

The only man not dressed as a cleric clasped her shoulders and pushed her toward another small room. In his haste the door was left half open, and she recalled peering at Gabriella's sleeping body.

At that very moment, another man had brought in a small bundle wrapped in satin covers, placed the bundle in the bassinet and pushed the top cover away from its face. She'd almost screamed. A dead, blue skinned, blotched face reflected in the mirror above the bed's alcove. Voices outside the door had frightened the group.

Dr. Durand had just returned. The slim cleric entered through a back door. "Get back in there, not a word or... "He'd showed her the curved blade of a knife with an ivory handle, which he'd tucked deep in the pocket of his cloak. "Do you understand? You and your husband on the guillotine before the end of the week!"

Nodding to the priest, he prodded her forward toward the just arrived physician, Gabriella and the dead baby.

"Ah, Eveline, come, I could not stay away. A few hours of rest did me a world of good. Back to work, thank you. It is your turn to rest. There is a comfortable room downstairs; please feel free to use it. Stay in the building. I may need your help."

Before she could respond the doctor strode to Gabriella's room. He hastily checked the bassinet as he picked up the black bag he'd earlier left behind and... froze.

Stunned, he whirled to Evelyn, who stood immobile by the door. "When did the child die?" He questioned the nun in an accusatory tone as he glared at the child. Nervous, the woman remained silent and quickly crossed herself. "The child took its last breath as we were standing over him less than a few minutes before your return," the stern voice of the pretender called out.

"Eveline?" the old man stared at his trusted nurse, tears filling his eyes. She nodded in acknowledgement, while the insurmountable fear that a wrong word might land her on the guillotine might come to pass.

"Funeral arrangements will need to be attended to," the old doctor said calmly.

"Thank you, Docteur Durand," a man dressed as an advocate donning a wavy powdered gray wig and wearing a long dark robe and white pleated collar remarked. He had materialized out of nowhere. "The Dowager has been contacted. We will handle it from here. Thank you."

"What of the Duchesse de Bourbonne? I will remain and take care of her."

"Madame will bear the burden of telling her granddaughter-in-law and her grandson of this great sadness. But now is not the time, with Monsieur being detained. There is only so much one can surmount, Docteur. Madame, as you are aware, experienced many losses. She seems unable to keep a child. No need to add to her great distress while she is fighting for the life of her husband. Our great leader, the Duke."

Durand bent his head. "Yes, yes, I will let the Dowager handle the matter. Bonsoir, Monsieur."

Evelyn recalled watching the old doctor walk to Gabriella's bedside, then touch her forehead with great care and compassion. "Yes, Gabriella, time will heal all wounds, your attention will need to center on your husband, dear child."

"Where are the documents?" From the entrance to the antechamber a man dressed in black with a low-lying cap on his head demanded.

Silent, the Docteur took in the new arrival, waited pensively as he fixed the man's face.

"There is no time to waste, Docteur, see that the documents are filled out immediately. Let me pay my respect to the Duchesse."

Dr. Durand ambled back to the desk, sat behind it and opened the drawers where a stack of papers had been arranged. He stared at the contents, sorted the needed document and dipped the quill in the mother of pearl inkpot to sign the copies of the death certificate. The man in the black suit reappeared and hovered over him. The gentle Docteur turned, sighed, lifted his head and clenched his jaw as he handed the vanilla-colored parchment to the Dowager's attorney.

"Tell Madame, that I remain at her service. I will express my condolences tomorrow. Meanwhile, I will return shortly to watch over Gabriella."

The doubtful lawyer spun on his heel and walked away. Evelyne recalled his every move as he stood with his hand on the handle of the gilded door for an instant, then turned and flung a murderous stare in her direction. She comprehended the code and remained stoic as he calmly strode out and closed the door behind him.

Docteur Durand watched and, almost as an afterthought, he called her back and handed her another printed document that he had copied and signed, the exact replica of the original—except that it was not a replica, it was the original. The one that she still kept.

"Evelyne, we have worked together for years. I knew your father and trust you like a daughter. Please bring these papers to the historical archives… immediately. It may look suspicious if I do it myself." He'd gone on his way. She'd never returned to his hospital nor taken the documents to the archives. Instead, a carriage awaited her. My drunkard husband, who'd understood despite his inebriated state not to ask any questions, sat next to me as the carriage departed of Paris for Switzerland. No one knew of the original copies she'd kept concealed in a secret compartment of her Bible these past six years.

Time was of the essence now, the story needed to be told. A child, if it was still alive, had been made an orphan through no fault of his own.

A surge of energy exploded within her. A sense of moral rectitude denoted the pride of a life well led until that dreadful early morning when, to safeguard her life and that of her husband, she had made the awful decision to choose her own happiness over that of an innocent child. The remorse and punishment had been worse than the fire of hell here on earth. These past six years had been filled with disastrous disenchantments. Her husband became even more abusive, and his gambling debts grew to such an extent, they had lived in abject poverty. Finally, she decided to return to the South of France in the small village in the Basse Alpes.

Amidst the incessant pecking of chickens, the grunting of pigs and the whinnying of horses, she stood again, and climbed with difficulty the four steps to her room. The cold breeze drifting from the open windows lifted the curtains as she made her way to the secretary where she kept the large Bible. She opened it and the parchment envelope the three folded documents written in impeccable script. She returned back to her bed, gasping for air. She laid down with great difficulty, too weak to lift the white cotton sheet.

Claude would never have allowed her to reveal a truth that could land them in jail for the rest of their lives or suffer the ultimate judgment—the guillotine. Nevertheless, she would be the first one to meet her Maker, and she had committed a mortal sin. She had been unable to even reveal the ordeal to her confessor... but now?

Her shriveled body moved onto its side. With difficulty she let her legs fall off the edge of the bed. She placed her stocking-covered feet into the tan felt slippers and searched for her cane. She stood, looking over her shoulder to be sure Claude would not surprise her and follow her. The sick soul was most probably gambling and drinking her hard-earned money in the back room of a local café.

She picked a small gold key attached to a red ribbon from a sock she kept inside her shoe, inserting it into a secret oubliette at the very back of an old secretary. She looked at the square envelope that she had kept secret for the past seven years. Her eyes filled with tears as she unfastened the thin cordon that sealed the envelope which revealed the secret live birth of Gabriella de Conte Thornsen de Pleyssis's son.

It had stood the test of time. She folded them neatly one more time, then dropped the package into a reticule she carried attached to a sash on her waist. She'd traversed the Place de Ville bordered by two restaurants and a café before she entered the Poste Nationale. Time for amends. With immense regrets she gave the clerk the address of Dr. Durand. The package was sent. Why she had not taken that step earlier? For the umpteenth time since her arrival in Levens, she had entered the church and stood before the statue of the Immaculate Conception.

She loved that sculpture and had prayed to her ever since her childhood. She had heard her voice and had followed the whispers of the Virgin. These past few years the whispers had ceased. She had walked alone.

"I am back," she said to the Lady in blue. Content, she slowly made her way home. Her life had not been a waste. Redemption was at hand.

Two weeks later the documents reached Dr. Durand's residence. The doctor had passed away a month earlier.

CHAPTER TWENTY-SIX

It was almost two o'clock and Evelyne, wearing her old blue and white button-down cotton shift, walked down the four wooden steps that brought her to a small terrace. A couple of green wrought iron painted chairs and a matching table mounted and nailed to the cement for safekeeping adorned her back patio. She felt safe on an unusually warm mid-March day, which she tried to enjoy.

The guilt she had felt for years reappeared even more succinct now than it had ever been. The end was near and she needed to make things right. She inhaled deeply three times and reclined in the lounge chair, the sun warming her tired body. The constant bloody cough and hacking kept her in a weakened state. Throughout these past years not one moment passed without her recollection of what she had done. She recalled that awful night, which had changed the rest of her life... for what? A love that had not been reciprocated.

She picked up Minette, the cat had been her constant companion throughout the last six years. Reclined in an old lounge chair, she faced the light mauve hillsides and began to narrate the nightmare she had kept within all these years. The animal, her sole confident throughout these fretful years, would never divulge the entirety of her secret. Meanwhile, the wrinkled brown bag filled with the documentation of the child's birth would be in Durand's hands by now. She'd made sure of that.

"I was in attendance as Gabriella de Pleyssis gave birth to a six and a half month living child," she murmured to the cat. "Dr. Durand and I had worked late into the night to save the infant as the mother held on to life by a thread. The young woman had been crushed to the cobblestones by a common carriage traveling *en sens inverse*, the wrong way, on the boulevard Saint Germain. She must have stopped by the patisserie on her way to visit Monsieur de Pleyssis, who was incarcerated in the Prison de la Santé during the six horrific weeks of the Paris Commune...

"Eh oui, Minette, those were the good old days when I was a remarkable citizen." The cat purred as she caressed his soft fur. "Gabriella's gray satin dress was spattered with almond paste and raspberry confiture."

She gazed ahead at the brilliant blue azure canopy as she recalled those atrocious days. 'Victor Jean-Louis-Pierre Gabriel, de Conte Thornsen de Pleyssis, if he should live,' Gabriella had murmured almost inaudibly.

CHAPTER TWENTY-SEVEN

As his horse galloped through the Faubourg Saint Germain toward his grand house, the coachmen and grooms urged the Percherons to follow closely. Pensive and reviewing the night he had just passed with Gaby, he wished he could have let his pride vanish and met with his former wife in the parlor, where she waited for him, but his arrogance had not let him. The spectacle he'd made of himself, both at the ball and in Gaby's bed, was pathetic.

A month away walking the Camino with Cunnan, his trusted Commanding Officer, also a naval colleague of his own father, who had sailed and fought with the de Pleyssis in times of peace and war. Jean-Louis-Pierre had no better friend than Cunnan. Gaby considered him to be a father figure. She adored him, and the feeling was wholly reciprocated. The long hike would surely clear his mind and cease the incessant gossips.

He slowed to a trot as the horses approached the two large wooden doors of the grand portal. The guards perched above in a turret recognized his arrival. The carriage followed close behind, *sans* one horse. The imposing gate opened and Jean-Louis's horse cantered in. Dismounting, he caressed Fury's mane and surrendered the reins to the young groom before stomping up two by two the marble steps of the grand entrance.

The coachman stopped and shouted for the guards to keep the gates open. The regal black carriage with the encrusted de Pleyssis coat of arms rolled in as young grooms hastened to take it to the coaches' hangar. They removed the harnesses from Jean-Louis's horse and walked it along to his proper stable.

The Duke, a somber expression on his manly face, marched inside where Cunnan awaited his arrival on one of the platforms of the wide and winding staircase.

"Where have you been?"

"I stayed at Gaby's," he responded.

Ne relevant pas la réponse, notwithstanding the retort, Cunnan kept silent and continued down the rest of the stairs. "When are we leaving?"

"I believe that Fernand is done with my packing. I need to eat and check my mail. We should be on our way within the hour." Cunnan followed the younger man inside the library. Luggage had been prepared and was waiting to be brought out.

"Monsieur, where do you want your petit déjeuner, in your apartment or in the morning room?" the old butler who had been part of Jean-Louis de Pleyssis's life for over thirty years asked respectfully as he tried to keep up behind them.

"In the library, Fernand," the Duke responded as he turned to Cunnan, "want anything?"

"I'll nibble on a few croissants, and a café crème. Merci, Fernand. »

The men strode along the long corridor where paintings of the long line of de Bourbonne looked sternly down upon them. Jean-Louis-Pierre strode to his desk where a pile of mail and two large cognac envelopes were arranged separately in a parchment folder secured by two red circular seals. He turned the package around, no aristocratic coat of arms, he paused and reached for his 16th century *coupe-papier,* that had been held in many de Pleyssis's hands, his family seal adorned on its handle. He ripped open the letters as a knock on the door focused his attention towards the gilded doors.

"Oui, Stephane?" His secretary stood there, sounding breathless as he said, "*Monsieur Durand fils, pardonnez-moi, Monsieur...* Dr. Henry

Durand came this morning before conducting his rounds, Monsieur. He wanted to talk to you, and he left these two envelopes for your review, Monsieur. He said that it was of the utmost importance, and that he would return late tonight to talk to you." The secretary's long and lean body bowed slightly as he began his retreat backwards toward the door. "Will I be needed, Monsieur?"

"*Non merci, Stephane*." Jean-Louis-Pierre opened the large envelope next without much interest. His languid glance and composed demeanor suddenly turned rigid. His body straightened, his jaws clenched and his left hand massaged the back of his head. He reread the note, staring at the document. "*Pas croyable*!" he murmured, his face tense, his left fist clenched on his desk.

He held out the envelope with renewed vigor and kept on reading the short note enclosed. He stared at the hundreds of books lining the wall of the library and then returned his sight to the two documents he had just plucked from the envelopes. Stunned, he tried to contain the tears that threatened to overflow from his bright blue eyes. One lone tear escaped as he turned to Cunnan and offered the documents. He kept the birth certificate in view as he evaluated every last corner of the dossier. The old man began to read the interpretation, consternation leaving him wordless.

"Our plans have changed," Jean-Louis-Pierre declared. "Let us wait and see what Henry will reveal, if anything." He pursed his lips. "I'll start the search for my child immediately. I hope you will join me, Cunnan."

"*Mais bien sur*! Let's take this time to figure out our next move."

The two men walked to the long mahogany tables set up in between the large bookshelves in the library.

"Should we request the help of Philippe?" Cunnan questioned. "And Gabriella, will you reveal to her this abominable deed performed in essence by the machinations of someone in your family? It is inconceivable, Jean-Louis-Pierre," the old weary sailor remarked.

"Not yet. Let's examine the list of nunneries and convents in England."

The servants brought in their breakfasts as both men, coffee in hand, proceeded to the table to consider the search at hand. Two hours later, piles of books lay haphazardly atop the table. Seated across from each other, the two men dipped their quills into the golden inkwell, both writing down addresses of all convents and nunneries in the British Isles.

"If alive, the child just celebrated his 6th birthday," the Duke remarked almost to himself with a sigh.

Cunnan did not respond. Their mood remained somber.

At almost eight o'clock Henry Durand was announced. Jean-Louis-Pierre and Cunnan started downstairs.

CHAPTER TWENTY-EIGHT

ENGLAND

It was the third nunnery they'd visited in England. They'd spoken to myriad Priors, Mother Superiors, monks, nuns, and religious people of many institutions. The result—absolute denial on all fronts. The child appeared irretrievable. He had vanished. Had he survived? Truth be said, he might have died while traveling to Calais or during the crossing.

"One certainty, the kidnappers were not aware of the subterfuge by the late Docteur Durand —the original copy of our sealed and signed copy of the birth certificate."

"This last development is the most worrisome," the Duke retorted. "If the kidnappers had been sure that they were in possession of all the documents, what incentive did they have to keep him alive? According to Henry Durand, his father Claude Durand believed that the child had died during his absence in the early morning hours. Had there been a hint of suspicion in Durand Père?" Jean-Louis-Pierre paused, his hands massaging the tense muscles of his neck. "I knew Évelyne, she was a trusted nurse to Durand—a woman of integrity."

Cunnan nodded and looked away. "A woman of integrity?" he questioned, shaking his head. "She ruined a child's life—your son!"

After two weeks of constant digging, they weren't any closer to finding out about the child. Upon returning to the inn, they cleaned up, met up in the foyer and walked over to a local pub. The place was filled, even at this late hour. The music was loud and played by four musicians on a makeshift stage constructed of dark planks pushed together and arranged on square wooden chests. Traditional music played on guitars and fiddles, the dark wood paneling and the free flowing, of thick and strong Guinness was the perfect place to gather, to talk and to drink together.

Cunnan explained, "They're like museums, the owner lives above his pub. At times, they are used as post offices or even mortuaries. I have heard stories from faraway villages, where hospitals or morgues were non-existent. The local pub was used as a resting place for the deceased while waiting for the family to claim the body."

Jean-Louis looked up and smirked. They entered the pub through narrow wooden doors at the entrance, then proceeded to a table in the far corner of the establishment, close to an exit. Four pretty damsels noticed their entrance, as well as their expensive overcoats and posh Italian leather boots. The owner of the place winked at a table filled with sorry looking gamblers, who looked prepared for a rumble. The two pistols hanging from the Duke's hips gave the men time to suspend their impulses.

The pretty young bar girls possessed the same goal—stealing their money - followed the two strangers as they entered the pub. All three surrounded Jean-Louis-Pierre. Cunnan smiled as he called to mind a novel by Toulouse Lautrec, wherein the young prostitutes extorted enormous sums of money through perverse, intricate plays and to which the painter retorted, "If *you ask me what I came into this life to do, I will tell you: I came to live out loud!"*

At any other time, it would have been fun. Jean-louis-Pierre smiled and passed along a small pouch of gold coins. These pouches might go a long way to help families of these destitute women, to help their children, or so he hoped. He had been discreet in the hope that their pimps had been blind to the transaction. Since they were not allowed to leave the *maison close*, a good many ladies of the night provided for their families the only way they knew how. They'd find a way to bribe a baker, a musician, a painter, a carpenter, or a wealthy aristocrat in

Paris and, yes, even in proper England, they'd extort any man who'd entered these houses of carnal love.

These men were never seen again. The prostitutes, debts mounting and always too much to repay, were essentially prisoners who satisfied men's sexual needs before they died of venereal diseases. If luck played a role in their lives, along with youth, beauty and wit, an aristocrat or merchant might take them out of their sordid existence and set them up in an apartment to accommodate their own pleasures, but it rarely happened. In many aspects England fared worse than France, while on both sides of the border these women lived horrific lives. The *maison close* was a means to an end; it helped to keep their families fed or their drug habits satisfied. Absinthe, a ghastly continuing plague.

Cunnan smiled. He loved the Duke and knew well the fabric that made up the young man's staunch demeanor. He gulped down his stout to the last drop and waved the girls away.

"In their defense, Jean-Louis-Pierre, all convents have shown us the records, the certified documents were kept in good order and the dates of arrival and departure of orphans were precise. Although... I feel that the Sisters in this last nunnery knew more than they wanted to share. The Mother Superior, in particular," Cunnan said pensively.

The Duke lifted his eyes to the wooden beams as he tried to recreate these last few days in this boisterous setting. Strange that Évelyne had been so exacting in the written note attached to the documents she'd secreted all these years. A revelation that would turn the House of Bourbonne on its proper continuing lineage, she'd written in a scholarly script.

"According to nurse Évelyn's diary, she had accompanied the newborn to Calais... but the inconsistency? Ships do not leave from Calais with a Dover destination? Her diary stated clearly that the kidnappers were comprised of 'men of the cloth'. Were these men priests? Monks? Impostors?" Jean-Louis-Pierre mused. He continued to read aloud, "'and uniformed military men followed two nuns endowed with nursing skills... they had taken the child from the bassinet to the anteroom? How many had taken the child to England? Not clear. Had Évelyne been allowed to follow them to England?"

"No stones have been left unturned and yet the results are devastating," Jean-Louis-Pierre said. He sipped the beer that had been brought to their tables and picked at the chips surrounding the breaded cod.

"Do not despair yet," Cunnan urged. "Tomorrow gives me hope. Abbott Pierre Easton was adamant about the retirement castle we will visit. Many former Abbots, who are now retired in the historical fortress, could possibly reveal a mysterious and sinister plot from that very time. Abbott Easton revealed that we should also visit a retirement priory, an ancient stronghold in Cornwall. Former Abbots and Priors of major Christian institutions in England reside there. Both are on our calendar.

"Let's hope so," the young man replied "although the last convent for retired prioresses and nuns we visited in Cornwall was dismal. All were tight lipped."

"The last monastery in England proved to be a stunning defeat, all physical traces of the child removed," Jean-Louis-Pierre murmured.

Cunnan nodded silently.

"There is no turning back. Abbott Easton's advice will be followed," the Duke stated as he touched his friend's shoulder. "I need to sleep, Cunnan. We will talk tomorrow morning."

Cunnan finished his stout and returned to his room. He sat on his bed and bent down to remove his boots. Perhaps tomorrow, the retirement castle for older monks might lead them in a new rewarding direction, he contemplated. He was always impressed with the Captain's sense of non-stop pursuit. He had braved unwinnable moments in war and always came out on top. Now the fight of his lineage was upon him—the continuation of his family's ancestry—but most importantly the child he had fathered with the love of his life, Gabriella. The only certainty was that Jean-Louis-Pierre de Pleyssis, Duke de Bourbonne, would not yield.

They started the new day under a gray, cloud-filled sky. Rain pelted their ermine lined coats.

"On our way!" exclaimed Cunnan as they threw their weight upon their respective horses, straddled the stallions and poked their spurs into the animals' flanks. Less than two hours later, on a low mount, they stopped to survey the Priory from afar. It was an old castle, its moat still visible, a few miles from a quaint village. Cunnan noted the cobbler's sign still showing the sole of boots on their colorful hanging signs.

"Interesting, in our day and age, we often forget that many still lack proper reading skills." The village's well, its '*puits*' as the locals called it, situated in the square across from a small Anglican church, appeared to be the place of congregation. Men sitting on its edges discussed the weather and the season's harvest. Everyone stared at the two men on horseback trotting toward the Priory.

None appeared to notice a young girl who'd materialized from the Minister's house. She dragged a bucket twice her size, sat it down, waited a moment to catch her breath and strenuously climbed onto the rough stones ensconced in the cement close to where the farmers sat on its edges. She then with a last great effort, attached the pail to the lowering rope.

"Need a hand, sweet child," Cunnan shouted as he dismounted his horse, tied the reigns to the post nearby, and approached the girl. He lowered the buckets into the well and lifted the filled pails to rest on the rim of the water hole. He noticed a few ironic glances from the men nearby and shot them a murderous glance.

"Where do you live?" he asked.

She pointed to a street adjacent to the Church.

"Show us the way and we'll meet you there." She hesitated at first, glanced at the farmers who now pretended not to have heard, and did as she was told. Crossing the crowded place, up the hill on a narrow dirt path, she stood by the door of the house of her employment—the seminary.

Quickly, she clutched the water buckets that were handed to her. She smiled at Cunnan. "Thank you," she whispered shyly before entering the dwelling.

"How old do you think she was?" Cunnan questioned.

"Ten perhaps, not much older. Life is rigid for so many." Jean-Louis-Pierre clenched his jaw. His son might not be in a much better situation. They returned to fetch their horses as many eyes followed their every move. They rode through the gates of the old village.

The ancient priory next on their list had been closed during Henry VIII's reign. Although the king rejected Papal authority, he was still a Catholic who burned protestant heretics! Some priories had been transformed into retirement homes for the superiors of convents and monasteries throughout England. Several abbeys in France sent their elderly clerics to this picturesque village. Both stopped their steeds to focus on the task at hand.

"Jean-Louis-Pierre, our last recourse at the moment in England is Father Henry," Cunnan declared. "The old priest from the village we just rode through, confided that his confinement to this faraway place was a penance. Strange that it happened just a day after our visit and inquiries to the Church he led? I understand he was pushed out of his position in London, and he is bitter about his forced retirement to the country. They gave him a coveted rank above many of the resident Abbots. Naturally, all dislike him greatly.

"He has no friends, no confidants, only powers to drive his inferiors mad. Let's take a look. There might be a silver lining. His anger may give us a new direction. One of his former duties was in an Abbey in France that took in orphans who were the unsavory result of many aristocratic indiscretions."

Jean-Louis-Pierre acquiesced and sighed. "Eh bien, on our way!"

He pressed his horse hard to a fast gallop down the hill, Cunnan close behind. They trotted down the narrow streets of the village, stopped for a moment in front of the church where they had met the young cleric the previous day. He stood in front of the church, watching the two horsemen proceed toward the castle. Both bobbed their heads and proceeded on their way until a young man showed up and opened the once impenetrable wooden gates to the former castle.

The two men passed the gate and slowed their mounts as the newly arrived Abbot, Father Henry, strode out to meet them. Both men were surprised at the Abbot youthful looks and sprightly demeanor. The cleric acknowledged their surprise. Both men dismounted their horses and shook hands with the short and stout director of the saintly institution.

As they walked to the stern structure, Father Henry vented his frustrations openly to the stunned voyagers. "I was sent here, Messieurs, to this sanatorium he proclaimed with great disdain and a forceful voice, TO REST AND ENJOY THE FRUITS OF MY SAINTLY LIFE, I was told. Realistically, the calm and serenity of the place creates more dismay. It startles my sensibilities into despair," he announced loudly. "I do better in a dorm filled dormitory with rotten little orphans," he smiled a kindly smile, "to be disciplined and taught well so that in adulthood they can find their place in a society that will not look kindly on their sort... and naturally lead a saintly life. Let us see if I can make your trip out here worthwhile, Messieurs. Follow me upstairs to my office."

They followed the Abbot, who stomped quickly through the gardens, the orchards and the long rows of denuded wine trellises. As they entered the courtyard and the long-covered corridors, a small door with bronze carvings opened to the side. They ambled through it. Large tapestries of the victories of the knights of St John the Hospitaliers of Jerusalem covered the stone walls.

"These beauties keep us nice and warm in the dead of winter when the cold and the humidity wreak havoc on our old bones!" the Abbott declared, nodding toward the long corridor that led to the refectory. "You should see these poor souls cowering next to one another during our communal meals."

Jean-Louis-Pierre and Cunnan remained silent.

No one was in his service. He opened the door himself with long bronze keys that he inserted into the lock. He pushed the knocker down and the heavy brown wooden door opened easily.

"Eh bien, sit down and tell me how I can be of service."

"I am searching for my son, who was abducted from his mother—at birth." Jean-Louis-Pierre announced.

The bluntness of the reply revealed a shocked expression on the Abbott's otherwise passive demeanor. He sat, looking uncomfortable in his large desk chair.

"When did this infamous event occur?" the cleric retorted promptly back to attention, his eyes questioning the veracity of the information at hand. His interest was not lost on Cunnan.

"Close to six years ago."

Abbot Henry paused and glared at Jean-Louis-Pierre. He swallowed hard as he raised from his tufted leather fauteuil and paused. His glare intently on the Duke.

"Eh bien, let's begin our search," Father Henry retorted, directing the men to a walled library. "I am listening."

The story of the lost child was recounted.

"If he has survived, his life probably resembles mine. I was an orphan brought up first in a convent and then a monastery. I made the best of it. My bottom pummeled often and hard in that sordid Irish monastery. Many tried to break me. I looked over my shoulders, always ready to raise my arms above my head to avoid the constant blows that were sure to follow on my back or face," the man reminisced. "Calm is stressful to me, they think..."

Cunnan stopped him. "They?"

The Abbot raised his shoulders quickly as if he could not care less, and did not answer the question, instead he said, "They think they are doing me a service by placing me in this frozen tundra's fortress, when it's actually hell on earth!" He smiled and lifted his eyes to the heavens, praying for a quick indulgence from his Maker above.

"Discipline seem to be the magic word, these children of God have more than their share of the school of hard knocks and because of the economic hardship," he stared at Cunnan's wide questioning eyes, the cleric patted his rotund stomach, "it was not always like that," he smiled. "I have put in my time, yes even us we are accepting more children that we have space to house and educate properly." The Abbott turned to Jean-Louis-Pierre, brazen, unabashed, "your kind, Monsieur is the reason behind the state of these institutions—your libertine lifestyles and your proclivities toward ridding your household of the bastards so as to not tarnish the family name."

Jean-Louis-Pierre's jaws dropped, an incensed form of unformulated riposte flashed across his manly face but he remained silent for a short while and swiftly intoned back: "I cannot say that I totally reject your statements, Mon Père, our culture of affluence needs to change." He placed his long fingers below his nose and laid his thumb across his chin.

"Do you have any clues and advice you could share with us on the whereabout of the child?" Jean-Louis-Pierre questioned calmly, shocking Cunnan with the self-restraint displayed.

"No," the elderly cleric replied after a long pause, staring at the Duke, "I have your address... if they even let me return to the monastery, I will inquire and send word to you."

Neither men held out much hope that the promise would materialize. They politely departed after spending an hour in the office looking at records.

"Wait!" the religious man called out, "I presume your child has been baptized Catholic?"

The Duke lifted his shoulders and nodded. "It would appear to be so. Nuns and monks were purportedly involved in the kidnapping, although they could have been impostors who cared little about our religious rituals."

"Northwest of our town, we have a nunnery." He looked for the address in a red leather notebook, found it and wrote down the directions. "Here is the address. It is usual to send an infant first to our sisters, the male child is returned to us at three or four years old, depending on their development. I wish you luck, Gentlemen. You have a hard road ahead... or perhaps none at all."

The two men thanked their host and took their leave. They stopped in town to have dinner prior to returning to the inn.

CHAPTER TWENTY- NINE

London

As both men returned to the tavern, a note awaited Jean-Louis-Pierre. The Duke reached over the desk to grasp the envelope.

"Send our dinner to my room and have the hostler take care of our horses. I will pay well for their comfort, thank you." He clasped the keys handed over by the front desk clerk and returned to the foyer where Cunnan waited.

While ascending the winding staircase, Jean-Louis-Pierre followed by Cunnan, began to rip open the envelope, no red wax stamp that usually sealed a letter, no coat of arms or name of the monastery they had just left.

Cunnan came closer and stared down at the note that had stopped the tall aristocrat in his tracks. "The writing—definitely from a learned man," the Duke murmured, "well-formed elegant letters, perfect spacing, the directness of the message is meant to stop our gerrymandering in England—definitely to the point."

Do not search for the child in England.
Ireland is a catholic country.

Both men spun on their heels and marched back downstairs to the reception desk.

"Who delivered the dispatch?" Cunnan questioned the clerk. "And how long ago?"

No one seemed to recall who had delivered the note.

"A young man or perhaps a girl... a long black fringe fell on his forehead. It covered half his face, the frayed gray cloak shielded the remainder of his body," the young man at the desk said. "Messieurs, his threadbare boots left mud tracks on our tavern's well-polished floors, *vraiment*," he tried to explain in French.

"We tried to engage and stop him, but he slid the card on the counter and ran in between the tables. Big Jack here tried to follow him, mind you, leaving dirt on our floors, but we are sorry. The little scoundrel was fast, and he escaped on foot into the forest. This debauched lad did not want to be retrieved, sir! I'm telling you! I know their kind! Little scoundrels always out for a penny." The waiter quick on his foot was slammed on the shoulder by a passing waiter. "Sorry, messieurs, I'm needed in the kitchen!"

The Duke turned to Cunnan and handed him the note, "let's return to the monastery early tomorrow morning."

Cunnan nodded and returned the note.

Jean-Louis-Pierre picked it up, folded it and filed it in the right inner pocket of his jacket. "It just comes to mind that Henry the VIII closed all monasteries and nunneries in the middle 1500's," Jean-Louis-Pierre said. "I should have thought of this tidbit of history prior to wasting our time in England." He sighed.

CHAPTER THIRTY

The following day was a ruse. The cold wind blew across the valley, sweeping through the brown and crackly autumn leaves that had fallen in heaps on the country's sodden earth. Black storm clouds overhead prodded their urgent goals, perhaps the note had been sent by another monastery or the nunnery they had visited earlier during the week of course under their acquired names or retirement homes. At this point total dismay and confusion set in. Father Henry refused to see them—was he even there? The Duke requested to see the assistant to Father Henry. It was granted.

"Father," he began, if our search were to take us to Ireland, we would like your blessing and furthermore your suggestions on how to retrieve this young boy who by no fault of his own was removed from his mother's womb and expediated unlawfully in another jurisdiction. Can you help us in our travail in locating both nunneries and monasteries in Ireland? I am the duke of Bourbonne, Jean-Louis-Pierre de Pleyssis."

He had added his title, well aware of the authority of England's aristocracy and its impact on the clergy, despite the key influence of the Church of England instituted under Henry the VIII. The cleric did not engage.

"I have nothing more to add to His Eminence's words. I know absolutely nothing on that subject. Your search in Ireland might be fruitful. I will pray for your good fortune. You will now have to excuse me, for I have much to do. Good day, gentlemen," he responded loudly.

“Monsieur,” Jean-Louis-Pierre questioned, clasping the cleric’s robe as he passed by him, “why was His Eminence removed from his position in London?”

The man stared down as the Duke’s fingers held on to his robe. Jean-Louis-Pierre did not release his grasp.

“Frankly, Monsieur, it is none of your affair,” the young prelate replied.

“Father Henry was working in the monastery we visited less than two weeks ago. He was not available then and within a week, he is retired—here. And then he is given an Abbott position? Do you not find it odd?”

“I am not accustomed to being placed in a prosecutorial position, Monsieur. I receive orders from my superiors, and I obey their commands.” His light blue eyes stared into Jean-Louis’s.

“This lack of cooperation, Monseigneur, will not be forgotten.” Jean-Louis-Pierre retorted in the same calm and guarded response. “Cardinal Conte de Thornsen will be made aware of your lack of collaboration in the search for his kidnapped nephew.”

The old bishop, who had followed the pair closely, stared down at the red Aubusson carpet, well aware of the retributions. His clerical career had come to an end. He’d been demoted from his formerly superior position as head of this Priory. “It will just be our penance, gentlemen,” he said loudly. He turned his back to the men and gestured to the wooden departure gates.

Both men rose from their high backed, burgundy velvet covered fauteuils. They turned their backs to the clerics and strode out.

CHAPTER THIRTY-ONE

Back at the inn, the populace enticed by the day of rest, Sunday, drank, danced and recounted bawdy jokes. The Duke stopped by the bar. Not willing to mingle, he picked up a couple of stouts that he brought back up to the rooms.

Both men sat silently across from one another at a large round wooden table. The lamb stew the maid had just delivered was getting cold. Both were ravenous.

"If I was not famished, I'd throw this dog food inside our privy," the Duke exclaimed.

Cunnan burst out laughing. "You've been in Paris too long, my friend. Recall the meals we have had to eat while sailing!"

Both sniggering, they dipped their spoons into the stew and ate heartily.

"Cunnan," Jean-Louis-Pierre declared. "I have it in my head to write to Philippe."

The old man stood, glass in hand and aghast. "Is he still in Paris?" he asked, hopeful that the Duke would follow through. "He could be most helpful with the Abbeys and Monasteries in Ireland. Would you reveal the full status of the situation?"

"How can I not? He hates me, but he adores Gaby, and knowing that a child of hers might have suffered such an injustice." Jean-Louis-Pierre sighed, his lips rolled inward. "There would be no limits to his dedication in finding the child."

"Correct, you will nonetheless need to share with him these yellow stained pages that disclose very intimate times in your lives."

The Duke stood, walked to the fireplace, silent for a long while, his elbow resting on top of the rustic wooden enclosure of the hearth. "Yes, he will despise me even more, but I do not see another way around it, Cunnan, do you? His religiosity and his intimate relationship with the Pope might give us entrance to the many monasteries and perhaps to the nunneries where these close-mouthed nuns and Mother Superiors might be enticed to reveal the truth."

Both men glowered at the yellow flames rising high in the hearth of the stone fireplace.

"Yes," retorted Cunnan, "we have had a dry well and this last dépèche by the Cardinal should not be taken lightly. We have left no stone unturned. It is time to check out Ireland. Write to Philippe, Jean-Louis-Pierre. He will be the rightful uncle of that child. He will not relent."

"My thinking falls along these lines, I have waited too long," replied the Frenchman. "I despise the man," he said with abhorrence that even Cunnan was stupefied, "asking any favors from him is total aversion in my head." He stared at the Louis XV's intricately designed desk that stood in between two long and narrow, floor to ceiling windows. It faced the rounded hillside where dry coteaux of sinuous vines looked like denuded skeletons as far as the eye could see. Although fruitless now, it waited for spring's eternal renewal to rejuvenate their blossoms and bring about the ripe, sweet grapes that Gaby loved to grasp and tear off the vine to enjoy.

He looked away, his thoughts never far from the love of his life as he recalled her mischievous demeanor when he'd told her that many viticulturists in the beautiful wine regions of France were despicable with tourists who'd dare to steal the perfectly sweetened crops. Her mouth filled with grapes, juice dripping from her lips, she'd retorted, "If you could fight and win a great battle against horrific pirates on the high seas, I have no fear that you will protect me from these pesky sommeliers!"

He'd kissed her arrogance right off her lips. They had been happy then, believing fervently that their lives had been touched by some heavenly might. And yes, he had been instrumental in throwing away these perfect moments."

"How will Gaby react to this mind-blowing discovery—a missing child, Cunnan, it will be monumental."

The old man remained silent, his head down as he studied the planks.

"The possible involvement of my grandmother in this sordid affair? The relationship will be strained. Just recently, Gaby had accepted my grandmother's compliments with a half-smile," he said, reminiscing about the scene at the opera. If proven correct that my grandmother was involved in the riddance of the child, I do not want to think of the ramification of this horrific affair."

Cunnan's eyes grew wide in utter disbelief at this last utterance.

"Jean-Louis-Pierre," the Irish seaman shouted, "have you lost all sense of righteousness?" Astounded, Cunnan raised his head. "Your own kin sent your son and my lovely Gabriella's infant to be orphaned and raised in a world where the child would be deprived of his true lineage forever, and you are wondering how to solve the feud between Gabriella and your grandmother? It's atrocious!"

Deep blue eyes filled with tears as he looked up at Cunnan. "You are right, Cunnan, my jealousy and possessiveness obstruct all sense of logic and decency. The news has been devastating and doubts flood my spirit about the legitimacy of that birth and how I will handle it."

"The bloody child is yours, Jean-Louis-Pierre!' Cunnan lashed out, "After all these years, how can you doubt my lovely Gabriella? I am sticking by you for this matter to be hopefully resolved. Gaby is too good for you!" he shouted and slammed the stack of pages on the desk. The leaflets flew in all directions.

Calmly the Duke stood and begun to pick up the pages scattered on the floor.

"You are correct, Cunnan," he agreed as he returned to the large leather chair and reached for the stout on his desk. For a long time, he remained silent. "The direction of the Abbeye was written down on the front of the envelope, along with the name of a fictitious Mother Superior. The nonexistent English address was a perfect ploy to confuse one who could have somehow found out the truth."

He grasped a piece of parchment stationery, dipped the quill into the ink pot filled with dark *encre de chine*, lifted it and held it there for a long moment in the air. He began to write.

"Are you writing to Phillippe?" Cunnan asked.

"Yes," murmured the Duke, almost apologetic.

"We can certainly use his influence. I think he'll come forth."

"Yes, our interests in this matter coincide. Gaby's well-being will always be at the core of our souls."

"Rethink your words and emotions, Jean-Louis-Pierre. Today, for the first time in your young life, you have disappointed me," Cunnan pronounced sternly. He strode across the room and stormed out, slamming the door with such force that the wood seemed ready to disintegrate.

The Duke stared at the door, then he pressed the quill to the blank sheet of paper.

Dear Philippe,

I need your help and influence on a most critical matter. The concern is our lives' mutual love.

Cunnan and I will leave for Dublin tomorrow morning. Please join us promptly and be discreet, reveal nothing of your trip to anyone. The names and addresses of myriad abbeys, nunneries, cloisters will be extremely helpful. Please, I repeat, be as private as is humanly possible. Thank you in advance for your consideration. Jean-Louis-Pierre

CHAPTER THIRTY-TWO

PARIS

On the avenue des Vosges, in the large Hôtel Particulier that had been placed at his disposal by the Catholic Church, Philippe sat alone in a dark green velour fauteuil at the head of a long mahogany table, waiting for his breakfast to be served. He anxiously awaited the visit of his cherished cousin, Gabriella.

A few knocks sounded at the door and his butler stepped into the dining room. "Votre Éminence," he said, a deep concern in his voice. "A courier is in the foyer, stating that he has a grave message to deliver."

"A grave message?" Philippe answered, suspicious. Everyone always had 'grave or critical messages. Today, he expected Gabriella. He wished for a moment of peace. "Did you ask him about the matter at hand."

"Yes, your Éminence, but he would not divulge a word. He says he needs to hand deliver the missive." Without much of a second thought, Philippe pushed away the breakfast tray that had just been served. He clasped the handle of his coffee cup, gulped a few sips and started for the library.

"Very well. Call Armand and Maurice to the library, and guide the messenger into the grand salon."

After the Commune, the Versailles government had instituted draconian security measures. France had been traumatized by the civil revolution. Now, both sides took extreme safekeeping precautions.

As the cleric entered the salon, all rose. The young man, followed closely by two burly guards, handed the envelope to the Cardinal.

Philippe took the envelope and turned it over. No seal adorned it.

"Who charged you with this note?" he asked the young man whose Irish accent could not be denied. The boy lifted his shoulders—a universal gesture of ignorance.

"Let us open it," Philippe suggested.

"Your Éminence, no!" the valet called out. "It could be poison!" He advanced toward the cleric, an embroidered purple and gold cloth in hand, ready to swipe the document from Philippe's hand.

Instead of agreeing, Philippe reached for the envelope and picked up the gold letter opener on his desk. He immediately ripped it open. The contents will reveal the identity, he thought. Recognizing the scholarly handwriting of Jean-Louis-Pierre, he read on. His facial expression changed from annoyance to intense inquisitiveness.

"Do you have a return passage, child?"

"Yes, Your Éminence."

Philippe turned to his audience. "Feed the young man and make sure his horse has been attended to." He then dismissed his entourage.

He strode to his desk, sat on the chair and re-read the note. Without hesitation, he composed a reply.

Jean-Louis-Pierre,
I will say High Mass on Sunday at the Cathedral. I will depart that same afternoon for Dublin.
PHILIPPE de CONTE-THORNSEN.

He dismissed everyone from the room. When the last servant closed the elegant floor to ceiling mahogany doors, he re-read the missive and reached for the ordinary red wax, often used by the lower rank members of the clergy. He sealed the envelope. He placed it in the hands of a trusted Cardinal envoy and sent the prelate on his ways across the Manche.

Letter in hand, the cleric strode to his vast and well stocked library across the room to search for the monasteries, cloisters and nunneries which served as orphanages in Ireland. Why would Jean-Louis-Pierre request the names of nunneries? Perhaps he had fathered a child he wanted to retrieve? I would not put it past him, the cleric thought.

The message still in hand, he repeated the words 'the love of our lives' de Pleyssis had written in his missive. He reached for his *lorgnette* and read it once more, intently... oh, DEAR GOD, it concerned Gaby. He buried his head in his hands, elbows pressing down on his desk. If Jean-Louis-Pierre demanded his help, it was a grave situation. A knock at the door reminded him of his cousin's visit. The butler entered.

"Votre Éminence, Madame Gabriella de Conte Thornsen de Pleyssis has just arrived," the servant said as Gaby let herself in and strode right behind the burly servant. The dearest person in his life had just arrived.

"Gaby, my dearest love," he exclaimed in an adoring tone. How he loved her. He gathered her close to his chest then gently pushed her away to take in her beauty. "Let me look at you, my dearest. You were sensational last night. I wanted to bask on the stage with you and share in your success."

"Your voice is magnificent, mon cher Philippe. Had I known you were in attendance, you would have been my Adonis. Few can equal your..." She stopped, recalling the castration in Rome. "Or perhaps a duet?"

Philippe roared, "Gabriella, seriously how could I say Mass on Sundays?"

"We are in a time of modernity, my dear Philippe. You may touch many who will see you as human and a lover of the arts. It is important to many these days."

"To the elite, Gabriella. People like you and your former husband. Think of all the people Baron Haussmann has ousted to the suburbs to embellish Paris—to make it the City of Light revered throughout our world. No, my dearest, not a good idea."

"I love you, Philippe. You are my world. I can always count on you to retrieve the person I was meant to be. I am famished, what can I devour? Or should we dine in town?"

"Perfect timing, my dearest. Juliette bought the most scrumptious, flaky croissants just for you, and Madame Bonnard spent all day on her one of a kind apricot confiture."

Gabriella giggled, her compelling laughter had Philippe staring into her emerald eyes a bit too long.

"I love you so, my dear cousin. A night here, just the two of us, will be splendid.

"Did Madame Bonnard prepare something a bit more substantial than croissants?" She untied the golden ribbons around her neck and tossed the hat on his canapé.

Philippe, as the man always prepared to assuage her every wish, winked. "Well, we will make her, Gaby. And if she refuses, I'll walk into my kitchen and attend to your wishes!" Both snickered only to be interrupted by the severe demeanor of Madame Bonnard, who'd just marched into the room.

"*Eh bien non*, not even Your Éminence enters my domain!" she exclaimed sharply. Philippe looked at Gaby, quieting her down.

"We had no intention to commit such grave error, Madame," the Cardinal replied politely as he sauntered to the side bar, poured his cousin a cup of coffee, adding cream and four teaspoons of crystal white sugar. He then crossed the room and offered it to her.

"*Madame, que désirez-vous ? Un bœuf à la Bourguignonne ?* It should be ready as I speak*?"*

"Parfait, Madame Bonnard, quel plaisir, merci." She sipped the coffee slowly while the aroma of the croissants and warm apricot preserve enticed the cousins to move from the library to the dining room. Smiling at her precious cousin, she walked to the elaborately set table and spread a generous helping of the preserve on to the croissant that she served to Philippe.

"Look at you Philippe, tall and slim, not a gram of fat on your athletic body! Two for you and one for me! *pas juste*, just not right," she giggled as she wolfed down a blueberry tart that she'd added to the platter of patisseries, the small, plump, purple, round fruit melting in her mouth.

"Oh Mon Dieu, Madame Bonnard, quel délice !" she complimented.

"I will go to Dublin tomorrow, Gabriella, for a week or so. I'm not quite certain. I will send for you as soon as I return. Will you remain in Paris? I heard you might take a short vacation in Venice? Is that correct?"

"I do not know, perhaps, Renoir is leaving for Rome and Monet and Camille Doncieux might join him. Perhaps? I am not quite certain, you know how much I love the South of France. I may just go and soak up the sun in Nice for a few days. Why are you going to Dublin?"

"An old friend called on me. Have you ever been to Ireland, Gaby?"

"No, let me know if you like it." The rest of the evening they spent reminiscing about their time on their plantations, their vacations in Mississippi, how their lives had taken a turn they would not have ever imagined.

"I met the painter Whistler a week ago. A charming individual. He will also be in Nice or Monte-Carlo, I am not certain. I would not mind spending more time with him."

"Isn't he called for?"

"He did not speak like he was. Anyhow from what I understand he is on his way to Venice. A very pleasant fellow, indeed." She stared at the painting of Villefranche she had given to Philippe after the break-up. "Yes, very charming."

"Have you heard from Jean-Louis-Pierre?"

"No, the last I heard from him was the morning after the ball we attended. He left my house without a word. Just as well. My feelings for him were re-emerging, and I even contemplated a reunion, a try-out if you will. Well, he has not changed a bit. He pretends a great attachment to me, but I have not seen him in over a month. I almost fell for him once more. Where he went, I do not know."

"Interesting, he made a total fool of himself with his uncontrollable drinking. I cannot fathom that you would have considered returning to your former life, Gabriella. What were you thinking? What happened to your 'I am no longer in love with Jean-Louis'?"

"Seeing him again was difficult, Philippe, more so than I ever expected. You were right I may not have been ready then, five years seemed reasonable enough," she sighed. I realize that he was my first love, my passion, my husband," she paused, reminiscing on the good times. "I will never forget him. We had some extraordinary years together, but my life will go on. I understand that now. I am pleased to return to New York for half a year. It will strengthen my resolve. By the time I return to Paris in December, I may fully be over him. Knowing Jean-Louis, he might be on another one of his expeditions."

"I hope so, my dearest Gabriella." Both began to enjoy the heavenly dishes served on their plates. She picked up a flute of Cristal. "To us, Philippe!"

CHAPTER THIRTY-THREE

LONDON.

The dispatch from Philippe had just been received. It was a cold night, but it did not keep the two friends from spending a few hours socializing in the London pubs.

"Our last night in London. Let's hit our favorite pub, Cunnan, and the gambling den nearby, the Albatross." As they stepped into the street, the rain fell in sheets of ice, drenching their coats, clouting their heads and faces. The mood was somber.

"I am pleased that Philippe will be joining us," Jean-Louis-Pierre murmured almost to himself.

Cunnan remained silent until they reached the pub recommended by the front desk clerk at their hotel.

Four hours later both were gambling heavily. A new man with a French accent picked up the seat of a bankrupt gambler who'd stumbled away. The man settled in. All at the table appeared to know him.

"Claude, any other good stories, chap? My wife and daughters are waiting for the sequence of the 'lost aristocrat'." The men laughed in unison. "Genevieve and my daughter Anne have very little compassion for the unfortunate soul, you know. In their defense, they work eighteen hours a day changing diapers and attending to these brats, wiping their arses, while continually apologizing for their apparent inept demeanor. Not a good lot, and they don't get any better as they advance in age! One less arrogant bastard is sweet justice to their eyes."

The man called Claude looked around the room before sitting down. He flashed a wicked drunken smile. "Will you purge my debts for my entertaining stories?"

"It depends, old man. Start recounting and try your luck once more."

Large sums of money and chips exchanged hands. Cunnan frowned and tilted his head slightly backwards and to the left. He winked and tapped Jean-Louis Pierre's forearm with his elbow. The discourse had not been lost on the Duke. His chin lowered, expressing understanding that had had good results for many years as they'd sailed and explored the world together.

"Last round, gentlemen," one of their table partners announced. "You've wiped me out tonight. My luck is running out, better get home to my good woman."

Jean-Louis-Pierre stood and walked over to the table where the Frenchman was still negotiating his debts.

"We are short one man," the Duke said in French. "My friend here has it in his head to write a good tale. Join us, entertain us, here are a few nuggets to lure you to our table." He passed some coins and chips in a rolled-up handkerchief into the hands of the man called Claude.

Surprised, Claude stared at Jean-Louis-Pierre for a short while, thought for a second and guzzled the whiskey. He pushed the table away, tripped and toppled face flat on the floor. He stayed there for a moment as the Duke and Cunnan tried to lift him out of his stupor and guide him to their table.

"My friend here is a writer, he finds your allusion to a stolen live child fascinating."

"Not any stolen live child—an aristocrat!" the man slurred.

Jean-Louis-Pierre wished that his consumption of alcohol had not been as elevated, but luck helped by knowledge of the subject. It had always worked in his favor. Perhaps out of the void that had filled their dead-end search, Madam Luck, oh so revered, was playing her hand!

Cunnan in his most direct and assured manner played on the man's inebriated limitations.

"Fabulously interesting!" he stated in a dramatic approach. "Have you just revealed that your wife, a midwife, that is, played a role in the usurpation of an aristocratic child for a dead infant of the Paris' morgue, for the sole purpose of paying your gambling debts? Out of pure love for you? What a romantic story line. Can you expand?"

At first, the man looked astounded at the directness. "How did you know?" he questioned.

"You have just told us!" Cunnan replied just as forcefully.

"Yes, yes of course," the man retorted.

"How can I be certain that this farfetched story is not taken from one written by an English prose writer. My creativity and professional life will be at stake, repeating lies could land me in the Tower!"

"True... but for a few more golden coins, I will give you the name of the illustrious family. How much are you willing to bet, my friend, for this once in a lifetime revelation?"

In a most cunning moment, Cunnan shifted his regard to the Duke, a quick blinking of Jean-Louis-Pierre's eyebrows gave him the answer. "You name your prize, my friend!" Cunnan swung the black velvet pouch, filled with large golden Louis in front of Claude's addicted, bloated face.

"I should have asked for more!" Claude thundered in a candid moment.

"Perhaps," Cunnan replied, "please continue, it might pique my curiosity, and if not, your life might be worth less than a shilling!" Cunnan calmly replied, his terrifying glare focused on the man called Claude speaking volumes.

Stunned, Claude tried to focus on the two men. He stared at Jean-Louis-Pierre, whose beard covered a large part of his face, and then slowly at the equally bearded Cunnan, as if there was a mite of recognition in his cobwebbed memory. His inebriated mind appeared to try to clear the fog as he shook his head and then looked down at the table. The heavy-laden black pouch at his fingertips waved away his suspicion. He might extricate a few more golden coins. A year of respite from work.

"Eh bien, Messieurs," he began, "my former wife was a nurse, a midwife as I said, in a doctor's practice in Paris. Our family's well-being had been endangered by my then reckless drunken demeanor. She was asked to replace an aristocratic child for a common dead child usurped from the city's morgue. The ploy was not discovered, our family was saved, my sickly ways were amended."

Claude straightened his torso and tried to appear to be the gentlemen that he wished he was. "My sickly and foolish wife is now dead and interred in the south of France. Our sons and I, oblivious of her horrific deed, learned of the act years later, not much to the story, sad of course, but completely out of our recourse. All I know, brother!" the drunken man stared Jean-Louis-Pierre in the eye, as if in his altered state, he knew that this man who pretended to be part of the proletariat was not.

"I often think that the Droit de L'Homme written in '92, mind you, had affirmed our rights... not for long! Three kings and two Emperors later, the advances of the common man have been dismal." Claude palmed and rolled his cognac glass in between his two hands and looked down on the gambling rug, one less of this sorry lot is revenge. "We should not weep over it. My wife carried the guilt to her death bed, literally. I had to toss into the flames—forever the brown paper bag she had kept all these years intent on revealing her 'evil deed'. God save her soul!"

Cunnan slapped Claude's back as a show of solidarity. "I agree with you, young chap. I hope you sent that child as far away from France and England as feasible! As you called it, one less of them is better for the rest of us. Where did your wife take him?"

"I do not know. Maybe northern England or even perhaps Ireland? She was not privy to his destination. The child, according to her stories, and I believe her—my wife was a good, God fearing woman, selfless and loving woman, as I said the child was abducted by a nun, a butler, and some uniformed men. She was told to leave immediately. We did, that very same night we escaped to Switzerland. We never returned to France."

Claude wanted to talk, and they willingly listened.

"There are many nunneries or abbeys in both northern England and Ireland. Perhaps even more so in Ireland. The Church of England does not weight much with the population, Catholicism is the conscience of the have nots! I do not know." Claude stared at Cunnan and then at Jean-Louis-Pierre, then asked, "Are you men aristocrats?"

Cunnan's head rolling backwards in a thunderous laughter stopped the questioning.

"Perhaps not, what about your companion?"

The same boisterous laughter echoed in the man's ears.

"Terribly sorry to disappoint you. We are sailors, making money is primordial. Your stories are not worth much, but in our present inebriated state, hilarity is primordial! Keep us entertained, brother, or else!" His gaze dropped down to his right pocket where a gun hung low on his hip holster.

"The sea is not a great conversationalist. It engenders a dark introspective view of our world, which is why I like writing. It takes me away," Cunnan declared.

Claude nodded, he picked up the black velvet pouch and stuffed it in his coat's pocket not before glancing around for any suspicious or curious eyes. A few stragglers remained, no one to be concerned about.

"Another round, then. If our maker up there hears us, I hope that the child will have found love and affection from a good woman—a good family. That is all a good man needs in life. "

This was the end of the line from this unexpected conversation. The man's head fell heavily onto the table. Not much more they could extract from him. They had crisscrossed England, but Ireland had not been in their research periscope. Time to delve into a country west of their present surroundings.

The two men forgave their losses and left the establishment.

"We have not learned much. Crazy karma... Although nothing that the documents did not reveal," Cunnan stated. "Time to explore Ireland."

The two men returned to the inn.

"Messieurs?"

They turned toward a young maid who stepped into the reception area just as they entered the foyer. The young soubrette who'd checked them in appeared. "Gentlemen, a man of the cloth, a Cardinal," her voice lowered with deference as she pronounced the title, "has arrived and requested your presence in his room. He is most insistent about speaking with you, Sir, Monsieur de Pleyssis."

"Good, please advise the Cardinal that I will meet him in his room in a quarter of an hour." Jean-Louis-Pierre shot a look at Cunnan before he strode to the safe located near his bed. He rotated the disk and opened the silver steel safe where he kept the documents affirming the live birth of the de Pleyssis's child.

CHAPTER THIRTY -FOUR

IRELAND

The following week, Jean-Louis-Pierre and Cunnan crossed the Irish Sea from a small village in Wales. Philippe sent a missive that he'd disembarked in Dublin and awaited them at a local inn. The men had met, the secret had been divulged.

The following week they'd visited a few nunneries with Philippe. Messengers were sent throughout the country with the help of the many churches, convents and priories.

There had not been any accusations from Philippe, although his first reaction had floored him. He'd turned white and asked for a Cognac. Unable to locate a bottle, they'd given him a few whiskeys—straight—on the rocks.

"How?"

"It is too painful to even contemplate, Philippe?" Jean-Louis-Pierre confided. "My own Grandmother? Perhaps my father's brother's wife and sons were involved? It is still a mystery. Our family's name grander than the life of a child? I can't fathom the scenario."

To his great surprise, Philippe had approached him and paused his healing hands on the Duke's shoulder. "Let's pray. If the child is alive, we will find him." Without another word, he'd marched to the great desk, "let's divide the work."

Less than a week later, offers to help research for the long-forgotten boy arrived daily from the multitude of Catholic institutions—all their means at their disposal. One of these leads was particularly interesting. They decided to visit it first. The friary was west of Dublin and distance wise the closest to where they were staying. The three men set out for the Cathedral on horseback. Philippe wore a pair of black trousers and, courtesy of the rigorous weather, a heavy coat, which hid his clerical habit.

The church and its steeple were noticeable from the mountainous path they traveled. Two hours later, they walked the manicured but still frozen gardens of an ancient monastery. Quickly they entered its great hall.

Sitting in an ornate office, the men faced the Vicar who was studying the records that Philippe had offered for his inspection. The Guardian in Dublin had told him that according to the dossier, the boy had spent a month in his institution prior to being sent permanently to his present destination. At first, the cleric had been shocked as he read the well-kept record. He paused, exhaled deeply and turned to Jean-Louis-Pierre and Cunnan.

"Messieurs, can I have a private conversation with his Eminence?"

Jean-Louis-Pierre on the verge to categorically refuse acquiesced to Cunnan who stood and tapped the younger man on the shoulder. Not pleased but submitting, the Duke stood, paused for a moment and looked down at Philippe, a man he had not learned to trust yet, and... reluctantly he strode to the door.

"Your Eminence," the Prior started when the two men of the cloth had been left alone, "why is it that Father Henry, who was then ensconced in London, had a say in the location of the child—on a farm of all places? Why is it that the location of the farm is absent? I have my doubts. All annals that you sorted out recently speak of his prodigious mind. He should have been with us here in the Monastery."

Philippe remained silent.

The following day—a similar agenda, except that a nunnery was the destination.

They'd arrived by ten o'clock and the Mother Superior was already awaiting them. Once more they were led through a somber corridor that opened on a vast room overlooking a very pretty garden where young children and sisters were busily planting flowers. A bit to the side, another group sitting in front of a statue of the Virgin Marie listened intently to what appeared to be religious stories as the nun pointed to the Mother of Jesus.

"This is our convent. The orphanage is located to the far left. I have been researching the whereabout of the child, Your Eminence, and I believe that I may have some news—good news. Please sit down."

"In effect, Monsieur de Pleyssis, a male child was delivered to the abbey, located right outside our village. Although the wrapper is discolored the date appears to be June 7th 1871. We have no knowledge of where the child was born or to whom it was born to. It stayed with sister Celeste and we know that she was devastated when three years later, the fathers decided that a monastery was more appropriate for the raising of a male child. Since many of these children join our religious orders, we agreed that a more acerbic upbringing was more appropriate in the life of a brother or a man of the cloth. We had to wait longer than necessary, for the child was a prodigy and far from humble about his gift. A more severe institution was required to break him of his pretentious and hard-core natural disposition. There are uncertainties and errors about his present whereabouts. It is not in our practice to lose or misplace documents, sir, but in his case, it is confusing. I am sorry." She paused and acknowledged a two years loss of documents. However, we were made aware two years ago that the child was sent to a monastery in Northern Ireland."

Unwilling to remain silent any longer, Jean-Louis-Pierre stood up. Exasperated, Cunnan clasped the Duke's shoulders hoping that his longtime friend accepts the slow meandering of the Mother's Superior research in the inconsistent record facing her.

"In effect, we even allowed Sister Celeste to visit her young protégé in the monastery. She returned even more distraught at the state her young baby was treated. She begged us to interfere, in tears, and when we did not and candidly could not as you know your Eminence, our power as sisters is limited, Sister Celeste had to be sent away to a sanatorium in southern Ireland. Her condition, I understand, has worsened, she has not returned to us and for that we are distressed." The old woman with circular gold rimmed glasses circling her beautiful blue eyes looked up, dismayed. Sister Celeste experienced a most similar fate, she had been sent to the convent at the age of two. Her fate was finely tied to the young child. Many of us in this institution do, Monsieur," she ended sternly.

Cunnan nodded. Not too enamored with the power of the Catholic Church and its strict restrictions on women and to a lesser extent, men, Jean-Louis-Pierre acknowledged the repentant Mother Superior. Philippe remained silent.

"Madame," the Duke began, "can you help us locate the child? We would be most appreciative."

"I have more than one abbey listed here, "she paused as she concentrated on the several documents in her hands. "Because of his prodigy status, he appeared to have been sent out to more than one institution. Are you staying in town? Let me send some couriers to find more information. I understand that you have traveled a long way, gentlemen. I would like to help." She faced Philippe with great deference and allowed herself a moment of reverence.

The submissiveness they showed to Philippe was estimable. The three men thanked her. Staying in town, they knew patience was imperative.

CHAPTER THIRTY-FIVE

The day was splendid, rare in these parts of Southern Ireland. On their horses, trotting along the spectacular pebbled roads that ebbed the high cliffs, they stopped their mounts and marveled at the furious Atlantic Ocean whose rolling waves pummeled the eroded ancient rocks. The fury of the untamed sea exerted a pull on the Duke. One of the happiest days of his life had been the day when he had purchased his first 'Tempête'. It had been delivered in Brest and he recalled sending a message to his father stating that he'd be gone for three months—he had sailed alone along the long stretch of the western, African Coast. All that travel had occurred before he'd been deployed to the South China Seas fighting for France in Indochina, Cambodia and Laos. The many conflicts he had fought for his nation had wakened a sense of adventure. That was the obvious reason behind his decision to fight for the Union in America instead of returning to the old continent. He loved the sea, it gave him a sense of freedom rarely felt in his overly ruled aristocratic life in France.

Cunnan was by his side, both men rode silent, still unable to fathom the developing story.

Jean-Louis-Pierre fumed at his senseless reaction when the kidnapping had been revealed. Requesting Philippe's assistance in the child's abduction had been his very first instinct, but his loathing of Gabriella's adored cousin had eschewed his usual unfaltering sense of logic. In less than a week, Philippe had reversed the trend that had plagued their search throughout their quest in England and now Ireland. The silence they'd faced throughout their visits and inquiries in the Priories, Monasteries and Nunneries, Friaries had turn into hours of research, delicious déjeuners that he could have gone without, and reliable interventions. Philippe in effect was an invaluable ally.

They'd arrived at the orphanage late in the day for the second time in less than two and a half weeks. For some unknown reason, the Mother Superior of the nunnery had immediately retrieved 'lost documents' covering the detailed history of the vanished infant.

"Supple and replete with information!" Cunnan whispered to Jean-Louis Pierre.

"Such a sudden recollection of facts is quite impressive, Madame." He glared at the sister while his arrogant retort remained unacknowledged.

Jean-Louis kept his aristocratic temperament in check. Although he'd already considered the punishment he would inflict on all these religious institutions that had proven to be less than transparent. Were they getting money for the safekeeping of the secret? Did they hate his kind? No, most Bishops, Cardinals, Prioress of convent came from the Ancient Régime. His family had always been more than generous to the church. Would a less affluent family have received better results?

"We are terribly happy that Your Eminence has found our humble abode," the Mother Superior cajoled. "A lot of good work has been launched here. Our work is deserving and many children whose dismal lives might have been taken by the forces of evil, have found instead the way of our Lord. Sister Celeste is one of these recipients whose sister had been a novice in our Sister Abbey. The older sibling did not have a vocation, she left less than a year later. However, her dedication to family and our Church has been a source of inspiration to many. The man she married, a farmer working his land south of here, has allowed her to take in orphans, they've done much good throughout the years and have taught many of these poor souls a good and saintly trade. Both sisters have some relationship with a French Bishop, who has just been appointed Abbot of a retirement Priory in Cornwall.

Sister Celeste will accompany us on our way South, Your Eminence. The child resides with her sister and brother in law and their natural child."

Jean-Louis-Pierre inhaled a deep breath, just the idea that his son, at age five or six, had been working on a farm was unfathomable. Philippe gazed in his direction, Cunnan stood and walked to him, gripping his friend's forearm.

"Do you know the name of the Bishop, Madame?" the younger man promptly retorted as he turned and glanced questioningly to Cunnan.

"No, it is not our place to ask questions, Monsieur de Pleyssis," the nun responded sternly. "We accept our sisters without inquiries, the only request is their love and devotion to our Lord and our young children."

The nun turned sideways and faced Philippe.

"Our guests' rooms are well appointed in our humble retreat, and it would be an honor to have you spend a night while awaiting Sister Celeste." She gazed at the two men sitting behind Philippe. "We have only a few rooms reserved for guests, I could send one of our protégé to the local village to secure a comfortable resting place for your friends."

Philippe spun his head and snickered at Jean-Louis-Pierre and Cunnan.

"Eh bien, gentlemen. Let's meet again tomorrow. I'll send word as soon as Sister Celeste arrives."

Cunnan smiled. The Duke, in no mood to be amused, nevertheless nodded, stood, and exited.

Cunnan followed close behind, placing his hand on the younger man's shoulder. "Let's not forget our main objective."

"A demain," Jean-Louis-Pierre's thunderous voice echoed in the room. He strode disdainfully to the door without turning his back.

The young man tending their horses hurried on the pebbled stones and handed the reins to each of the men. "They've been fed and brushed down, gentlemen."

"Thank you," Cunnan said as he reached for the horse and furrowed in a side pocket for a red burgundy pouch that he gave to the child. "We will return tomorrow."

Both men mounted their horses and waited for the young boy to open the large wooden doors. Their inn was less than five miles away from the picturesque village where the convent was located. The tide had turned.

CHAPTER THIRTY-SIX

A common carriage arrived in front of the nunnery the following day. A tired looking Sister in a simple black habit, stepped down on the pebbled entrance, a large bronze cross hung on her belly from a black cordon tied around the waist. Her round face was corseted in a white starched cloth stretched tight across the forehead, around her cheeks and binding under the chin. She appeared haggard before her pale blue eyes shifted to Jean-Louis-Pierre and remained solely on him as if a ghost of long ago materialized across from her. She marched to him, lifted her face to his and glared.

"You are Ian's father . . ." She paused. "you . . . DEVIL!" she whispered with a thick French accent as she accused him, striding so close to Jean-Louis-Pierre that her habit grazed his coat, her scowl fixed on his face. Consternation reigned.

"He was taken from me at age three, Monsieur . . . we loved each other, after three years you demanded that he'd be moved to the monastery. Have you no shame? He loved me more than the world!"

She took a step backwards to better take in his countenance. The unrelenting tirade flummoxed those present. "As if he had not endured sufficiently at his tender age... He was easy to lose, *n'est-ce-pas* when convenient for his 'Grace,' but it was not enough, was it? You inflicted more punishment on his tender soul at three years old—the hardship of a monastery!" she shouted.

Jean-Louis-Pierre was stone faced.

"A nefarious deed, "she bellowed in a madwoman's tone, uncontrollable tears running down her face as if the scenario had been memorized by heart for the past seven hours and regurgitated like the gush of a springtime river struggling against a large boulder barring its natural flow.

"Sister!" the Mother Superior declared harshly—a sign that this awkward outburst had come to an end. "Follow me inside, much needs to be discussed and elucidated."

The three men stood silent. The Duke had been ready to swallow his pride and ask her about the child, his description, how had he ended up in a farmhouse in Southern Ireland. But silence reigned, her revelations too difficult to acknowledge.

Philippe was the first one to react to the emotional outburst. He approached the sister who, accustomed to ecumenical orders, had silenced her frenzy. He calmly grasped her elbow. "Sister, much needs to be known and clarified. Your presence is of utmost importance in our talks." He spoke in French with his peaceful voice.

She responded to him in another torrent of tears. "Your Grace, my brother..."

The Mother Superior turned suddenly and silenced Sister Celeste. "These eruptions will cease! Sister, the infirmary is still open. If you cannot control these emotional surges, Sister Marie-Josephine can give you proper medication to help your confused state." Sister Celeste frozen facial expressions spoke volumes. She started to respond, then closed her mouth before a sound escaped. "We understand your great love for the child, but I am starting to understand that we were mistaken in asking for your presence in this delicate matter," the Mother Superior ended.

Philippe did not rebuke either woman. He raised his palm to Cunnan, who'd had just about enough of the drama unfolding before his eyes.

"We will travel south tomorrow, and you will join us, Sister Celeste. I look forward to learning about this young child that, for some unknown immoral reason, was taken from his birth mother and orphaned in a foreign land. I look forward to hearing about your brother, did you say Father Henry?"

Sister Celeste halted. "Yes, Your Imminence," she answered quietly. Swallowing hard, she straightened her rotund form as unshed tears in her limpid blue eyes spilled free. She bowed her head, sighed and continued to walk behind the Mother Superior, at times looking backwards to glance at the Duke.

The Mother Superior glared daggers in her guests' direction, but she remained silent. At the end of the marble staircase that was climbed quickly by all parties, the nun opened the floor to ceiling double doors to the salon. At the far end of the room close to another door, twelve small chairs were aligned in a half circle around an old piano.

"This room serves as a music room for our young wards," the sister called out as she came around her desk, waiting for Philippe to take a seat before sitting. She rang a small bell. An old woman with a contorted spine and a disfiguring wine birthmark that covered most of her face entered the room.

"Bring a chair for His Eminence and some refreshments, as well," she ordered the servant who carried a small brown leather book. She took copious notes of their preference with their teas and pastries.

"Thank you, that will be all," the nun said, waving the woman away.

Fauteuils were brought in a round table style with everyone taking a seat. Philippe sat in the large tufted leather Chesterfield chair. "Sister Celeste," he began, "it is no longer a secret that you care deeply for little Ian. Do you recall who brought the child to you?"

"I do not know. I was called into the office and asked to bring the child back to the nursery where the other orphans were kept. I did as I was told."

"Was the child enveloped in rags or fine blankets?"

"Nothing extravagant that would have differentiated him from the others."

"With all the infants that you have taken care of, why did you develop such a binding attachment to Ian?"

"I do not know, he was so sweet and good-natured and his story broke my heart." She paused for a few minutes, casting a furtive look to her Superior. "I mean... all these children have a wretched story."

Not much more new information was delivered in that meeting, however, tomorrow in the carriage, Philippe would have more time to question her without any possibility of retribution from her Superior.

CHAPTER THIRTY-SEVEN

The following day both men awakened early. They filed down the tortuous staircase that led to a small dining area whose walls were covered with yellow, blue and pink wildflowers *papier feutré*.

The scent of porridge and sausage filtered through the air and became more appetizing as they approached the breakfast salon. Both chose a table close to a wide window that revealed the awe-inspiring sight of Ireland's thousand shades of green paysages.

Cunnan stared at his younger friend. "Are you ready for the next stage?"

The tall aristocrat nodded.

"Curious about my reaction had I been in this situation? My childhood has not always been easy—my emotional childhood, that is. Certainly, this ordeal has been enlightening, especially regarding our cruel and class divisive culture. How will Ian react to me, to you, to his mother? How will she react to him?"

They ate silently, both pondering the ideas brought forth.

"You have retrieved your son, Jean-Louis-Pierre. Soon you will be reunited in the ancestral home. That is the most important discovery, he will forgive you both. Maybe not now, but in the years to come. Gabriella was not at fault, neither are you."

Both men savored the last drop of their coffee, even more so since tea had been the *boisson* of choice since they left for Calais. "Eh bien, on our way!" They stood and walked out of the auberge. Quickly a servant girl arrived to clean up the table. "Merci, Messieurs," she uttered with a pronounced Irish accent as she picked up the generous tip.

They stood on the steps of the inn as the paltrier brought along their horses. He was a young boy, half hidden in between the horses that he brought about to be hitched to the well-worn but comfortable carriage. Cunnan opened one of the doors and looked inside. "We can all fit in, however..." he sighed "request a couple of extra horses, we may want to follow close behind if the Sister intends to continue the disparaging vitriolic statements of the land holding classes."

"It got a bit tedious. What do you make of her? I wonder if a remote connection exists with Father Henry in England?"

"The message sent to the hostelry in England seemed to have come from him. As if he wanted us to find the child. His removal from Cluny was bizarre. But I do not understand Ian's removal to a farm? Another confusion that perhaps Philippe might uncover. You are correct. Let's have a couple of horses at our disposal."

Quietly in the courtyard they mounted their horses, the coachman straddled his bench, took the reins, checked his whip inside its hollow steel tube and waited for the men to pass him. The postilion lashed the four hitched horses, and the two friends started through the village and onto the rocky road that led them back to the monastery, the carriage following close behind.

The Mother Superior with Philippe and Sister Celeste were awaiting on the smooth dirt path facing the entrance of the convent.

Cunnan and the Duke dismounted their horses.

"Bonjour Philippe, did you sleep well?" Cunnan asked in English.

"As well as can be expected." The cleric stood and stared at the two men.

"Eh bien, a moment of silence. Sister, Jean-Louis-Pierre, Cunnan, today will be a revelation for us all." The sisters dropped to their knees on the cold stones that lined the flower bed, Jean-Louis-Pierre and Cunnan remained standing and Philippe blessed them all.

"Will you both join us in the cabin?" Philippe asked.

The Duke shook his head. "The topography is phenomenal, I will ride and enjoy the sights of this magnificent land." Cunnan, close faced, smiled inwardly as he opened the door and helped sister Celeste inside the carriage. Quickly, he glanced back to Jean-Louis-Pierre and winked prior to climbing the steps.

The two hours ride South to the location where the child had been discovered began. All occupants became lost in their own thoughts.

At one of the resting places, Cunnan did not return to the cabin in the coach. He detached one of the horses, climbed on and rode alongside the carriage. The murderous stare Sister Celeste flung in his direction was no longer acceptable. It spewed venom.

Sympathetic to the emotions suffered by his young friend, Cunnan rode closer to the Duke. Both men followed. Philippe lingered inside. He rapped the velvet covered baton against the window, and the assemblage continued on their way South.

A couple of hours later at the summit of an insignificant hill, they heard the coachman shout, "Your Eminence, Sister, Messieurs, I believe that we have reached our destination."

Sister Celeste parted the curtain, her gaze drifting from one side of the field to the next.

Fields lined a narrow stream where myriad workers toiled. Farmhouses were built in the center of these fields with land extending in all directions, not unlike the sixteen stately avenues that formed the Étoile on the Champs-Élysées.

Phillippe focused intently on the nun seated across from him, watching her study each young worker in their respective row. He saw no recognition in her expression.

The carriage descended closer to the fields. Jean-Louis-Pierre and Cunnan, now riding alongside the carriage, observed the nun's every glance. The Duke swallowed, displaying his hardened jaw line.

Cunnan stared down the fields as the carriage descended closer to the laborers. A moment of despair. Silence reigned as the carriage descended the hill.

"Here he is!" Sister Celeste exclaimed to Philippe. *"Ici, voyez vous, c'est le plus grand, a coté de la ferme*, here, next to the farmhouse, the tallest of all. Here he is ! *Allez, Allez*, ride on, ride on, *on l'a trouvé, le voilà, arrêtez Monsieur* ! Oh Mon Dieu, Ian, I am here!"

Everyone kept silent. Sister Celeste knew. In all likelihood, the boy was found,

"Where, Madame?" the Duke responded.

"The second one from the right of the farm, Monsieur. Je suis sure, I am sure," she repeated in English. She swung open the door, but Phillippe arrested her move.

"Sister, his father needs to take action now." Regarding the poor woman, filled with emotion she could not suppress, he promptly shut the door and gathered her in his arms.

"I feel your pain, Sister." He held her close as she sobbed uncontrollably in his arms. Philippe had taken control and Jean-Louis-Pierre had let him. The cleric suggested that they observe the young man who wore a large straw peasant hat while he worked in the fields among his new family. But then the boy who had been designated as Ian was joined by another young man. Who the real Ian was remained a concern for everyone. Sister Celeste was unrelenting. The Duke chose to stand by her.

All came to a halt.

A cloud overhead emptied out its watery charge obscuring the view. It had not seemed to annoy the working family down at the bottom of the hill. They continued to grasp roots embedded deep in the soil... a field of potatoes perhaps. Just as quickly as the rain came, sunshine filtered through, giving the group a clear view of the sloping hill with the two boys whistling away as they worked alongside one another.

Which boy was his son remained a mystery. Both boys were of similar stature. The Sister had climbed down from the carriage and, with the Duke's binoculars, focused on her protégé. Jean-Louis-Pierre bent down to listen to Sister Celeste's every word as she spoke.

"Thank you, Sister," he said in a rare moment of humility. "I will make sure that you will be a part of his life in the future."

He looked down at his son as he took a moment to control his unraveling emotions.

Silence reigned in the anticipation of the children's reactions.

Jean-Louis-Pierre ordered the rest of the company to remain behind.

Slowly, he began his descent into the field where his son worked, his eyes focused on the land below. The two boys worked the rows of planted potatoes, pulling, checking the root, examining its ripeness and sometimes burying it back in the soil. As he reached the outer edge of the field, the Duke dismounted from his horse and tied it to a post as he ambled toward the children.

The young boy under the wide hat covering most of his face looked up, curious. The Duke attached importance to that familiar air. The muscles in his throat tightened, and he felt the surge of tears in his deep blue eyes. The child facing him was his son.

"Hello," Jean-Louis-Pierre said in English. "Hello" was his guarded response. Both man and boy stood, staring at one another.

Simultaneously emerging from the barn, an older man who had taken refuge from the misty rain quickly strode toward the group. The coach that had started the descent a short while after seeing the Duke facing his child, came to a halt in front of a haystack.

"Ian, go inside, my boy!" the man who'd come out of the barn kindly asked the boy. Docile, the child obeyed, although he kept on glancing back at the group as he advanced toward the farm house. A few minutes later, Jean-Louis-Pierre caught him peering from the parted drapes in the window. He could not draw his eyes from the window.

Philippe and Sister Celeste stepped out of the carriage. Cunnan, by the carriage, watched the unfolding drama.

As the child named Ian watched Sister Celeste step off the coach, he instantly removed himself from the window seal and ran out of the house. Instant recognition lit up the child's eyes.

"Sister!" he shouted as he ran toward the carriage where his protector stood.

"Ian!" she responded with uncommon passion.

They flew into each other's arms.

Philippe approached the curious farmer.

"Sister Celeste is my wife's natural sister, Your Eminence," he explained. "She practically raised the child, Ian, from infancy. "We could not have been prouder when Celeste, Sister Marie-Thérèse, worked her heavenly kindness and asked us to raise the boy."

Philippe nodded.

"We have but little, but our love of family is immense."

The farmer recovered his manners when faced with a Cardinal. "Please, Your Eminence and... gentlemen follow us. My wife and I have been expecting you."

Ian still curled tightly to his former caretaker Celeste. Philippe and Cunnan all followed behind until they reached the modest farmhouse.

The poor child, thought the Duke. Another difficult separation on the horizon for his son. He swore he would amend and ease the struggles the child suffered in his young life.

All sat at the rectangular table in the kitchen, including Conner, the farmer's son, and his wife, Catriona.

The Duke stared at his son as the story of his birth and connivances from a still unknown party was revealed. The boy stared back.

"Will I be taken away, once more, to a different household or a monastery?" he stoically asked. All could see that he tried hard to hold back the unshed tears in his eyes.

"Yes, you will, Ian, I'm taking you to France with me, where you should have been all along."

The tears began to drift slowly and steady on his cherubic face. He had faced separation so often already.

"Very well," the lad said, his face streaked with dirt where he wiped away the flow of tears. "I shall be ready in the morning." He stood and began to walk outside to finish his work.

"Ian," the farmer said, "Conner and I will finish the work on your plot. You need to get to know your father. Stay here, Child, by the hearth. Lots need to be clarified."

"Can sister Marie-Thérèse stay?"

"No, child."

Ian walked to Celeste and hugged her with so much love, Jean-Louis-Pierre almost permitted her to stay. He recalled the love he felt for his nurse Marie, in Loire.

"No, that is your time with your son," Philippe stated firmly.

Both father and son walked toward the hearth of the fireplace where a black cauldron hung above the ascending, trembling orange and yellow flames.

"You will have a good life, Ian, I promise you that."

The boy nodded with a half polite smile. He'd heard that line many times before, although his father did not respond with 'if you're a good, obedient boy and follow the rules.'

CHAPTER THIRTY-EIGHT

Along the dark cliffs of the splendid Irish coast, Ian, Philippe, Jean-Louis-Pierre and Cunnan boarded a waiting boat that would take them across the Manche's choppy seas, onto the French continent to Brest. From there, they would reach the Duke de Bourbonne's ancestral castle within hours.

Upon arrival, father and son began their quest for some semblance of a family life.

The child left speechless at the grandiosity of the massive medieval castle whose Renaissance additions had been added by the famed Leonardo Da Vinci while he stayed at the castle in Amboise during the reign of François I. The door of the carriage left ajar by Jean-Louis-Pierre, exposed to full view the rows of the liveried staff standing in attention as the Duke strode toward a tall and very thin woman, standing alone at the very top of the marble staircase. Ian remained in the carriage as fear and suppressed emotions paralyzed him to his seat.

"Have we arrived, Monsieur?" he questioned Cunnan, stuttering as he focused on the Duke and the servants onto the wide path leading to the entrance. Ian turned his head and was confronted by the Jardins spreading as far as the eyes could see, large avenues crisscrossing, enabling many carriages to pass through leisurely. "It is spectacular," he murmured. "I learned about these châteaux in the monastery." The child swallowed hard and turned to the cleric, a questioning regard shot to his emerald eyes who were trying in fact to make sense of his new world.

"Yes, this is your new home, Ian," Cunnan retorted as Philippe who had been seated next to him took his hand in his and tapped it gently. The child grasped the Cardinal's fingers tightly.

"Yes, my dear child, all waiting to make your life a happy one," Philippe added calmly. "Do not be overwhelmed."

"Who will teach me to plant in these well-manicured gardens? I have not learned to garden for beauty, your Eminence, but I am an avid learner, and a hard worker" he rejoined childishly. Both Cunnan and Philippe smiled.

"These servants and gardeners will be YOUR servants, Ian. There will not be any need for you to learn and perform any menial tasks unless you so desire. A new life, my child. I see your father returning with Marie, his loving former governess who never left his service, she will love you as much as she loved and still adores him."

"Will Monsieur le Duc leave me here? Is he returning with you to Paris?"

Before they could answer, "Ian, please step down," Jean-Louis-Pierre's voice echoed, "I want you to meet Marie. Both of us will be here for you as you explore your new home." The woman named Marie came close. Her sharp features and slight stature dressed in a mostly black dress with white sleeves alarmed the child. He stepped forward and the fearsome lady kneeled down close to him. "Hello Ian, welcome," she spoke in English, "we have been expecting you and we are mighty pleased for your safe arrival. Madame Bonnard has not left her kitchen in two days, as she's learned from the pastry chef how to prepare Irish desserts. Come with me," she spoke with such a charming voice, that her strict countenance was immediately effaced. Ian smiled at her, "thank you, Madame," he responded politely.

"Come with me, dear child, I will bring you down to meet her. You will appreciate the delectable *patisseries* she baked just for you. You must be ravenous." She clasped his hand and led him down the alley to the main house, as they marched in between the two rows of servants, curious to meet the new addition to the household. Ian looked backwards having not asked permission to follow the lady called Marie.

"Go on Ian, I have just been reranked to a number two position," Jean-Louis-Pierre shouted. Ian turned and question whether it was admissible to have followed his governess.

"I apologize, Monsieur." He shouted back as Marie shook her head, amused. Uncaring the older woman pulled him along the big house's entrance and bent down to Ian, "your father is just jealous that you will have the first pick of the magnificent desserts Madame Bonnard has prepared just for you." Stunned Ian stared at her then at his father. He was not aware that his familial situation preceded him.

***

Two weeks later, Cunnan and Philippe had returned to Paris. Jean-Louis-Pierre and Ian had gone hunting, although he'd caught Ian frightening rabbits and birds who'd taken umbrage in the bushes.

"Have you ever hunted for your food, Ian?" Jean-Louis-Pierre questioned.

"No," was the prompt retort, "I love all animals."

"But I saw you eat meat?"

"Yes, Monsieur, I have to but I prefer not to," the boy responded candidly.

"Eh bien, I am pleased to know that certain foods do not agree with your palate or sensibilities." Still a bit startled, the Duke pursued, "what about fish?" the boy grimaced, "any food that has a face," he replied facing his father, "but... I will eat whatever Madame Bonnard places on my plate," he continued, not wanting to offend.

"This is your home, Ian, and you will eat only what pleases you. Talk to Marie, she will pass on the information to the head cuisinier, chef that is," Jean-Louis smiled.

"Eh bien, since our hunting times have come to an end, what would you like to do?"

"I like to hike and listen to birds, I know quite a few..." The boy looked up and scrutinized his father's face, adding quickly, "I would also like to learn how to ride a horse."

Jean-Louis-Pierre had been at a loss for words with the birding interest, but riding was a success.

"Let's dump our rifles and walk to the stables. If it's a horse you want, a horse you will get!"

The boy looked thrilled, then greatly concerned. "Now? My own horse? I have never ridden a mule, never mind a stallion, Monsieur, I am sorry if I gave you this erroneous impression." The boy's head dropped to his chest.

Jean-Louis-Pierre smiled and rumpled his hair. He nodded, picked him up and replaced his light body in front of him on his mount. "You will learn. On our way, Ian."

To the Duke's surprise the child had good reflexes and was fearless or, at the very least, he contained it well. He could not help but remember the first time he'd seen Gaby on a horse. These long-ago dreamy times in Villefranche where he'd realized that his heart had been stolen by the beautiful American plantation owner. At times, he wished he could speak to the boy about his mother, but he had not asked and both had remained silent on the subject.

They rode and hiked where they spoke of their prior lives. Jean-Louis-Pierre took him overnight to Brest, the port where the Tempête's refurbishing was well underway. First, he wanted to initiate Ian to the ocean, as well as the beauty and hardship of a sailor's life. The Duke had sailed around the world several times.

They'd climbed a high cliff with an awe-inspiring view. The bluff surveyed a steep descent to a strip of white sandy beach battered by a tumultuous ocean. The immensity of the rough waters facing him mesmerized the young boy, who had been navigated from a closeted convent to monasteries, to who knows where in between. Gawking at the immensity facing him, he began to stride down the thorny slope.

"Can I run down to the beach below?" he questioned almost as an afterthought?

"Let's!" Both began the descent to the ocean. Ian did not stop on the beach. Instead, he kept a steady pace to the water—still dressed, shoes and all.

"Do you swim?" the Duke called out after the boy, running behind him.

"No, but I'll learn!" he shouted, meters away from a menacing wave that rolled toward him.

Plunging into the waves and scooping him up to return him to shore, Jean-Louis-Pierre propped him up on a high boulder. "Not so fast, Ian. I lost you once young man, and it will not happen again. Lesson number one, respect for the sea, primordial my son, it will control you, you need to learn her ways and adjust to her ever-changing moods."

The boy understood or appeared to comprehend the oddity of the situation. Both dripping wet, he smiled his mother's devilish grin, "Frightening," he murmured, "but exciting! Is your ship nearby, Monsieur?"

"Yes, as a matter of fact, we will reach Brest in a couple of hours. Your first night at sea. But first we need to dry up and change. There is a small inn nearby, let's go."

The Duke was astounded and greatly pleased at the facility of the major adjustments. The boy never once asked about his mother, and he would not breach the subject.

Weeks passed and the relationship between father and son grew deep. The boy did not seem to like Marie's early to bed and late to rise schedule. More than once, Jean-Louis-Pierre would hear some pitter patter coming down the stairs. Sure enough … tonight as he sipped a cognac from a silver snifter, the door creaked and slid open on the varnished parquet. The Duke considered this new apparition - Ian stood on his bare toes, holding down the brass lever, waiting to gain entrance to his father's vast and well stocked library.

"Oh, it's you, Ian. Having trouble sleeping. Come, I can call for some warm milk."

"Thank you." Without much ado, the boy directed himself to the rows where his father's English language book collection was located. He sat in the big leather chair his mother loved, his feet not reaching the horizontal part of the leather cushion.

Jean-Louis-Pierre smiled. He had used the library previously. "You seem to know your way around here quite nicely."

"Yes, Monsieur, my tutor has asked permission from Madame Marie. I have been working on my French language skills. Monsieur Tiberon says that reading and translating and voicing out loud is the quickest way to become proficient in a foreign language. I am usually alone in your library, Monsieur."

"Are you sure? At twenty-three hours?"

"No, Sir," he replied in English. "I usually come in after our déjeuner." He paused, big green eyes sad as he faced his father. "I know you are leaving tomorrow. When will you return?"

An inherent sadness wrought a shade of melancholy in his youthful visage.

"When will I see you again, Monsieur," Ian questioned.

"I will return next week, I have business to attend to in Paris, meanwhile Marie will help with all of your essential needs. I loved her dearly as a young boy and still do. You will appreciate her loyal and loving demeanor. Soon you will accompany me." The boy sighed but a shy smile upon his lips indicated that perhaps this time he would not be disappointed to be left behind. His father had never lied to him.

Two days later, trunks were carried out in the wide alley facing the stately residence. The Duke gave some direction to the coachman and returned to the boy who stood alone in the marble foyer at the entrance. Another separation, he thought.

"A smile, Ian. Just one week. Soon, you will return with me to Paris," Jean-Louis-Pierre said as he stepped into his carriage. He saw Marie approach his son and place her hand on his shoulder.

Both waved at the carriage as it departed down the circular driveway.

CHAPTER THIRTY-NINE

Close to a month later after Jean-Louis's departure, Gaby was angry with herself for envisioning a reunion. She stormed out of her room. Jean-Louis had not changed. Narcissism controlled his life. No one had heard from him. Perhaps he had fallen off the face of the earth. Life with her friends, Élise and Lilianne, who'd just returned to the capital from the Côte d'Azur accompanied by two of their adorable children, was charming. Paris was great fun—her adopted home. A magnificent hôtel particulier had been placed at her disposal. Élyse had shared, "only downside to the location, Gabriella, it's a bit too close to Jean-Louis-Pierre's ancestral home, but he no longer lives there. The home reminded him too much of you and your idyllic times there."

Gaby sighed, about to retort that he should steep in his own drama, but she recognized that Jean-Louis, Élyse, Rimbaud and Luke had a relationship that would not be derailed. After the break-up, his friends had offered a third-floor apartment overlooking the place de la Concorde in the Palais de Crillon. The two identical buildings separated by the rue Royale, had been constructed in 1758 by King Louis XV and revised to display façades of 18th century architectural designs.

The second owner, the architect Trouard, had purchased the property and transformed it into a sumptuous home. In 1788, the Duke de Crillon had purchased the residence. Unfortunately, during the French Revolution, it had been confiscated to house Louis XVI and Marie-Antoinette. The monarchs had not had to walk very far to the guillotine, where they lost their heads on the Place de la Concorde, directly across the street from their temporary residence. Later it housed the Royale, the Royal Navy, for a short period of time.

"If anyone deserves to live in that home it is certainly Jean-Louis-Pierre," the pretty blonde stated flatly. "Although, I would not put it past Jean-Louis-Pierre to return to live next to the love of his life!"

Élyse stood, clasped her friend's elbow and quickly passed her arm under Gaby's. She led her out of the café where they had stopped to sip on a café crème and a mille feuilles and naturally to view the Beau Monde as they took their afternoon strolls.

On the grand avenue of the Bois, where carriages and beautiful landaus strolled to show off the latest in millinery fashions, both girls playfully skipped down to their carriage and chanted, '*Quand on est deux amies on est toujours unies sur le même chemin on va main dans la main,*' a burst of laughter highlighting every hop!

CHAPTER FORTY

Snowflakes covered the cobblestones on the banks of the Seine. The limbs and branches of the platanes, unburdened from their spring and summer foliage, appeared to stand guard along the quays. Notre Dame, also dressed in winter white, worked her religious magic amongst all who stood on her *parvis*.

Gaby stopped to admire La Grande Dame and walked inside the cathedral. She lit a candle in front of the Lady of the Immaculate Conception and walked, head bowed, to her privileged dark mahogany pew at the very front of the altar. It still displayed her former name, Madame Gabriella de Pleyssis, Duchesse de Bourbonne carved on a golden plaque on the Prie-Dieu facing her. She stroked the thick but soft red velvet upholstery.

Why would she return to those pews? The scent, the memories of love and passion perhaps? Phillippe had wanted to place her on the other side of the aisle after the separation. At the time he had been the Cardinal assigned to Notre Dame. She sat back on the seat and watched the faithful stride along the perimeter of the Church, some stopped in the sanctuaries, others crossed themselves and prayed fervently in the chapels of the Virgin Marie and of Saint Joseph, both most popular.

Gaby wondered what these men and women asked for in their impassioned prayers to the Almighty with their chaplets in hand. Her prayer now was simplistic. “Please God, give me strength to keep my relationship with Jean-Louis manageable and simple!” A big demand. Perhaps another attempt at reconciliation? No! Too much to ask. She remained seated, lost in her thoughts for a very long time. As the

Church began to empty out, a young sacristan politely taped the velvet covering of the prie-Dieu.

"Madame, we will be closing the side entrances, I can accompany you to the other entrances if you desire to stay longer," he respectfully said.

"No, thank you very much. I will be leaving."

She reached for her gray fox coat that she had thrown over to the next pew, stood and turned toward the side exit to avoid the crowds as she walked home. At times like this, she wished that Jean-Louis was her companion, the wondrous times they had spent in these very streets. Not willing to return home, not just yet, she sat at the terrace of a nearby café and asked for a cup of hot chocolate. It arrived quickly along with two small brioches aux raisins, her favorites. They knew her taste here, or perhaps they wanted her to drink up and leave the terrace. A woman alone in a café was not appropriate.

Jean-Louis had no compulsion about taking her to the Café Athénée in Montmartre or other venues where men of wit and artistic talents spent hours in front of a glass of Absinthe. She loved Baudelaire, the great flâneur, the observer of the passing time, Sarah Barnhardt, who had thought her some attractive theatrical comportments that she'd utilized in many of her operas. Then there were the great salons of the well-known courtesans, the fascinating Valtesse, whose agile mind and curious temperament made her salons one of the most sought after in Paris. Jean-Louis had no qualms about taking her to these salons. He was always welcome! She laughed now at his force of character and audacity.

Instead of the stimulating conversations she would have preferred to engage in, she strode briskly to her favorite *salon de thé*, Madame de Sévigné in the Faubourg Saint Germain for le 5'oclock as it had been modishly named by the celebrated courtesan Valtesse de la Bigne. Warmth from the well-stocked hearth melted the icicles that hung from her silver-gray fox fur. Hot chocolate from the Islands and her favorite palmiers set in a silver basket lined in a white brocade napkin with the initials MDS embroidered on its front side.

She entered the sweet-smelling patisserie, looked at the display of croissants, *petits gateaux à la crème, mille feuilles,* and myriad of sugar topped *fruits confits, chocolats fourrés and petits fours* behind the glass vitrine. She strode to her favorite spot, a window seat overlooking the busy boulevard with a bird's eye view of the river.

The season almost over, she started to think of her new contract in New York. She had not returned to the United States since February of 1868. Her return to Paris for the Christmas season would resume in early December. Sarah Bernhardt, Sarah La Divine, the acclaimed French actress, had shared that she might stop in New York prior to a short trip to South America. She liked her immensely and while sitting in the Bois, she'd learned some of her theatrics, the ones she'd tried to conceal from many. And what a season it had been! One that she would not have dreamed of. She was signed for the next five years, after her tour in New York, every year from late September to late February, Paris was her destination.

Her impresario and agent had accepted many recitals. Rehearse, rehearse and rehearse again with the world's greatest tenors. She loved it all. She would depart early June to America to open at the Met, then return to Paris for the holidays. Jean-Louis had hinted about a return to the United States. They would grow apart, and that was best. He'd forget her, probably marry, and have many children for his namesake and the glory of his family lineage. That was the calling of the aristocracies, fighting the great wars, accumulating lands as the great families intermarried and provided new heirs for the continuation of their names and privileges.

Many of her friends had been passionately engaged to women - and men, as well - out of their social circles, but eventually family businesses, lands, and heredity came into play, maturity prevailed. Falling out of love or lust, logic dominated and attendance to their ancestral affairs became a priority.

Élyse was such a person. She recalled hating her when she'd arrived in Cannes. The feeling certainly had been mutual. She had adored her Count to the point of accepting his marital status and philandering. One morning she'd wake up and had seen the light. Years later, Élyse had married a very wealthy aristocrat from a solid family in Provence. Interestingly enough, her own lineage, along with Philippe's on their mother's side of the family, had noble descendance in the city state of Piedmont Sardinia. Nowadays, all states were reunited under the Italian flag.

Yet, in France, she was an American plantation owner—a farmer essentially. She grasped the heavily starch white napkin with the heraldry of the Marquise of Sévigné, the 17th century letter writer who extolled anything chocolate. She requested another cup of chocolate with a couple of choux à la crème. She would forgo dinner this evening.

Sitting by a window, she heard her name murmured by the Maître d'hôtel, she looked up and recognized the voice of the secretary of the Director of the Palais Garnier, who strolled to her table.

"Bonjour, Madame," he said as he entered the salon. "Je suis désolé to interrupt, but I happened to glimpse at the window and there you were, Madame."

She gestured to the chair across from her and invited him to take it. "Have a collation, Jean-Jacques."

He gave a sad look as he perused at the platter filled with confiseries facing him. "Oh, how I wish I could, but your singing keeps me on the run from morning to night, the season is phenomenal, Gabriella, and all because of you, ma chère!" He smiled as he gently caressed her hand. I would not have it any other way. But Madame, I have great news for your family. Your father's secretary just contacted us for tickets for this evening's performance, you know that you fill up the house nightly," the young manager smiled grandly at her with a *double entendre* wink, "a secret not well guarded, Madame. All subscription seats are taken but great luck, Monsieur Thiers has canceled this evening, so we gave them the Presidential suite! Regretfully, Madame, we were not aware that they were in Paris," the overly worked young man stated, discomfited.

Flabbergasted by his announcement, she had no knowledge of her father and his family's whereabouts. She let the news sink in for a short period.

"Jean-Jacques, cancel the Presidential suite. If there are no seats for Monsieur Thornsen and his family, they will just have to catch my performance elsewhere," Gaby replied in no uncertain terms. Before the young man could finish his sentence, she sipped her hot chocolate and reached for a tartelette. "But thank you. Now are you certain that I cannot entice you with this lovely plateau filled with sweet nothings?"

The poor man, utterly confused, promptly took his leave. "I look forward to your performance this evening, Madame, eh bien, *à ce soir*," he said as he hurried to the door.

"But Monsieur," his aide called back after him, "the tickets have been given to their servants."

"Advise them otherwise!" he ordered, leaving the patisserie in a rush.

A dark cloud stormed over Gabriella's face, not an ounce of remorse in her usually considerate demeanor.

CHAPTER FORTY-ONE

PARIS

As she rehearsed in her music room, a knock at her door stopped her voice exercises. She paused and gave a sorely needed break to the violinist who accompanied her.

"Wonderful surprise, Madame," her servant intoned joyously, "you will be delighted. Someone downstairs is waiting for you." Instinctively, she glanced at the mirror and mussed up her new very short hairdo. Jean-Louis had commented on how adorable she looked. "Trés mignonne, Madame." She wore wigs for the different roles she sang. The scissors had played a role—parting with the past. She recalled vividly holding her contract in Naples while stepping in a large tub—she had thought about ending her life then, as long strands had unfurled in the white porcelain bath. Instantly, like a spring her wavy former locks had rolled up to her scalp! A split with the past. She had kept it short and naturally over the past five years it had regrown. Now it played a part in her reality—again breaking with the past. Of course, it had been a shock for many, including Jean-Louis. Happy with her reflection, she descended the stairs.

"Ha ha ha, great surprise, my dearest Gabriella, I have missed you!" Cunnan howled, his bombastic voice filled the foyer.

"Cunnan!" She flew down the rest of the circular staircase. Like a little girl throwing herself in her father's loving arms. "When did you get back? I am so happy, I missed you so. When must you leave again?"

"Gaby, I have just arrived. I wanted to see your last performances."

She burst out laughing and came closer once more. She hugged him with all the love she felt. "I love you so, Cunnan, thank you so much for coming. I know it's a long voyage." She took his hand and led him to the sofa. "Madame Poulard... you remember, Jean-Louis's wonderful chef asked for a temporary transfer to my service when I returned to France. He was hardly home. She is here tonight, she will fix anything you wish."

"Wonderful, I am starving. Where is this wonderful lady?"

Gaby rang her little bell and two servants appeared. "Ask Madame Poulard to come, please."

"Where you in Spain... you walked Campostello?" she questioned.

"Well... Gaby. We were..."

At this very moment, Jean-Louis's overbearing voice hollered in the foyer. Gaby looked up to Cunnan. "Jean-Louis-Pierre and I were to walk the Camino this past month. We were to meet in Bayeux," he murmured almost apologetic, "but... we decided otherwise, Jean-Louis-Pierre will tell you all about it." Happy with himself, he shot a triumphant glance at the younger man.

"Eh bien, you two, you look awfully cozy," the Duke intoned as if he was master of the house, returning home from a long day at work. "Did Cunnan tell you that we were together walking the path for a month. You would love it, Gaby!"

"No, he shared otherwise, Jean-Louis." Gaby raised her brow.

"The man cannot keep a secret!" he retorted as he drew her into his arms and kissed her. "I missed you. Your hair, Gaby?" he whispered so intimately, that for a short instant she accepted his loving ways as if they had never parted.

"Gone" she smiled as she stood on her tippy toes to admire herself in a mirror facing the grand salon. She looked up to him. "You like it?"

"You are beautiful!" he retorted sweetly. The adoration in her eyes was gone, he noticed. He directed himself toward the side bar as Madame Poulard walked in. "The exact person I'd hope to see. What do you have in store for us, Madame?" Jean-Louis inquired playfully.

"Will you be staying, Monsieur?" The cook asked deferentially. "Yes, your reputation in the culinary skills precede you, Madame. I would not miss your omelette, Madame Poulard."

"Very well I will surprise all of you with a splendid feast worth a Louis d'or from Louis XIV!" the rotund renowned chef from Normandy proclaimed. "And for you, Madame," she came closer with a grin and whispered to Gaby "your favorite blueberry tart. Jean has just returned from Deauville, these juicy delights are immense and glorious and oh, mon Dieu, so sweet!"

Madame Poulard was the only servant that the Duke liked. She had worked in the ancestral home for as long as Gaby remembered, but Marie, Jean-Louis cherished governess, had placed her and her daughter in the service of Jean-Louis in Paris, when all the properties had passed on to him after the death of his father. She adored him, and he reciprocated her dedication. When Gaby had returned to Paris, she had asked for a transfer to her household. Of course, it had been immediately granted. Had it been planned? Perhaps!

The afternoon had been great fun like old times. The wine and meal softened her disposition while the note she'd received from her father yesterday had left her in disarray. Without a second thought, she opened up to these two men who essentially knew her life's history.

"My father is in Paris, Jean-Louis," she stated flatly without emotion, "along with his family. They are staying very close to the de Crillon. I am to meet him next week in one of the salons. His wife and daughters are in Italy with his younger son, who's on his Grand Tour. Why there, Jean-Louis?" she questioned.

"I will find out, Gaby. Does he know that I reside there at times?"

"No, I do not believe so. I think he wants to revisit my inheritance of the plantation, La Justine. Our lawyer, Aidan... Hartley, that is, essentially told me and Philippe so. He has offered his legal expertise. He adored my mother, as you know. Jean-Louis, they were lovers for many years and he will never let my father rest until the old man is behind bars. I have the notion that it is his life's work."

"Let your father approach you, Gaby. Nothing is wrong with the de Crillon. It is the home of naval operations. I will be there."

The conversation carried on late into the night. Cunnan sighed and yawned.

"Eh bien, Cunnan, will you return with me to our home?" the duke demanded as he winked at Gaby.

"Sated and too exhausted," the older man retorted as he elongated his arms above his head and yawned. "I will stay here if Gabriella permits."

Delighted, Gaby called upon the servants to prepare a room.

"I have seen too much of you this past month. I need a pause." Cunnan retorted. Jean-Louis-Pierre laughed a happy guttural laugh. The older man stood and staggered toward the door. "Gaby, my whiskey has been spiked?"

"Fernand took pity on you, Cunnan, I saw him more than once refilling your glass. Sleep tight. We will talk tomorrow." She blew kisses to him.

"*Eh bien*, I will bring the warm croissants," the younger man teased. "Will stay at home tonight, much closer, my dear, unless Gaby will let a stuffed to the brink, inebriated man share her bed?" he questioned, his devilish smirk directed at his former wife.

"No!" came the curt answer. "Good night, Jean-Louis."

Six hours later, he returned, two large paper bags in hand. The butler let him in and glanced at the large Frenchman's shoulders with a grin as he climbed two by two the stairs leading to his former wife's apartments.

CHAPTER FORTY-TWO

The butler held the double doors open as Gabriella entered one of the large salons in the elegant residence. She noticed in the back corner of the vast room, on both sides of the fireplace, her father ensconced in a large red velour fauteuil while his two eldest sons closed in behind him. A sick tableau, she contemplated. Family portrait in Paris, she should send a note to Manet. He painted with great details these types of enigmatic figures, exposing a wild ironic depiction that many failed to distinguish.

"Hello, Gabriella, thank you for coming. You recognize your brothers, Armand and Henry."

Blank faced, disdain pouring out of her glare, she remained silent. Instead, she crossed the room and took a seat across from her father on a wide Louis XVI beige and rose settee.

Momentarily ill at ease, the old man stirred in his chair. "Yes, they've grown up, not solely in stature, but both are great businessmen," he declared with pride.

Gaby glared at the picture-perfect men across from her. Not a word passed her lips. Appreciating that his comments did not generate much interest, the patriarch tried to sweeten the conversation by complimenting her on her great professional advances.

"We are very proud of your accomplishments, Gabriella. Just the other day, Simone and I acknowledged how much New Orleans misses you and Philippe, both of your voices touched so many hearts." He smiled first at her and then turned to his boys for approbation. Compliments on her singing zipped by like a speeding train.

"Eh bien, gentlemen, we all know that your suggestion to meet has nothing to do with my voice, profession nor my diligence. Therefore, why did you call this meeting, Mr.Thornsen?" The impertinence stung. There were no reactions from any of them for a lengthy moment, until the old man visibly annoyed, retorted.

"This was uncalled for, Gabriella. I am your father."

"You never acted like one," she countered calmly. "What is the reason for this meeting? My plantation?"

"YOUR plantation? Please!" the father snapped, amusement in his voice, an ironic stretching across his wrinkled lips. His demeanor? A wise above the fray adult deriding a child as he said, "You know quite well, my dear child, that these plantations are mine! The Justine and River Boat, Philippe's land. I want my boys to take over my properties. As you are aware, I allowed your mother to place your name on the deed to appease her soul while in prison. It pleased her. I was considerate of her love for you."

"I have heard enough!" Gaby sliced. "*La Justine* is mine. Philippe will have to decide as to his inheritance. My grandfather willed it to my mother with emphasis 'her sole property' stamped on its front cover. I have the documented legal papers. Not surprising, I never met him, but even then, de Conte surmised that the emphasis needed a legal dossier. His impression of your honesty was less than clear. Clairvoyant, I would say. *La Justine* is well managed, one of the few plantations in New Orleans that stayed lucrative during and after the Civil War. La Justine escaped the financial ruin many of your friends experienced with their lands. The plantation is well administered. I am quite happy with its dividends. It will continue to profit. I was a young child when you tried to swindle my estate. Thanks to AIDAN HARTLEY, my mother's lawyer... "

"Her lover, you mean?"

Gaby looked away, well aware that she had to choose her battles. “The documents were served to you and you accepted their conclusion. I am no longer a child. The answer is still NO! I will not, I repeat— I will not pass the deed to your children under any circumstances.”

Stunned, the old man held his anger back... not for long. “And tell me, Gabriella, who will then inherit YOUR imagined land when you pass?”

“Samuel and his family, the very ones that have kept the land lucrative, are my designated inheritors. My mother hung for her beliefs. That is the very least I can do for this generation of freed men!”

“Niggers!” he shouted. He stood, before his sons reacted to her words, Thornsen crossed the room toward her, “Niggers over your own blood? You’ve gone mad?” His anger stunned even his progeny.

Gaby stood just as promptly and started for the door.

“Come back here!” he screamed at her, his blood red aquiline nose attempting to catch a breath. Beady pleuritic gray eyes darted left to right, his expanded chest and stomach blubber pulsating above the tightly woven cummerbund around his waist, he approached her with his cane airborne. Quickly, she ran for the door, turned the knob and ask the butler to summon Jean-Louis. He was waiting.

Calmly, the Duke strode into the salon. “Eh bien, Monsieur Thornsen, I see that your cowardly behavior extends to women as well! Why is Gabriella so displeasing to you? All adore her in Paris.”

The old man stopped immediately at the unexpected entrance of the large and fierce Frenchman. Thornsen had been on the receiving end of his blows years ago in the restaurant’s courtyard in New Orleans. A repeat performance would send him to meet his maker.

“My daughter and I had a business discussion, which is frankly none of your business!” the old man replied brazenly.

Gaby’s temerity is inherited from this lineage, the Duke presaged.

"Before we pursue this pathetic conversation, she does not..." the old man took a deep breath and began to gasp for air.

"Does he need medical attention?" Jean-Louis questioned his sons.

Before an answer was formulated, Thornsen came forward flaming with wrath.

"Do you know what this unhinged young woman, who is barren and who's most cherished cousin is gelded, has in store for my land in my State of Louisiana?"

Stunned, Jean-Louis did not respond.

"She wants to pass on my plantation to a nigger and his family! You're a landowner and businessman, a member of the privileged class, how can you reconcile such insanity?" he concluded irately.

"I reconcile it well. It is her property left to her to do as she chooses. What I do not reconcile are your thugs who beat me, starved me and left me for dead in one of YOUR infamous prisons, Thornsen. I was lucky. I'm an influential man across the seas, and I was delivered from the living hell you've put me through. Inconveniently for you, I was actually saved by the very man you now try to deprive. You're on my turf now, Thornsen. Our prisons are a tad better than yours, but trust me I can make life very difficult for you here and abroad. My banks could cancel out loans that you have taken recently in the hope to steal back the Justine. Continue to annoy Gabriella with your rodent businessmen and you and your family will find yourselves eating in your kitchen house—outside with your nigger servants. Understood? As of now, you and your sons are under arrest in France until we find the connection between you and Mr. Matelier's search for documents in Gabriella's home less than two weeks ago. The change of guard in Rome was bizarre, non, Thornsen?"

The Louisianan reddened and abruptly stood up from the large *bergère,* he strode impulsively and nervously to the fireplace, turning his back on the Duke and Gabriella. The sons froze. Stunned, Gabriella looked up at her former husband.

"He became historian almost overnight after Mr. de la Rontelle became seriously ill and unable to resume his contract as the distinguished historian Gabriella trusted," Jean-Louis continued casually. "I understand the man is still quite ill in a Rome hospital. Suspicious, isn't it?"

"You're a demon, de Pleyssis! the old man raged. "I should have fought your freedom from prison in our State. This is where you belonged, and that is where your truant life should have ended."

"My truant life?" the Duke replied calmly as he advanced toward the old man. "You have made a grave error," he whispered in the old man's ear. "You will not be allowed to leave France until the financial affair with Gabriella's inheritance is settled."

"You serpent! I will get revenge!" the old man cried out.

Jean-Louis nodded. "I understand, your wife, daughter and son are enjoying their Grand Tour immensely in Tuscany?" The Duke smiled as he watched the old man's fiery green eyes freeze with shock.

"My family? How do you know their itinerary, de Pleyssis?"

"Good intelligence in France. You will just have to spend some extra time in the City of Light. Now let me tell you what I want from you. We will meet tomorrow once and for all to settle the legality of the plantation. Understood, Monsieur Thornsen? A carriage will pick you up at your hotel at ten o'clock tomorrow. I would advise you to be there."

"Your words are feces, de Pleyssis! French law does not extend to Louisiana!" Thornsen retorted triumphantly.

"True, but my assets in the United States speak volumes. I would dislike it immensely to see your children dig ditches at your former cotton plantations. They do not appear to be predisposed to hard labor!"

The old man stood and waved for his sons to follow him.

Jean-Louis scanned for a chair, strode to one and sat, staring at his former wife's family. His booming voice instilled fear in everyone in the room. "Sit down, Thornsen. This matter needs closure. Now hear me well." Intimidated and fearful, the sons marched in unison far away from the man whom they perceived as a mad French aristocrat. Their father followed closely, less apprehensive, but eventually all regained their former seats. A few steps behind her former husband, Gaby settled back in a white and rose satin upholstered bergère.

"Good. Let me skip to the problem at hand." Jean-Louis focused on all seated for long moments.

Gaby's glances questioned her former husband's demeanor, seeming to ask, 'where are you going, Jean-Louis, with the information I provided?'

"I understand much cotton was burned by the Union during the war, huge plantations and their great houses razed to the ground. True?"

Thornsen kept silent.

"Furthermore..." he continued, his eyes resting calmly on the men in the room, "large bales burned... in Columbia, I believe. Could it be that thc cotton was set on fire to confuse the financial community of the planters' voracious losscs? The Confederacy had been invoked. I recall our ships were not too far away. Where did you hide your assets, Thornsen. Up river?" The Duke remained silent. He expected a détournement, a rerouting, but none came.

"Be there tomorrow or my wrath will be unleashed on your precious possessions. The Cotton Exchange does not look kindly on crooks—connections or not. They like to be paid on time!"

At the mention of the Cotton Exchange, the old man ceased all discussions. He lifted the palms of his hands to his sons. Calmness for now—required.

"Very well, Monsieur de Pleyssis. We are gentlemen and my sons and I know when the battle has been lost. I will have my lawyer, who happens to be in Paris as well, attend the meeting with us. If it pleases you, of course." He extended his hand, which was not taken nor shaken. Jean-Louis-Pierre stood motionless, his eyes fixed on Gaby.

"We will meet at the agreed upon time." Jean-Louis walked to Gaby, who had not budged from her seat near the door. He took her hand and squeezed it as he led her outside.

"Let's see what he will do tomorrow."

"How did you know about his unlawful secreting of his cotton assets up river?"

"I have my informants, as well." He bent down and brushed a kiss to her temple. "You cannot refuse to have dinner with me tonight, Gaby."

"No. Everything has a price, I presume!" she scoffed as his hand wandered to her waist and below. Swiftly, she removed it. "But... thank you."

As it happened they spent the day together. Him pressing for more favors, her showing some resistance while not quite ready to leave his company.

CHAPTER FORTY-THREE

Gossips ran rampant. Jean-Louis-Pierre and Gabriella were a constant at the many soirées, recitals, and plays of the moment. Cunnan had set his sight on their reconciliation. Le Beau Monde was now spreading the rumor that perhaps the breakup had never really existed.

"Just a ploy to give Gabriella a bit more liberty to ease into her highly controversial profession," said Juliette de Moribanal, a well-known Parisian socialite who sat next to Cunnan at a supper given by the American Ambassador. "He refuses her nothing. A shame if you ask me. Quite vulgar! His grandmother is chagrined by such a lack of politeness toward our likes," Juliette had explained to Cunnan.

"Aren't you enamored with her singing?" Juliette's very handsome and very young escort continued, "We spent seven days in Naples two years ago just to attend her concerts. It appeared to me you could not get enough of that splendid voice!" The young man pulled his shoulders back and straightened. He smiled as he reached for a *tasse de café-crème*. He sipped it slowly as he forked his apple tart, a half smile lifting the edges of his mouth.

Juliette shrugged and batted her eyelashes as if the poor fellow's comment was unsolicited and not relevant. "It is just not proper!" she concluded in a tone that made further comments a non-starter.

Meanwhile, Jean-Louis-Pierre did not want to press Gaby. He had two months to play his cards well. He took short trips to the ancestral home to visit their son and returned to show up unexpectedly at her door. As predicted by Élyse, he'd set up his offices in the Saint Louis's home once again, closer to Gaby's residence, *naturellement*. He'd entertain his friends and business relations. Spring was on its way.

CHAPTER FORTY-FOUR

Weeks later, their relationship was in full swing once more. Her singing contract terminated for the season, Gaby now lived in Paris as if she had never left it. In the late afternoons, she practiced with Maître Lauriot, always rejoined by the Duke who was never far away. Plagued by countless insecurities, he'd ambled with great désinlvoture in her dressing room ten minutes before the end of the opéra.

Her home was now his new residence and not once had he balked at the arrangement. His wardrobe sent over daily after the reconciliation, rendered his household staff insane with the back and forth. His businesses attended each morning from the Saint Louis's home, and his prompt return to her in the early afternoon became a source of curiosity. In many ways he had not changed much. He monopolized her life with so many plans and outdoorsy types of activities they both loved, seeing her old friends became difficult.

"I'm like warm bread, the scent follows me and so does Jean-Louis," she'd recounted with amusement to Élise and Ribaud.

"Are you happy, Gaby?" Luke had casually questioned.

"Yes, but I will admit to some anxieties." She sighed. "I have made a decision that I hope will not fail me."

Élyse stood, approached her friend, and hugged her tightly. "*C'est la vie*, Gaby, leading a life on the edge is living not existing."

Gaby did not respond.

A month before Gaby's return to the United States for her opening at the Met, Jean-Louis-Pierre's American friends had arrived in Paris to accompany their son and two daughters in the Grand Tour. Jean-Louis had not extended an invitation to the dinner he planned to host in their honor. Pained but unwilling to acknowledge the slight, she'd invented a singing arrangement that she would attend with her friends.

As he entertained in his grand fashion, a walk by her old home was *de rigueur.* She quite relished the amusements on the quais along the Seine, its various bookstand sellers, who with the hope of selling the classics, often revealed the obscure sections of the stories' denouement! The artistes peintres, as well, sitting on their woven cane, armless chairs frequently had the artsy desire to divulge their innermost sentiments about the Seine, the boulevards, Notre-Dame, often including the 'whys and the whens' of their visions of the world that had changed their lives.

"*Pour ouvrir les yeux du monde, Madame*!" To open the eyes of the passersby, many communicated. "Regardez, Madame, Monsieur Paul Gauguin, un agent de change à la Bourse de Paris et aujourd'hui un peintre pas assez reconnu... mais attendez, il sera grand maître un de ces jours! "

The fellows managing these make shift boutiques were always ready to talk, complaining about the weather or extolling the beauty of their capital. Yes, her life had changed immensely, she reminisced on the anxious days upon her arrival in this splendid city and... her life now... so many uncertainties.

As she strolled by the wide wooden gate, the security guards outside the large home recognized her, relayed that information to the gatekeepers, who opened the doors to permit her to enter the courtyard of her former home. She hesitated.

The impressive marble flight of stairs that led to the grand entrance welcomed her. Former personal maids, Maître d'hôtel, doormen welcomed her, even one of her favorite cooks, Madame Bargayllon, who had taken over Madame Bonnard's duties, came rushing out from a side door. Even new stable boys peeked from behind the horses to take a look at Gabriella de Conte Thornsen, the renowned diva and former Madame de Pleyssis, the previous queen of this magnificent home.

"Oh Madame, quel plaisir!" her former secretary greeted. "Monsieur is in the sitting room. I will advise him of your arrival." She nodded and entered the grand home.

No turning back now, she thought as she sauntered inside. Gaby sighed and took a deep breath. With her million dollar smile, she lifted her skirt and stepped onto the thick Aubusson rug. She nodded at the faithful servants and let Fernand help her with her dark green cape, lined with brown mink.

Her eyes darted toward the left wing of the house. Her theater remained. Her life six years ago flashed before her eyes. To her surprise, the gut-wrenching torture that she'd experienced after seeing Jean-Louis taken away to prison in chains did not register. Thank God, because the incident had subtracted years of happiness. Nothing had changed. The house was one of the few in Paris that had not been requisitioned by the Prussians. Jean-Louis had been imprisoned then. The enemies of your enemies are your friends!

As she waited in the foyer, reminiscent of days gone by, her former husband's boisterous and energetic voice called out from one of the smaller dining rooms facing the gardens.

"Gaby, you've come! Splendide! Come join us, we've just sat down." He took her hand, pulled her to him and kissed her. "Did you cancel your plans to attend the *déjeuner?" he asked.*

"Sophie was *enrouée*, hoarse, silly to chance catching her cold. I have to sing these next few weeks," she lied. In effect, she had no plans to go anywhere but he had not extended an invitation.

"I am delighted that you chose to join us. My friends' eldest daughter is not part of the *grand tour.* You will like her when we reach New York. She is intelligent and very social."

Gaby shot a sideways glance.

"Gaby, she is but twenty! "he exclaimed, pretending utter shock at the insinuation.

"Let me remind you, mon cher, that I was a mere twenty-one when you seduced me!"

He burst out laughing and pulled her into the library. "Should I refresh your memories, Madame?" he whispered in her ear. "My recollection of the momentous event was most different. I recall distinctly the great strength of character it took to gently push you away, while you, *ma chère...* "

"Cease," she pulled away, turned on her heel and started toward the door.

He caught up with her, turned her around and kissed her. "I should not have wasted the first weeks!"

"Introduce me to your friends!" she replied flippantly.

They strode into the dining room.

"A great pleasure, Madame," Jean-Louis's friends said as she advanced to the table. An additional table setting was placed next to him, and the afternoon conversation continued happily. Gaby's favorite soufflé had been lovingly prepared by her cook. She was home.

"We will be in New York prior to your opening at the Met, Madame. The Duke has told us that you will be quite surprised at the elegance of your new home. I understand you have not yet seen it. These long separations must be quite difficult."

Stunned, Gaby looked up at the elegant old man and grinned. "Jean-Louis and I have been divorced for the past seven years, I would not have known any of his architectural plans!" She smiled, amused.

The handsome French man burst out laughing. Gaby was about to embarrass him a bit more until the young girl next to him asked, "Is Marie-Hélène aware of your... separation, Monsieur?"

"Gabriella has a devilish demeanor and a humor that one needs to appreciate. Nothing is sacred with her. Quite fun, I must say."

All had a good laugh and shortly thereafter the family departed, still not quite certain if the couple was married.

As the carriage exited the wide and thick wooden gates that enclosed the home, Gaby turned to Jean-Louis. "You actually had them believe that we were still married? How, Jean-Louis?"

"I had no desire to court or to be courted, Gaby. That is all." His tone of voice indicated that the matter was closed. She did not pursue the questioning.

CHAPTER FORTY-FIVE

Their passion rekindled, they were seen in Paris together more often than not. Jean-Louis-Pierre always appeared alone if not accompanied by his former wife, Gabriella. As a couple, both were more social and flirtatious.

Paris was confused, and tongues wagged. Yet, the Duke, Phillippe and Cunnan kept a secret that might unravel the relationship. Against Cunnan and Philippe's advice, Jean-Louis concluded that time was of the essence to divulge the birth of their son.

Ian's arrival at Garnier, Paris' new opera house on the Grands Boulevards, was a scene to behold. His deep green eyes goggled every inch of the magnificent building. He looked radiant, standing next to his father in a matching dark burgundy fitted dress coat and matching trousers. The outfit completed with a white satin vest and silver buttons.

The child stood by his father as friends and government ministers came to pay their respects. Many on the parterre and the adjoining loges were looking at that child who was the exact replica of his father as a young child. Many remembered the young future Duke standing beside his father and stepmother.

This young man in the official loge was a de Pleyssis or, at the very least, part of the great lineage. The dowager was absent from her box, while all awaited Gabriella de Conte Thornsen. Could the couple have hidden their relationship to ease Gabriella's entrance in the world's great opera houses? Was the child their very own? Or was the boy the love child of one of the Duke's many escapades? The opera house was filled and with this latest apparition, the rumors and gossip ran wild.

The one most curious about this new appearance in the family's lineage was Jean-Louis's cousin, Henry. In his loge, one floor removed, he whispered to his wife, who coyly tilted her head to the side to watch the child.

"A strange and new complementary outcome, indeed," she murmured. "Cardinal de Conte-Thornsen is in their presence... they despise one another. A strange turn of events. What are we coming to... such a faux pas, Henry. I swear this new modernity is turning our world upside down!" She stared at her husband who, with great difficulty, diverted his regard to the stage once more.

"I will learn more in the halls as soon as the opera begins. I'm delighted that Grand'Mère is not in attendance this evening. This scandalous appearance is utterly shocking."

"Your dear cousin can do no wrong in her eyes," Marie-Anne whispered back. "This child, if legitimized, will be adored at the expense of our sons," his wife whispered while casting resentful sideways glances at Ian. "Do you recall, we expected great disapproval when he decided to fight in the American Civil War and even more abhorring his anointed marriage to an American soprano. I love Gabriella but... "

The orchestra started the prologue. All fell silent awaiting the magnificence of the spectacle. And what a spectacle it was!"

Ian kept silent, nodding and smiling rather than breaking his self-imposed silence—his Irish accent would be recognized immediately. Meanwhile, Philippe and Cunnan were pointing out the finer sculptures and stagecraft on stage of a rendition of Jesus arriving on Palm Sunday in Jerusalem.

Mesmerized by all that confronted his senses, the boy took it all in. He let the two men pass him, pretending an avid interest in a woven tapestry commemorating a hunting scene. Inconspicuous, he turned around to check if anyone was looking. Satisfied that he was not the center of attention, he pressed his hands together, lifted his eyes to the heavens, and whispered, "Thank you."

Philippe, who had caught up with him, smiled and winked at him as he placed his hand on the boy's shoulder.

"Father," an embarrassed and bewildered Ian began. Philippe had been introduced as a family friend, but only until the time came when the secret birth could be revealed to Gaby. "I wonder if you could ask the Duke to introduce me as Jean-Marie-Marc. It is the name of Monsieur de Pleyssis's grandfather. Madame Marie said the Duke admired him greatly."

Phillippe bent down, kissed the boy on the cheek and nodded.

"Your father will be proud," Philippe replied solemnly.

The boy smiled and suppressed the urge to touch his robe. Instead, he returned to the edge of the balcony to admire all that adorned the stage.

"The apple does not fall far away from the tree!" the Cardinal whispered to Cunnan who had just heard the last of the request. Both men focused on the scene a while longer, considering the decision taken by Jean-Louis-Pierre—bringing the child to the opéra. Both men had been against the decision.

"Too soon, Jean-Louis-Pierre," Philippe had declared, "give it a couple more months." Cunnan concurred. The Duke thought otherwise.

Many drafters scanned the loge, fast at work on their yellow pads.

"What will the Gazette reveal tomorrow?" asked Cunnan.

"The boy and his father look alike. There is no denial," Philippe replied. "And there is also no denying that the color of his eyes and his smile are Gaby's... and mine. That grin. belongs to our side of the family tree. Will the drafters capture that trait? Will she recognize it? Gaby reads the newspaper daily. What will be her reaction?" Philippe continued almost to himself, "Will the documents convince her of the veracity of the story?"

Cunnan stared at the cleric, fully aware of the hatred both Philippe and the Duke felt toward one another. A young child had just entered their lives, complications to that relationship were sure to ensue.

"Now that Jean-Louis-Pierre has rebuked Gaby's father and his family, I thought Gaby might be amenable to a reconciliation as friendly as friendly can be, considering the passion that animates these two souls," Cunnan said, pensive as he walked away from Philippe and stood closer to Jean-Louis-Pierre.

Myriad persons of significance entered the loge to pay their respect. Ian looked behind his shoulder as the commotion intensified. A look of terror developed on the child's face.

The new Minister of Defense of the Thiers's Versailles government came around to shake Jean-Louis-Pierre's hand.

"Good looking young man, mon cher."

Ian smiled. A beam that betrayed his mother's winning grin. Cunnan and Philippe standing nearby focused on him a moment longer than necessary.

Very much aware of his pronounced Irish accent, the boy returned the smile but remained silent. Curious, the Minister tried to induce the young man into a conversation. "Do you like opéra, young man?"

Silently Ian nodded, excused himself silently as he ambled along to the front of the loge. He smiled politely and proceeded quickly to the balcony overlooking the stage mesmerized by the splendor of the venue. He stood alone staring at the parterre for a long time tortured by the thought that perhaps he had failed his father by not responding in accordance to the aristocratic protocol.

Marie had told him not to be afraid to be rude. "Privacy is important and expected by your father." Consequently, he'd adapted to it—with much difficulty. In this particular instance, his accent would have been a revelation. He recalled his time in the monastery, he would have been severely rebuked by this last insolent conduct, maybe five days on bread and water.

Good manners were of utmost importance in these institutions and lately he seemed to cross all that he had learned in the early days of his life with the monks. He did not want to embarrass his father with his pronounced accent. His tutors had told him that, at his age, it would disappear quickly and Ian worked for hours on his speech. He had asked for a vocal coach.

"Un tuteur de diction, Ian?" Jean-Louis questioned.

The following day the tuteur materialized and, for almost two months now, they had been hard at work daily by the brook that bordered the castle properties. His French history tuteur had restricted the budding friendship he'd developed with one of the cottager's children. The mother reminded him of Mam O'Reilly, the wonderful woman he loved so very much and had been so broken-hearted to leave behind when the three aristocrats had appeared on the farm's doorsteps.

He recalled the day so vividly. He had been hard at work, collecting and raking the hay for the stables. "Winter is still in our mist, boys, let's keep our farm animals happy and well fed throughout the season," Father O'Reilly would say every evening as he picked up his cello to soothe the aching muscles after a hard day's work.

The past two years had been the most loving. The closest he'd ever come to family life. He did not mind the hard work, and he'd felt important as he often helped Father O'Reilly with his well-honed reading skills. Billy, the older son, and Conner had been good friends as well.

Two wonderful years! All had come to an end as the Duke, Captain Cunnan and Cardinal Thornsen had suddenly appeared in his life. Again, his life had been turned upside down. They had traveled from

Brest where the ship had moored late at night and had arrived at the Duke de Bourbonne's castle.

One day happy as a lark as a farmer's charge, another as a noble man in this immense castle where everyone attended to his needs. Liveried servants had been awaiting their arrival and the following morning, a gentle governess had come to his service. All were very nice to him, and Madame Marie was kind and understanding. His father had spoken highly of her dedication and his love for this woman, who at first sight had frightened him with her stern appearance.

The men had returned to Paris a fortnight later with a promise to return the following Sunday. His father had returned two days earlier than expected. While waiting for the return of his father, Madame Marie had sat next to him at the never-ending table while his own butler could not do enough to please him. Even the cook who'd just entered the dining room stared adoringly in his direction. According to His Eminence who'd come and tap him on his shoulder prior to their departure, Madame Poulard and Madame Bonnard were a no nonsense, authoritative culinary queens. "Whatever you do, Ian, always thank Madame Poulard and Madame Bonnard for their fabulous dinners, I have been told more than once that they could be your best friend or your worst enemy!" Then he'd smiled his gentle smile and kissed him on both cheeks.

"A bientôt, Ian."

He'd waved back politely.

"These small blueberry tarts with the crème fraiche in between the layers were your Maman's... pardon me, the Duke's favorite." He'd skipped the blueberry tarts entirely and pushed the dish away.

His heart had skipped a beat as he recalled vividly the moment. "You know my Mother, Madame?" he'd exclaimed.

She'd smiled and had changed the subject, switching his attention to the magnificence of the tapestries that lined the walls. After an elaborate dinner and delicious desserts, he'd returned to his room. He'd hoped that his manners had not insulted anyone. So many knives, and forks, for meats and fishes, so many glasses and cups and small bowls with lemon slices swimming in the water. He'd glanced conspicuously to his right and left to adjust to the proper table manners in France. Aside from using the soup spoon to dish out the crème fraîche, he believed he'd skipped a faux pas.

Late that very night, a horrific winter storm found him covered in heavy blankets at the very end of the ornate bed. Every roll of thunder made him shiver as he recalled Madame Marie opening his door to connect him to her room and her own bed. All seemed well now.

What would happen in the next few years? He did not know. All of his questions had been answered... but evasively. He knew one thing for certain - the Duke was his father. The truth of all the other stories? A big question mark. What had been revealed to him came from his friend, the cottager's son.

"A great love story," he'd said, quoting his mother. "Unheard of in French aristocratic circles, Ian, according to my mother. The wedding was held here in the Castle. The Duke married an American soprano. And all of us, cottagers and villagers alike, shared in the festivities for three whole days," his friend said.

Had this woman been his mother? Daniel's father had been non-committal on the subject. Ian had asked if he remembered his father's wife when he came the following day to help out around the farm.

He had been told, "Daniel has a lot of work. We appreciated your help, but we find this situation out of the... ordinary, and we would prefer this relationship to end."

Daniel's father was stern. Ian obeyed. The following Sunday in the village church, where Madame Marie had taken him to attend Mass, the father and mother had nodded in acknowledgement. Daniel, however, had turned his head toward the Sacristy. The hint was clear.

His friendship was not valued or wanted. He turned his attention to his studies. He chose a hidden spot close to a frozen stream, where he sat for long hours on a severed tree trunk with his books.

The weather was freezing cold, but it felt wonderful. As well, a little freedom amongst the beautiful rolling hills was a respite from the confusion surrounding his new life. On the two occasions that the Duke visited, he had taken him to the stables and chosen a horse for him. He'd been frightened but had shown no fear.

He'd learned self-control after his transfer to the severe monastery he had been sent to from the nunnery. He missed Sister Marie-Céleste, who loved him so. He knew he'd been fortunate after hearing dreadful stories from some of his peers at the monastery. "Better show no fear, Ian. These monsters thrive on the fear they inflict on you young ones with their whips and batons. You will survive a good whipping, but your cries and protestations of no wrongdoings will only excite these half men to increase the severity of the beatings—to make you a strong man physically and emotionally! Like them! A sad joke if it was not so tragic. Stick to yourself, my boy. You must be smart to be here at such a tender age. You will overcome."

That very speech had given Ian strength when the beatings were painful and numerous. He refused to shed a tear at the very young age of four and half. As compared to many others, he had been spared the rod more often than his peers. The transfer a year and a half later to the O'Reilly farm remained a mystery. He didn't question his good fortune. Why? He was happy!

CHAPTER FORTY-SIX

The ringing of the bell … the musical curator walked up and down the marble staircase as he announced the beginning of the opera. Jean-Louis-Pierre, who had been engaged by many of his peers in the back chamber, re-entered the box. Ian, from his vantage point, admired the impressive opera house. He glanced back and noticed that statesmen and longtime friends had returned to their own loges. He made his way to the last seat on the far right of the box on the second row. These seats were designated for lesser guests who had been asked to join the grands for a performance.

Jean-Louis-Pierre strode to him, winked as he clasped his hand, and led him to the central bergère. "Sit down Ian, you will enjoy the performance better from this vantage point."

Love, respect and admiration reflected on the child's face. Ian came closer.

"Monsieur," he whispered recalling his French tutor's pronunciation, "perhaps you could call me Jean-Marie-Pierre or Jean-Marie-Marc?" he whispered in English.

Jean-Louis smiled. The child fell silent, cheeks flushed with embarrassment as he stared at the stage. Before the Duke could answer, the musicians began the prelude. The curtain rose. In the parterre, all seats were taken, all the aficionados waiting anxiously for the presentation of Georges Bizet's Carmen. A part that no one could sing with as much passion and ironic value as the young Louisianan Diva.

Gaby entered in all her splendor and stood center stage as the orchestra performed the prelude. She had instituted a lovely tradition.

Prior to her performances, she would appear on stage and talk about the opera at hand, first thanking the script writer and the artists involved in the drama or comedy. Her charming accent kept the audience captivated. Within minutes after the enchanting presentation, she blew kisses to her audience and returned to her dressing room.

Philippe, sitting nearby, passed on the lorgnettes to his nephew. "Watch this amazing diva, Ian," he said.

The child beamed, his eyes filled with love and gratitude.

"You're about to hear one of the most beautiful voices in the world of opera," his father said, leaning nearer. He retrieved another pair of lorgnettes stashed in his back pocket. "You can keep these, they're yours. They belonged to my... your great grandfather. Look," he whispered and pointed to the intricate coat of arms of the family.

The child swallowed hard as if the weight of the world's burden balanced on his shoulders. "I will study hard and will make you proud, Messieurs. Roman said my accent will recede. I am young, determined and very intelligent—I have been told," he insisted.

"You have suffered enough because of my mistakes, Jean-Marie-Marc," Jean-Louis-Pierre said, using the first name suggested by his son. "It is time for you to enjoy the wonderful life that is ahead of you."

The boy regarded his father.

"Enjoy the performance!"

He recalled Daniel's comments referring to the American soprano. Surreptitiously, he observed his father as he stared with an adoring gaze at the young woman who had just re-entered the stage—that very woman might be his mother. The admiration in the child's face turned from enchantment to fury as he recalled Gaby's enlarged photographs in the myriad European opera houses. Even at such a tender age, the child comprehended that the woman cavorting on stage, singing with unrestrained abandon to her adored audience, had abandoned him.

He hated her. He walked to Cunnan first and stared, then Philippe before he directed an irate gaze at his father. The emotion traversing the young boy's body was palpable. He turned on his heel, tears streaming down his cheeks. He ran out of the loge, forgetting scarf, coat and lorgnettes, tossing to the carpeted floor the program that showcased the performance.

Taken by utter surprise, they all stood still for a moment. Then the truth of the situation unfurled before Jean-Louis's eyes. He gave his coat to Cunnan and began the chase that ended with him at the bottom of the famous staircase into the formal foyer. There, he seized his son's trembling body and pressed him to his chest.

"I am so sorry, Jean-Marie-Marc," Jean-Louis whispered, not letting go.

"Please, Monsieur, I want to return to Marie in Normandie," he said in English.

Without returning to the loge, father and son boarded the waiting coach and returned to the ancestral home in Saint Louis, the ride home silent. Upon their arrival, father and son disembarked from the carriage.

Silently the young boy walked up to his apartment, straight and proud at first. Then he ran, leaping up the steps two at the time, sobs overwhelming his youthful body. Throwing himself on the bed, he released his sadness.

Jean-Louis-stood still, his hands on both sides of the gilded wooden arches leading to the child's room. He watched helplessly as his son cried himself to sleep while dreams of Ireland and Mrs. O'Reilly and his adopted family danced in his head.

Early the following morning, he woke up still thinking that a day's work in the O'Reilly's farm lay ahead of him. He lifted the coverlet and a distinctive scent awaited him. Still half asleep, he looked for his pants and shirt. He bumped into the armrest of the sofa that divided his bedroom from a sitting area. He quickly turned around.

An aroma of strong Ethiopian coffee permeated the room. Jean-Marie-Marc dropped the eiderdown coverlet that dragged behind him. It fell to the floor. His father, seated in the large fauteuil where he learned his lessons by heart, was sipping the dark scented concoction as he read by his bedside.

"Good morning, young man," Jean-Louis smiled. All is ready for your trip back. "Pull the cordon," he nodded to the right of the headboard, "your breakfast will be brought in. Let's return to Normandie, Jean-Marie-Marc,'' said the Duke in English.

The boy stared for a long time as his father stood and walked to the windows.

The tall Frenchman parted the curtains to let the sunshine in. "Quite cold, the denuded branches of the trees look like skeletons ready to burst through the window and swallow you up!" he joked.

The boy glanced his way, a petrified stare on his beautiful face.

Jean-Louis returned to the bed where the boy now sat. "Relax, Jean-Marie-Marc, your choice of reading material may need some adjustments. Quite frightening, the material you read."

"I like bloodcurdling stories, Monsieur, but I am often terrified by the characters. The series I am presently reading suggests that the dead might return during winter and consume the living!"

The questioning stare on the poor child's face softened his father's stance. He lifted the boy out of bed and carried him to the window.

"Nothing to worry about Jean-Marie-Marc," he clasped the child to his chest and held him tight. "All will be fine. The old adage 'nothing to fear but fear itself!' is one to live by. Continue to read your bloodcurdling stories, you'll soon realize that your creativity will be sharper, your self-esteem profounder and your strength of spirit fiercer than most. Just words, Jean-Marie-Marc, just words."

''Will you accompany me, Monsieur?"

''Yes, of course.''

"Really?" Jean-Marie-Marc asked, stunned. He then flashed his magnificent smile, eyes filled with joy. "Thank you, thank you very much." He would have his father all to himself.

As the carriage hobbled down the paved Parisian streets, and then the non-paved roads leading out of the capital towards the Loire, the boy read The Count of Monte Cristo by Dumas Père, looking relaxed as he sat next to the window.

"I found it impressive that you chose this difficult novel, Jean-Marie-Marc. I posit that you discovered it in the library?"

The boy turned red. "Yes, Monsieur, I will return it promptly. Monsieur Luthod suggested it, and I found it on the lower shelf prior to coming to Paris. I hope I have not offended."

"Jean-Marie-Marc, I admire your interest at your tender age. No, you have my permission to peruse at any time in the library. It is impressive. I am very proud of the adjustments you have had to make. You're a remarkable young man and my love for you is infinite. I will always be there for you."

The boy burst into tears, unable to control his sobs for a long time. "I will make you proud, Monsieur."

"You already have," Jean-Louis-Pierre answered solemnly as he clasped the child's wrist and gathered him into his arms. "You already have, Jean-Marie-Marc," the Duke repeated, holding his son close to his heart.

The coach continued its route to the ancestral castle in the Loire. Jean-Marie-Marc, like any young child who had experienced more than his share of emotional distress, fell soundly asleep in his father's arms.

An hour and a half later, the Dukes' favorite inn was in sight. "I am famished, young man. Let's stop, stretch our legs and we will then,

I forgot the English words, *nous dégusterons un bon déjeuner*." Father and son climbed down the steps of the carriage. Jean-Louis-Pierre began the conversation which he knew was in the boy's mind.

"What happened last evening at the opéra, Jean-Marie-Marc?"

"Is Madame Gabriella de Conte Thornsen, my mother, Monsieur?" the child blurted out, staring at the aristocrat like any six-year-old too young to control his emotions.

Flabbergasted, Jean-Louis-Pierre remained silent for a long time. The boy, just as relentless, continued to stare at his father.

"Yes."

"Why did she throw me away, Monsieur," the boy retorted, tears once again flooding his eyes. "Why do you stare at her with such love?"

Jean-Louis-Pierre reached for the child and brought him back to sit on his knees. "Did you believe me when we recounted to you on our way back to France on the ship, the story of how we came to realize that a child of mine was living in an orphanage in Ireland?"

The boy nodded.

"Now you will have to believe that your mother Gabriella to this very day is not aware that she has a living child, Jean-Marie-Marc."

Even at that young age, the boy sadly looked away, trying to return to his seat. The ironic glance seemed to say—even you try to deceive me. His father kept his arms firmly around his waist.

"Let me tell you what happened. Your mother of course knew that she was expecting, as she crossed a street, a carriage hit her, she lost consciousness and was taken to our family doctor who worked all night to revive her after he'd delivered you. When she woke up, she was told that you had died. Since she had lost many babies before you, it was not a great surprise. You are a miracle child, Jean-Marie-Marc. You know the rest of the story."

"But why did you let them take me away?" he declared angrily. "Where were you?"

"In prison," the Duke replied, his tone stern.

"In prison? YOU?" He stared in shock at the tall Frenchman.

"A long story. Gabriella was on her way to visit me and too quick to cross a street. It was a very difficult time in French history. I will explain one day, but for now you need to understand that your mother is unaware she has a son who is very much alive and well. Let's return to the carriage. It will be dark before we reach the castle. We have time, Jean-Marie-Marc."

Arriving at the impressive castle de Bourbonne, late in the evening, Marie was surprised to see father and son arriving alone. The boy, exhausted from the long journey, needed no supper, just a warm bed and a soft pillow to lay his head upon. His father followed him to his apartment, watching as the young master succumbed to fatigue.

Jean-Louis-Pierre stared at the Louis XVI clock positioned atop the mantle of the large fireplace. Two logs had been lit by the young servant, Armand, the flames reaching high into the hearth.

Staring at his son, he recognized that imperturbable glare—Gaby's exact expression when he'd thwarted an activity she longed to pursue. He had been so afraid during their marriage for her safety, she wound up as a little bird in a cage. Her singing at the opera had been forbidden, an immense sacrifice for her. After all, her operatic contract had been the reason for leaving America. His insane jealousy, both in Paris and Italy, had also caused her great loneliness and sadness. He was often gone, especially while in Italy, so sharing her with anyone became an insurmountable task for him.

Sometimes, her emerald eyes left nothing to divine. Jean-Marie-Marc's glance after the revelation did not leave much to the imagination, either. His mother's impertinence shone through. No doubt the boy had not believed or accepted the facts that his father had just shared.

Unconvinced, the child had not pursued the questioning. He loved Madame Marie, and he was returning to her. Concerning his father, he no longer knew how he felt toward him. His mother had finessed this sordid story to get rid of him and continue with her singing in the large opera houses of Europe. He had been a burden that she'd quickly discarded. One thing was for certain as far as his mother was concerned, he still hated her, even more so now, aware that she had lied to his father!

The following morning, Jean-Marie-Marc walked down to the main kitchen for his breakfast. In the absence of the Duke, the practice had been overlooked, however today the master was in the house and there was no question to serve breakfast to the young master in the servant's quarter. Promptly, Marie gathered him and brought him back to the morning room. Jean-Louis-Pierre awaited his arrival.

"Good morning, young man. You slept well, I reckon."

"Yes, thank you. I was not good company last evening, Monsieur."

His father smiled and remained silent for a long time. Desiring to give a rest to the subject abhorred the day before in the carriage, Jean-Louis-Pierre complimented him on his academic progress. He would have lied a million lies to catch that smile.

"I will have to return to the United States for approximately three months, Jean-Marie-Marc. I will return in late September for a short time and then again in early December. We will feast our first Christmas together. I want you to continue to study and excel in all subjects, Jean-Marie-Marc, for before I leave I will register you at the Lycée Louis le Grand. You will stay in the ancestral home and will be taken to school. It's a short distance from our hôtel particulier."

"Will I be left alone in that large home?"

"Of course not, the servants are there and Madame Bonnard will delight your stomach with her culinary feasts—everyday. I was sent away to boarding school, it was difficult, as you well aware know. You will stay in your home." The child's expression expressed sorrow.

"Will Madame Marie stay in Loire?" he asked waiting to be disappointed.

"Of course, not. Marie will stay with you during the week, and the two of you might decide to return to Normandie or in Loire for vacations. That will be her decision, as well as your teachers."

Jean-Marie-Marc's face lit up. He jumped back on his father's knees and, without thinking, kissed him on both cheeks. "That will be just fine," he murmured, "just fine." Staring outside of his bedroom window onto the unfurling hills, he rested his head on the Duke's chest. "I will be the first in my class, Monsieur, and will receive the Médaille d'Honneur monthly," he declared. "Thank you."

Jean-Louis-Pierre ruffled his son's hair and held him for a long time before the boy moved into his dressing room. Washed and dressed, he returned to the salon in his apartment and put on his shoes. "On to breakfast, or rather to the petit déjeuner, Father," he caught himself and continued in French, flashing his beautiful smile.

After leaving the castle in Loire, Jean-Louis-Pierre contemplated that perhaps, if a full reconciliation occurred before June, Gaby might decide to take the boy with them. He could return him in time to start school in late September.

Too much dreaming and far away plans. Time to focus on the work at hand, he reminded himself.

CHAPTER FORTY-SEVEN

Gaby woke red-eyed from a sleepless night. She slipped into her red satin robe embroidered with white roses. She tied the sash snugly around her waist while ambling to the window, a half-eaten croissant with raspberry jam in her hands. Her maid had brought two newspapers, along with the operatic gazette that included the latest critique of her performance, and naturally the sordid details of the child and his almost immediate departure from the loge.

The article continued with images of the child running down the wide veined marble staircase, Jean-Louis close on his heels. Both father and son had been caricatured by the many drafters while waiting for the couple to step into the Duke's carriage before the horses bounded forward to an uncertain location.

Jean-Louis had not returned to his loge that night, and Philippe and Cunnan had left soon afterward, she'd been told. She shook her short bobbed coiffure and allowed a few tears to slip down her lovely, heart shaped face. "I presume I should tolerate once more Jean-Louis's lack of civility," she murmured, "How quickly he had forgotten their love... or perhaps a mistress had been there all along?"

Lately, she'd thought that perhaps a reconciliation had been possible. Once more he'd betrayed her and Philippe had witnessed the event. He must have known. Was he there to soften the blow? She picked up the paper once more and stared at the child who appeared mesmerized by the venue's magnificence. She possessed not a single doubt that the boy was his. The resemblance, uncanny.

Why would he inflict such pain and embarrassment when now the *tout Paris* recognized that a reconciliation might be in the offing? And

Philippe and Cunnan? She swallowed hard and, feeling dejected, dropped the paper onto the thick carpet.

A knock on the door brought her out of her thoughts.

"Madame, His Eminence is downstairs."

She nodded. "Let him in, Madeleine."

A few minutes later, unwilling to attend to her toilette, she trailed her maid down the stairs. Philippe and Cunnan both awaited her in the foyer.

Philippe came forward first.

"We need to talk, Gabriella, an important development has occurred that will affect your life and all those who love you. I have taken the opportunity to cancel your next two evenings at the opera."

"Philippe, have you gone mad?" she retorted, furious as her emerald eyes sent daggers at the cleric.

"It is important, Gabriella," advised Cunnan, walking right behind the prelate. "We cannot divulge the new development in this affair, but your presence is paramount in the unfolding story. Do not fear, Gabriella, the ensuing result will be rewarding and heartwarming, but that is all we can reveal at this time." Cunnan came closer and enveloped her in his arms. "Everything will be alright, Gabriella."

Stunned, she pushed him away, stumbling slightly prior to steadying herself by grasping the intricate bronze railing of a nearby rosewood table.

"I think we should leave for the ancestral home in Loire, as quickly as possible, Gabriella." Philippe said unperturbed.

"For the Loire? Have you both lost your minds? Does it pertain to Jean-Louis and the child? I do not care!" she screamed. "Just another impropriety from my former husband. Please let me be. I am perfectly fine. His intrinsic infidelities while I tried to save his life from the guillotine will never, never be forgiven. I was betrayed... again. I saw the child. No one can refute the resemblance, but life goes on and my life is quite good, so there is no need for this great theater to rehash its sordid ending. Jean-Louis has a son. Good—his lineage is now guaranteed. Another woman gave him what I could not. All good. It's been over in my heart for quite some time. Please, let me be. It is not such a great surprise."

Both men stared at her. An answer was not necessary.

Philippe strode to a canopied chair by the start of a long corridor and sat. "It is more complex than that, Gaby. We will wait for you. You know how much I love you, my dear cousin, and Cunnan has always been devoted to you. But this situation is so uncommon, you must trust us. Only Jean-Louis-Pierre can shed light on the story and, although you've always known my dislike for him... my reservations about his wayward attitudes... I will not excoriate his reaction to a most unusual circumstance."

"Cunnan?"

"I cannot add to Philippe's statements, Gaby. We need to take the road as quickly as feasible."

Flabbergasted, she nodded. "All has been taken care of, Philippe?"

"Yes, Gaby."

"Very well." She turned on her heel and headed upstairs. On the first landing, she stared at the two men she adored, knowing that her well-being was foremost in their hearts as well. What had Jean-Louis schemed to distress her this time?

***

The three hour ride to the ancestral home in Loire took place in silence. By early afternoon they'd passed the Duchesse de Pleyssis's estate. The Chapel, erected to the right of the property, was barely visible from the path except for its unusually high steeple.

Cunnan had lowered his head to Gaby. "I recall a certain young beauty from Louisiana walking down the aisle of this venerated chapel."

"I recall distinctly wishing to escape Jean-Louis's grasp and forego all vows on my wedding day," Gaby scoffed.

Cunnan burst out laughing.

"In retrospect I should have," she responded bitterly.

He looked at her with a half questioning smile.

She smiled back. "No, perhaps not. Those heady early days together were some of the happiest moments in my life." She sighed and glanced back at the vanishing castle. "I paid dearly for the bliss! And after all these years, I am still entangled in his disturbing and controlling life. What am I doing here, Cunnan? Philippe?"

She stared at both men. "For God's sake, explain!"

Philippe reached for her hand. "You will soon know, Gaby. We are here for you, but it is not our place to explain."

Angry, she pulled her hand away and turned her back to her most trusted friends, then parted the covering on the window and stared at the river that tumbled against beds of wide flat rocks. At times, small cascades drifted on white and gray shining pebbles, only to resume its raucous descent into the heavy brush of the forest. She'd spent so many hours hunting with Jean-Louis in these very same woods as they'd entertained frequent guests.

Less than an hour later, Cunnan bobbed his head to the castle. "Are you ready, my dearest?" he questioned with obvious concern.

She shrugged, resigned. "I've been through worse!" she replied.

The old Scottish seafarer grinned. "I quite admire your lack of decorum in your prompt retorts, Gabriella—very American." He clasped her hand and tapped it gently.

The wide alleys of the breathtaking manicured gardens reminiscent of Vaux Le Vicomte's castle, the former propriétée of Nicholas

Fouquet, Marquis de Belle île, former Superintendent of Finances under Louis XIV, who'd been imprisoned by the monarch for a supposed diversion of French funds. Vaux le Vicomte had from most accounts been the inspiration for the architectural prowess of the Sun King's palace, Versailles.

Fouquet, a brilliant, life loving, member of the Noblesse de Robe, a class of nobles who had been given titles and lands or at times had been part of the Judiciary and administration, had with his superb soirées and extravagant feasts and lifestyle angered the monarch. The poor man paid with his liberty, twenty-nine years in prison and the confiscation of his properties.

Jean-Louis-Pierre's lineage came from the Noblesse d'épée, the oldest class of nobility who owned large estates and owed military allegiance to the nation. Jean-Louis-Pierre had been raised in this affluent milieu, and his grand castle in the Loire told of his privileged ancestry.

At the entrance of the castle, the usual calm and guarded manners from the guardsmen in the *guérites* appeared questionable.

"*Madame, bonjour, quelle joie*!" Bertrand communicated as he looked inside the carriage. He quickly bade a younger man to the main estate to announce her arrival.

Upon the carriage's arrival in front of the grand entrance, all the household servants were lined up awaiting her appearance. Many she had depended upon during the terrible days of the Commune when the Duke had been imprisoned. Others new and curious, most certainly aware of the gossip that pre-dated her present fame, looked in her direction.

She nodded her head as she stepped down from the carriage and beheld Marie, Jean-Louis-Pierre adored governess, who anxiously ogled the incoming group. Dressed in a stern gray dress with a white, starched officer collar, the skeletal mistress walked down the wide marble stairway holding firmly to the balustrade to greet Gaby personally. Quickly she re-directed her gaze to Cunnan.

"The Duke left three hours ago. The boy and his tutor went missing early in the afternoon."

"Where?" Cunnan replied, looking stunned. "Where is Jean-Louis-Pierre ?"

Philippe marched closer, Cunnan's distressed glare sent chills up his spine. Like his former relative, the man never appeared unnerved. "A new development, Philippe," Cunnan shared softly, his glance to the former Duchesse. "The child and Claude, his teacher, have gone missing." Aghast, the cleric looked back to Gabriella, who sauntered toward her old familiar grounds.

Gaby now alone by the stairs, dismissed the staff and swept in the foyer of the residence, toward her former music room. Nothing had changed. She sat on the piano bench, not touching the keys, reminiscing of days gone by.

The Duke's study was located on the East side of the estate. The two men entered the impressive room, Marie following close behind. She closed and locked the door.

"We're all indisposed," Marie exclaimed. "Bertrand and Yves have been in the village and to the houses of the cottagers along the path. One young shepherd seemed to think that he saw Claude and the boy sitting by one of the tables where they regularly had their *goûter,* snacks, outside of the property by the stream.

"I usually let my sheep graze nearby and they always share their lunches with me," he told Fernand, the butler and I. He continued on with too many inconsequential details, but then he mentioned that he saw a servant in livery attire step down from a carriage, which he believed belonged to the dowager de Pleyssis. A heated discussion followed with Claude and the boy, and the three climbed into the carriage and departed. Naturally, after Jean-Louis-Pierre learned of the situation, he left immediately for his grandmother's castle. We have not heard anything since then, which was about five hours ago, Messieurs. Daylight is on the wane. I'm beside myself with worry."

"Do not fear, Marie. Philippe and I will go now. Please take care of Gabriella and be silent over the provenance of the child. We will send word as soon as we have arrived at the Duchesses' castle. Please send word if he should return by another route."

Both strode to the stables and grasped their own saddles. Philippe lifted his chasuble and tucked it inside the belt of his pants. His many years riding on his plantation South of New Orleans proved to be helpful throughout his life in Europe, even in Rome at Vatican City. He'd assisted Pius the 9th, dressed as a peasant, as he'd escaped from Victor Emmanuel I as the Piedmont Sardinian monarch tried to consolidate the Italian peninsula. Of course, they'd lost the Papal States and Rome had been reunified with Italy under one king, but they still had their heads and the Pontiff remained the undeniable master over Vatican City.

Less than thirty minutes later they were en route to Madame de Pleyssis's residence down the road closer to Vouvray and the river banks. Darkness was setting in. The last remnants of leaves crushed under their horses' hooves crackled. they rode as fast as their mounts could take them. An hour later, night had set in. The castle was within sight. They gave their name to the men in charge at the *guérites*. At first no impression was made and the Duchess's security kept them at gun's length, until Philippe showed his identity card—Cardinal of Notre Dame. The stamp as the Pope's Nuncio in Paris kept the guard interested. His simple stature inserted doubts in the man's demeanor.

Aristocrats had suffered unimaginable deaths during both the 1789 revolution and the Civil War that followed the Prussians invasion of Paris in 1871. The landowners of the Vendée, the belly of the Loire, had been persecuted to a horrific extent. Security was on its guard.

"We are friends of Jean-Louis-Pierre de Pleyssis, the Duke, and if he is here, can you please announce our arrival. That is all that we ask. We will wait here."

"Unmount your horse and come with us!" the chief ordered without relenting his skepticism.

They obeyed the request respectfully.

Less than a quarter of an hour later, Jean-Louis-Pierre entered the cramped room. He smiled as he shook his head and dismissed the guards back to their post. He continued to stare as they walked away, until they reached the entrance to the castle.

"The boy is safe," he spoke with a great smile. My grandmother read the papers and essentially as he sat daily with his tutor in the prairie outside the estate, she came calling each day in her carriage, bringing sweets and amusing anecdotes about my childhood. Essentially my grandmother had been talking to Jean-Marie-Marc prior to our soirée in Paris at the opéra unbeknown to me. Neither of them thought that it would be inappropriate to learn about MY childhood! Seriously, I never knew I had that much restraint in my bones to withstand the present situation." A great sigh of relief came from the two men. Jean-Louis-Pierre walked back outside and called out to the guards. "Bring us some well-aged whiskey-a full bottle, perhaps half a dozen!" He let his tall and muscular body fall in the old chair that could not have accommodated comfortably a lesser man. Cunnan could not suppress a smile.

"Gabriella is in the castle with Marie, I promised to send word. Tell one of the guards to harness their mount quickly. We will stay here tonight but I want them to relax knowing you've handled the situation and that the boy is safe."

"Thank you, Cunnan. I presume you divulged the truth to Gaby?"

"No, we have not."

The Duke appeared relieved. "Thank you," he retorted solemnly.

"But Jean-Louis-Pierre, what was the boy's tutor thinking, seriously?" Philippe questioned.

"I was ready to strangle him, but like his mother, the boy stated that it was his fault and no one else's. My grandmother? *Eh bien,* she was contrite as well. I no longer know what to think. We have been talking all afternoon." The tall aristocrat raised his chin, staring at the beam in the ceiling. "I just do not think that she could have ordered such an act. I was her world as a child and most assuredly still am. She would not have taken the heir of our illustrious family and sent him to an orphanage."

The two men looked at one another as two accomplices disbelieving what they had just heard. "Your grandmother abhorred Gabriella from the very beginning!" Philippe shouted, obfuscated. "The lies that she fed you after your imprisonment—and her perfidy that you chose to believe over my dear cousin's total devotion to you caused your separation!"

He nodded, and for an instant, his deep blue eyes filled with tears. He swallowed hard, inhaled deeply and promptly retrieved his composure. "All true, Philippe, although she disliked Gaby, your and Gaby's roots are Piedmont Sardinia's old lineage aristocrats. There is the fine line that I hate to evoke."

"Essentially, if Gabriella had been of a lesser birth, sending a common child to an orphanage would have been a right decision?" Philippe retorted.

The Duke did not respond.

"Would you have married Gabriella if she came from a peasant background?"

His reply did not take long. "Yes, a million times yes. Gaby stole my heart forever."

Cunnan bought into it. Phillippe's half belief spoke volumes. Essentially, the cleric doubted the aristocrat and everything he stood for.

"Will you give me the benefit of the doubt, Philippe?"

The cleric did not reply.

"You do not erase centuries of culture in a day, Philippe, you of all people should know that."

"Two wrong does not make a right, Jean-Louis-Pierre," Philippe answered calmly, his thoughts returning back to his ten-year-old self in the surgeon's office of the Vatican. He had not been razed fully, 'just in case' the assistant to the doctor had said. Two years later, the operation had been unsuccessful, his voice had changed, he had not been chosen for the chorale and he had been sent back to New Orleans—castrated.

"My grandmother thinks it might expose a dishonorable conduit on the part of my cousin's wife to safeguard the fortune her sons would inherit if Gabriella remained barren. I do not know. My sister in law..."

"The wife of your cousin, Admiral de Pleyssis?" Cunnan murmured in shock.

"Like me he was in the Northern Sea. However, she, Josephine, was in Paris. She is Madame de Pleyssis, as well."

"According to my grandmother, she's dying of consumption in the Aquitaine where she is from. She might have had more to gain from this desperate situation—her children certainly."

"Enough excuses, it might be, Jean-Louis-Pierre, that Madame de Pleyssis is correct, but if you want a reconciliation with Gabriella after the revelation, I would advise strongly to take her side, no matter what you think or would like to believe. Your grandmother's lies destroyed your marriage. You're at the crossroads again, Jean-Louis-Pierre. She might give you another chance, but let's be clear. Gabriella needs to be first and foremost, you're one and only consideration in your decision." Cunnan did not mince his words.

"I know, and I will. If it takes my lifetime, Gaby will always be my one and only." The Duke nodded and reached for the glass offered to him by the guard. He twirled the dark brown liquor in its crystal glass and gulped it down, prior to serving himself another glass.

"The two of us have grown. Jean-Marie-Mark is now part of the equation."

CHAPTER FORTY-EIGHT

Later that evening, after the arrival of the servant's announcement that the child had been retrieved safely at the dowager's castle, Marie found Gaby in the library, reading while sipping a cup of chamomile tea.

"Madame, we have just received word that the gentlemen will return tomorrow early."

Gaby nodded.

"The cook has prepared a *pigeon en blanquette,* one of your favorites." Marie blushed. "Which room would you like us to prepare?"

Gaby smiled. "Our room will serve well, but I will take my dinner in the dining room. Thank you," she added.

Her luggage was taken to her ancient night spot on the second floor. She followed the servant, strode into her former apartment, and discovered that nothing had changed.

The large mural picture, the Kiss by Francesco Hayes, next to Bernini's bust of Louis the XIV, a Bourbon King, and as the queen of this ancient household her painted portrait by Claude Monet, a close friend along with his wife, Camille Doncieux, still loomed high above the fireplace in the salon. She ambled down the corridor which led to Jean-Louis's study, his big desk in the same place. She touched the deep veined oak. Here, too, not much had changed, portraits of the two of them during their idyllic years framed the desk on all three sides. She sat in his chair, staring at the long and wide burgundy velour and satin canapè. They had been so happy then.

Marie walked in. "Dinner is ready whenever you are, Madame."

"Thank you, I'll wash up and be right down."

She strode to the rose Italian marble bathroom, her very favorite, to her surprise, Shalimar, her perfume in its original vaporisateur from the house of Guerlain founded in 1822 still occupied the center of the marble table on its purple velour pillow in her dressing room. Even more surprising, she discovered that most of her gowns were still perfectly hung with their matching slippers below. She smiled. "Return to past follies!" she murmured to herself. After she washed up, she made her way downstairs.

She returned back to the bedroom an hour and a half later. Her bed looked inviting, the sheets turned down. She caressed the satin cover of the down eiderdown and fluffed the white embroidered pillow case, slipped off her boots and began to remove her dress and petticoats.

After all these years, she'd kept up the practice that her former husband had begun when he'd bought her first dress at Madame Chapotier's store on the rue de Rivoli. The seams on the side of the torso covered with tiny pearls matching the silks or velour of the attire - 'much more practical, Gaby, for our passionate existence'- he'd laughed, spreading his large hands under the tiny buttons of the opening to fondle and caress her waist to her voluptuous breasts. Their lives had been passionate.

The practice of side openings she had maintained for the sole reason that it provided independence when she returned late at night. Most of the time she did not require a maid to help her undress. Funny how simple, insignificant tasks or words compiled simply for an ordinary sentence brought to recall a particular individual stuck from one's past. She slipped into one of her old nightgowns, which to her astonishment was recently cleaned and pressed. The scent of lavender teased her senses.

Stop with stupid memories, Gabriella! The child obviously had been delivered as she'd lost their own son. Nothing but a farce. She rolled in bed, angry at herself to have caved under pressure from her two friends. Tomorrow is another day, and I'll soon return to Paris.

The following morning ,Juliette, her former chambermaid, came in with croissants, café crème and raspberry jelly.

"*Bonjour Madame, vos préférés.*" She placed a wooden bed tray and covered it with a white embroidered tablecloth as she expertly transferred over the silver tray with the petit déjeuner.

"*Je vous remercie, Juliette, de bons souvenirs en fait.*" The servants could not do enough to please her. She'd been missed and it pleased her. She ate, dressed and went downstairs. What today would bring, no one knew. It was not long before the men returned. She looked out the window. This time Jean-Louis accompanied them, the boy followed closely. She watched Claude, the teacher, march with his head down toward the apple orchard where he and his father shared a cottage. Marie joined the group, holding Jean-Marie-Marc in a long and warm embrace.

She'd always wonder how this homely person, who personified a severe and unyielding demeanor, could offer unconditional tenderness and acceptance to those she loved. She became beautiful!

As the men gave the reins to the stable boys, she watched as the child held his favorite mare not wanting to let go.

Gaby advanced to the great doors.

The boy walked in first. "I am happy that you are safe and sound, Jean-Marie-Marc," she said softly in English as he passed by.

Tears filled his brilliant green eyes as he stared at her and held her gaze. She was mesmerized.

"Merci, Madame," he replied.

Taken back momentarily by the bizarre sense of recognition of someone other than Jean-Louis, she felt his hands clasp her elbows, turned her around and draw her into his arms.

"I adore you Gaby!" he declared for all to hear and kissed her. That behavior had not changed. It had his signature on it. She waited for the boy to be taken away by Marie.

"Now I want to know, why was I brought here?"

"Let's move on to the sitting room," Jean-Louis-Pierre urged, clasping her hand. She shoved it aside, but he strode behind her, anyway.

Philippe marched quickly to Gaby and Cunnan winked.

"The news is good. Let's not look as if we're going to a funeral. The arrival of a child in a family should be celebrated." He winked a second time at Gaby, but she did not smile in return.

"We are no longer a family, Cunnan!" she countered promptly.

As usual, when the old seaman sensed that his silence brought more rewards than a specific retort, Cunnan bit his lips and gave a smile that spoke volumes. It usually amused her. At this very moment, it did not.

The boy had slipped unnoticed into the corridor as he waited to be admitted into the same room as the adults. The protocol of the ancient French nobility and its attitude towards young children still to be absorbed and practiced by Jean-Marie-Marc. The reply by his mother had taken its toll. His facial features froze with dejection. He finally followed his governess in the grand dining room.

Gaby turned and observed the boy as he stepped into the dining room. His appearance reminded her of someone, but who?

Jean-Louis had loved her, of that she was certain. Perhaps he had been attracted by an English woman who resembled her. Perhaps not a mistress at all. Perhaps, he had succumbed and accepted the ideals of a lineage with aristocratic descendance? Something she could not offer to him. She almost wished the boy was his cousin's child, a love child from the Admiral?

She looked at Cunnan as she walked to the large bay windows and solar openings that brought in the crisp winter clarity that she'd so treasured years ago. Her music room had been to the right of the salon—with the same exposure. In winter, trees stripped of their leaves, erect in stature reached to the sky. At times they gave umbrage to squirrels covered in thick winter fur while they burrowed deep into their trunks for warmth and a spare cubicle where nuts could be retrieved easily.

Miniscule birds perched on the stripped limbs. What sustained them besides the bowls of grains she'd placed in strategic places she did not know. The practice had ceased when the gardener had stated that prolonged feeding by humans hasten their deaths. "Quickly they'd come to rely on a provenance that may not be forthcoming, Madame," he'd reproached her.

In the spring and summer, all the windows would be open and her voice reached octaves that sometimes surprised her. A significant time kept her staring out the window. She turned back, caught in happy reminiscences and faced Jean-Louis-Pierre as he observed her.

"Good memories, I hope," he said.

She did not respond and noticed the child standing by the open doors. She smiled at him.

Jean-Marie-Marc appeared a bit more relaxed when the servant offered refreshments.

"Cognac for Monsieur, whiskey, Monsieur Cunnan, Your Eminence?" he asked. "And Madame, we have a special reserve of Cristal just for you. Monsieur Jean-Marie-Marc, *une surprise*, *un flan Irlandais,* an Irish pudding... still warm, just for you." The old butler smiled as he bent painfully forward, reaching for the pot on the silver platter held by a servant. He offered it to the child prior to exiting the room.

"Thank you so very much, Monsieur Fernand. I like it immensely. Please convey my appreciation to the sous chef, Madame Linette."

Immobile, the boy lingered in the doorway. Both Philippe and Jean-Louis-Pierre turned and noticed him.

"A little ghost is following us," Cunnan remarked kindly.

The duke could not return the smile.

Philippe and Gabriella stared at one another.

"Jean-Marie-Marc, I did not notice you. Where is Marie?"

"She was needed in the kitchen," he answered without elaboration. "I wanted to say, Monsieur, that it was not Claude's fault. It was mine." His convictions brought him forward and closer to his father. He turned to stare at Philippe "Your Eminence, I do not want Claude to be punished for a deed that I have committed. He fought hard against the idea... "

"Very well, we understand, Jean-Marie-Marc, but he's nineteen years old and you're six. He should have known better," the Duke replied, annoyed but ready to place this affair behind him. Gaby needed to know what had happened.

"Monseigneur Henry find me thick headed, Monsieur, 'you're a force to be reckon with Ian,' he would say." Philippe and Cunnan stared at one another, stunned.

"Did you say Monseigneur Henry?" Cunnan repeated.

"Yes," the boy replied sheepishly.

"Not England? In Ireland?" Cunnan pursued.

"Yes Sir," he responded with his Irish accent, visibly perturbed.

"But," he pressed as he approached his father. "Monsieur, Claude is not at fault. I am. Please, he is a wonderful teacher," he said in broken French, his emotions forbidding him to explain himself distinctly in a foreign language. "I have learned a valuable lesson. I will abide by Claude's rules in the future, Monsieur. Please."

Gabriella sensed that Jean-Louis was exasperated.

"I understand, Jean-Marie Marc, but now please return to Marie. Topics of importance need to be discussed."

Gaby stepped forward.

"Jean-Louis," she said in French, "we are no longer in the Middle Ages when whipping boys received the punishments for the aristocratic protected class. The boy stated it was his fault. Accept it and go on, please."

She turned back to the boy. "You know, Jean-Marie-Marc," she began, "I lived on a plantation in New Orleans in the Americas."

"A plantation?" the boy interrupted, "with slaves?"

"Until recently the law permitted it, Jean-Marie-Marc, a horrific practice," she said softly in English, "but one that lasted for over two hundred years."

"Were they black?"

"Yes."

"The Masters beat these men if they did not bring in their... how do you say it? Their 'cotton quotas'?"

"Yes, some did. Let me tell you of a story that may apply to your case today. Phillippe, His Eminence, and I lived next door. His plantation and mine are about the same size. Our parents owned slaves to work the fields. In our houses, we had servants like your father has. Their lives were somewhat better than the fields' hands. I know that my mother gave a small salary to my maids and butler." She sighed, blush arose almost immediately from the base of her neck to her cheeks. "One thing was certain, Jean-Marie-Marc, my favorite people to this day were my servants, Tita and Auguste, who raised me and loved me and gave me wonderful rules to live by."

Jean-Louis's shocked expression spoke volume, but he kept quiet.

"Where were your Mother and Father?" The boy asked.

"Both were in New Orleans, but very busy, too busy to tend to their children."

"Philippe and I..."

"Your Eminence?" He confirmed, staring at the Cardinal.

"Gabriella and I are first cousins, Jean-Marie-Marc," Philippe replied.

"Cousins? Oh, my God!" He took a few steps backward.

"One of the men we both adored and who loved us back immensely was a Negro called Toby," Gaby continued. "My mother appointed him to watch over us simply because of his size. He was enormous, Jean-Marie-Marc, and kind to the very core. Philippe and I had wanted to ride on the banks of the river for a very long time to meet up with one of our good friends down river. Toby had forbidden it. A lot of unsavory men conducted business in that area. One morning at dawn, while Toby still attended to his many chores, I mounted my horse and rode to Philippe's plantation. All were sleeping save a few sla..."

"... slaves, "the boy said. "Harriett Beecher Stowe, Uncle Tom's Cabin ... our tutor in the monastery read us the novel, Madame."

"How long ago was that, Jean-Louis-Marc?" Philippe questioned, flabbergasted that a novel that had essentially forged the path for the American Civil War in 1852 had been read to a five-year-old.

"I'd just turned five, Your Eminence. Four of the other pupils were seven, *l'age de raison.*"

Gaby looked up to Philippe, "yes, it was a terrible time in our history, but returning back to our story," she said as she moved closer and knelt down in front of the boy, "I brought Philippe his horse, and we both galloped down alongside our beloved Mississippi River. Naturally we were caught, returned to our respective plantations and guess who received the punishment that we so deserved—Toby." She paused for a moment, a vivid memory of being made to watch this man being secured to a post and whipped until the skin on his back bled.

"Did they whip him?" the boy asked.

"The moral of the story," she replied, "is that our actions matter, at any age."

The story was over for the boy. His eyes turned from utter interest to deep disgust as he glared at her.

"Yes, Madame," he replied in English with his Irish lilt, "our actions do change lives."

Stunned by his words, she did not speak.

The Duke called for Marie. She walked in and scrutinized the boy, who was studying with great intent his father's reaction. The child himself broke the uncomfortable silence.

"I am sorry, Monsieur, for my ignorant actions that caused you some worrisome moments. It was my fault." He turned on his heel, too proud to pause by Marie and show his tear-filled eyes.

All stared at the little fellow, so seasoned at his tender age.

"Jean-Marie-Marc," the tall aristocrat called after him, "tell Claude to resume his lessons. I believe he returned to the cottage with his father. Dinner will be served in two hours."

The boy turned back to look at his father. "Thank you, Monsieur, I'm on my way." Without a second to spare, he smiled at his audience.

Philippe gawked at Gaby, who did not acknowledge in the child the evidence of her very own smile. With his tear-soaked cheeks, he dashed out the door. Marie grinned at this little fellow, who reminded her so much of Jean-Louis-Pierre as a young child under her tutelage. She winked at him and followed the boy into the foyer.

CHAPTER FORTY-NINE

The Duke glanced at all in attendance. "It is time," he said.

He paced to Gaby, clasped her elbows with the intent to lead her out of his study. Once more, promptly, she pushed him aside.

He sighed. "Let's walk to the library."

All followed. Something momentous was in the air, Gaby realized as she silently scanned her companions.

Arriving at the mahogany paneled room, filled floor to ceiling with ancient, revered books and manuscripts stacked in orderly rows, Cunnan was the first to settle into in a great cognac leather chair. Philippe stayed close to Gabriella.

"Please sit on the sofa, Gabriella," Philippe murmured as he tried to take her hand and direct her across the vast library where a comfortable salon faced an immense fireplace that could have engulfed her and her companions.

She stiffened, banning all physical contact, shoved aside her cousin's hand. She'd had enough of their senseless secrets. "I want to leave immediately!" she shouted in pure frustration.

Philippe clasped her hand. "Come, Gaby, let's sit. It is of great importance—essential, my dearest, that you listen."

She stared at all present, flabbergasted. She swallowed hard and made her way to the sofa.

Her former husband perched on the corner edge of his desk, a small manila envelope within his reach, a larger packet wrapped in common brown butcher block paper tied neatly by an extra wide, black knotted cord.

"Well?" she questioned, waiting for the great secret to be divulged. She stared at her former life partner.

"Gaby, Jean-Marie-Marc is our son," the Duke stated calmly.

"Jean-Louis-Pierre!" Cunnan jumped from his seat, unable to comprehend what had just happened. He had expected a softer approach, even from Jean-Louis-Pierre.

Philippe gripped Gaby's hand, horrified by Jean-Louis' blunt statement.

Gaby stared him down with rancor. "You have reached a new level of baseness, Jean-Louis. Our son?" she murmured. "Are you mad?"

"Cunnan and I did not walk Campostello," he said. "Instead, we traveled to England and then to Ireland, where Philippe met us and helped us retrieve the child."

She stared at all of them as if she'd entered another medium. "Philippe?" She covered his hand with hers and tried to sit up. He caressed her hand as he nodded his confirmation. "Jean-Louis spoke the truth."

"You were expecting when I was in prison," Jean-Louis persisted, although his voice broke for an instant.

"Yes, I lost the baby. Nothing new... you know that. I was not meant to create another life." Swiftly, she stood and shook her mane. "I saw the corpse in the bassinet next to me, Jean-Louis. That night, Durand saved my life! That was also the night that the good doctor, the first man I trusted in Paris, died of a major aneurysm. I went to the Cathedrale a month later when they honored his life with a high Mass. He saved my life that night," she repeated, probing the fog of those long-ago memories, "that very same life that would have done everything in her power to save yours! A grave error in retrospect!"

He acknowledged the statement, his jaw tightening as he studied her.

"Evelyn was there... I recall, he fought hard for me and promised I'd have a pretty bébé... I'd made him promise to do everything in his power to have the child recognized as a de Pleyssis, to have your name in case my days were numbered..." She sobbed and demanded, "How can you? How can all of you, people I trust and adore, make me relive those horrific moments? Philippe... I shared with you, the turbulence in my room, someone talking about England..." She stopped, a frisson of pure shock jolted her memory as she rifled to retrieve the traumatic moments.

She pressed her fingertips to her forehead. "I heard a cry when the child was delivered." She swallowed hard, swiping at her nose.

"You did, Gaby. It was Jean-Marie-Marc," Jean-Louis-Pierre lifted the small package. "The incredible story is here, Gaby." He lifted the envelope and the small package that he'd received the day before they were to leave for Spain. "A lot of facts still need to be exposed, Gaby. I cannot refute his resemblance, your emerald eyes and smile, Gaby. Jean-Marie-Marc is ours."

"I saw the child, the following morning, he was dead... blue! "she shouted.

"Jean-Marie-Marc had been kidnapped by then... swept away and taken first to England and then to Ireland. The child in the bassinet was a dead child from the Paris morgue."

Gaby stood suddenly, then dropped onto the dark green Aubusson rug. Marie, who had just entered the room, rushed to Gaby, knelt beside her and quickly waved salt crystals under her nose. She regained her wits as the men picked her up and placed her on the leather sofa.

"Couldn't you have been gentler, Jean-Louis-Pierre. What sort of a monster are you?" Philippe demanded angrily. "Poor Gabriella!"

"No, Philippe, I do not know how," was his terse response.

A soft knock at the door... the effect caused everyone to turn around.

"Monsieur, Madame." The young man walked to the sofa where the men surrounded Gaby.

Marie again placed the salts in front of Gaby's face. She opened her eyes. The scene had not changed. Jean-Louis' story was true then. The child... her child was staring down at her.

It was obvious that the scene had not been lost on Jean-Marie-Marc.

He came closer to his mother. "I am sorry, Madame, I will not be bothersome. I understand the enormous gift God has granted me. I will study hard and be a productive member of this illustrious family," he pronounced solemnly.

She smiled at the sweet face staring down at her. Finding the will to sit up, she extended her hand to Philippe for assistance. He clasped her hand and sat next to his cherished cousin on the canapé.

"Jean-Marie-Marc, please come," she tapped the empty space beside her. Obediently, the young boy strode to the sofa and complied to her wishes but instead he sat at the opposite side from where she sat.

"Jean-Marie-Marc..." she inhaled deeply, "had I known about your existence, my life would have been all about you," she pronounced simply in her American clarity. "I'd prayed and visited Notre Dame every day when I was expecting, hoping that if God would take your father away from me, I'd have given this world, a part of him that would outlive us both. You are this miraculous child, Jean-Marie-Marc and your life will be blessed and filled with happiness from this day onward. Both your father and I will see to that. I am bringing you back home to stay."

The boy glanced at his father. His expression clearly stated his dismay at yet another separation when he'd thought all of life hardship had been in his past.

"Am I leaving you, Monsieur, to live with Madame." His facial features revealed his anxious emotions, his obvious fear that she would find a way to dispose of him.

"You are not going anywhere without me, Jean-Marie-Marc. Your home, your ancestry, your lineage has its place in these lands. They will be yours when I leave this world. You are returning to Paris with us," Jean-Louis-Pierre stated. "We will take you to New York, when Gaby... when your mother leaves for her performances in America." He turned to Gaby.

"Yes, naturally," Gaby instantly replied.

The boy looked away. Like his parents, he knew how to conceal his private thoughts.

That same night, Madame Bonnard finessed a magnificent celebratory dinner. There had been much celebration amongst the adults. After all, thought the Duke, it had not been as traumatic as he'd envisioned. He had his son, and Gaby had agreed to a somewhat communal living. Her home that he had purchased years ago for her was just a few homes away from his. Children rebounded much faster than he'd previously thought... and Gaby, well she was formidable, a true angel that he'd adored from day one. He lifted his flute once more. The last of the desserts had been served and the candles under the sifters filled with aged cognac were warming nicely. Not too fond of Champagne, Jean-Louis's flute was almost full.

"Eh bien, Gaby, Philippe, how about a duet? Jean-Marie-Marc, you have never heard your Mother and your uncle sing. A musical experience like no other. You know they used to sing at the Cathedral in New Orleans on Christmas Eve. They called your mother, 'the voice' on account of the purity of her sounds. Gaby, please? Philippe?"

Both smiled and stood. Philippe strode to the grand piano, prompting Gaby to follow him.

"Do you have a favorite song, Jean-Marie-Marc?" she asked.

The boy shook his head.

"Very well, if Philippe can recall, let's try Jacques Offenbach's widely popular opérettes from La Belle Hélène, and the Boule de Neige. Do you sing, Jean-Marie-Marc? The Ave Maria?"

"Yes, Madame, we had to know it by heart, in Latin."

"Very well."

"Jean-Marie-Marc, come here, you will not want to miss their theatrics." The Duke reached for the boy's hand and gathered him close.

The music began to rise in the grand, spacious dining room, and Gaby as gay and happy as if she was on stage began the aria. At first the boy was quiet, staring at the duo. However, like all children who spontaneously respond to happy sounds and dances, he began to gesture from his position atop his father's lap while sipping surreptitiously the tasty liquid in the flute before him.

By the end of the second aria, he slid down his father's legs and amused everyone as he placed one of his long forefingers on top of his head and started to whirl round and round the room like a marionette. Gaby simultaneously closed in on the act and clasped his hands to steady him. She burst out laughing as she glanced at Jean-Louis, who at the very moment lifted his empty flute.

"I presume it tasted better than lemonade!" he murmured sheepishly to Cunnan.

At the end of the musical duo, the boy clapped and clapped. Up above, on the balcony and in the alcoves overlooking the dining area, the household help looked on in awe of the performance they had just witnessed.

"It has been a long time since such a small and happy gathering revived this beautiful home. Thank you, Madame, Your Eminence," Marie, always in control, whispered. With a glare up at the balcony, everyone promptly dispersed.

The boy just let himself fall unceremoniously onto the satin sofa. "What great fun!" he declared. It was not long before his eyes closed and his beautiful little face rested against a satin pillow.

"It's the first time he's acted like a six-year-old child," Cunnan laughingly said. "He needs a lot more of these moments, Gabriella, *sans le champagne*."

"A momentous time in all our lives," she said softly. "I would like to read the documents at hand, Jean-Louis. It is inconceivable that an act of such horrific magnitude could have transpired." She released a great sigh, fell on the opposite sofa from the sleeping child and hid her face in her hands. Jean-Louis-approached his former wife.

"I know how difficult today and these past hours in particular have been, Gaby." He sat next to her, one arm across the spine of the sofa.

"You're admirable. Our future plans with Jean-Marie-Marc will come to fruition, Gaby. I promise you." The double doors opened once more and Marie entered, gesturing toward the child with her two hands joined, tilted and slipped under her right cheek.

"Yes, excellent idea. I will bring him to his apartment, Marie." Jean-Louis turned to the soprano. "Gaby, will you join us?"

She quickly searched in her skirt side pocket for a mauve embroidered handkerchief. She dried her cheeks and stood behind Jean-Louis-Pierre as he picked up the child. Both climbed the imposing marble staircase and turned left toward the young man's suite, the very same rooms where the Duke had spent a great deal of time during his childhood. He placed his sleeping son onto a pillow and drew a blanket up to his neck.

"Jean-Louis-Pierre, the child needs to undress," Marie exclaimed.

"Let him be!" The Duke laughed. "He had a great day. Let's leave it at that."

The governess shook her head. "You're incorrigible!" she responded as she checked the logs in the fireplace and replaced the burgundy, velour cordon on the eiderdown next to the child's hand. On her way to the door, she approached Gaby, gathered the young woman into her arms and kissed her tenderly. "Do not be sad, Gabriella, a beautiful new addition will complement this age-old family. Jean-Louis-Pierre will ensure his happiness. I assure you, magnificent days are ahead with our little Jean-Marie-Marc. It is a miracle that he has found his way to his grand family."

She lifted her head to the heavens and reached for a golden chain beneath her blouse where a médaille of the Virgin Mary hung. She pressed it to her heart. "A real miracle, dear Gabriella."

The couple waited until Marie had left the room. Gaby had not moved an inch as she stared at the child in the bed. Jean-Louis came close and put his arms around her.

"An imaginable *sang froid*, Gaby. I realized how horrendous the revelation has been. I had sufficient time to get acclimated with the truth, Gaby, but you were plunged into an arctic frozen lake."

He looked up to the decorated ceiling as if an inspiration could descend upon him from the painted heavenly figures. "This blessed denouement works for us, Gaby. I am awestruck at your demeanor today. All your acting skills honed to its utmost for Jean-Marie-Marc's emotional well-being. You were spectacular. I wish it could have been otherwise."

"You had a full three weeks, Jean-Louis! I need time alone now to absorb and make sense of this disclosure." She exited the child's room for a guest room salon nearby.

The Duke kept quiet but clasped her wrist as she walked past him in the hallway. "Gaby, please let's talk—in our room. Time is of the essence."

She paused and looked up to him.

"Yes." She stepped closer to Jean-Louis. He caressed her hair and kissed her forehead. "Marie is correct. It is a miracle that we have retrieved the child. Less than two months ago we were not aware of his existence. The most difficult part of this ordeal for me, Gaby, is that our child has experienced a hard life at such a tender age. I will find the culprits and they will pay for it, wherever the dice fall," he vowed. "You look devastated and exhausted, I will return to our friends in my study. Go and rest, Gaby."

He opened the door. Together, they entered their old room. That night, she knew she may not spend the night alone.

Once the household fell silent, Jean-Louis-Pierre left his library to rejoin her. As he rolled into bed next to her, he dropped a kiss on her short curly hair. "I have no more doubts, Gaby... *l'amour existe encore*."

He drew her to him and, although his engorged manhood was difficult to ignore, he held her for a long moment. Her passionate nature awakened as she recalled the intimate nights spent in that very bed, and she succumbed to the sensuality of the handsome man lying next to her.

"Just tonight, Jean-Louis," she whispered.

He did not answer. Instead his lips searched for hers, silencing her as he ripped her night shirt from her and kissed every inch of her willing body.

"I adore you Gaby," he whispered.

CHAPTER FIFTY

Two days later they all returned to Paris. Philippe and Cunnan departed early in the day. The trip to Paris was quiet. They stopped for a quick déjeuner in Vouvrey.

At times, Gaby felt the need to pinch herself as she struggled to come to term with this new turn of events. A child. A living child that she had carried in her womb. She glanced furtively at him as he read. Would he want to spend time with her in her hôtel particulier? she wondered. He appeared very comfortable in Jean-Louis's ancestral home, it would be the same in Paris. These de Pleyssis' adapted to all sorts of environments.

Upon arrival in Paris, the carriage passed her house. "You'll be staying with us tonight, Gaby?" her former husband tested.

"No, I cannot. I have an early rehearsal tomorrow morning." She turned to Jean-Marie-Marc. "I should be free by treize heures. Maybe lunch?" she asked in English, because the boy always addressed them in English.

Jean-Marie-Marc looked up at his father.

"Am I invited?" her former husband questioned with a broad smile.

"No," she replied emphatically. "A little time alone might do us both a world of good."

She smiled at the former love of her life, who looked at the still questioning child. This situation was not going to be easy, but she stood by her guns. You give up now, she thought and you lose all control. "I will buy the tickets for le Guignol, it should be fun."

The boy did not return her smile and stood stiff when she approached him to hug him. The steps had been unfurled. She stepped down and swallowed hard. The cold air hit her in the face. He will learn to love me, she told herself. She turned on her heels and waved a last goodbye as she headed for the door of her carriage. "A demain!" she climbed in as she lifted her skirt and passed the doors kept open by a new young servant.

Quickly she reached for her coat and put it on without waiting for the old butler to help her. "Merci, Fernand." Her carriage was waiting, the steps curled to their original positions by the footman. She hopped in. Her grand smile disappeared and tears began to spill down her face.

Another difficult odyssey. Jean-Louis had not thwarted the idea of her being alone with their son, although she knew time was on his side. A trapped bird. That was precisely how she felt. The tall aristocrat knew that she would bend the knee sooner or later. He just needed to wait until their return to America. He would not be foolish enough to have Jean-Marie-Marc cross the Atlantic with him on The Tempête. Still three months away, she mused.

She had no time to ponder the past. The likely event was that the child would not deny her lack of knowledge and personal involvement in his six years of horrific experiences. He hated her. Despite his polite demeanor, she hadn't missed his hatred filled glare when he was certain no one was looking. She adored him already, and she would do anything to give him a happy and loving childhood. The price she would have to pay—she knew too well.

The carriage stopped in front of her estate. She waited for the steps to be unrolled and then quickly walked inside and strode right to her apartments on the second floor, oblivious to the questions voiced by her servants.

Less than a week later, Jean-Louis-Pierre strode into his library. He sat in his old Chesterfield chair, this particular fauteuil having accommodated many generations of the de Pleyssis's back sides. He scoffed as he stretched out his long legs and reached into the golden cigar box Gabby had presented to him for his birthday. The double blade cigar cutter sat on the edge of a large ashtray next to the box. Two light taps on the back of his chair surprised him.

"I did not hear you come in, Jean-Marie-Marc. I thought you'd returned to your lessons with Claude. Come sit with me."

The boy sat on a huge fauteuil, which engulfed him. His feet dangled from the edge. "No, I finished my reading yesterday in the carriage." He sighed and then took a deep breath. He seemed on the verge of changing his mind, but he stayed in the chair.

Jean-Louis-Pierre glanced at him, amused.

"I was wondering if I could return to the Loire. I really like it there, and so do Marie and Claude. I know that my behavior disappointed you immensely... but I will never repeat my conduct, I promise you that."

"Immensely is a rather big word, Jean-Marie-Marc. Your curiosity simply got the best of you. An inquisitive mind is excellent. There is a lot to see and do in Paris, and you've only been here for less than a week."

He thought of himself at that age. He could not wait to go to Normandy or the Loire. He hated Paris, especially when all of his friends would return home after the season. "But... yes, you could. I'd have to talk to Gaby... to your mother."

"Oh, that is truly wonderful! Can we leave tomorrow morning?"

"Of course, not. You have a déjeuner with Gaby, with your mother!" he answered. "You will have fun." He paused for a moment, wondering if he should invite himself along. No. Gaby needed time alone with her son. "If you still want to return to Loire with Marie and Claude, I will accompany you."

"Thank you." The boy stood and walked to the shelves that surrounded the great library. His father watched him. He knew exactly where he was going. He pulled out a thin leather-bound book that had been set in the far-right corner where the English novels were categorized. He returned, sat back in the chair and pulled surreptitiously his mother's white velour blanket over his legs and feet. He looked up, smiled and continued his reading.

"Dickens? There is a French translation if you wish to practice the language. I can see that you have been here already."

"Claude and I came here after dinner last night." He looked startled as he glanced at his father. "I asked him to come. I hope I was not impolite."

"No, I am impressed," Jean-Louis-Pierre retorted.

"Thank you. Yes, for enjoyment I prefer English. It is easier." He lowered his gaze to the book.

Jean-Louis-Pierre gazed at him more intently. A force to be reckoned with. Gaby had a tall order facing her. Jean-Marie-Marc's dedication to him was resolute, poor Gaby, he had seen the rogue glances zipping in her direction when no one watched.

Both father and son returned to their reading until Marie called them to dinner.

CHAPTER FIFTY-ONE

In early July, they had taken him to New York, and although Jean-Marie-Marc had no intentions to love the woman which he continued to believe gave him away to pursue her profession, his affinity with his father was of greater importance. He played the loving son well and for all intents and purposes, it served him well.

While Jean-Louis-Pierre sailed his ship across the Atlantic, the child and his mother had embarked on the ocean liner the SS Great Eastern, the largest of its kind. It had been launched in 1859 and could carry in excess of two thousand passengers. He had his own room in a lavish suite reserved for the notorious diva. They had breakfast, lunch and dinner together as she spoke of common interests. The clever young boy forced niceties out of his mouth. She appeared to be content with them, he thought. Perfect, he assumed his father would be happy.

Her retinue included voice coaches, musicians, masseurs, and God only knew who else.... His father had been waiting for them in New York. Although there was a magnificent apartment at their disposal on Park Avenue, next to the Fitch's magnificent home, Gabriella insisted on staying at the Waldorf Astoria. The view was extraordinary and while his mother rehearsed her arias for the Grand Gala at the opening season of the Met, he walked along the avenues with one of his nannies in the mornings. 'The afternoon is dedicated to us,' Gabriella repeated incessantly.

Although he barely tolerated the myriad images of the extraordinary Diva advertised at every corner of every street, she was interested in the arts and took him to every imaginable museum in the city. She was interesting, unassuming and very gay, laughing easily, he could see why his father was madly in love with her. Well, they would have to share the great man. He did not need to love her—he would simply pretend.

The wharves where the Tempête was docked had been of great interest to him—mostly because his father had taken him there. The plan for the following week was to sail along the New England coast to Newport in Rhode Island where his father owned a magnificent estate overlooking Narragansett Bay. Gabriella was in New York, singing to an adoring audience. He called her Gabriella in her head, "mother" not a word that came easily unless there were no other options while in public.

Both father and son strode down Bellevue Avenue in the picturesque small town on the Narragansett Bay. A stable located close to his estate had provided two great horses, and they had ridden around the Seventeen Coach Road. A spectacular site that overlooked the tumultuous waters provided stunning views of the rocks that bordered the elegant estates being pummeled.

George Washington, it was alleged, had stayed in the mansion next to Jean-Louis's—The Clift House. The chef prepared a delicious déjeuner of raw oysters, baked shrimps and lobster tails. The young lad and his father were munching on the firm meat that Jean-Marie-Marc tried desperately to tear off the carcass helped by the fish cutlery his father had brought from France. The youngster recalled how embarrassed and famished he had been at one of the great dinners that had feasted his return to the ancestral estate in Loire. Just a few friends, Marie had secreted.

Over seventy guests had passed through the grand portal! His father's closest friends! It was difficult for him to entertain just one! While the repast took place, he was at a loss with the serving cutlery and glasses. Although famished, he denied himself all sorts of wonderful appetizers that he eyed with envy in the guests' plates. To his rescue, under the guise of placing a napkin on his knee, Auguste, the butler had whispered: "Start from the outside in."

Grateful, the following morning he wrote a poem to the aged servant, who had been with the family from a tender age. His family had tended to his father's ancestors—essentially his very own. He carried the papyrus he wrote it on down to the kitchen himself. The help, definitely less formal in that setting, quieted down and stood promptly. He looked around and could not find Auguste.

He smiled and asked politely, "Is Monsieur Auguste in the house today?"

"Non, Non, Monsieur, he is in his office." A young woman detached from the group. "I am Annette, in your service, Monsieur, let me take you to him."

Sure enough, consternation was visible in the older man's always stern attitude as Annette, followed by the young master, entered the spartan room. A desk covered with well-arranged papers in vertical columns, a lamp, a well-worn leather great chair, and a bell.

"Thank you very much, Monsieur Auguste, for the suggestion last evening. I was famished but did not want to embarrass my father with my lack of manners. I would have gone to bed hungry like a naughty boy without your consideration. Here is a poem that I wrote for you. Thank you, a million times thank you and please feel free to instruct me in the conduct of my peers."

Not knowing how to respond to such an uncommon display of appreciation, Auguste rose and ever so formal: "You never cease to amaze all of us in your service, young Sir. I will cherish this poem for as long as I live," the older man responded. He placed the parchment in the inner pocket of his jacket. His voice quivered a bit before he nodded to Annette to disappear.

"I will walk you back to your room, Monsieur." And sure enough, he had done just that.

Sitting on a rock on the Seventeen Coach Road, Jean-Marie-Marc threw flat rocks in the turbulent water of the Atlantic Ocean. The *galets,* small pebbles ricocheted many times over the waves that smacked against the steep rocks of the Atlantic coastline. His mother had agreed to let him return to France with his father on the Tempête. The wait was almost unbearable. Gabriella still had four concerts prior to their return, which meant they would weigh anchor in late October. Upon his return to France, he would make his father proud by studying hard to prove to all that he was worthy of the generosity showered upon him. He was a de Pleyssis, the future Duke of Bourbonne, and he'd be proud to honor the accomplishments of the previous Dukes of the long lineage.

Tomorrow his father would take him to Boston and the following month, they would embark on the Tempête. What an adventure! Footsteps behind him made him turn his head. His father took a seat next to him.

"You can change your mind and return with your mother on the Britannia, Jean-Marie-Marc. The crossing will not be a cup of tea, as my English friends often remind me."

"Oh, non, Monsieur, please." He still had not used the word 'father' when speaking directly to Jean-Louis-Pierre, "I was just thinking that the adventure will be one more wonderful highlight of my new life. Please, oh please, let me accompany you on the Tempête."

His father smiled. "I look forward to it as well, Jean-Marie-Marc. An adventure it will be. Ask your mother." The boy smiled to please the man sitting next to him, his Father, the very man he had come to love with all his heart.

CHAPTER FIFTY-TWO

Return to France from New York Harbor

Three weeks later, Jean-Louis-Pierre and his son were ready to embark. Provisions had been brought on board, and the crew was anxious to depart. The young lad was so proud in his long leather pants, gray woolen shirt and leather vest. He sat alone on the edge of the bow as he focused on his father and Cunnan, the first officer having joined them less than two weeks earlier. Both ordered the equipage and its rank to finesse their watch and check every detail.

The crew appeared to respect his father and Cunnan, most had sailed with the Captain and first officer for many years. The boatswain's mate revealed to Jean-Marie-Marc that he had fought with the Duke in Indochina. The man called Henry James had a Scottish accent and appeared weathered, but his bright light blue eyes revealed that he might have been younger than his outward appearance.

No one paid much attention to the young lad. He took in as much as he could. Later that night, his father invited him to join the Captain's table.

"Are you up for the eight days crossover, Jean-Marie-Marc? You still have time to change your mind."

His retort was immediate. "Absolutely, Father! I have watched and learned from Mr. James." He smiled that beautiful smile, his mother's Gabriella. "I am ready and will not be a burden to anyone."

In an emotional moment, Jean-Louis-Pierre hugged his son. "First time you called me Father, Jean-Marie-Marc, I hope that it will continue. I like it much." He picked up the boy and pressed a kiss to his forehead. "Yes, my son, I like it much." He winked and lowered him to the deck. "I was not much older than you when my father and Cunnan took me across the Manche. This voyage is twice as long. It will be arduous but I hope you will enjoy it."

"*Trés bien*," the Captain responded. "You may retire if you wish."

He did not have to be told twice, exhausted but unwilling to show any fear and weariness, the boy filed right out of the dining mess. The conversation between the Captain and Cunnan and the two other deck officers continued late into the night. The sea lanes had to be charted, early November always an uncertain time to cross the Atlantic. Jean-Louis returned to his cabin in the early morning hours. His son, like an angel, slept soundly. The Duke suddenly had second thoughts; perhaps a six-year-old on board might be an encumbrance to the crew. He had followed his late uncle at an early age as well, the indelible experience shaping the remainder of his life. They would travel with minimal risks if they left within the week.

CHAPTER FIFTY-THREE

Five weeks later, Gaby returned to Paris awaiting word from Brest. Her own Liner had not returned to the original port. The winds had battered the coast for the past month and waves the likes they had not seen in decades assaulted the cliffs, enabling ships to seek shelter in the deep grooves of the many ports in *Bretagne*.

Philippe remained in Paris, he tried to paint rosy pictures to Gaby, stating that the route had most certainly been altered because of the violent storms.

"They most certainly sailed toward the *Manche*, to re-enter French international waters. You will hear from them once they reach Cherbourg. Jean-Louis-Pierre has sailed the world over thrice, Gabriella. They will all return safely."

On the 21st of December, remains of the ship had drifted toward the Île Rè. All hope vanished. The ship with all those on board had sunk. The wild waters of the Atlantic had taken its precious cargo. Gabriella canceled her repertoire for the season, but then Maître Lauriot persuaded the great singer to return and finish the season.

"Chère Gabriella, music has healing power. Return to us, my dear." He'd embraced her. "My dearest, let music be your only passion."

She'd surrendered to his wise advice.

Jean-Louis-Pierre's nephews had contested his ancestral home. She'd acquiesced. "Essentially it belongs to the de Pleyssis, I have no right over the property," she'd told Élyse.

"But absolutely Gabriella, it is absurd, it was Jean-Louis-Pierre's will. How can you?"

"I have no determination to fight over a home. It is not important. My memories are mine, and mine solely, Élyse. I had some lovely moments in my house with the people I cherished most—for a very short period of time." She stared off into space. "Financially, I will never need anything. I will never remarry, and I will never bare another child. I am married to music now, Élyse."

Élyse strode to her friend. "I love and treasure you, Gabriella. You can always, forever, count on me, my dearest friend." The elegant blonde embraced Gaby. "Not yet thirty, Gabriella. You will love again. You deserve to love again and you will. Let life decide."

CHAPTER FIFTY- FOUR

For the first night in many months, she had answered her dear cousin, Cardinal Philippe Thornsen, request that she sing the Ave Maria at the midnight Mass at Notre Dame.

During the Offertory, as Philippe blessed the gifts, a stupefied hum coming from the parishioners traversed the knave of the Cathedrale.

Gaby, sustaining to the last note, waited for the priests to descend from the altar with the host. She stepped aside, followed by her troupe of musicians as she descended the steep stone stairs to partake in Holy Communion. Rounding the corner of the wooden staircase, she followed the parishioners. Little attention was paid to the mounting murmurs and the silent elbowing of people clearly shocked by the appearance of a ghost in their ranks. Gaby joined her hands together over her heart and continued down the aisle.

The enormous crowd in the cathedral turned their attention away from the altar, timidly at first and then rapidly to focus on the back of the church where a celebrated man sat. Gaby, with her troops of musicians on the second floor, was blind to the phenomenon occurring down below. As she appeared in the center of the aisle, she took little note of the tumultuous attention given to her entrance. After all, she'd halted all her performances since late November.

Philippe bowed to the Tabernacle, lifted the Chalice and turned to face the parishioners. Blind as a bat, as Gabriella likened his less than distinct vision, he proceeded down the altar.

One of the older priests in a white chasuble approached him, pointing with his five fingers extended, to the tall man seated in the back of the church in the commoner's pews.

Ignoring the priest, the Cardinal pursued his duty—that of blessing the Host. Once more, the aged priest approached him, this time whispering to Philippe that the Duke, or someone whose resemblance was uncanny to that of the celebrated Captain, walked behind Gabriella.

The Cardinal raised the wine and glanced at Gaby and then beyond ... the blessed chalice fell from his hands. Bewilderment ensued, priests and *Enfants de Coeur* shifting to the altar, all unable to touch the blessed Sacrament or replace the wine in the cup. Philippe slowly moved away from the altar. He stared at the man ambling behind his cherished cousin with his distinct grin.

As Gaby approached the kneeling station, she looked up at Edouard Goncourt, a man who stood against every principle of the Catholic Church. He had just lost his brother, Jules, the previous September. The painful separation from his beloved brother had brought him to the Cathedrale to find solace in the blessed rituals of Midnight Mass.

Philippe, terribly perturbed, waited for Gaby. She had not seen him this disturbed since the taking of the Papal States by Victor Emmanuel II. He strode to her, clasped her wrists and pressed her to his heart. Gently, slowly, he released her, reached for the blessed Chalice and offered the Host that remained.

Clueless, she accepted the Lord and glanced sideways. She crossed herself, ready to return to her pew, the very same one that still held her former title as the Duchesse de Bourbonne written in gold letters on the arm rest of the Prie-Dieu, a piece of furniture consisting of a kneeling surface recovered with red velvet posited for kneeling, and a narrow and higher wooden platform recovered as well with matching red velvet to rest one's elbows when praying. The Prie-Dieu had not been removed from the great church.

As she crossed herself, she lingered for a moment, stared with reverence at the Cross and then dedicated a prayer for the souls of her family. She pivoted, ready to return to her seat. Stunned, she came face to face with her former husband ... heat emanated from every pore of her body... she fainted.

The Duke seized her before she crumpled to the hard marble covered with a long, thin, red carpet.

Philippe shivered violently and attempted to reach for the chair that had been brought forward to support him.

"Should I continue the service? I have not been ordained, but from the looks of it, it appears that the congregation has just seen a ghost!" Jean-Louis-Pierre exclaimed.

In essence, the press had not stopped covering the great drama that had occurred in autumn. It had touched many Parisians' hearts. An immense crowd had followed his coffin from his home on the île Saint-Louis to Notre Dame. It had been a day of mourning in the provinces as well. Today, all the parishioners in the ancient Catholic Cathedral stood aghast at the apparition.

Jean-Louis-Pierre smiled as he carried Gaby to the vestry where he placed her on a forest green velvet sofa. He kneeled next to her as a priest, who had just entered the chamber, swung a pouch filled with salt back and forth close to her face until the beautiful diva regained consciousness.

Suddenly composed, Gaby pushed up to a seated position and then stood. Still on his knees, the tall aristocrat waited for a response. It came swiftly. She struck him with all the force that she could summon. "Where have you been? Where is Jean-Marie-Marc? Where is Cunnan?"

The stunned Duke stood promptly. "Gaby, they are fine. In Loire. Jean-Marie-Marc is staying with my grandmother, Cunnan in our home, recuperating. I wanted to be with you on Christmas Day," the adventurous Captain replied. "Perhaps a messenger announcing my arrival might have been more appropriate."

She sighed and sucked in a long breath of air as Philippe entered the vestry.

Many parishioners, curious as this great turn of event unfurled, pushed the great wooden doors of the priest's chamber inward, and stood aghast at the sight of Jean-Louis-Pierre. Many had paid their respect less than three months ago as his assumed body lay in state in a closed casket in the imposing cathedral.

"Jean-Louis-Pierre, what happened? They found part of the Tempête à la dèrive on the île de Rè?" Phillippe sighed.

"Yes, we lost it. It is a miracle that we all survived. No one lost. The perfect storm rolled the ship. Thank God, presaging a disaster, we had embarked on the navire de sauvetage beforehand. Out of pure luck or divine intervention the strong underwater current deposited us on a still unnamed island to the northwest of La Rochelle. Cod fishermen discovered us as we fished for our daily meals."

He turned to Gaby, and smiled. "You will be pleased to hear that more than once our son invoked the warm croissants with raspberry jam you're so fond of. Apparently … like mother, like son!"

She smiled, his charming accent warming her heart as he spoke to her in English. Unable to contain herself, she threw herself into his arms. "Don't you ever leave me again! Not ever, Jean-Louis!"

He caressed the long mahogany mane that unfolded in long waves down her back. "Never again. I promise, Gaby."

THE END

www.ingramcontent.com/pod-product-compliance
Lightning Source LLC
LaVergne TN
LVHW041924090826
845145LV00015B/294

* 9 7 8 0 9 8 5 4 4 1 9 2 0 *